# ETERNALLY
# BOUND
## SPIRIT GUIDE BOXED SET

TJ MICHAELS

# CONTENTS

# ON THE PROWL

"Move over, Secret Agent Man, Michaels' heroine, Delaine, is a spy queen. Her moves on the sheets and off make this a page-turner."
-Romantic Times BOOKReviews

## T.J. MICHAELS

Dear Reader,

This book, originally published as Primed to Pounce, was my debut novel. It was the first book to ever be contracted and published and was the beginning of my career as a professional author. It received a wonderful reception and great reviews.

When the rights reverted from the publisher back to me, it was republished to ensure that you could still enjoy this particular world. So, here is On the Prowl in its entirety and original form. Enjoy!

With the greatest respect,

~TJ

# CHAPTER ONE

"Thank you for flying US Airways. We'll land at Charlotte's Douglas Airport in approximately thirty minutes. Cabin crew, please prepare the cabin for landing."

All Delaine heard was "Yada, yada, yada, yada..." as she thought of her husband, well, her now ex-husband, for the trillionth time since he'd left her.

What the hell kind of man sends his wife an e-mail to tell her he's leaving her?

*It's been a year and I still can't believe what he did*, Delaine fumed inwardly, remembering that fateful morning as if it was yesterday. Her husband Gary had kissed her on his way out the door for work. Hell, he'd even told her to have a wonderful day. The last thing she'd expected when she arrived at her office was an e-mail from him giving her a two-day notice of his intentions to move out.

Delaine had been hurt and confused after reading his long rant of a jabbing e-mail. But when the light bulb in her head flipped on she'd been livid. No one simply blinked their eyes and had a whole new life, a new apartment and a new girlfriend without a little prep time. The bastard had planned his cowardly actions for weeks, maybe even months.

But unlike Gary, Delaine didn't have the option or desire to abandon her family. So she'd held it together, saw their twins off to college and was on her way to North Carolina on a new assignment for her agency.

She caught her reflection in the window. Dark brown, almond-shaped eyes twinkled intelligently in the dim overhead light. A slight smile graced her full, heart-shaped lips. She looked like a big kid in her baseball hat, leather bomber and jean shirt. Her cinnamon skin was flawless, and she couldn't see a single, easily identifiable wrinkle. In top physical shape and curvy in all the right places, at thirty-seven Delaine looked ten years younger. And her husband had left her because she had a habit of leaving her clothes on the bed? Shaking her head on a snort, she yanked her hat down over her brow and scooted down into the cushions of the leather chair. Well, at least she was headed to Charlotte first class.

She gazed out the small window at a beautiful pink and purple sunset, but all she saw was her hands wrapped firmly around Gary's neck as she squeezed. Hard. The image faded as Delaine's spirit guide whispered soothingly in her mind.

*He is not worth the effort, Suta Winyan. He was not a worthy mate.*

'I know, Sapa, I know,' Delaine sighed inwardly, sending the tired thoughts to the black mountain lion that shared her conscience.

*The Great Spirit says this is meant to be. Good things are coming to you.*

They landed without a hitch and Delaine was standing at baggage claim within fifteen minutes of deplaning. A loud siren blared, signaling the start of the conveyor belt just as a graying older gentleman, dressed in a classic black chauffeur jacket, white shirt and black trousers, approached. The sign he carried held her initials written in bold, black letters.

"Ms. D.J.?" he asked politely.

Delaine nodded with a friendly smile at the man's welcome attempt at discretion. After all, she was undercover. It wouldn't do to have her name plastered on a sign for all to see.

"My name is Timmons, and I'll be your driver tonight," he said, with a tip of his hat and a slight bow. "I'll retrieve your luggage and we'll be on our way shortly, ma'am."

Delaine waited patiently in the arriving passenger area while Timmons brought the car around—a white Crown Victoria limousine, courtesy of her company, Aegis Analytical. Her belongings were quickly stowed in the spacious trunk, and a very polite Timmons settled her into the spacious backseat. Without a word, he passed her a large sealed manila envelope, climbed into the driver's seat and they were off.

She flipped on the reading lamp and kicked off her shoes. The big backseat was perfect for sprawling, and Delaine mentally thanked her boss, Geri, for arranging a private car to take her to her new home.

Delaine allowed her tired body to sink into the plush leather cushions then carefully opened the flap on the envelope. It was stuffed with several items, some she would need immediately. She pulled out the keys to her new house and a note from her boss confirming the date of delivery of the rest of her belongings. Also the spare keys to her car, which she'd gone without for the past couple of weeks so it could be shipped ahead, and another note from the transport coordinator—the car was now parked in her driveway just waiting for her to arrive.

The envelope also contained the results of a few

special strings Geri pulled in consideration of Delaine's unexpected status of single mom—a bank receipt for a hefty moving bonus, already deposited in a bank in Charlotte, and airline e-tickets for her children, who would fly to Charlotte for their Christmas break instead of Denver. Thanks to Geri, the exchange of the plane tickets hadn't cost a dime.

There was a second manila envelope buried in the bottom of the first. Delaine tucked it into the side pocket of her carry-on bag. She knew from experience that this one pertained to her mission. She'd wait until she was in the privacy of her home before she opened it.

Delaine flipped the reading light off, leaned her head back against the seat and peered out the window. It wasn't all that late, but the winter days were short. If she'd been thinking, she would have flown in earlier so she could see the surrounding landscape. It was completely dark out and she couldn't see a thing except the lamps illuminating the highway.

As they sped along the interstate, Delaine felt a strange mix of apprehension and giddiness. She called out across the psychic bond she shared with her spirit guide and Sapa immediately came to the forefront of her mind. The black lioness was always in her head, able to communicate thoughts and feelings. When directly summoned, Delaine could actually see the image of the big cat behind her eyes and even call her onto this plane in a physical form. It was pretty neat to watch the expressions cross Sapa's face when she'd been summoned in the middle of pouncing on some imaginary prey. But tonight, the big cat felt Delaine's anxiety and sought to comfort her charge.

*Do not be afraid. You will be happy here, and I will always be with you,* Sapa said calmly.

'Of course,' Delaine pushed her thoughts to her lifelong companion. 'But this is the first time in years

I've been off on my own with no children, no husband. I don't know where anything is, don't know anyone here except Pam. And what about this guy I'm supposed to get the goods on? What's his name? Baker?'

*You will be successful, as you have always been.*

Delaine basked in the warmth and acceptance Sapa sent along the bond. She drifted into a light doze and the lioness retreated to a small corner of her mind.

They were both snapped out of sleep by the sound of Timmons' voice ringing through the limo's intercom.

*Ah, we have arrived. Our new home is fit for the princess you are.*

Delaine blushed. Sapa had such a way with words.

The limo pulled into a paved half circle driveway on a wide, quiet street. The outside lights were on and Delaine's mouth dropped open as she gazed at her new home through the window of the car. They'd arrived, all right. She'd lived in a nice house in Denver, but nothing like this. This was a large executive mini-mansion. Absolutely breathtaking, it was two stories of beautifully laid brick, with two sets of stairs that led up either side of a wide columned porch. The nearest house seemed half a block down the well-lit, tree-lined street.

'Wow, Sapa, this is amazing. I can't wait until morning to get a really good look.'

*If you wish, I will lend you my sight so you can see the outside of the house now.*

'Nah, that's okay. I can wait until morning. All I want right now is a bite to eat and a comfy bed.'

*As you wish,* Sapa purred on a yawn of her own.

Timmons maneuvered around a car in the driveway and pulled up in front of one of the sets of stairs that led up to the front door. Delaine inwardly sighed with relief. The car in the driveway was her black Jaguar, which appeared to have made the journey just fine.

They climbed the stairs together, Delaine helped

Timmons put her bags in the foyer just inside the front door. She bid him goodnight and slipped a generous tip into his palm before she closed and locked the door behind him.

Her eyes roamed around the large marble foyer and admired the vaulted ceilings and hardwood moldings. Off the foyer the huge sunken living room, centered by a wide wood-burning fireplace, had her wowing. It was like someone had placed the living room in a beautifully matted picture frame, where the furniture, mantle and fireplace were the picture, and the steps down into the room were the frame, all the way around. And it was huge, perfect for the coming Christmas holidays. The kids would have a ball decorating the place.

Delaine kicked off her shoes and strolled from room to room. Her toes sank into the thick pile of the creamy winter white carpets in each room and allowed her body to appreciate the matching winter white leather furniture in the living room.

In addition, the first floor had a large stone floor gourmet kitchen, a beautiful dining room laid with lacquered wood floors and several more empty rooms. She'd turn one into her office and let the kids fight over the rest of them. At the top of the curved staircase was a landing that could be used as a loft or entertainment area. The rest of the upstairs was her bedroom with a large master bath from heaven.

She could live in the bathroom alone! The tub was the size of a small pool and sunken into the floor. A shower big enough for four people had a wall of creamy tile with two massaging showerheads and a rain-like waterfall showerhead between them. Two walls were made of glass brick with built-in bath benches. Done up in white glass and ceramic tile, miles of glass, gold and sparkling mirrors, it looked like something out of the ancient world.

Sapa purred at the opulence surrounding them and encouraged Delaine to relax and enjoy their new home. She unpacked her suitcases then made her way back downstairs to the fully stocked kitchen for a bite to eat. The fridge was full and the pantry was packed. It seemed her boss really had thought of everything. After a quick dinner she picked up the phone in the kitchen and dialed her girlfriend's number.

"Hey, Pam, it's me. The flight was fine and I got in about an hour ago."

"How about breakfast in the morning?" came the excited, familiar female voice on the other end of the line.

"Sure, but it'll have to be early. Tomorrow is my first day at the new job."

"You don't get any time to settle in first?"

"Nope, but it's not a problem because this sistah is hitting the sack within the next half-hour. I'm wiped out," Delaine said on a genuine yawn.

"Well, hurry up and get a pen so I can give you directions to my favorite breakfast spot."

Pen and notepad in hand, she leaned against the kitchen counter and said, "Go ahead, I'm ready."

That done, Delaine spent the evening exploring the rest of house. Later, she ventured outside to the back porch, leaned against the wood railing and looked up at the night sky to quiet her mind. Her head seemed to be everywhere at once, her thoughts bouncing from tremendous pride in her children who'd recently headed off to college, to missing the physical companionship of her idiot ex-husband. Then there was the sense of peace and fulfillment at knowing she could be alone and still be satisfied. After all, she had herself and her spirit guide Sapa. Moving to a new place and meeting new people was actually exciting, and this new assignment was the most important of her life. She had a dangerous target to take out and she couldn't wait to get started. The thrill of the hunt was an indescribable mix of eagerness and caution.

Despite her reeling emotions, she silently thanked the Great Spirit for so many blessings. Her lips tipped up into a grin. If Gary's trifling butt hadn't cut out on her and the kids, she probably wouldn't have accepted the opportunity to move to the East Coast for this assignment. Nor be in this fabulous house, nor reunited with her good friend Pam. She sighed. Well, thank God for small favors.

Delaine climbed into bed, checked her Taurus PT99 handgun, made sure there was a bullet in the chamber and tucked it under her pillow. She lay sprawled under the warm blankets and comforter then remembered the envelope she hadn't opened earlier. She bounded to the floor, headed for the gigantic walk-in closet and flipped on the light. She pulled her carry-on bag from one of the many cedar shelves and retrieved the envelope from the side pocket.

Back in bed, she ripped it open and dumped the contents into her lap. There was a picture inside of a handsome man with blond hair, emerald-green eyes and a too-perfect smile. So this was Brian Baker? This clean-cut, Opie-Taylor-looking man was her target?

Her spirit guide became restless. Delaine, so used to Sapa's presence, ignored the cat's agitation. She studied Baker's picture and began to plan a strategy to find out what he was up to. Where might he keep any evidence and what would she have to do to get it?

The longer she thought on the man, the more Sapa's agitation escalated until it flooded through the bond in torrents. Delaine finally gave up trying to strategize and quieted her mind. She meditated until she had the cat's full attention then summoned her directly.

'Come to me, Sapa,' Delaine whispered in her mind.

The lioness stalked forward, her image visible to Delaine's eyes. Sharp incisors were bared and the fine hairs on her neck stood on end. Obviously something about Baker disturbed the big cat.

'What is it? What's wrong, Sapa?' Delaine asked, sending concern to her spirit guide.

The black lioness turned gleaming grey eyes on her and continued to brood but said nothing. Delaine nodded off with Sapa pacing back and forth in her head, a quiet, menacing growl resonating along the bond.

\* \* \* \* \*

Baker walked into his office, closed the door firmly and turned the deadbolt. It was six-thirty in the morning and no one was around yet, but if nothing else, he was cautiously meticulous. He sat down, opened his briefcase and pulled out the file he'd been looking over during breakfast. He laid the manila folder on his desk, flipped it open and pulled out a picture of the new production process specialist being brought in.

Her name was Delaine Jeris, a technical expert newly assigned to his business unit to develop the new neuromuscular drug Zalactin. He would have to remember to reward the woman in Research & Development for getting him this information. Since the Jeris woman was coming on as a consultant and not an employee, neither Human Resources nor he had been involved. If not for his little bitch in R&D, who'd nicked the info from the dupe she was sleeping with in Purchasing, Baker would never have known someone outside of his "special circle of friends" was joining his team. Yes, he would have to thank…what was her name? Sarah Ann, yes that was it. He'd have to thank Sarah Ann for alerting him. A quick screw up against a wall should do it. He didn't have the time or patience for a slow one.

He picked up the picture in one hand and studied it closely. This Delaine was a fine-looking woman. Her résumé said she was an expert in systems, database and process analysis. Very impressive. Very beautiful.

A hand found its way down to his crotch and stroked his burgeoning erection through his trousers as he eyes moved over her photo. He noted the intelligence in her dark brown almond-shaped eyes and her flawless cinnamon skin. Imagining his fists knotting in the long natural curls of her hair, he leaned his head back in his chair, her photo in one hand, and unzipped his pants and freed his rock-hard cock.

Baker closed his brilliant green eyes, the image of Delaine Jeris etched firmly in his mind. He spilled his seed into one of the handkerchiefs he kept in a drawer for these occasions and wondered if the woman could be bought or, depending on who she worked for, sold.

\* \* \* \* \*

Justin Cooley flipped the secure cell phone closed and grimaced at the new intel he'd just received. So a new investigator was stepping into his case, eh? It was a woman who was coming in as some kind of techno-geek. Her cover was to map out the production process and data sources for the new medicine that Brian Baker's team was developing. So was Baker her target? Justin had no idea. He also hadn't a clue who she was or what she looked like. But since he wasn't supposed to know anything about her at all, it was no surprise the information he'd been given was sketchy. His partner Derrick was trying to find out more. Justin would check in with him later.

Thankfully, the manufacturing and corporate facilities at Astin Pharmaceutical were huge. He blended in with everyone else, surveyed who came and went and who had access to what.

Keeping an eye out for this new agent should be easy enough. He was finally closing in on Baker. The last thing he needed was a newbie coming in and spoiling what had taken him months to set up.

# CHAPTER TWO

Delaine circled the parking lot at the Arboretum Mall for the third time, relieved to finally luck out on a parking space close to the restaurant. She flew into the spot, jumped out of her sleek black Jag and hurried to the door. She was supposed to meet Pam more than ten minutes ago. Her fingers closed around the door handle when she was nearly tackled by a very excited female.

"I really missed you," Pam said with a toothy grin. She released Delaine and dragged her through the door to the table where their breakfast waited. "Hey, I ordered some of that frou-frou food I know you like, so eat up."

"Thanks, woman. Sorry I'm late," Delaine said, quirking a brow at her friend as packet after packet of sugar disappeared into Pam's coffee cup. Ick! She shuddered visibly then laughed when Pam stuck her tongue out at her. Delaine took a healthy bite of fruit, yogurt and granola Breakfast Banana Split. Her eyes rolled heavenward in appreciation then her nose wrinkled in distaste when Pam took a gulp of syrupy coffee.

"I'm so excited to see you, Delaine! Girl, I still can't

believe you're here!" Pam exclaimed, squirming in her chair like a little kid with a new toy at Christmas.

"I know, I can't believe it either!" Delaine beamed, just as happy to see Pam. It had been eight years since the two women had left their homes in California. Delaine had moved to Denver, and Pam had been all over the place. She still couldn't believe they'd both ended up in North Carolina at the same time.

"So tell me again why you didn't like Houston?" Delaine asked around another bite of yogurt heaven. "You were there for, what, two years?"

"Too hot, too humid. Not enough gorgeous men," Pam jested as she leered over her shoulder at the butt of a nice-looking man being seated across from them. "I had a pretty good clientele, but it got old fast."

Delaine tilted her head in question and said, "But why Charlotte, of all places? It's just as hot and humid as Houston. Besides, last year you said you were going back home to Cali."

"I know, but I changed my mind. You know I've always wanted to live on the East Coast somewhere. I didn't want to live in New York. Too crowded, too expensive. But I didn't want to live in Florida either."

"Too many hurricanes," Delaine mumbled around the napkin she wiped her mouth with.

"You've got that right. So I settled for Charlotte. It's almost right in the middle of the Atlantic states. Close enough to New York to get in plenty of shopping and close enough to Florida to get plenty of sun. And, baby, the Miami strip is just waiting for me."

Delaine almost laughed at Pam's screwy logic, but for her friend, it made perfect sense. Pam moving to North Carolina because it sat between New York and Florida fit her personality perfectly. Sun, fun, shopping and hair were her life.

"You've been here six months. How long before

you're off to somewhere else, girlfriend?"

"Well, I've always wanted to see the South of France. Hey," Pam exclaimed, changing the subject. The woman was like a gnat, flying from one subject to another and never in a straight line. "My salon is right on the other side of the mall. You only live about fifteen minutes from here. Why don't we meet here for breakfast again? Afterward, we can walk over to the shop and I'll do your hair, just like old times. And while I'm hooking you up, you can tell me what you're doing here without your husband."

Delaine grimaced. Other than her kids, she'd shared her situation with nobody but her boss Geri, and even that conversation hadn't been too deep. At the time, Delaine just couldn't handle getting into the morbid details. She hadn't wanted to think about how her husband had abandoned their family for the most unbelievably dumb reasons. He'd claimed she wasn't supportive around the house, but what wife would support a total nag? Especially when he'd nagged her and the kids around the clock. And god forbid there be a dish in the sink! Or a dryer sheet left on top of the clothes dryer. In all his selfish whining, he'd never thanked her for buying him whatever he wanted and standing by him in anything and everything he wanted to do. Not to mention the endless years of boring, uninspired sex. Funny, he was always the one with a headache. It was a wonder they'd ever had children.

She'd been too ashamed to talk about it before, but now she felt stronger. Maybe she should talk to Pam and release the disappointment and hurt once and for all. Besides, she'd known Pam since the Stone Age. If anyone could be trusted with her private business, it was the woman sitting on the other side of the table.

Delaine took a steadying breath and let the words tumble from her mouth.

"Gary and I are divorced, Pam. We've been separated for more than a year and the dissolution was final last week." She watched Pam closely, not realizing she held her breath until her chest started to ache. To Delaine's surprise, Pam looked relieved.

"Oh thank god! It's about damn time," Pam said, sticking a finger up in the air while doing a seated version of the happy dance. "I never told you this in all the years we've been friends because I didn't want to speak against what made you happy, but I've never liked Gary. You gave and gave and gave to him, but he always made it seem like he was some kind of martyr for being married to you. It's about time you cut that loser off your apron strings."

"He left us, Pam," Delaine said, the heat in her voice directed at her no-good ex rather than Pam's revelation that she'd never liked him. When Pam's face fell, Delaine giggled at her friend's incredulous expression. She obviously hadn't been expecting to hear this. But Pam, being Pam, recovered from the shock quickly and was as pissed off as Delaine had ever seen her. But she didn't miss the hint of sadness in the woman's dark brown eyes.

"After all you've done for him, he left you? Left your children? I don't believe it! The bastard! That son of a …"

Delaine quietly cut her off mid-rave.

"Pam, it's fine. I've moved on. It's been tough being alone after so many years, but I'm fine. Really."

"I know exactly what you need. You need to get out and meet some new people."

Delaine immediately shook her head, adamantly mouthing the word no. Pam kept right on talking.

"Hey, I have an idea," Pam squealed, setting her cooling cup of coffee down once and for all to silently clap her hands. "There's a group called The

Charlotte/Mecklenberg Professionals Group. It's where folks who are new to the area can meet other professional singles to hang out with."

"Look, I'm not interested in the meat market thing, okay?" Delaine said firmly, pointing a single finger at her friend.

"No, girl, it's not like that. It's a place for professionals, like yourself," Pam said, warming to the topic. "They do a lot of recreational stuff, you know, they network, go boating, dancing, take trips to the mountains and junk like that—not a teeny bopper, get-me-some-coochie type group."

The lioness had been content to doze in the back of Delaine's mind. Now, Delaine felt Sapa sit up on her haunches, fully alert, her ear pricked forward as she listened closely to what Pam was saying.

"Is it safe?" Delaine asked. The lioness and she both tilted their heads thoughtfully.

"Definitely. You won't find anybody like me in the whole place!"

Delaine's laughter drew the gaze of a few nosey folks seated at the table next to them. She pulled her outburst down to a chuckle and looked up at Pam through lowered lashes as she thought about her suggestion. So there was a place for professionals looking to meet up with others? Definitely not Pam's style. She'd be more comfortable at a titty bar. One-stop shopping, no intellect required. The woman had always been a free spirit, not afraid to tell a man she wanted a good lay and a good bye. Not like Delaine, who'd settled for less than mediocre sex for the entire length of her eighteen-year marriage. But now the divorce was final. Was there a reason she shouldn't get out and meet people, get on with her life?

"It's an exclusive, invitation-only group, Del. I'll try to get you into the social this Friday night. I put you down to get your hair done on Saturday so you can fill me in on how it went. Oh, and wear something nice. They're meeting at the Duke Mansion this time. Real swanky place."

When Pam pulled out the appointment book she never went anywhere without, flipped it open and penciled her name in, Delaine resigned herself to her fate with a sigh. She entered both her hair appointment and the social into her PDA and packed it back into her briefcase.

"If it's not your type of thing, how do you know so much about it?" Delaine asked, pulling a few dollars out of her wallet for the tip.

"A client of mine runs the outfit. She'll arrange VIP treatment, so no worries."

"All right then. I'll see you Saturday. And this social thing better be fun or I'm gonna talk about you bad when I walk into your shop." She smiled, kissed her friend on the cheek and rose from the table. "I'll see you later. Gotta go to work."

"Work? At seven a.m.?"

"I like to get a head start on things. Thanks for the breakfast, Ms. Pamela."

\* \* \* \* \*

It had taken her most of the day, but she'd finally slipped away from the annoying Sarah Ann person from R&D. When Delaine arrived at work this morning, she'd been surprised to find the woman waiting for her, looking rather uncomfortable as she sat in a chair outside her office. The cute little dark-haired woman behaved as if her interest in Delaine was simple Southern hospitality for the new kid on the block. But Delaine was no idiot. The woman was shadowing her, but on whose orders? Perhaps her target, Baker, whom she'd met her first day on the job just yesterday.

She shuddered at the memory of meeting Brian Baker, a handsome Englishman with a chilling smile and the coldest green eyes she'd ever seen. The moment they met, Delaine heard the lioness growl deep in her throat. Sapa had kept it up the entire time Delaine was in his presence. And when they'd shook hands, the way he looked her over and held her hand much too long had totally creeped her out.

Delaine had always been a fair, "innocent until proven guilty" agent, no matter what. But something about this Baker character made her want him to be guilty of what he was suspected of.

She pressed her identification badge against the card reader and the doors to the elevator slid open. She pushed the button for the basement and scanned the hallways as they closed, thankful Sarah Ann hadn't popped out from around the corner. Removing a small silver tag from the hidden pocket on the inside of her waistband, she held it against the digital lock on the control panel. In seconds the little device deciphered the encryption and the elevator began to drop rapidly.

The labs were much deeper than she'd thought. When the elevator reached the floor indicated by the last button on the panel, it just kept going. There were no buttons on the panel for these floors and she had no idea how far down she'd traveled. She took a deep breath and steeled herself for whatever and whoever might be down in the subterranean labs. The doors slid open with a quiet hiss.

'Okay, Sapa, we're on high alert now,' Delaine thought.

*I am one step ahead of you, Suta.*

She poked her head out and looked around before stepping out. The doors swished silently closed. Delaine stood in the near darkness and allowed her eyes to adjust. She stood in what looked like a maintenance area. Little pathways led through and between what looked liked large water or sewage pipes.

Walking softly on the outside edges of her feet, her high-heeled boots made no sound. Halfway down the path she'd chosen, the lioness' ears pricked up. Someone was watching.

*Shall I see who watches?*

'No worries. As long as they stay hidden, we're all right,' Delaine replied. She kept walking, not wanting to alert whoever watched that she was aware of their presence. She flipped through a small stack of quality reports in her hands and busily reviewed them. She painted on an intent expression and confident body language that said something was important on the papers she rifled through. Anyone looking should believe she had every right to be down here. The lioness remained alert, but no one appeared.

The dimness of the little pathway gave way to a large room lit by blue lamps mounted high on the walls. The room led to a series of tunnels that ran off in all directions. Which way should she go? If she picked the wrong tunnel, she could end up at a dead end, or worse, at the entrance to one of the labs where Baker was reported to spend most of his time. He wasn't supposed to be down here this early in the morning but she couldn't be sure.

'Come to me, Sapa. I need your guidance.' She silently called the great cat onto this plane, and the large body of the black mountain lion shimmered into existence.

Delaine would never get used to how big Sapa was. The top of her muscular back was higher than Delaine's waist when she reached out to ruffle the soft, wiry hair between the lioness' ears, glad no one else could hear or see the big cat, even in her physical form.

'Sapa, I don't know which way to go,' Delaine said

softly into her mind. Immediately the hunter rose up, calm and sure of her power, ready to aid her charge.

*Take what I offer,* Sapa spoke along the bond.

The black cat lent Delaine her keen sense of sight, smell and hearing then shimmered away. The aura of the lioness prowled ahead and explored each passageway. Within moments, her thoughts flashed through the bond, telling Delaine which way was clear before fading away.

Delaine took off at a silent clip down the tunnel farthest to her right.

* * * * *

*What the hell is she doing down here?* Justin wondered as he watched Delaine make her way through the maze of pipes and pathways. She had to be lost. In fact, he couldn't think of a single female on the list of those allowed into The Vault. Hell, he wasn't even supposed to be down here. He had an hour, correction, forty-five minutes, to get back up to the locker room and slip the badge and encryption key back into the lab coat pocket of the scientist he'd nicked it from.

He remained in the shadows, hidden behind one of the large steel and PVC units that delivered fresh air, electricity and water to these floors. Her height was average, but that's where average stopped. Her features were exquisite, her skin smooth and clear. Even in the dim lighting her dark brown eyes held a depth of intelligence and ruthlessness that caused his lips to draw down in a pensive frown. What caused a woman this fine to have a look like that in her eyes? Like she was after someone, and if the person was smart, they'd be running for the hills.

He let her pass by and then poked his head out from behind his hiding place to get a good look. He almost gave himself away.

Dayum! He exclaimed silently, his eyes glued to her firm, round butt. His mouth fell open as he watched her move into the room that led to the maze of tunnels. He could tell she was athletic by the nicely formed biceps and shoulders under the fine gauge of her coral pink short-sleeved top. The contrast of her tasteful sweater against her mocha skin made him think of chocolate-covered strawberries.

But fine or not, he'd better find out who she was and what she was doing in The Vault. Was she the investigator he was looking for?

The beauty disappeared down one of the tunnels off to the right that led to the quality lab for Baker's secret little projects. As soon as she rounded the corner and disappeared from sight, Justin popped open his secure cell phone and dialed.

"Derrick, it's me. We might have a little problem."

\* \* \* \* \*

"Mr. Baker, I'm so sorry. I followed her to the ladies room on the fourth floor then I lost her. I tried to keep an eye on her, I swear I did."

Sarah Ann flinched when he pierced her with a malevolent glare. Such a wicked look shouldn't have been possible from such a handsome man. Blond hair, green eyes, perfect white teeth. And brilliant. She was surprised to realize she didn't even like him, and hated herself for needing him.

"You know, Sarah Ann," Baker said, rising and circling around his desk to stand directly in front of her chair, "you're assigned as the R&D specialist to my project. If you can't carry out simple tasks then perhaps I should have your boss assign you to someone else." He almost smiled when she blanched.

"I know I failed, Mr. Baker, but please... I-I'll do

anything. Please, can I have some, Mr. Baker? Just a little?"

"What will you give me? I couldn't possibly let you have it for failure," Baker sighed nonchalantly, knowing exactly what he would get for his high-grade pharmaceutical candy.

He smirked when she dropped to her knees and tore frantically at the belt holding up his classic cut wool trousers. In seconds she had his limp cock in her hands and plunged her mouth down over him. He stroked her hair and said, "Perhaps just a little bit. Only good girls get a full dose."

Sarah Ann removed her mouth from his stiffening cock, her eyes wide with need.

"I can be a good girl, Mr. Baker. I swear I can!"

He thrust a hand roughly into her hair, tightened his fingers at her scalp and snatched her head backward, effectively quieting her too-loud pleas.

He snarled directly into her face, "Prove it."

She was off her knees in a flash. Baker looked down at her bobbing head and gasped as she stroked him expertly with lips and tongue. Her cheeks hollowed as she took him so far down her throat, he felt his engorged head bump against her tonsils. He kept hold of her hair, driving himself brutally into the back of her throat over and over, until his balls tightened and the tips of his toes start to tingle.

Just the sight of her swollen, wet lips wrapped around his shaft turned him on more than the tongue that stroked his length. Her mouth made him think of another pair of wet, glistening lips he'd much rather slide between. Suddenly he pulled away, ignoring the confusion in her wide eyes as she looked up at him.

Without bothering to tuck himself back into his pants, he strode across the room to a line of several dark pine file cabinets fitted into the wall of the elegantly appointed office. He reached into one of the drawers, opened a small safe hidden in the bottom and retrieved a small brown bottle. From it came half of a single tiny pink tablet,, the remainder, of which he put back into the bottle and secured in the safe. The little pink half-tablet teetered on the edge of his finger. Sarah Ann watched it hungrily as he approached.

"Remove your clothes," he commanded blandly, not really caring whether she obeyed or not.

Baker watched through hooded eyes as she stood and yanked off her sterile white lab coat and tossed it on the floor. His lips twitched up into a sardonic smile when the chit almost ripped her blouse and the buttons on her pants in her haste. She had a gorgeous body. A bit short for his tastes, but what she lacked in height was made up for with lush, full breasts, a tight hot cunt and a willingness to do any nasty, gutter trash sex act he wanted. And she was a good scientist. Expendable, but good.

When she was completely naked, he gave his next instruction.

"Sit on the desk and spread your legs."

He stood between her thighs and raised his hand. She automatically opened her mouth and lifted her tongue, sighing as the little piece of tablet was placed underneath. Baker took a step back, dug a small stopwatch and notepad out of his lab coat pocket and marked down the exact second the reaction began. He watched closely as her eyes glazed over slightly. Her breathing deepened, her small hands smoothed up and down her body, finally settling on her sensitive breasts. She squeezed them softly at first then brutally as she threw her head back on a ragged moan. Her fingers tweaked and twisted the hard, elongated nipples until they were swollen and red. She keened pitifully while her legs opened and closed as her clit swelled rapidly, painfully.

Thirty seconds this time. Baker was impressed with the progress he'd made in how quickly the drug began to work. He set the watch down on the dark wood top of his large desk and stepped closer to the writhing feast laid out before him. He was glad he'd had the foresight to cover the desktop with a thin sheet of plastic. It simply wouldn't do for Sarah Ann's juices to ruin the fine lacquered finish.

"Sink your fingers into that wet pussy and spread some of your cream over your ass."

Her limbs trembled uncontrollably as she obeyed, spreading her own dewy liquid over herself. Baker's eyebrow lifted at the unexpected turn of events—the trembling was new. Somehow, the effect of the drug had escalated. He'd have to look into that.

Sarah Ann shook, whimpered and undulated her hips, begging, ready and willing to have him any way he would take her.

"Please, Mr. Baker!"

"Are you sure you're ready?" he asked sarcastically, teasing the very tip of his throbbing cock up and down the length of her weeping slit. He didn't care whether she was ready or not. Neither did Sarah Ann. The drug saw to that.

"Yes, yes I'm ready. Now, please."

Her pussy leaked so much, her juices ran down around her ass to coat the tiny opening more. He raised her legs over his shoulders and pushed against the tight, slick hole, gasping when the head popped past her sphincter. She ground down hard and tried to impale herself on him, but he pulled back each time so just the tip remained inside. He held her firmly by her hips, dipped his head and sucked one of her breasts with hard, rough strokes of his tongue until he felt her pussy flutter through the thin barrier between him and her cunt. Just as he bit down on her nipple, he plunged and sunk deep.

She screamed. The pain tore into her, pushed away the haze of the drug for a moment as he ravaged her ass. A part of her brain was thankful he wasn't all that big, disgusted that she gave herself to such a devious man, let alone spy and risk her career for him. Another part of her, the part affected by the drug she craved, didn't care about the pain or the consequences. That part only wanted to be pounded by a hard cock until her eyebrows burned.

Baker continued to pump in and out while he observed the mental tug-of-war going on behind Sarah Ann's eyes. He was pleased when the drug won the argument. A blond brow shot up when Sarah Ann sank her own fingers into her pussy, stuffing her sex as he filled her ass. The extra stimulation of her fingers against his rod triggered his own release. His head fell back on a shallow gasp as he pumped into her once, twice more, and blasted his seed deep.

The drug was more potent than the last lab tests confirmed. The woman had come four times to his one and still begged for more. He pulled out of her with a plop, cleaned himself with a wet sanitary wipe from his desk drawer and tucked himself back into his pants. He tossed a bottle of sterilizing solution and a roll of paper towels onto the desk next to her naked thighs.

"Clean my desk, get dressed and get out," he called over his shoulder, stopping at the file cabinet again. A strong antibiotic was in order seeing he'd taken Sarah Ann's backside without a condom. He popped a dose of Zithromax penicillin, locked the cabinet and walked out. He didn't bother to lock the office door behind him.

Sarah Ann ignored the bottle of sterilizing solution and frantically pulled and rubbed her clit until she exploded against her fingers three more times. When her legs steadied enough to hold her weight, she slid off the desk and cleaned it and herself. Once dressed, she slipped out of his office and practically ran back to her cubicle in the Research department.

The whole episode had taken less than fifteen minutes.

# CHAPTER THREE

Pam had been right. The Duke Mansion was definitely high class. Delaine stoically oooh'd and aaah'd as she walked up the front stairs of the columned entrance and across the expansive patios. Once inside, she blended in with a few other ladies as she walked through the large French doors. She admired the historic paintings and tapestries on the walls until they reached the entrance of a soaring double foyer where a good-sized crowd merged into a growing line. Obviously this was the place to be on a Friday night.

A smartly dressed, balding gentleman walked down the long line and through the crowd, checking names against a list. Delaine was so far down the line, one more step and she'd be practically outside. She mentally kicked herself for not coming a few minutes earlier. When the man reached her, he checked her name twice before giving a tight-lipped smile.

"Pardon me, madam. You are not required to wait in line. If you would follow me please?" He extended his arm and personally escorted her forward to the great hall. Delaine made a mental note to thank Pam for hooking her up.

An attendant in jet-black livery retrieved her from the great hall and led her to an elegant dining room. He waited while she slipped her heavy wool cloak off her shoulders and handed it to the woman manning the coat check at the door. He then showed her to one of many small round tables, the perfect size for four people and a full-course meal. She ordered a glass of sparkling wine and discreetly surveyed the poised and professional men and women filling the room.

She wasn't sure why, but as her tablemates for the evening were seated, she grew nervous. It wasn't like she'd never found herself in a group of veritable strangers before. Her job required her to frequently acquaint herself with people she didn't know, get into their circle, obtain information they had no intention of giving her and get out. But this wasn't work. This was no mission. Work, Gary and her kids had been her life, and she hadn't been out to play as herself in a long time. Perhaps the fact that this particular soiree was for pleasure rather than work had her uncomfortable in her true skin. Or was something else rattling her cage?

'Sapa?'

*I am here. Why are you concerned? There is no danger here.*

'I don't know why I'm nervous. I feel like something is going to happen, or someone is watching.'

*It is the latter.*

And that's all Delaine could get out of the damned cat.

* * * * *

Justin looked up from the Earl Grey tea he was drinking and almost choked. The woman he'd seen down in The Vault a few days ago was being escorted to one of the dinner tables across the room. Her table filled up quickly with other women, but none as gorgeous as her. She seemed to hold herself apart, observing rather than participating while the others at her table introduced themselves, ordered their dinner and chatted. He was sure the guy and two ladies at his own table were mingling as well, but he tuned them out as soon as he'd laid eyes on the beauty across the room.

He set his cup down, leaned back in his chair and stared long and hard. Damn she was sexy. There was confidence in the set of her shoulders, just as he'd seen in the few seconds he'd watched her before she disappeared down the tunnel in The Vault.

Her little black dress, high-heeled pumps with matching leather handbag and upswept hair all oozed class and femininity, but her strong legs and toned arms screamed "fighter". Her natural curls were swept up into an elegant chignon, with wisps curling around her face and down her neck. Justin even liked the shade of lipstick she wore. It reminded him of ripe Bing cherries and complimented her dark skin.

Her mouth looked just perfect for kissing, and anything else his mind could conjure. He had no business even thinking about getting with her until he knew who or whose she was. And her appearance here tonight didn't change the fact he'd seen her walking around in a place she certainly shouldn't have had access to. She either worked with Baker or she was the agent he'd been keeping an eye out for. He couldn't compromise his mission sniffing after her. But damn, he couldn't help himself.

He picked up his cup and took a gulp. The beauty chose that moment to look away from her chattering tablemates and directly at him. He raised his cup in salute and grinned when both her brows shot up a good inch. He chuckled when she craned her neck to look behind her. When she turned back around she seemed genuinely surprised he still watched. He held her gaze until she lowered her eyes and looked away.

Justin reluctantly gave his attention to the waitress taking his order, or rather, trying to take his order. She cleared her throat for the third time and asked him again what he wished to eat. With emphasis on the word eat, the waitress' eyes slid boldly over his body, settling on the crotch of his pants. There was no doubt what the waitress offered off-menu. His tablemates' shocked expressions had him suppressing a grin. The girl's invitation was blatant, but Justin couldn't have cared less. His mind was full of the beautiful woman across the room who was now completely ignoring him.

He ordered a steak, rare, with a side of mashed potatoes and mustard greens, then tried to focus on the people at his table. He was supposed to be getting to know them, but his eyes kept straying to the tastefully dressed woman whose dimples appeared when she laughed. Who motioned with her hands when she talked. And eyes, so mysterious and exotic looking.

A chime sounded, marking the beginning of the social. Until dinner was served everyone was expected to stroll around the room and drop in on any table with an empty seat. The point was to make a new acquaintance, chat a bit then move on to the next table. The beauty never got up to mingle. She didn't have to. Justin clenched his jaw, surprised at the impatience he felt at not being able to speak to her. Every time he got ready to make his way over, any empty chair at her table was quickly filled with another man.

It was almost comical to watch them time their arrival with the departure of the man before. Justin watched the I-want-you musical chairs go on until the dinner bell chimed and everyone returned to their original tables to dine.

He watched her smile up at the waiter who brought her dinner, then attack her food like she was mad at it. She'd seemed to be enjoying herself, but now she looked stiff and annoyed. Her back was ramrod straight and brows drawn tightly together. Had one of the men who'd dropped in said something to make her feel uncomfortable? If he found out who'd done it, he'd give them a little wall-to-wall counseling for upsetting her.

Now he'd have to wait until dessert was served to go over and talk to her. That was fine. He'd already decided that before the night was over, he would know her name and anything else she chose to share.

* * * * *

"Here I am eating a delicious dinner in a swanky, first-class mingling establishment, and I'm sitting here talking to myself," Delaine grumbled under her breath, hacking her asparagus into itty bitty pieces with her steak knife.

*But you are not speaking with yourself. You are speaking, or rather arguing, with me,* Sapa whispered sarcastically into her head.

'I am NOT going over there to talk to that man!' Delaine growled back along their bond, stabbing her knife into a steak fillet so tender she could have cut it with a fork. The lioness was trying to get her to talk to the gorgeous redhead eyeballing her from across the room. But the cat was clearly crazy.

*You know you want to meet him, Suta.*

'Who the hell cares whether I want to or not? There's no way I'm making a fool of myself. I did that for eighteen years, and I am SO done,' Delaine fumed at her spirit guide.

*Pride versus opportunity, Suta Winyan. Choose one. He's interested. And quite tasty looking.*

'Puh-lease! A man as fine as that, interested in me? Riiiiiight.' It was times like this Delaine wished her spirit guide would go on vacation or something, but no such luck. The attractive man had caught the big cat's eye.

*A possible mate, yes?*

'NO!' Delaine wailed in her head.

More than confident at her job, Delaine just wasn't that bold when it came to trying to develop a love life. She'd been with the same man since her nineteenth birthday. At thirty-seven, she had no clue how to play dating games, and there was no way between here and hell she was putting herself out there with a total stranger. Besides, if the father of her children didn't want her, then who would?

*You admit the puny Gary person you were married to was right?* the lioness asked on a sly purr.

Delaine bit the inside of her cheek to keep her mouth from falling open. What an ah-ha moment. Sapa was right. What the hell was she thinking, allowing that bastard Gary to make her feel unworthy and unwanted? She'd been more than good enough for him. He was the first man she'd ever dated, ever made love to, and unfortunately, settled for. But she would never settle for a mealy-mouthed, untrustworthy, spineless, selfish asshole again.

Mr. Handsome-As-Sin with the piercing eyes didn't look like he fell into the mealy- mouthed category. He was stunning. He must be intelligent or he wouldn't be in this group. She would never know if he fit the rest of the bill if she didn't take a chance.

'Okay, Sapa, let's do this,' she said, and took a deep breath as Sapa appeared behind her eyes, ready to give any aid Delaine might need.

Delaine squared her shoulders and pushed to her feet. The butterflies in her stomach grew kite-sized wings the moment she locked eyes with him. He didn't look away. If anything, he stared harder. The man had no shame. The expression in his eyes was primal, like he had an unsatisfied craving for something. So that's what lust looks like? Her knees felt peculiarly weak, but she kept right on walking.

She told herself to relax, painting on a calm facade. He stood and waited for her as she made her way over to his table. Lord, he was so tall and powerfully built. Forcing her eyes not to widen like a startled owl's, she took in the length of his legs. He had to be at least six-foot-five to her five-foot-seven inches. His gray fine-gauged sweater accentuated the width of his shoulders. A pair of jet-black, tailored trousers showed off a trim waist, flat stomach and super long legs.

Sapa purred in her head as Delaine entertained thoughts of sliding her hands over the well-developed deltoids and thick biceps that bulged through the material of his sweater. His wavy, dark red hair was tastefully cut, with the sides and back cut shorter to fade into a neat line at the nape of his neck. His eyes were the most vivid, breathtaking blue. Like perfectly cut Caribbean Sea gemstones. Jeweled topaz blue. Damn, she'd always been a sucker for blue stones.

With a slight bow, he held out his elbow to her. As soon as her fingers touched his arm, she felt a peculiar zing dive-bomb straight between her legs. Woo, goodness! Delaine gasped silently. Her painted-on smile faltered a bit from the intensity of the unfamiliar sensation, and Sapa purred and panted as though she was in heat.

Delaine lowered her lashes, sent a mental "cut it out" to the big black cat and then looked up at the tall, ruggedly handsome man. Lord, he was fine. What had she been thinking, walking over here like this? Her stomach churned and her thighs burned. Oh please,

please, please let her steak and veggies stay down. Water. Maybe a sip of water would unclog the lump in her throat. Then he smiled and Delaine felt her barely-in-place facade melt completely.

The two women sitting at his table glared daggers at her while the man glared daggers at the two women.

"Time to go," the attractive hunk said in a voice so smooth, it made her think of Luther Vandross on a rainy night, sprawled out on a plush fur rug in front of a fireplace. Delaine prayed harder for her veggies when his eyes twinkled mischievously. He winked, and steered her toward an empty table in a corner of the room.

He pulled out a chair and motioned her into it. "Good evening, gorgeous. I'm Justin." His chest tightened with what could only be described as pure male satisfaction when her dimpled cheeks turned a sweet shade of caramelized pink. "Glass of wine?"

He ordered a glass of rare white merlot for himself and nodded in appreciation of good taste as Delaine ordered a small glass of their best dessert wine...Sandeman's Twenty-Year Tawny Port. When she also ordered an apple tart for them to share, he tilted his head to the side and embraced her with his eyes. Skip the apple tart— he looked like he'd rather just eat her.

"So, what brings such a beautiful woman here tonight?" Justin asked charmingly.

"I, well, um," she stammered, but caught herself quickly. She forced her breathing to slow so she could answer the damn question. Whew, he was just too good looking for words. And Sapa ran around in circles in her head like a fool. Looking down into her glass, she respectfully asked the great lioness to quiet down and lend her some of her quiet, royal strength. Sapa immediately quieted and sent a flood of calm confidence through their bond.

"I just moved here," Delaine finally answered as

calmly as she was able. "A friend of mine suggested this group was a good way to meet other professionals. I'm a bit too old for the meat market, wham bam, dance club scene." Whoa! Had she actually said something so blunt to this man? Perhaps Sapa had given her too much gumption? Oh, he was definitely turned off now. Good. Better to get it over with so she could go home and throw up then kick herself in the butt for being such a babbling idiot.

Her annoyance with herself quickly became surprise and then utter amazement when he reached across the table and dipped his finger into the whipped cream of her apple tart.

"I like a bold woman." His grin could only be described as sensuously wicked. And way he locked eyes with her as he licked the frothy whip off his fingertip? Oh lord!

She watched his tongue swirl around the cream on the tip of his finger before his lips wrapped around it and sucked the rest of the whip away. Okay, the upset stomach was a thing of the past. Her heart beat so fast she figured she'd just pass out and wouldn't have to worry about throwing up after all.

"So what kind of work do you do?" he asked, still eating the whipped cream from his fingers. She kept telling herself to stop looking at that long index finger as it disappeared into his mouth but her eyes wouldn't listen.

*Stop looking! You cannot have a decent conversation if you are drooling, Suta Winyan.*

Delaine mentally nodded, thanking Sapa for intervening in her major duh moment, and took a fortifying gulp of rich, sweet port. The potent wine tingled as it slipped down her throat and calmed her churning tummy. Justin wiped his fingers on a linen napkin. Good, no tan lines on his ring finger. She looked up to his face and her gaze settled on his mouth. She'd never seen a white guy with lips like this except on television. This man had full, Steven Tyler lips. Firm, kissable lips. Oh lord, she had to get a hold of herself. Must be the wine. Sapa snapped her out of her examination of his mouth.

*He asked what kind of work it is you do, remember? Of course, you cannot tell him.*

'I know, Sapa. Geez, I'm not that far gone.' Delaine thought she heard a sarcastic snort resonate along the psychic bond as she answered the man's question. "I'm a technical consultant," she finally answered.

"Technical, as in…?" he queried.

"Technical, as in pharmaceutical and biotech manufacturing hierarchy development."

\* \* \* \* \*

Justin lifted his eyebrows with a perfected dumb-as-a-rock, need-more-information-please look. He knew it had the intended affect when Delaine chuckled.

"I work for a company that specializes in providing analytical solutions to pharmaceutical and biotech manufacturers. We help them map out their production processes in a hierarchical manner. Then they can retrieve data from multiple databases for any part of their process. It enables them to do analysis just like that," she explained with a quiet snap of her fingers. "My job is to work with my customer's business community and scientific process engineers. I help them determine how they plan to use their data for analysis then we can build the graphical representation of the process, or hierarchy, appropriately. Make sense?"

Justin nodded. He knew exactly what she was talking about, but he kept his expression neutral. This woman was alluring, sexy as hell, and he was instantly attracted to her. But she'd just confirmed that she was definitely involved in what he was investigating at Astin Pharma. When he'd sighted her in The Vault, it hadn't been an interesting coincidence after all. Damn.

"So, Justin, what do you do?" Delaine asked. Mimicking his behavior, she dipped her own finger into the whipped cream on their dessert then licked it off with a mischievous grin.

Justin's eyes zeroed in on the pucker of her mouth as her dark cherry lips curled around her finger. He couldn't decide if he should choke on his wine or swallow his tongue. So he did both.

Out of her seat in a flash, Delaine circled around the table and starting thumping him right in the middle of his back. Damn, the woman has a strong hand, he thought, wondering if he would have bruises where she whacked him in her effort to clear his windpipe.

"Are you all right? Oh goodness, my first outing in this town and I've already half killed a man!" Delaine growled, and kept right on beating the hell out of him. Justin's hacking cough turned into a raspy chuckle. She'd sounded so sincere, he couldn't help laughing.

"I'm fine, Delaine, really," he wheezed around a final hack. He held up his hands to ward her off in hopes that she wouldn't pound him again. Well, the physique he'd glimpsed when he'd watched her disappear down the tunnel in The Vault obviously hadn't been a play of the dim lighting. He smiled big and shook his head in delight. The woman was a treat. The smile vanished when, all on its own, his mind filled with thoughts of his tongue sliding along her smooth cocoa skin to discover what this rich treat tasted like. His cock filled right along with his mind. Hungrily he watched her pretty almond-shaped eyes turn all soft and feminine, then widen as he reached out and took one of her hands. He leaned forward and spoke quietly, his fingers a feather-light caress over the back of her hand.

"Thank you for saving my life, beautiful."

Delaine settled back into her chair, her face on fire with a fierce blush. She'd totally overreacted to his little bout of choking, but here he was thanking her. And looking at her like she was the most beautiful female on the planet. His gaze slammed into her and those damned butterflies stirred once more.

She could only nod. His expression was so lusty she couldn't look into his eyes another second. It did funny things to her belly, made her want to pull him across the table and jump his bones on top of the remainder of her apple tart.

"Delaine, I know a little jazz club not far from here. You game?" he asked, not bothering to hide the huskiness in his voice. He watched her body language closely and her eyes flashed such a wide range of emotions so quickly he couldn't catch them all. His eyes followed her tongue from one side of her inviting mouth to the other as she licked her lips nervously. For a moment, he thought she might turn him down. Relief stilled an uneasy flutter in his gut he hadn't noticed was there until she nodded and allowed him a glimpse of her dimples once more.

"Wait here, I'll be right back." He left the table, strode to the coat check. From a distance Justin could have sworn she was mumbling to herself, but as soon as she saw him approaching, she stilled. He slipped the heavy black cloak around her shoulders and put on his own coat before offering his arm to her again.

She looked up at him warily, her brows knit in a tight furrow of suspicion. He hadn't realized until this moment that he hadn't asked which coat was hers but had simply retrieved the one his investigator's mind logically picked out—an ankle-length black cloak with fox fur around the large hood that said "class" loud and clear. He knew exactly what she was thinking. Softly, he said, "Baby, I've watched you from the moment you walked in the door. You're the only woman here classy enough to wear something like this." He fingered the thick, soft material at the neck and secured the clasp, grazing her soft cheek with the backs of his fingers.

\* \* \* \* \*

Arm in arm, they stepped out of the dining room and made their way out of the mansion. Claim tickets in hand, the valets were immediately off to retrieve their vehicles, leaving Delaine and Justin alone under the cloud-covered moonlight.

To Justin, the four seconds it had taken the attendants to turn their backs and move off into the night was four seconds too long. As soon as they were out of sight, he gently pulled Delaine to him, just close enough for the front of her cloak to whisper against the smooth leather of his jacket. He leaned forward, his voice a deliberate and seductive whisper.

"I've wanted to get you alone all evening," he breathed into the soft down of her hair.

Usually ready with a smart-assed reply, Delaine's throat closed up and every thought flew right out of her head. Her hands lifted to touch his shoulders all on their own while she fought with the rest of her body to keep from rubbing up against him. He moved closer, blatantly inhaling the scent of her skin as his lips gently explored the soft contours of her face. The kiss that wasn't quite a kiss had her practically melting. Damn, it was so erotic, she barely felt the chill in the air as her body warmed from her scalp down to her pinky toes. She wanted him. Badly.

Justin gently rubbed his nose against hers. His nostrils flared as he inhaled her natural scent. She smelled like allspice and ginger. Spicy, sweet. He liked it. He rubbed his lips against her cheek, brushed over her mouth and nibbled along her jawbone. She wore hardly any makeup, skin so baby smooth he could stand there and rub his cheek against hers until she tired of him doing so.

He worried her diamond stud with his teeth. After endless moments of bathing in the sensual fog that was Delaine, he managed to string together a few words against the tempting lobe of her dainty little ears. "May I kiss you?" he whispered against her skin.

Unable to gather enough air to speak, Delaine mouthed the word yes, almost desperate to feel his mouth moving against hers. Her head screamed, Hurry up and kiss me already! She couldn't tell if it was her, Sapa or the both of them. Strung so tight, her whole body hummed with the effort it took to stand there and look like a woman halfway in control of herself.

By the time he finally got around to it, she was ready to grab him by the collar, rise up on her tiptoes and lay one on him. She'd never had this kind of physical reaction to a man. Neither had Sapa, so beside herself, if she purred any louder in Delaine's mind, she was sure even Justin would be able to hear it. Oh lord, she almost hoped he would say something stupid to ruin the moment. Give her an excuse to shut down and bow out. All this stomach fluttering was just too much.

Justin played it out for as long as he could, but now he couldn't wait another second to claim her lips. He slanted his mouth tenderly over hers but couldn't hold it there. It just wasn't enough. Pulling her body flush against his, he deepened the kiss like they were in a private room with nowhere to go but to bed. When she began to move her mouth under his, his arms tightened around her until she was wrapped completely within the cocoon of his large body. He groaned brokenly when she eagerly opened for him, allowing him full access to her lovely mouth. He tasted, teased and then plunged deeply, entangling his tongue with hers. She was delicious, like apples and fine wine. Her ready response made his thighs flex and stomach clench wildly with need. She made him feel…untamed.

A quiet uh-hem caught his attention. The valets had arrived with their cars. Damn, already? Broke the kiss on a sigh but couldn't resist another taste or two. His mouth kicked up into a half grin when she smiled up at him, lips parted, and slightly dazed.

Justin stepped back, admired the sleek machine idling at the curb and caught Delaine's unabashedly smug expression. She drove a black on black Jaguar convertible. Exactly like his. Yep, the woman had class.

He pulled open her door and settled her behind the wheel. "Follow me, beauty," his sensual whisper a promise of things to come.

# CHAPTER FOUR

Delaine followed Justin to a jazz club about a mile from the Duke Mansion. The four-minute drive gave her too much time to contemplate her ridiculous physical reaction to the man. What was it about him that made her want to jump him? How did a man she'd just met turn her on more with a look than her ex-husband ever had with his whole body? This just wasn't like her.

Thankful for the few minutes she'd had to get herself together, she managed a small smile when Justin appeared and opened her car door for her. He ushered her into the club with his hand at the small of her back. She couldn't help tensing at the intimate contact. His fingers burned through her coat, sending an uncontrollable tingle up her spine. Damned traitorous body.

The place was large and tastefully decorated with dark leathers and leopard print chairs. They sat in an intimate corner at a table just large enough for two. Mauve linen tablecloths, the subtle scent of fresh cut flowers and candles set the perfect atmosphere for lovers.

They listened to the band do covers of some of her favorite jazz songs. In the middle of a smooth Anita Baker set, the hackles on the back of Delaine's neck stood at attention. She felt the lioness rise to prowl back and forth for a moment before speaking calmly but firmly to her charge.

*There is an enemy is in this place.*

'Who is it?' Delaine queried along the link that secured their bond.

*The one you hunt.*

Baker was here? Of all places for the man to be on a Friday night, he had to be at the same club she was. Double damn.

*Excuse yourself, Suta Winyan. Take us to the ladies room.*

"You all right, Delaine? You look a little peaked," Justin asked, concern etched across his smooth brow. His fingers sought hers from across the table and stroked the back of her hand.

"Oh sure, I'm fine. Justin, would you please excuse me a moment? I need to run to the ladies room." Heat crept into her cheeks on a blush when he stood up with her and kissed the back of her hand. Such a gentleman, drop-dead gorgeous, tall, nicely built... Sapa prodded her out of her reverie and she hurried off with sure, solid steps.

Delaine stood in a typically long line for the bathroom. The lioness prowled restlessly until she could duck into the first available stall, lock it quickly and close her eyes. She blocked out the sounds of the club, pushed the saxophones and deep bass far away. The smooth, sultry voice of the lead singer floating through the speakers in the ceiling faded into the background.

Delaine summoned her companion with a thought. 'Please assist me, Sapa.' The lioness sprang forth and a vision began.

Through her spirit's eye, Delaine saw a short blonde woman sitting in her very own living room pleading for Delaine's help. Then the vision flashed to another woman sitting in a chair. Her hands were tied tight behind her back and a large canvas bag was over her head. This woman appeared to be in a large dark room that was completely empty. In the background, Baker's face drifted in and out, a maniacal gleam in his jewel-green eyes. Then the vision winked out and Sapa was back in Delaine's mind, growling low in her throat.

'Thank you for your foresight, Sapa, but what does it mean?'

*It was not revealed to me, but you will know when the time comes. I will be with you, my Suta. Now go, enjoy the rest of your evening. The one you hunt departed while we waited in the long ladies room line.*

The vision showed Baker was involved in something sinister, but she'd already known that. The identity of the women and their part in this play was a mystery. These women had to be important. Sapa only shared these kinds of visions if there was danger. At least one good thing had come out of her little trip to the restroom—Justin hadn't been in the vision.

* * * * *

Justin stood as he watched Delaine make her way back to their table. He held out her chair and was gifted with a brilliant smile. She seemed to have a bit more bounce in her step. That must have been one hell of a special trip to the ladies room, he thought.

"I ordered a drink for you. Hope you don't mind," he said, flashing a smile of his own.

"No worries. Thanks." But her expression was distant, far-off. He caught a glimpse of the wheels turning in her head and knew he'd given her too much time to think about something other than him. For some reason, jealousy rose up in his chest at whatever or whoever had her attention. Probably not good, but he wanted her focused on him and him alone. He reached across the table, took her hand again and looked directly into her beautiful root beer colored, almond shaped eyes.

"I love the shape of your eyes, the way they tilt up at the sides. You look…exotic." She looked at him like she didn't believe him, but he was genuinely interested. "Let me guess. You're mixed with Indian, perhaps?"

"Actually, I am," she said, impressed he'd totally hit the mark. Most people thought she was part Asian or Mexican or something, then took one look at her long, kinky, curly hair and were completely confused. "I'm black and Native American. My family on my mother's side is Blackfeet and Lakota Sioux. And a little bit of Choctaw mixed in, though I'm not sure how since that tribe is so far south of the others."

"That's pretty cool. We have a little bit of Cheyenne in our family, but it's so far removed I couldn't begin to tell you anything about it. What about you?"

"Well, I have an older brother who actually speaks Lakota fluently. I only know a few words," she said, deciding how much to reveal about herself. Just because she felt she could trust him didn't change the fact that they'd just met. "My kids and I powwow every summer with our adopted family. In fact, my daughter and I are both pretty good fancy shawl dancers and my son is a serious grass dancer. Won first place last year at the Annual Golden Powwow."

"Golden?"

"Yeah," she said slowly, a bit of unintentional "duh" in her tone, "as in Golden, Colorado. It's a town. You know, where they make Coors beer." She laughed when he wrinkled up his nose and made a disgusted sound at the thought of actually drinking Coors beer. "So you're a beer snob? Say it ain't so!"

His hand flew to his heart in a dramatic gesture. "I'm afraid it's much worse than that, beauty. If it comes in a can that doesn't say Coke, it doesn't get anywhere near these lips."

His lopsided grin appeared, and the butterflies in her stomach came out to play again. The damned things should have been exhausted by now. Did butterflies take naps?

"So what does get near those lips?" she teased and propped her elbow on the table. She rested her palm in her chin and regarded him boldly. Whoa! Since when did she know how to flirt? Goodness, how many times was she going to surprise herself tonight?

*Perhaps this man brings it naturally out of you?*

'Shhh, Sapa.' She'd never heard the big cat sound so saucy. 'You're going to make me laugh out loud, then he'll think I'm crazy,' she growled silently, trying to keep her expression steady.

"So you want to know what gets near these lips?" he asked, giving her own question back to her. "Only the best, I assure you."

Their drinks arrived and Delaine burst out laughing. The man had ordered Shirley Temple drinks for both of them, and hers had an extra cherry!

The best? Definitely!

* * * * *

Justin heard himself talk her into a slow dance. He took her in his arms and immediately regretted it. Barely managing to behave, his fingers itched to slip low on her back and tease the luscious curve at the top of her ass. Arms wrapped securely around her firm body, his nose buried itself in the top of her soft curly chignon, careful not to disturb the elegant style. Nudging her chin up with his nose, he urged her to lift her head so he could kiss her then kiss her some more. Mmm, she tasted and felt so good. And when she gave him delicious slow slips of her tongue and little nips of her teeth, he got so hard he could have played nine innings with his dick. Damn, if he didn't get her off the dance floor soon, he'd come in his pants.

To Delaine, Justin's kisses were like chocolate—rich and addictive. She couldn't hold back her soft moans as he nibbled and sucked on her tongue. He pressed closer and she gulped. Lord, the man was hard as a rock and huge against her stomach. Feeling his arousal did wicked things to her body. Good thing her wardrobe hadn't been delivered yet. That little inconvenience meant a pair of granny panties was getting soaked under her little black dress instead of her usual itty-bitty thong. All hail granny panties! A thong would have been drenched and completely good for nothing by now.

They returned to their table and talked, kissed and held hands until well past two in the morning. As he saw her to her car, Justin was genuinely pleased he'd shown her a good time. Unable to resist one more kiss, he leaned down far enough to take one more kiss as she sat behind the wheel. Delaine responded hungrily, as if she'd never see him again and had to get her fill of him right now. That lip lock singed the hair on his toes and left him clenching his teeth, fighting for control as he closed the door and stepped away from her car.

She pulled away from the curb and his smile faded. He started his Jag and flipped on the secure cell phone link hidden in the dash. A few seconds later the beep signaling the end of transmission sounded. The digital photo he'd quietly taken of Delaine was sent.

* * * * *

"Hey, Geri, it's Delaine. Sorry to call so late but it's the first chance I had today."

"No problem. What's going on?"

"So far so good at Astin. I met Brian Baker. A real sleaze," she grunted into the phone, fighting with her high heels, trying to toe them off as she sat down at her laptop. "You're a genius, by the way. My badge got me access to The Vault. How you managed to get the encryption key to work, I'll never know."

"That's why they pay me the big bucks," Geri chided. "That, and getting your butt out of there in one piece. Have you come up with any evidence yet on what Baker is doing?"

"Not quite, but I'm working on it. I've got a tail, Ger, and she's slowing me down. Can you check her out for me?"

"Sure, send me a digital."

Delaine pressed the send button on the encrypted e-mail program and said, "It's on the way to you now. Her name is Sarah Ann Crosby," she said on a wistful sigh.

"What was that?"

"What was what?"

"That dreamy sigh you just let slip is what," Geri said matter-of-factly.

Delaine should have known better. Geri Studebaker had been a top agent back in her day. She didn't run the most secretive law enforcement agency for nothing. The woman didn't miss anything and her deductive reasoning was second to none. Hell, she could probably figure out what Delaine's motive had been for things she'd done back in grade school.

"You're not going to believe this, but I met someone tonight. Ger, he's so fine, and smart."

"What's his name?"

"Justin."

"Justin what?"

"Oh my god, I have no idea," Delaine said in amazement. A name, a whole name, was usually the first thing she got out of a person when first meeting them. She had no idea of his profession either, having just asked about his career when she'd gotten the grand idea of teasing him with that stupid apple tart. The end result—Justin had almost choked to death and she'd pounded on his back like she was tenderizing a tough side of beef.

"Just be careful, Delaine."

"Will do, boss. Good night."

Delaine shut down her computer and then walked around the house, checking security. Once in bed, she tucked her gun under her pillow and summoned Sapa onto this plane.

'Come to me, Sapa.'

The black lioness shimmered into a relaxed heap on the floor next to Delaine's bed. She licked her paws and replied, *Yes, Suta?*

Delaine hadn't been this wound up in, well, never. She reached down and rubbed Sapa between her ears in a gesture that soothed both her and the great cat. "What do you really think of the man we met tonight?" Delaine asked anxiously.

*He will make a worthy mate.*

"I just met him, Sapa. How could you possibly know?" Delaine paused as an idea popped into her head. "And why didn't you tell me whether Gary was a worthy mate or not?" Delaine ground her back teeth, agitated at having asked the question before she'd really thought it out. She already knew the answer, and Sapa, if anything, was straightforward and a lover of I-told-you-so's.

*If you recall, Suta, I expressed dislike for the Gary person several times before you married him. Yet, I am your guide, not your master. You will do as you will.*

"Yeah, yeah, I remember," Delaine sighed. The fact

that she'd never shared Sapa with Gary spoke volumes. "By the way, thanks for the heads-up in the ladies room. Who was the blonde woman in my house begging for help? I assume the woman tied to the chair was a different one. What did the vision mean? Who are those women?"

*I was not told or shown. But do not worry. We are never given a glimpse of things to come in order to hurt us, always to aid us. Now sleep. We must rest for tomorrow.*

"Tomorrow? Other than my hair appointment with Pam, there's nothing going on tomorrow."

But Sapa only purred, her long feline tongue lolling to the side as she began to disappear. Oh lord, the lioness was grinning.

"Sapa, you come back here!" Delaine called. "What happens tomorrow, you stubborn old thing you!"

Sapa sent serenity and reassurance along their bond as she shimmered away to her quiet place inside Delaine's mind.

Delaine was asleep in seconds, her dreams filled with a redheaded, six–and–a–half– foot, gorgeous hunk of a blue-eyed man.

## CHAPTER FIVE

Who in the world could be calling her this early in the morning? Delaine grumbled, rolled over in her bed and snatched the phone off the hook. "Hello?"

"Hi, Mom!"

"Hey, babies! How are you?" she said happily, bolting straight up in the bed, now wide awake. "What are you two doing today?"

"We're working in La Boulainge for brunch," said Tanna, her oldest.

"Then we're going to play a round of golf. Finally!" Michael declared. He was Tanna's spitting image, born only a few minutes behind his sister. Both were enrolled in the Le Cordon Bleu culinary bachelor's degree program, and Delaine was infinitely proud of them. They'd taken the departure of their father with amazing grace and rallied around her like little soldiers during that rough time. They still had a relationship with their dad, though by his and his mistress-turned-new-wife's choosing, it was somewhat cool.

"We just called to check on you. How do you like Charlotte?" Tanna asked.

"It's nice. Lots to do, plenty to see. You'll love the house. Most of my upcoming assignments are on the East Coast, so I'll be staying here for a while."

"Will our stuff get there in time for Christmas break?"

"Yep. And I can either set up your rooms before you get here, or wait until you arrive so you can pick which rooms you want."

"It doesn't matter to us. Can't wait to see you. The next two months are going to feel like forever, Mom," Michael's deep voice filled the line.

"I look forward to seeing you too, sweetie."

"We've gotta run," Tanna said, always the diligent one. Shooing her brother off the phone she said, "We'll call you next week, Mom."

Delaine felt a tug along the bond. "Oh, Sapa says hello to you both. She misses you as much as I do."

"Hi, Sapa!" they chimed in unison. "Love you, Mom! Bye."

"Love you too."

Even as tired as she was, she was so jazzed at hearing from her children she couldn't possibly go back to sleep now. With that, Delaine was out of bed and headed to the shower.

While she lathered up in the oversized stall, thoughts of her children filled her mind along with a nagging guilt she hadn't felt in a long time.

Tanna and Michael still had no idea she was a spy. Front companies like Aegis understood that agents, especially those with families, needed to maintain as normal a life as possible. Since she had kids, and used to have a husband, most of her traveling had been limited to short take-downs where they were pretty sure who was up to no good. All she had to do was go in, get the evidence and get out. It usually amounted to a few days here and there with the pretense that she was away training pharmaceutical manufacturers how to use her company's software or help them map their production processes. Perfect cover for her high-tech persona.

She used to question why she couldn't share her profession with her family. After all, she was providing a valuable service by taking scum off the streets by infiltrating their organizations and taking them down. But after so many years of firsthand experience with the kind of ruthlessness these criminals possessed, she was glad neither her ex-husband nor children knew what she did for a living. Ignorance was the best form of protection. And Aegis protected them well. After all, Delaine Jeris wasn't even her real name.

The steam felt good, but her conscience nagged. She'd just met a fabulous guy whom she wouldn't mind seeing again, but it had been forever since she'd had to do the "hide my identity" thing with a potential lover. She cringed at the memory of how she'd almost slipped and told him her real name last night. With Gary, she'd had years to adjust until keeping her job secret was second nature. But what face should she wear with this new Justin guy? And why did she wish she could wear none at all?

'Come to me, Sapa,' she whispered to her best friend and guide.

*I am here, Suta, but I will not get into that water with you.*

Delaine laughed at Sapa's dry humor. She'd learned as a little girl that the lioness despised playing in water. One summer while visiting her grandma on the reservation, her cousins tossed a non-swimming Delaine into the lake. Floundering to stay afloat, she'd screeched for Sapa to help her. Her cousins thought she'd suddenly perfected her dog-paddling technique. What they hadn't seen was Sapa's big black back holding her head above water, trying to get her to shore with all haste. Delaine's threats to tell her grandma sent her cousins fleeing, while a very angry Sapa wished she could sink her fangs into their backsides. Never mind the fact Delaine only had to put her feet down to touch bottom. Sapa had growled, hissed and, to Delaine's surprise, cursed a blue streak until her supernatural fur dried out.

Delaine pressed her lips together as the lioness' corporeal form stalked around the large bathroom. A giggle bubbled out of her throat just as Sapa chose a nice cool spot on the tile floor near the sunken bathtub, flopped down and regarded her charge. Delaine laughed outright at the sound of Sapa's droll voice.

*It is a dreadful memory.*

'I'm sorry, Sapa, but it's funny. Now. At the time I was terrified. But that's not why I called you to this plane.' With that, Delaine stuck her face under the shower of water and groaned. God that felt good. Too bad her mind couldn't enjoy it.

'Sapa, what's going on with me? I feel so…unsteady.'

*There is nothing wrong with you, Suta. Your name, Suta Winyan, means Strong Woman. You are, and have always been, a strong woman. Even now when you feel unsure.*

'But why do I feel this way? I've never had a problem doing my job before.'

*Performing your duties is not the issue. Deceiving our mate is the issue.*

'He is NOT our mate,' Delaine protested hotly, not sure why.

*And you know this how?*

Delaine scrunched up her face and regarded Sapa like the stubborn little girl she'd been when they'd met. She rolled her eyes instead. The great hunter lay on her side yawning, not paying the least bit of attention to Delaine's face. But then, she didn't need to.

'God, what is it about this guy? I don't even know him and I want to tell him everything. What makes me want to…hell, I don't know. I've never been affected by anyone like this. Not even my ex-husband, and I was married to him forever.'

*Do you have to mention the puny Gary man? It makes my stomach upset and gives me the urge to eat grass.*

"Sapa, you only eat grass when you feel sick or nauseous."

*Precisely.*

Delaine snorted at her spirit guide's matter-of-fact tone, then Sapa said something that rocked her back on her heels.

*You do realize the puny Gary man hid more from you than you did from him, yes?*

Delaine hopped out of the shower, sputtering like a drowned rat in a shower cap. Yeah, she'd known all right. She was, after all, an undercover agent. If there was anything she was good at, it was ferreting out the truth, even about her own husband. The cheating bastard.

'Enough said. Sometimes I wish I weren't the only one who could see and touch you. It would have been nice for a chunk of his ass to disappear and he'd have no idea what bit him.'

*I would not have dared bite such a vile creature. Just the thought…* Delaine's eyes went wide as the lioness actually shuddered and made a nasty gagging sound! *I must depart in search of some grass to eat. I am feeling somewhat unsettled.*

Delaine laughed as she grabbed her favorite aromatic oil and worked it into her damp skin. With genuine thanks, she responded, 'I'm fine now, Sapa. Thanks for keeping me company.'

*Anytime, Suta, but do not fool yourself. Justin is for

*us. It is expected that you would want to keep no secrets from our mate.*\*

"Uh, sure," she drawled, not giving in on the mate business. Not yet.

With that, her spirit guide faded into the back of her mind, leaving Delaine with more to think about than she'd had on her mind before summoning the big cat. Shower cap tossed aside, she strode to the closet to dress. The phone rang again and the tactical gear she'd selected from the sparsely occupied shelves landed on the closet floor. Thinking her kids must have forgotten something had her flying back into the bedroom. Her towel hit the floor as she dove across the bed for the phone like a third baseman for the Colorado Rockies.

"Tanna? What'd you forget, honey?" She tensed when a deep, sexy voice greeted her enthusiastic hello.

\* \* \* \* \*

"Good morning, beautiful."

Justin? Oh my god. She wasn't ready to talk to him yet. What to do? What to do? Okay, now just calm down. The man wasn't standing here looking down at her completely naked butt, he was on the phone. But on the phone or not, her body responded to the smooth tone sliding over the phone line. Her breasts pressed into the soft jacquard comforter, which felt unusually abrasive against the sensitive tips. Delaine wondered if the small droplets of water on her back were starting to steam. She cleared her throat, bent her knees and allowed her feet to kick back and forth in the air.

"Well hello, handsome. How are you?"

"I'm great, but I'd be doing better if you were having breakfast with me."

"Breakfast? I…uh…" She had to what? Come on, girl, think of something!

"Have you eaten already? I know it's a bit late."

Whew! He'd just bailed her out. She guessed she should be thankful considering the state of her frozen brain. Wait, what did he mean by a bit late? Her first glance at the nightstand clock convinced her that the cheap plastic thing was lying. She couldn't wait until her things arrived from Denver so she could have a clock that was reliable. There was just no way she'd slept the morning away until eleven o'clock! Time to get moving if she was going to be on time for her appointment at Pam's. Damn, she hated rushing.

"I can't do breakfast today. I have a hair appointment in an hour, then I'm going to work."

"Where's your hair appointment?"

"Arboretum Mall. My friend Pam has a salon there."

"Well, why don't you meet me at Le Peep restaurant? It's at Arboretum, right?"

"Yes, but by the time I'm ready and get over there, we wouldn't have much time to eat."

"You're not just blowing me off, are you?" Justin asked directly but playfully.

"Oh please!" Delaine laughed. "I might have taken the time back when I was twenty, but now, handsome, I wouldn't bother to blow you off. I'd just tell you to go suck wind." Her tone was good-natured, but she wasn't kidding.

"I've never met a woman more subtle," he chided in return. "How 'bout a rain check?"

"You've got it. Next weekend?"

After two hours of sitting in Pam's beauty chair getting her hair done while spilling the details on the great time she'd had at Duke Mansion, Delaine finally made it to work.

She flashed her badge at the front door and stopped to speak amicably to the security guard before making her way to the elevators. From the numerous monitors on his desk the plant looked all but deserted, thank goodness. Nothing like surveillance on a Saturday afternoon. Humph, it reminded her of a bad song title. Surveillance was her favorite part of every assignment. So why didn't she feel exhilarated?

*Because you would rather spend the afternoon with our mate.*

'Hush, Sapa, nobody asked you. At least not this time,' Delaine whispered in her head, unable to keep the grin out of her voice. She received an answering chuckle. God, how weird people would think her if they knew she had a chuckling black mountain lion in her head. And the lioness seemed to understand her heart better than she understood herself. But there was no way between here and hell she'd admit it to the big, arrogant fur ball.

She put her game face on, stepped into the elevator and froze to the spot.

\* \* \* \* \*

"Hello, Ms. Jeris."

Eewwww! Baker's voice slid over her like oil. Black, thick, crude oil. The last person in the universe she wanted to see occupied her elevator. Sapa sprang to the forefront of her mind with a snarl, ready to lend her speed and strength should there be a need.

'It's all right, Sapa. I've got it under control. Go scout the building and see who's down in The Vault.' As soon as the thought was completed, Delaine felt the great hunter's presence dim in her mind as she took off to perform her task.

"Hello, Mr. Baker," Delaine said brightly behind a perfect smile. "How are you?"

"Fabulous, thank you. What floor are you going to?" His eyes practically glowed when his hand brushed

60

against her as he reached for the control panel.

"Headed to my office. There are a couple of pieces of the process that are eluding me. I just can't seem to wrap my mind around them," she said in the most confused voice she could muster. "Thought I'd work on them while it's nice and quiet around here."

Both their offices were on the ninth floor, and that button was already lit. Damn it! The man's timing sucked. She'd been on her way to Research and Development one floor below. Since R&D took up the entire eighth floor and none of those people were in the building, technically she didn't have any business on that floor. She'd have to snoop later. And what the hell was he doing here on a Saturday afternoon anyway? From what she knew of him, probably the same thing she was.

The elevator doors slid closed and Delaine busied herself looking for something in her purse when the first image from Sapa flew into her head.

The Vault was empty, all of the tunnels that led to the labs were dark with the exception of two of the fifteen. Images streamed into her head of what looked like janitors or interns cleaning the floors and such. Excellent.

As Delaine continued to fumble in her purse, the cool handle of the gun on the bottom of the large bag teased her fingers. When Baker's jade green eyes traveled from her face down to her breasts and then lingered, she wished she could just put a slug in him. God, the man made her skin crawl. Okay, she needed a distraction. She tried to engage in polite conversation, but it turned out to be a true test of her patience. He said very few words and kept his eyes plastered on her chest until he had the gall to let them stray to the vee at her crotch. Nasty bastard.

Almost to the haven of her office, he sprung a doozey

on her. "Why don't you come to my office? Perhaps I can assist you with the piece of the process that's, ah, eluding you?" Oh joy, an offer she couldn't refuse.

They stopped at her office, grabbed her documents then headed down the hall to his. She'd been inside before but not while he was in it. This was the most help he'd been since the day she met him, and god knows she'd been more than content without his aid.

Okay, time to do the process analysis dazzle. Spitting out everything she knew about the manufacturing process for Zalactin, minus a couple of key parameters and components, she sat back and let him take the lead.

The bland expression on his face screamed bored, loud and clear, but his eyes flashed green fire. The man was either turned on or pissed off, she couldn't tell which.

He quickly filled in the missing pieces she'd deliberately left out and she gave him a big toothy smile as she packed up her stuff and left. Ducking into her office, Delaine wished it was farther from Baker's. The docs she and Baker worked on were deliberately spread out on her desk.

An hour later a quiet knock sounded on her open door.

"I'll be leaving now. Have a good evening, Ms. Jeris."

She looked up and found a too-good-looking Baker in her doorway. "Thanks, Mr. Baker, you too," her voice fading on a distracted murmur. Her head snapped up from the papers she pretended to be reading as she said, "Oh, and thank you for your help earlier. I think I've got it now." She motioned to the dataflow diagram on her whiteboard and flashed him a satisfied smile.

The second she heard the ding from the elevator she tucked her gun into the waistband of her pants, pulled her sweatshirt down over it and stuck her head out of her office door. The coast looked clear, but she backtracked past Baker's office just to make sure. She knocked on the door. No answer. The doorknob didn't budge. But she had the feeling someone was watching her.

'Sapa, is Baker in the building?'

*He is gone, yet you are still not alone.*

'What does that mean?' But Sapa didn't answer. Fine. She didn't have time for this. Striding toward the elevators, Delaine snapped open her secure cell and hit the send button.

"Okay, Geri, I'm getting ready to go down. The homing beacon is active. If you don't hear from me in two hours, send in the cavalry." She snapped the phone closed, flashed the encryption key against the elevator's control panel and braced herself for the plummet down to The Vault.

* * * * *

Justin watched Delaine disappear into Baker's office and felt his stomach knot up with disgust. Baker was the slime ball of the earth. So this is what she meant by "go to work" on Saturday, eh? A smile kicked up on the side of his mouth because it's exactly what he would have meant if he'd said it to her.

Even in her loose-fitting sweats, the woman was impressive. Nice wide hips, slender waist and an ass to die for. Damn, she looked as lovely as she had last night. Then she'd been all sultry and soft, a high-heeled goddess. Today, with her hair down in all those twists and curls he liked so much, sweats and sneakers, the woman was all business, ready to kick butt and take names. But still lovely.

Relief coursed through him when Delaine waltzed out of Baker's office seeming none the worse for wear. Glad for the atrium in the middle of the building, he sat two floors up, able to reposition his scope to see into Delaine's open door. She appeared to be working. Her mouth was pulled down into a frown as she concentrated on something on her desk. She leaned back in her chair and stretched her arms over her head, arching her back on a yawn. Damn, that was sexy. He wondered what it would be like to be the one making her arch and stretch like that. His cock stirred and he cursed.

The scope now set on Baker's door, he watched the man lock his door, stop at Delaine's for a second and then head to the elevator.

Justin packed up and headed for the stairs. But not before taking one last look at Delaine in her office. If only he could go down and talk to her. But he knew he was the last person she would expect to see here. But he wanted so bad to see her. Was drawn to her until his throat clogged with the urge to run for the stairwell, down to the ninth floor and around the atrium to her office. Just to inhale her natural scent, touch her hair. And he couldn't do a damn thing about it.

For the first time in his life, Justin despised his job.

A quiet beep sounded on his earpiece. Baker was making a call. By the third ring, Justin pressed a series of numbers to kick off the tracer program Derrick had written to attach to Baker's cellular signature. Both of them would hear the call.

"Sarah Ann, this is Baker. I'm at the facility. I'm leaving now to make our appointment. Do you understand?"

"Y-Yes, sir."

The call was disconnected. Two more phone calls revealed Baker's plans for the next couple of days. And little did he know, Justin would be right there with him at each of his destinations. So much for spending time with Delaine this weekend. Strangely enough, knowing he'd see her when she came back to work made him look forward to Monday morning for the first time in his entire career.

# CHAPTER SIX

"Justin? What are you doing here?" Delaine's eyes went wide for a split second then her instinctive game face snapped into place. Thank goodness her body knew what to do because her brain had completely checked out.

"Hey, beautiful! It's nice to see you. What are you doing here?"

"I asked you first," she countered, unable to think of anything else to say.

"I'm a contractor for Quality Control. I'm usually up in the QC labs."

"Really? I don't recall you saying you worked here in our previous conversations." A grimace almost peeked through her painted-on smile when Sapa began to growl. And she was growling at Delaine, not Justin. The man had called her every day since they met and she'd purposely avoided the subject of work. The guilt was eating her alive.

"We didn't really talk much about work. You told me you were a production process something-or-other but I didn't know you worked in this facility. There are several pharma and biotech companies in South Charlotte these days. But you're a contractor, right? How long will you be here?"

Was that a flicker of guilt in his eye? Maybe it was her own conscience getting to her. Whatever it was disappeared so quickly all she had to go on was her own unease as Sapa's thoughts insinuated into her head.

*You will tell him in time, Suta, but not today. Ask him to lunch.* Before Delaine knew it, she was doing exactly what Sapa told her to. Now that was a first.

"Uh, how about lunch, Justin?" His smile lit up her world.

*Very good, Suta. You have just made our mate very happy.*

'Will you stop calling him that?' Delaine blushed in her head. Sapa just seemed so sure, but she just wasn't. It wasn't a feeling she was familiar with.

*Ceasing to call him mate will not make him any less ours.*

'Damn it, Sapa...' Justin's deep voice snapped her out of her private conversation.

"Listen, I just need to return these samples to the lab and I'll meet you...uh, where?" he asked.

"I'm parked in Lot J, Slot 2. Say, ten minutes?"

* * * * *

"Derrick, I'm in deep here. I just ran into Delaine Jeris in a secured elevator. I can almost guarantee she was on her way down to The Vault."

"How do you know?"

"Because that's where I was going, damn it. If she hadn't gotten on that elevator I'd be down there right now looking for evidence. And I have a feeling she's thinking the same thing."

"And how's that?"

Justin wanted to say "relieved" but held his tongue. The last place he wanted Delaine to be was down in those labs. The thought of her running into Baker down there made his gut clench so tight he had to fight to breathe. A subject change was in order.

"I've managed to keep out of Delaine's sight while managing to watch her all week."

"It's not your job to watch her. You're after Baker, not a piece of Jeris' ass."

"Last I checked you were my partner, not my boss, Derrick!"

"Whoa, slow your roll, Justin," Derrick said firmly. Justin didn't miss the long drawn out sigh from his partner before he continued. "Look, Jus, I'm just concerned about you getting sidetracked. We've been boys for ten years and I'm just looking out for you, man."

Justin felt contrite for his outburst to his friend. Well, almost. Delaine was nobody's business, except his.

"I appreciate your concern, Derrick, but I'm all good. I can handle it. I know what my job is, but part of that job is to not get caught. If I rush this I could blow it. Listen, I think Delaine is being followed and I want you to check it out for me. I've seen a woman around Delaine, ducking in and out of Baker's offices…"

"So?"

"…and down in The Vault."

"Aw, hell."

"Yeah, my thoughts exactly. I've already sent you a digital of the woman. Check her out and get back to me."

Justin clicked the cell shut, dropped off the sample cart and headed out of the building to Lot J. He was amazed no one was on to him yet. If he was lucky, it would stay that way until he could get the goods on Baker and get himself and his woman out of here in one piece.

He shook his head and sighed. He already saw Delaine as his, and he couldn't tell her a damned thing about what he suspected was going on in this place.

* * * * *

"So where do you want to go?" Delaine asked as he slipped into the passenger side of her Jag. As soon as the door shut Sapa started dancing around her head as she did every time she heard this man's voice. It was damned disconcerting to have her spirit guide behave so giddily. Even when talking on the phone the lioness pranced, growled and rolled around like a loon. Amazing. Sapa's actions mirrored what she wished she could do. She looked toward him and his smile twisted her brain. Lord, could she even string two words together?

They pulled out of the parking lot and headed toward the highway. "It's cold as I-don't-know-what outside. Pam told me about this place on South Kings Street called Austin's. If you're up for some nice, hot Caribbean food we could go there," she suggested kindly. His startling blue eyes darkened to a sultry midnight hue, glittering as if she were the treat of a lifetime.

"Nice and hot?" his voice smooth as silk. "Yeah, I think I could go for some of that."

"Lord, you are such a flirt," she grinned back.

"Guilty, baby." His hand reached across and slid underneath her cloak to rest on her thigh. The skin tingled but she didn't flinch or pull away. His fingers felt like they belonged there, even when her breathing took off and her grin split her face in two. She knew she was blushing so hard, her scalp felt on fire, but she just couldn't help it. It might have been forty degrees outside, but underneath her coat was at least ninety-two!

'Sapa, send me some relaxation or something, quick! This man is sending my temp through the roof!'

"So how's your process hierarchy thing going at work?" he asked, his thumb tracing lazy little circles across her knee.

Her face fell, like she'd been doused with cold water. No need for Sapa to help her calm down after all. What could she say to him other than the typical oh-my-project-is-fine? She certainly couldn't say "oh, well my surveillance is going fine, I'm on to the bad guy and I've managed to elude the woman who's been following me."

"You all right, Del?"

A tremulous smile replaced her giddy one. All she could afford to spare him was a glance as she said, "Sure, Justin. Just great."

\* \* \* \* \*

Justin could have kicked himself in the teeth. His question about her work had put her completely on edge. And that was the last place he wanted her. He knew what it was like to be asked that question. He hoped Delaine wouldn't go there and ask him—he didn't want to lie to her. But she was a smart woman and would probably pick up on his hedging sooner rather than later.

When they pulled into the parking lot at Austin's, before she could get out of the car, he turned in his seat, reached for her and practically hauled her into his lap. Justin poured everything into that kiss. Everything he couldn't say and everything he wasn't supposed to feel rippled through him as his lips unerringly found hers. He couldn't remember ever feeling so anxious.

Delaine pulled back with an alarmed expression on her face. Breathing ceased and he just knew he was busted. Why else would she be looking at him like that?

Then the deep lines in her forehead softened. He leaned into her hands as the smooth leather of her gloves glided over one side of his face.

"Justin, honey, what's wrong? What is it?" He liked it when she called him honey.

"Nothing, beautiful. Just," he sighed, "a lot of things on my mind." That was putting it lightly. "One of which is when I'll have some time alone with you. Rain check, remember?"

Her smile twinkled up to her eyes and the iron grip around his lungs loosened. Maybe she hadn't figured him out after all. At least, not yet.

Inside the luncheon spot, she ordered for him and he enjoyed ox tails, jerk chicken, beans and rice and some kind of meat pie that was out of this world. And she'd been right. It was nice and warm, with the perfect amount of spicy heat. Just like her.

Back at Astin, he jumped out of the car, ran around to her side and opened the door for her. She gaped up at him, drew her brows down into a serious frown, then her expression brightened again. What the hell was going on with these cartwheeling emotions he'd felt rolling off her the whole time they'd been together today? They'd shared an easy conversation over lunch, along with soft touches of hands and sweet kisses. But when it was time to return to the office Delaine had been all over the map. One minute she was happy and smiling, the next she was wary and then sad. And seeing her in such a tangle of emotions just wasn't palatable. The need to protect her welled up in his chest. Even if it meant shielding her from her own feelings.

He stood in front of the car door, not letting her out.

"The weekend starts tonight and I'm still waiting on my answer." He was glad she didn't pretend not to know what he was talking about.

"Call me in the morning," her voice sultry and warm

as she traced a finger over his bottom lip before snatching her hand back with a giggle when he tried to bite her.

Backing up a step, Justin watched her climb out of the car with fluid grace and walk toward the building. The wink she cast over her shoulder made his heart flip-flop in his chest. He tried not to watch her move away, but damned if he could help it. Even through her long wool cloak, her ass seemed to call to him on a cellular level, along with her smile, her charm, her strong but sweet personality. Damn, he could really love a woman like her.

# CHAPTER SEVEN

Delaine groaned and rolled over on her back, shielding her eyes from the bright light seeping through the drawn curtains. Lately it seemed like she was always waking up to the ringing of her telephone. One eye cracked open to check the clock. Ten a.m. She swung her legs over the edge of the bed and sat up with a start. Crap! Here she was again with only an hour to make it to Pam's.

The ring of the phone was beginning to get on her nerves. Maybe she'd just hit the shower and let the answering machine get it. Thoughts of warm water sliding over bare skin caused Justin's face to pop into her mind. She wasn't going to call him, so she called out to her spirit guide instead.

'Come to me, Sapa.' Delaine wiggled her toes in the thick fur on Sapa's back when the lioness appeared underneath her feet, sprawled out on the carpet.

*Wondering what our mate is doing?*

"I am not," she denied weakly, knowing she'd never successfully lied to Sapa before. And she did wonder what he was doing. On the fourth ring she picked up the phone.

"Hello?"

"Time for that rain check, beautiful. Pick you up in half an hour for breakfast?"

Justin! Damn, speak of the devil. Her stomach started doing the jelly-jiggle thing at the sound of his sexy voice. She thought about the way her name sounded on his lips and all the jiggle went bye-bye. After all, it wasn't her name. "Can't. I've got just enough time to shower, grab a bite then make my hair appointment."

"You spend a lot of time at your friend's beauty salon."

"So," she teased, ready with a retort of how all women needed to be pampered.

"I like it. Your hair makes me want to play in it."

Dayum! Not the answer she expected. And his voice was all smooth silk. Oooh, the quivering tummy was back with a vengeance. Sapa's corporeal form stalked back and forth across the room, her tail swishing in what Delaine called her 'happy ass'.

"Well, if we can't do breakfast would you allow a man to cook dinner for you?"

Her eyebrows shot straight up. "Say what?" Boy did that slip! There was no way she intended him to hear the shocked tone in her voice.

"Well, beauty, don't you think you deserve to have a man cook for you?"

"Is this a trick question?" she asked, smiling so hard she was sure all of her teeth were showing. Rolling over onto her back, her fingers trailed lazily over her bare breasts as she imagined his wicked grin and sumptuous kisses.

"Why don't you give me directions to your place? You can eat a little something while I drive over to pick you up. I'll take you to your appointment, go grocery shopping and pick you up when I'm done. I'll bring you back home, and we can have dinner. Sound good?"

Good? Hell, it sounded better than good. He'd thought of everything and Delaine couldn't find a single reason to object. And she certainly looked for one. Hard. Besides, no man was this damned perfect. Right?

*Wrong.*

'Hush, Sapa,' she thought, sending the ultra-weak reprimand along the bond, grinning too hard to put any weight behind it.

\* \* \* \* \*

Justin hung up the phone in his living room, slipped his arms into the sleeves of his heavy leather bomber jacket and headed out. Once in the car he flipped open his secure cell, unlocked the keypad and hit the speed dial.

"Harris here."

"Derrick, it's me. What have we got?"

"You were right about the Sarah Ann woman. She's tailing Delaine, but we don't know why or on whose orders. We can assume Baker's behind it, but we have no idea how he would have obtained any information about who we think Delaine is. We think she's with Aegis, a front company for Interpol US operation. But she could be with any number of black ops orgs. Even ours."

"Uh-huh. Well, I'm on my way to pick her up now."

"Is that smart? I mean, she's being tailed."

"Delaine's got a tail, I don't. Besides, I've already made the plans." Hell, even if he was being followed, he'd still be tempted to show up at her house. He'd never admit it to anyone but Derrick in a million years, and only because they had ten years of trust between them. "This is hard for me to admit, Der, but I don't know whether I'm coming or going with this woman. There's just something about her. I mean, damn, the woman has everything a man could want. Smart, fit, beautiful. Hell, I even love her laugh."

"Her laugh? Are you on crack?"

"No, man, I'm serious. When she laughs, it reminds me of all the naughty things I did when I was a kid and nobody was looking. Deep, like she has some dark, sensuous secret."

"Well, it's probably a good thing you're hooked on her. You need a strong woman to keep your ass in line."

"Oh, and you should talk?" he laughed into the mouthpiece. "So what's the plan?"

"Spencer wants you to concentrate on Baker. He doesn't have any problem with you getting with Jeris as long as you don't compromise your cover. Besides, getting with her may be the fastest way to wrap this thing up. Appears she's one step ahead of us, even though we've been working this case for months."

"How the hell is that possible?"

"Don't know. But there's also the possibility that somebody's outted her."

"I'll stick close to her. And as for hooking up with Delaine to use her to gather intel, you tell Spencer he can kiss my ass." With that, Justin clicked the phone shut and disconnected the call.

He'd been an undercover agent forever, and because of the hazard and secrecy of the job, he'd never enjoyed the companionship of a woman unless it pertained to a mission.

But Delaine was no mission. She was special. He didn't know how he knew, but he knew he was right about her. Right then, Justin made a decision that might cost him his career. It meant he would have to tell her exactly who he was and as soon as the time was right, he would. First he had to win her. Then he would keep her.

* * * * *

Delaine was ready when Justin rang her doorbell twenty minutes later. She opened the door and almost fainted dead away. Did men get better looking after a little bit of sleep? He smiled and pulled off his dark sunglasses before stepping over the threshold into the foyer. The only word she could think of to describe him was "yummy". He was dressed in a pair of worn jeans that fit his body perfectly—not too tight, not too loose. His leather jacket was unzipped and revealed a huge muscled chest wrapped in a black, tight-fitting Under Armour shirt, the kind the guys at the gym wore when they worked out.

She looked up at the ceiling and said a silent prayer. Lord, please don't let this man take his jacket off. If I'm going to make it to my hair appointment, don't let me see his chest now, lord. She was so busy trying to keep it together, she didn't notice the sizzling looks Justin sent her way. After all, her dark blue Under Armour shirt looked painted on too.

"Did you forget something?" he asked.

"Huh?"

"You're looking up towards the stairs. Did you forget something?" He stepped close enough for her to get a whiff of his cologne. Oh, he smelled so good. She jerked back like he'd slapped her, ignoring the tilt of his head at her odd behavior.

"Uh, yeah, I just remembered that I forgot something," Delaine said lamely, knowing her words didn't make any sense but glad she'd left her purse on her bed. It gave her an excuse to flee the room. "Is it cold out?" she asked over her shoulder as she headed up the curved staircase.

Justin watched her glorious butt fill out her jogging pants and called out a chilly forty degrees as she hurried along. He bit his lip to keep from telling her how nice her ass was.

While she scuttled around upstairs, he took the opportunity to look around her house a bit, noting how meticulously clean it was. Sterile was a better word. No photos on the mantel. No pictures on the wall. He knew she'd just moved here and probably just hadn't had time to do any decorating. Or did she plan on leaving soon? The thought bothered him. Hell, he'd just decided to pursue her, no holds barred, and her leaving Charlotte anytime soon didn't jive with his goals.

He didn't know what drove him to win her. Frankly, he didn't give a damn. It never occurred to him she might have other plans. Besides, if she felt the same spark between them that he did, even the best-laid plans could be changed, namely hers.

He leaned against the mantel, his eyes glued on the stairs as he waited for Delaine to descend. She made her way down, completely composed and distant. It was second nature for an agent to hide behind a mask of calm acceptance, and he understood that. Understood her life firsthand. Never having the luxury of getting close to anyone. Sometimes moving from place to place, either to chase down criminals or for your own safety. But the thought of her disappearing from his life after he'd just found her…Nope, not gonna happen.

A bomber jacket tucked under one arm, she stuffed her hands into a pair of navy leather gloves and headed directly to the door without even looking at him. An icy chill slipped up his spine followed by a tide of emotion that washed over him so completely, he felt like he was drowning in it. Such depth of feeling all because of this one woman? He could deal with that.

He marched across the room and swept her into his arms. His mouth crashed down over her, desperate to wreak havoc on her senses, needing her to want him the way he wanted her. By the time he let her up for air, one of her legs was wrapped around his calf as she moaned softly into his mouth. After another kiss, this one sweet and calming, he spoke softly from his heart.

"Delaine, I know we're just getting to know each other, but don't pull away from me. Don't shut me out."

She didn't answer, but the question in her eyes was clear.

"I saw it in your eyes when you came down the stairs," he said against her temple.

She met his gaze and looked deeply, trying to decipher the raw, open expression in his glittering eyes. Justin was the type of man to bare all, but he wanted her to see what he was feeling, to see what he wanted. As much as he liked her, he hoped she could give him what he asked for.

"Look, Justin," she said, trying to push away. He didn't let her. "It's been a long time since I've done the dating thing and I'm just a little unsure."

"I understand. Just give me a chance, baby, that's all I'm asking."

A double assault, she thought with a wry grin. Justin pressed her gently from the outside while Sapa pressed from the inside. Well, at least the lioness liked him. That alone almost made up for not knowing him. Delaine sighed, laid her head against his chest and snuggled into his arms for a warm hug. She could really get used to this. Damn. She would have to meet someone like him while she was on assignment.

* * * * *

"Girl, you are really feeling this man, aren't you?" Pam asked, her eyes wide as she questioned her friend.

"Yes, ma'am, I am definitely feeling him. Pam, he's smart, funny and not to mention gorgeous. And it's all your fault. If you hadn't talked me into going to that professional single mingle group thing, I don't think I ever would have met him."

"Hey, if you want to give me the kudos, I'll sure take 'em! So what's his name?"

"Justin."

"Justin what?"

"Pam, you're the second person to ask me that."

"Huh?"

"Never mind. He and I are having dinner tonight. At my place," Delaine waggled her eyebrows.

"Isn't that moving a bit fast, Del? I mean, what do you really know about this guy?" Pam asked, not really sure why.

"Concern about moving too fast? From you?"

"Look, I'm known for doing the dip-n-dash on a first date. But this is you, Delaine. You're the cautious one. The careful one…"

"The divorced-after-eighteen-years one," Delaine reminded her. "Hey, I've been careful all my life. What did it get me? And this conversation is getting old fast. One more guilt-inducing word and you won't get a tip, woman."

"Okay, okay," Pam conceded, raising her hands in friendly defeat. Besides, Delaine deserved some happiness after having her life shattered by that nincompoop Gary. Without faith, strength and money of her own, his abandonment would have been really hard on her and the kids. "I've gotta give you credit for bouncing back after that milksop you were married to, so I'll leave you alone about your new man. Hell, your ex is such an unappreciative pig, even I want to cut his heart out with a spoon," Pam said quietly, dropping the subject.

"You almost done? Justin will be here to pick me up any minute."

"Pick you up? What's wrong with your car?"

"Nothing. He gave me a ride then went shopping for dinner. He's cooking tonight."

A man cooking for Delaine? Wow! "He's cooking for you? Maybe I need to go to the professional single mingle thing," Pam said with raised eyebrows.

Just then, the chime on the door sounded and Pam looked up to see the most stunning, rippling muscled, well-built white boy she'd ever laid eyes on in her life. He had wavy red hair cut into a fade on the sides, a strong chin and piercing blue eyes. The man could have been the next James Bond. He held his leather jacket tossed over one shoulder, showing off solid biceps and wide shoulders. What was he doing in her shop? Whatever he wanted, she'd be glad to give it to him.

"Hey, Justin's here. I gotta run."

"Justin? Where?" Pam asked in a daze, staring at the gorgeous hunk walking toward her.

"The man you're drooling over, girlfriend. Snap out of it and take the rest of these twists out so I can go, will ya?"

"Girl, that's Justin? He's good looking and cooks too? Lord Jesus!"

He strode directly to her chair. Pam felt equal parts jealous and happy for her friend, even as she eyeballed the man shamelessly. He put his hands on the armrests and bent over to plant one directly on Delaine's lips. Pam finger combed the twists Delaine often wore loosely curled down her back, and still he kissed her. Nope, the man had no shame, not an ounce. He'd walked into a beauty shop full of sistahs and put one on the woman like they were alone in the dark. If her girlfriend had been chocolate, she would've melted into the chair.

Justin broke the kiss and stared at a dreamy-eyed Delaine. All his attention was focused on her as he spoke in hushed tones.

"Hey, baby."

"Hey, you," she said breathlessly, worrying one side of her bottom lip with her teeth.

"Almost ready?"

"Uh huh."

He grinned at her giddy, breathless expression and said, "I'm parked right out front, all right?"

"Sure."

He straightened and Delaine visibly shivered as his fingers traipsed over her bare forearm. Then she seemed to remember to be polite.

"Oh. Justin, this is my good girlfriend Pam. Pam, this is Justin," Delaine said, happy she had something to concentrate on, like forming words into coherent speech.

"Nice to meet you, Pam," Justin said with a friendly smile. Delaine noticed it wasn't one of the sizzling smiles he seemed to like laying on her.

Justin shook Pam's hand and left something in it.

"That's for her hair," he said, and turned and headed back toward the door.

Pam unfolded the paper in her hand—a crisp fifty-dollar bill.

"But it's only thirty-five for a wash and set," Pam called after him.

"Her hair is beautiful. Consider the rest a tip." He continued right out the door without breaking stride.

Pam and Delaine gaped after him, along with every other woman in the shop. Delaine snapped to her senses and hopped out of the chair.

"Girl, I've gotta go. Later, Ms. Pamela."

She snatched her coat off the rack and pulled it on as she made for the door in Justin's wake. She turned back to Pam to give her a hug and caught the strange shade of green in her friend's eyes. She quirked her head and stepped back, her hands on her friend's shoulders. "Girl, you all right?"

"Yeah, sure. Go enjoy your dinner. Put you down for an appointment in two weeks?"

"Yep. And I'll call you this week so we can get together for breakfast too," she said, kissing Pam on the cheek and flying out the door.

\* \* \* \* \*

Delaine showed Justin to the kitchen and ran upstairs to change. She trotted back downstairs in a big tee shirt and pair of jean shorts to find him already busy cooking.

"What's that smell?" she asked, striding into the kitchen. He stuck a pot under her nose and she pulled her hair back and stuck her nose into the saucepan while he continued to stir. She sighed in appreciation, "Mmmm, now that smells really good."

"Homemade teriyaki sauce. I've got this covered, but do you mind helping me with the rest of this?"

"Sure. What do you want me to do?" she replied with a smile.

The twinkle in his eyes should have told her it was a setup. She gladly accepted the task to wash a head of lettuce and cut a few tomatoes for a salad. It took her forever to do those two simple things. And it was all his fault.

While Delaine washed the lettuce, Justin came up behind her to rinse green onions for the stir-fry. Then he needed to rinse the carrots and bell peppers, one at a time. Then he filled a pot with water and rinsed off the rice before setting it on the stove to steam. And each time he needed to use the sink, he came up behind her, pressed his chest against her back and reached underneath her arms to get to the spigot. The crook of his elbow teased the sides of her breasts as he moved whatever he was rinsing back and forth under the flow of water. Before he moved away to his side of the counter, he took a moment to breathe in the scent of her hair while pressing his stone-hard erection into the curve of her butt. Oh lord, she should have expired from his teasing at least twice over.

Her pulse pounded and a fine sheen of sweat broke out over her brow. Her fingers trembled and her hands were damp, and not from rinsing the stupid lettuce. By the time she was done with her small task, her breasts tingled unbearably, and she was uncomfortably wet between her legs. Here she was in an industrial-sized kitchen, with gourmet everything and more counter space than every display at Home Depot combined. But it was too small for just the two of them. She was so hot and bothered she could have skipped dinner and just had Justin for dessert.

Even with her arousal at a constant hum just beneath her skin, Delaine actually enjoyed their meal of chicken teriyaki stir-fry and fresh tossed salad with fresh balsamic vinegar dressing. Afterward, she led him into the living room where she left him sitting while he ran to the garage and hauled in a few logs for a fire. With a blaze in the hearth, they sat on the floor in front of the couch. Delaine paid no attention as one of her favorite classic action movies played on the flat screen plasma TV mounted over the mantle. She'd smiled when Justin pulled the DVD out earlier, but now she couldn't care less that James Bond was in the middle of laying some whoop-ass on a nasty bad guy.

Delaine sat sideways in Justin's lap, toes curled into the carpet as she snuggled into his big body. Her shoulder leaned lazily against his chest as he reclined against the couch. His masculine scent filled her lungs, enticing her to nuzzle into the crook of his neck while his fingers traced tiny circles up and down her arms.

Justin pressed light kisses on the top of her crown then dipped his head to plant light kisses over her forehead, her temples, her cheek. Her stomach flipped over when his soft lips traced the shell of her ear, blowing lightly. His fingers strayed to her shoulders and massaged the tense muscles there. Her breathing deepened at the insistence of his hard cock pushing up against her butt through his jeans.

His touch was tender and often, as if he savored caressing and arousing her. She took delight in the affection he lavished on her, even as her body heated and her blood simmered. His touch was magic. A deep, needy groan traveled up her throat when one of his large, strong hands traced the line of her neck, teasing each individual vertebrate as he worked his way down. His free hand slid across the quivering planes of her stomach and around to her waist to hold her tightly to him.

His growing erection told her how much he enjoyed touching her. It royally turned her on to feel him harden and stretch underneath her. Slowly, so slowly, her hips began to writhe, seeking more of the hardness pressing against her. Her eyelids drooped closed as body and mind accepted his sweet attention on a sigh.

Her breasts swelled and ached, the tips so tender she gasped with an erotic shiver when Justin's forearm accidentally scraped against them on the way to wrap around her body.

Oh please, please touch my breasts, she willed him silently with each tormented breath pulled from her chest. As her body reached out for him, Delaine felt Sapa slip completely away from her. On the verge of panic at the sudden emptiness in her mind, the bond vibrated softly. Sapa was giving her privacy. Privacy to mate.

Delaine lifted her head from beneath his chin. Her tongue flicked out and tasted the sweet muskiness of his skin, salty from the sweat she hadn't realized was there. His skin felt hot against her lips. She opened her mouth against his throat and allowed her tongue free reign. Licked and tasted with wild, carnal slides of her tongue along the column of his throat, smiling against the taut muscles of his neck when he leaned his head back with a moan and ground his hips up against her ass.

Justin leaned forward and whispered in her ear. "You feel so good in my arms, Delaine. You're driving me crazy, baby. I can smell your heat and I'm trying really hard to keep my hands to myself." His breathing deepened with each word.

She stretched sensuously against him and said, "I don't want you to keep them to yourself." Delaine reached for his hand splayed across her hip and placed it boldly on her breasts. She closed her eyes on a swift intake of breath as Justin proved he could more than take it from there.

# CHAPTER EIGHT

Delaine was a starving woman, arching wildly into Justin's hands as they closed firmly around her aching, tender breasts. She wanted him to wrap his fingers around them and knead them like fresh bread dough. She couldn't hold back a long, needy moan as he found her nipples through her bra. He tweaked them, then smoothed insistent fingers over the stiff peaks. It didn't take long before she needed more.

Her back against his chest, she wiggled down between his legs until she was on the floor between his thighs. Delaine reached back and slipped her arms around his neck, stretching into him like the sleek cat who shared her conscience. Her oversized tee shirt rode up to expose the smooth milk chocolate skin of her belly and she quivered as Justin slipped his hands underneath the fabric, his rough hands seeking, moving up her body to explore the ridges of her washboard stomach. Long, warm fingers skimmed over the goose bumps around her waist and teased the top of her pants. Her hips swiveled all on their own, seeking the thick ridge of his cock through his jeans. He nibbled and kissed his way around the back of her neck, making her hungrier. She felt the clasp on the front of her bra snap loose. The second her breasts spilled free, he lavished them with attention.

"Mmmm, your hands feel so good. Oh yes, touch me, Justin," Delaine moaned.

Justin grabbed her underneath her arms and picked her up as if she weighed nothing, turning her around to face him. Settled her on her knees, her thighs straddled his and her hot channel came down directly on top of his straining erection. He took her mouth almost brutally, tasting her, pulling her into himself. He lifted her up again and his head disappeared under her tee shirt. The way she cried out when he took a delicious, dark nipple into his mouth made him want to wring that sound from her over and over again. Made him want to suck, feast and ravage her flesh until she trembled uncontrollably.

Every desperate sound she made evoked powerful feelings of possessiveness in him. When her cries became desperate, the need to be inside her right then and there raged through his blood without restraint. He released her breasts and wrapped his arms around her in a sensuous cocoon. He kissed her neck and along her jaw, grinding the steel bulge in his pants hard against her clit. Delaine held onto his neck as if she was drowning and he understood exactly how she felt. Leaning her back a bit, he buried his face between her breasts long enough to get his breath.

"Justin." It was a whisper so heavy with passion, it made him feel so untamed he wanted to rip off all her clothes and take her right there on the carpet.

"I have to make love to you, baby," he rasped through gritted teeth. "Tell me you want me."

"Justin, please." Delaine ground her hips against his hardness, needing to satisfy the throbbing between her legs. Oh, she wanted him, all right.

"Then tell me," he hissed, sliding his large hands

over her ass, fingers pressing up against her weeping slit from behind. She almost came on the spot.

"Oooh, Justin," she wailed, "yes! I want you!"

"Stand up for me, baby."

She rose on wobbly legs and reached for the waistband of her pants. She jumped when, quick as lightning, Justin's hand shot out and pushed hers away.

"Don't…move."

His voice was hard, desperate. Delaine dropped her hands to her sides. He began to undress her. It was torture. Sheer, unadulterated, bliss-filled torture. His lips traveled over every inch of skin as he exposed it. Inching her shirt up, his mouth kissed its way up her stomach, gobbled up a breast on the way, then nibbled and licked a path up her neck, around her nape and down the other side. He found a sensitive spot where her neck met her shoulder muscles. He bit down gently and made her squirm and gasp as the knee-buckling sensations shimmied down her spine. Her shirt and bra hit the floor and he moved on to her pants.

Justin slowly moved the waistband of her shorts down a bit and kissed his way around her waist. Her stomach rippled when he licked her navel, so he did it again and again, worshipping her body.

He moved around behind her, nipped and licked the cheeks of her ass as he lowered her bottoms. Delaine shuddered when he gently raked his short nails over the sensitive globes. His teeth lightly grazed her flesh. Mmm, he's a biter. Oh lord, that feels so good. The grazing of his teeth was replaced by the sweet suction of his full lips as his mouth settled on her left ass cheek. Next came hard, intense sucking. Her pussy clenched violently. Justin caught her when her knees buckled. He kicked her shorts out of the way, swept her up in his arms and headed for the stairs.

\* \* \* \* \*

He set Delaine's feet on the floor long enough to push the covers back. He picked her up again, laid her on the edge of her bed and leaned over her to tease and torment her with his lips and tongue. Nudging her thighs apart, he slid his fingers between her legs. He gave her a lopsided grin when he withdrew his hand and licked off the evidence of her arousal while gently easing the fingers of his other hand inside her slick flesh. She was a quivering mass of muscle and bone, but he was nowhere close to finished with her. He wanted to hear her scream. See her scratch the sheets off the bed. He wanted her so far gone, she would give him anything and everything he wanted.

He stood up to remove his clothes and Delaine bolted up in the bed.

"Don't leave me!" she cried, her eyes full of longing while her body trembled uncontrollably.

For a second he wondered at the panic in her voice and was even more determined she would never have to worry or wonder about his need for her. Before the night was over she would feel beyond cherished. Then again, maybe he'd tell her that he needed her so badly he wanted to lay a hurtin' on her pussy that would have her begging him to leave her alone. Instead he simply said, "I won't leave you, baby, but I can't wait another minute to feel my skin sliding against yours."

Justin's gaze never left hers as he peeled his shirt off over his head, exposing the wide planes of his body to Delaine's hungry gaze. With each movement, her eyes followed the ripple of taut muscle. He'd never been stuck on his physique before, but now he felt a strong sense of pride and prowess as he watched Delaine admire the power of his honed body. She sat on the edge of the bed and ran her palms over his large biceps, then across broad sculpted pecs, savoring the feel of the downy soft, reddish-blond hair sprinkled there. Her eyes traveled down his chest to a chiseled, ripped stomach.

He stepped back, made short work of his pants then stood and let Delaine look her fill. He watched her tongue travel across her lush, full lips as she took him in. Her eyes traveled down past his hips and grew wide as she stared at his cock in wonder. It jutted out from his body, huge, jerking with a life of its own. He wasn't sure he'd ever been this hard. The thick mushroom head was moist and weeping. If he wasn't beyond ready, his cock certainly was.

"Oh lord," she gasped, breaking out of the sexual stupor she'd been floating in. "You're going to kill me with that thing!" Survival instinct kicked in, propelling her body backward so she could scoot away across the bed. Her lust evaporated into uncertainty and more than a bit of fear.

Justin chuckled, but his need didn't diminish one whit. He grasped his wide base and stroked his length as he stalked toward the bed.

"Don't worry, beauty. I know what to do with it." But first he had to get her mind off the size of his cock. He reached out, grabbed her by an ankle and pulled her forward until she sat with her legs spread on the edge of the bed. Leaning down, he licked her across the mouth and silently smiled to himself when her eyes fluttered closed and some of the tension leached from her body. His teeth captured her bottom lip and worried it a little before pulling it into his mouth like a ripe piece of juicy fruit. Her arms wrapped around him, breasts writhing flush against his chest.

"Just lie still for me, baby. Close your eyes and let me taste you," he whispered against her lush mouth.

Delaine looked like she wasn't sure of what he was talking about, but she let him rearrange her on the bed.

Her lashes fluttered closed as he stroked her thighs, encouraging her to ease back on the bed to give him room to kneel on the edge. Pushing her thighs farther apart, he lifted her legs over his shoulders. Then came the hot swipe of his tongue up her swollen cunt.

"Oh lord!" she cried and almost shot straight up off the bed, more than a little self-conscious and obviously glad she'd shaved down there this morning.

He lifted his head long enough to ask, "Hasn't anyone ever loved you like this, beauty?"

She shook her head dumbly, her breathing sharp as his fingers played with the smooth skin just above her clit. His thumb dipped down and pressed up against the swollen bundle of nerves and her hips jerked forward, eyes closed on a strangled cry.

"Lie back. Relax," he ordered gently and then dipped his nose into her sex and inhaled. The delicious scent of her tender folds called to his blood until the need to please her as no one else ever had overrode all other desire.

"God, Delaine, you smell so good. Like cinnamon and spice. I need to taste your sweet, pretty pussy."

He then licked her from the top of her slit to the bottom, smoothing his hands up and down her quivering thighs as he dove headlong. Whipped his tongue across, up, down and inside her until she writhed and cried out in a frenzy of need. He moaned against her and deliberately sent a titillating humming against her clit. But when he sucked the sensitive knot roughly, as deep as he could get it into his mouth, she yelled to the rafters. Delaine grabbed his head between her thighs and bucked wildly, coming long and hard. But Justin didn't stop lashing her with his tongue, just kept at her until she exploded again.

"See how good you taste, baby," he whispered, sliding up her body to cover her mouth with his. The taste of herself on his tongue was such a turn-on, she latched onto the talented pink organ, sank her fingers into his hair and sucked his tongue like a piece of candy.

Justin broke the kiss, sat back on his knees and pulled her hips up his thighs to position himself at her entrance. He needed to feel her wrapped around his cock, needed to feel the slick walls of her pussy holding him tight. But first, he needed to hear the words.

"I need to be inside you right now," he ground out, teasing the head of his throbbing dick against her swollen, slick flesh. "I want to fuck you, Delaine. Now, tell me what you want."

Instead, she tried to shimmy herself up his legs and impale herself on his hard length.

"Tell me what you want, baby," his request was a tight-lipped command, barely in check.

"I-I want you."

"You want me to what?" Her eyes were wide with need, but Justin could see her starting to think. But he didn't want her to think, he wanted her to feel. Still rubbing himself against her slick heat, he made it very plain what he was after.

"Listen to me, baby. I'm nasty as hell. A total freak. I want to lick, suck and fuck you all night, but I want you right there with me. Hot, creaming and screaming for me. So tell me what you want. I won't take you until you do."

Delaine wasn't sure she liked this kind of control. But maybe it was because her ex had never exerted it? With Justin, it felt right. It blew her mind that she actually wanted to be dominated in the bedroom. She wanted to be ridden hard, taken. By him. But she had to be woman enough, bold enough, to tell him what she wanted.

"I want you to fuck me, Justin. Please, honey," she whispered. A little unsure but determined, her palm reached out and stroked what she wanted. Her fingers wrapped around his dripping, hard cock. When he moaned and bucked against her hand, she grew a bit more bold. "I want you hard and deep. Fuck me until I'm so hot, my hair is on fire."

"Guide me in." Eyes closed, he let her guide him into her hot, soaking wet channel. When the thick, almost purple head of his cock was positioned at her entrance, he flexed his hips and slowly inched his way in. He knew he was big and tried to take his time so he wouldn't hurt her. His eyes flew open when Delaine raised up on her elbows, put one foot on his chest, the other flat on the bed and pushed forward with all her strength. He slammed home and bumped against the entrance to her womb. They threw their heads back on a unified yell. At this rate, they'd both be hoarse by morning.

He leaned forward until he lay on top of her and then gathered her into his arms. Skin to skin, breast to breast, he slowly stroked into her as he whispered how beautifully sexy she was. How much he loved being inside her warmth. She moaned non-stop, but he wanted more. He wanted to mark her, brand her as his. He'd never felt this primal with a woman. Tried to rein it in, but after a few moments of gritting his teeth against the urges, he gave up the fight.

On his knees again, he took her with him until only the top of her shoulders were left on the bed. Stomach muscles tightened as he clenched his teeth and withdrew his length until only the head of his cock was in her creamy, moist heat. He pistoned into her but gave her only that little bit. Her hips rose to meet him stroke for stroke, but he wouldn't give her any more than that.

She'd been so unbelievably full of him, reveled in the deep plunging he'd been giving her. Now he teased her with quick shallow strokes and Delaine was on fire, desperate to have all of him inside her again. She had no shame as she grabbed the sheets and ripped at them with her nails. She yanked and pulled at his body, trying to get more of him. Her head thrashed back and forth and her hair became a wild silky tangle. Every other word from her lips was his name.

Then she begged, and he completely lost it.

"Justin, stop teasing me! Oh, god! Please... please! Give it to me!"

It was over for him. He didn't need any more encouragement to sink back into her depths. In fact, he couldn't wait another second. He leaned forward, supported his weight with one arm and held Delaine by the hip with the other until she was tight against his body.

He plowed deeply until he thought he'd see his cock behind her eyes. Damn she was tight, and felt so good, so right as he rode her hard. Sweat poured off him and mingled with hers until he was wet to the scalp with it. He growled, swore, moaned and pumped until his name was one long word out of her mouth.

"JustinJustinJustinJustinJustin!"

He ground down and felt Delaine's wet heat flutter and tighten around him, milking him as he panted wicked words in her ear.

"Ah, baby, you feel so good. Come for me. Milk my cock and give me that cream." And she did, tightening almost painfully around him, squeezing then scalding him with her flowing juices. He came with a shout right behind her. His fingers dug into her hips, back arched and head fell back as he let loose inside her. Justin erupted, filling her with his seed until it flowed out of her dripping honey pot and down onto the sheets.

He lay on top of her for long moments and relished the soft stroke of Delaine's fingers over his back and shoulders. Finally her caress slowed, then stilled. She'd drifted off to sleep, but he couldn't bring himself to leave her body just yet. Carefully positioning her limp form until they lay spoon style, he reached down and pulled the covers up over them and settled down to untangle her beautiful hair with his fingers.

\* \* \* \* \*

Delaine woke in the middle of the night to the feel of hard, warm male behind her. Tucked underneath a strong chin, solid thighs were pressed behind hers, a well-formed arm thrown over her hip, and her head lay on a thick biceps instead of her pillow. Goodness, she was surrounded by strong man. And she liked it.

Justin tightened his embrace, sighed in his sleep and then eased his hold. She rolled slowly away and got up to go to the bathroom. When she climbed back into bed, she lay on her side for a moment, sorting through her thoughts and everything she'd seen and heard since she'd arrived in Charlotte. In the end, all she could think about was how cold the sheets felt way over on this side of the huge bed. Then she was suddenly surrounded with warmth as Justin encircled her waist and hauled her over to his side. She snuggled close and said one simple word for the most mind-blowing sex she'd ever had in her life.

"Wow."

"Hmmm?" he sighed sleepily.

"Well, I've never had an orgasm before," she muttered sheepishly.

Justin was wide awake now and peered at her through the darkness. "What? You were married for eighteen years, had two kids and the man never made you come?"

She blushed. "Well, Gary wasn't the most attentive lover. I didn't know I could do it until you made me tonight."

Her ex-husband was obviously an idiot. She deserved

so much better. Deserved someone attentive, caring. Someone like him. Before he met Delaine, he wouldn't have entertained these kinds of thoughts to save his life. Settling down wasn't something he'd planned on, especially in his line of work. But now that he'd talked with her, touched her, these kinds of permanent thoughts felt right. He didn't even question wanting to be with her. Instead, he kissed the top of her head and nuzzled the back of her neck and shoulders.

She tilted her head to give him better access to the tingly spot he'd found earlier. She took a quick intake of breath when his hand slid up from her hip to caress the underside of her breasts. It amazed her that he instinctively knew what she liked and exactly how she liked it. Reaching up to wrap her arms around his neck, her fingers brushed against something that hadn't been there when she'd fallen asleep. Gingerly she touched six neat fat braids, three on each side of her head. It was the sweetest thing anyone had ever done. Hot tears pooled behind her eyes and spilled down her cheeks until her shoulders shook with emotion.

"What is it, baby? What's wrong?" Alarm seized the inside of Justin's stomach. He held her tighter, pressing her back tight against his chest. A lump formed in his throat at her wracking sobs. He simply couldn't bear to hear her cry.

At his soft, caring words, Delaine rolled over and buried her face in his chest and bawled like a baby.

"Please, baby, tell me what's the matter. I can't stand to hear you cry," he said softly into her hair, placing soothing little kisses everywhere his lips could reach.

She hiccupped and sniffed, "You braided my hair."

"Hell, I'll take them out if it upsets you that much. I love your hair and thought you'd want it out of the way while you slept," he said as he reached up to take the braids down.

"No!" she screeched. He snatched his hands back quickly and for the first time in a long time, Justin had no idea what to do. Her next words pierced his heart.

"No one has ever combed my hair before," she sobbed. "It's such an intimate, sweet gesture, I don't know what to say. Justin, look, I don't know where this is going, or if we'll even be together next week, but thank you for making me feel so special tonight."

"You're welcome, beauty. It was my pleasure." He gently took her tear-stained face between his hands and kissed away the trail of tears. His mouth took hers in a sweet caress. Their tongues dueled lazily, but he found himself as hard and fiercely needy as the first time. Justin pulled her leg up over his hip and caressed her lovely, round ass. A finger disappeared into her pussy from behind and her hips circled against his hand. She was already wet and more than ready.

"Are you sore?" he asked, thinking if she wasn't tender from the pounding he'd given her earlier, she should be.

"Mmmm." Lord, how could he make her feel so hot and needy with so little effort? His touch made her cream, her womb clench, made her crave the finger stroking in and out of her body. He added another finger and she arched against him with a ragged moan.

"If you're sore, baby, I shouldn't make love to you again."

"Then no...not sore." Breathless, she wiggled her hips, wanting him to sink his fingers deeper.

"Are you lying, Delaine?" He playfully nipped her ear then soothed the bite with a swipe of his tongue.

"That's my story and I'm sticking to it. Now, do you think you can make me come again? I just want to be sure I can really do it," she queried playfully, her tears a thing of the past.

"Do you think I can make you come again?" he

asked, loving their word play, sliding his fingers as deep as he could get them up her creamy passage.

"Oh, yes. Yes, I definitely think so," she breathed out in a rush as his fingers were replaced with a thick, throbbing cock.

# CHAPTER NINE

"Good morning, beautiful."

"Good morning, handsome," Delaine replied into her speaker phone as she ran her fingers through her thick hair to undo the twists she'd put in before she'd gone to sleep. She'd hoped he would call, and he hadn't disappointed her in the two weeks they'd been seeing each other. She was glad he couldn't see her looking at herself in her bathroom mirror, grinning like a loon.

"I enjoyed spending time with you last night," he said seductively. "When can we get together again?"

"Well, you don't waste any time getting to the point, do you?" she asked saucily.

"Baby, I don't have any time to waste. If I see a priceless jewel should I reach for it? Or should I pretend I don't see it and hope it's still there the next time I happen to come around?"

Well, didn't he have a way with words? He made her feel all warm and gooey inside, like melting caramel.

"How about dinner tonight?"

"I'm not sure if I can make it tonight," she said, disappointed that it was true. She really needed to do some surveillance. She was really close to getting what she needed on Baker but was frustrated because she wasn't further along in the case. That damned Sarah Ann was on her like white on rice since that day Delaine had shaken her off her trail.

"Have another hot date lined up already, eh," Justin said, half-serious.

"Sorry, but this sistah can't move that fast," she teased.

"Baby, I happen to like your moves," he crooned into the phone. "So how about it? My place, say, seven o'clock? If we get through dinner early, we can work on getting my bed to smell like hot sex and you, like your bed does."

"You are such a freak," she giggled.

"Yeah, and you like it."

"All right, I give!" she laughed, knowing he was out of her league when it came to sexual banter, but she was catching up. "I'll come as long as I don't have to eat delivered Chinese food."

Justin's totally male laugh made her breath catch as her insides danced at his masculine chuckle. Lord, she just loved his voice. They finalized their plans and Delaine headed out the door for what was becoming a habit of Sunday morning breakfast at Le Peep with Pam.

If Pam noticed Delaine was dressed in black tactical gear and SWAT-issued boots, she didn't mention it.

\* \* \* \* \*

Justin parked several blocks away from Astin Pharma, snuck in the back gate and into the building through a back door some idiot left propped open so they could take a smoke break.

It was Saturday and there shouldn't be anyone in the building except the process engineers on the main production floors. But lately, Baker hadn't been sticking to his regular schedule. If the man was anything, he was meticulous and predictable, and Justin wondered if Delaine's presence was the reason for his out-of-character behavior.

He made his way to one of the restricted elevators, flipped open his cell phone, hit the speed dial and spoke quietly.

"Okay, I'm in. Do your thing," he whispered into the mouthpiece. He held the display panel of the phone up to the badge scanner. A moment later a beep sounded and the elevator doors slid smoothly open. Another beep and a click later, it started its descent. Justin spoke quickly into the mouthpiece.

"Thanks, Derrick. Now tell me what you did in case I have to explain my way out of it later."

"I hacked the database and saw that Baker recently gave the Sarah Ann chick who's been tailing your girl access to The Vault. I displayed the barcode from her badge onto the screen of your digital cell. The reader in the elevator doesn't know the difference between the badge and the phone."

"But what about the logs that show who's been in and out of the elevator?"

"Baker tried to be slick by programming Sarah Ann's badge with a fictitious name, but that works to our advantage. The system won't show that either you or she were ever there."

"You're a genius. Thanks, man."

"No problem. By the way, I'm still working on getting more details on Delaine. We're almost one hundred percent sure she's with Aegis, which is good for us. Spencer's calling one of his contacts to verify. And there's a small problem."

"What?" Justin asked impatiently, not liking the hesitation in his partner's voice.

"You're going to have to keep an even closer eye on Delaine than you already are."

Justin's brow furrowed as a lump formed in the pit of his stomach. This couldn't possibly be good. Hell, he'd been spending so much time with Delaine, if he watched her any closer he'd be living with her. While that particular thought held appeal, he pushed it away and focused on the conversation with Derrick.

"What do you mean keep a closer eye on her?"

"Because Baker knows she's undercover. I don't know how, but she's been compromised."

This was not what he wanted to hear. Baker was a dangerous son of a bitch and the thought of anything happening to Delaine at his hands made the blood behind Justin's eyes boil. He was so angry, he literally saw red. "Shit!" Justin fumed, raking his hand through his thick red hair as the elevator continued to plummet.

"My sentiments exactly. All indications are the two of you are on the same side. Why don't you just talk to her about what we know?"

"Are you crazy? And have Spencer fry my ass?" Justin growled into the mouthpiece, squeezing the phone so hard it was a wonder the thing didn't break in two.

"Look, Justin, you've never been this crazy about a woman in the ten years I've been working with you. I know you care about her. Besides, Baker is your target, not Delaine. I'm not saying you should blow your own cover, but talking to her about Baker may be the only way she'll let you help her. I know you can come up with some way to talk to her about Baker without telling her you're D.E.A."

"Look, Derrick, there's no way in hell I'm lying to Delaine! I'll just have to watch her back without her finding out."

"You don't have authorization for that, man. You know regulations."

"Fuck regulations! She's my woman, damn it! And I'm not going to let Baker get his hands on her just because the regs say I can't get involved in another agent's case without auth!"

"All right, man, I feel you. I'll run it by Spencer and get back to you."

"What the hell do I do in the meantime?"

"If Delaine hears from someone else that you're working the same case, she's going to fry your ass and you won't have to worry about Spencer. She's a sistah, and they don't play. Trust me, I know. And there's the possibility that if Baker knows …"

"…then someone else knows too," Justin reasoned quickly. "Damn it! I may have no choice but to talk to her, but not today. I'll catch up with you later, Derrick. I'm going to lose the signal any second. Almost at the bottom."

"Good luck, man."

"Yeah, thanks." Justin disconnected the call and turned off his cell completely. He flipped it over to make sure the homing beacon still flashed faintly, then slipped it into his back pocket just as the elevator doors hissed open.

* * * * *

Delaine walked right through the front door, her long cloak hiding the jacket and black tactical gear. She headed straight for her office, locked the door and did a little creative hacking. In minutes she'd bypassed the main security camera program and fed the digital photos she wanted the security guards to see into the system that controlled all the camera links. The program would only run for ten minutes, which was more than enough time to get into a restricted elevator unseen.

Her badge and digital key worked perfectly, just like

before, and in moments she was speeding down to The Vault. Before the doors opened, she checked the guns in the holsters under her jacket, a lethal black bowie knife tucked in her boot and the homing device hidden behind her ear.

She knew exactly which lab she needed to break into, having explored all the tunnels over the last few weeks. Every tunnel led to a legitimate research and development lab, except for the two tunnels on the far right. Both these labs were always locked. The first, which she'd successfully broken into, appeared to be scrubbed clean after every use. Whoever had been using it left no evidence of what they were doing in there. She'd found no dust, no residue. Not even a fingerprint. The second tunnel led to an identical lab she hadn't been in yet. It was larger and had another door near the back. And she headed straight to it.

She encountered no one as she slipped her gloves on and picked the lock. Once inside, she eased the door closed and slid the deadbolt home. A quick sweep of this front room found it clean but not spotless. There were a couple of used vials, a pair of tweezers and even a small dissolution test kit. On one of the metal tables she found a small bit of some kind of pink powder. Delaine put a sample in a small glass vial, careful not to inhale or get it anywhere on her skin or clothes. Sealed and secured in a plastic baggie, she tucked it inside her inner jacket pocket and made her way to the door at the back of the room.

Closing the door softly behind her, she threw the deadbolt and stepped fully into the room. Her gut promptly twisted. This room was soundproof and would prevent her from hearing anyone approach. She'd have to work fast. She passed by the lab equipment, three doors that she assumed were closets for storage, along with file cabinets, and went directly to a wide-screen monitor with playback equipment hooked up to it. The playback cables were connected to three video cameras arranged in front of small neatly made beds, and a medical table with stirrups on one end.

Delaine went to the digital video camera. There was still a tape inside. She popped it into the playback unit and Baker's face immediately came up on the screen. The date and time at the bottom of the screen was six-thirty yesterday morning.

Baker moved away from the screen and a blonde woman Delaine had seen a couple of times in the lunchroom sat on one of the beds naked. Her arms were crossed over her breasts, her legs clenched tightly and her head down. She looked up at Baker through lowered lashes and appeared decidedly uncomfortable. But this blonde wasn't the one she'd seen in her vision.

In the video, he approached the woman with a little pink tablet balanced on the end of his finger. Delaine's hand immediately felt for the vial inside her jacket, wondering if the residue inside was from the same stuff. Baker placed the tablet under the girl's tongue and the timer on the video started counting.

At thirty seconds, the girl still sat on the edge of the bed, but her eyes were now wide and frightened. Her hands dropped to her breasts and she watched her hands massage and pull on them as if she couldn't believe what she was doing to herself.

At a full minute, the woman writhed on the bed, pumping her hips at something that wasn't there. Her legs fell open and she ground down into the mattress. As she panted and moaned, her eyes followed Baker's every movement.

At two minutes, she wept and begged Baker to take her. The perverted bastard obliged.

Delaine watched the tape and almost gagged when he approached the bed with his skinny hard cock poking out of the fly of his pants. He lay down on top of the woman and her legs immediately wrapped around his hips. The woman was like a wild animal under him and screamed, yelled and clawed at his back while he pumped into her body with his pants, shoes and shirt still on. The woman came on a tormented scream. Then Baker flipped her over, told her to get up on her hands and knees and took her from behind. She screamed as she came again.

No wonder the walls were soundproof. Baker had plowed his blonde guinea pig for fifteen minutes and she'd come several times. When he was done, she still writhed and rolled around on the bed. Then Sarah Ann came into the picture. Before the blonde collapsed from exhaustion, she'd come almost non-stop, compliments of Sarah Ann and a dildo.

Sapa roared loud and long in her mind. The lioness had obviously been trying to warn her about something, but she'd been so absorbed in the disgusting video, she hadn't been paying attention. Delaine snapped out of her incredulity at the turn of a key in the lock. Shit! She snatched the tape out of the playback unit, stuffed it into her pocket and moved silently to the first closet door. Hell, it was locked and there was no way she'd have time to pick it. On to the second door. Locked. Relief coursed through her when the third door opened and closed smoothly just before Baker stepped into the room.

'Sapa, I need a little help with my hearing,' Delaine called to her spirit guide. The great hunter's keen senses flowed through the bond and manifested inside Delaine's body. Through the door, she heard everything going on in the lab as if she were sitting right there. Crouched in the dark, she listened while Baker fussed at Sarah Ann for dead-bolting the doors and leaving the lights on.

Ready to take the bastard down, she silently unsnapped the secure strap on her holster to slide her gun free. Delaine had all the proof she needed.

A wicked, sharp knife pressed against her throat from behind. She didn't move a hair further.

# CHAPTER TEN

Justin couldn't believe it. The woman was supposed to be having breakfast with Pam, not nearly getting herself killed. He was furious.

"Don't make a sound, Delaine, or we're both dead," he hissed as he removed the blade from her throat and pocketed it in the sheath hidden in his boot.

She hissed to her spirit guide, 'Damn it, Sapa. Why didn't you warn me Justin was here?'

*Because he is not a danger to us.*

He pressed so tightly against her back, she was practically in his lap. Against her will, her skin heated and her nipples tingled. She didn't need this, not right now. She needed to concentrate on taking down the bad guy.

"What the hell are you doing here, Justin?" she whispered furiously to her man crouched behind her.

"Can we talk about this later and concentrate on getting out of here in one piece?"

"I'm a law enforcement officer. Don't interfere with the arrest I'm about to make," she warned in a no-nonsense tone.

"Don't think so, baby. Baker is alone in this room, but he's not alone in the facility. If we're discovered, we'll find ourselves 'disappeared', and probably with lots of pain involved."

She cocked her head to the side. "Baker has allies here? In the building?" She clearly wondered how much he knew that she didn't.

"Justin, who…"

"Later, Delaine."

"No, now. All we can do is wait until Baker leaves. I think we've got time."

Her tone was snide. He was so pissed, he didn't care. "I'm not willing to wait that long," Justin snapped quietly then flipped open his cell phone and turned it on. He breathed a sigh of relief while grumbling about poor signals in a state-of-the-art facility.

He whispered into the mouthpiece. "Hey, Derrick, it's me. We're stuck in Baker's lab. Confirm the passage behind door number three." After a couple of seconds, he said, "Excellent." He clicked the phone shut and listened. It sounded like Baker was having hot and sweaty sex with Sarah Ann. Good.

"Sounds like the perfect time to get the hell out of here. Stand up, and step where I step." He pressed a button on the back of his cell phone and a thin beam of blue light appeared, just bright enough to see the floor of the little room.

She followed silently, her back stiff with anger and her brows drawn so tightly together she felt the beginning of a fierce headache. Delaine couldn't remember being this angry since the jacked-up e-mail from Gary a year ago. It had been a long time since she'd been this frightened for someone she cared about. And she didn't like it one bit. She was royally pissed. If she said a single word, it would be a very long, loud mistake.

\* \* \* \* \*

With Derrick's guidance, it took Justin less than a minute to find and open a small hidden hatch set into the wall at the back of the closet. It was one of many that had been used to get building materials down to The Vault when it was being secretly built. Once through it, he turned off the small flashlight built into his phone and they moved silently up a narrow hallway until they reached a steep stairwell. It took them another twenty minutes to climb up to the first floor. They emerged outside at the rear of the building covered with dust and cobwebs, their lungs burning from their adrenaline-fueled jaunt up those endless steps. By the time they reached the rear parking lot, they were both huffing, puffing and sneezing all over the place.

Justin packed Delaine into his car and sped her home. He clenched his jaw to keep silent, not trusting himself to speak to her just now. He knew his reaction to discovering her down in the The Vault ready to draw on Baker was unreasonable. She was, after all, an undercover agent like himself. It was her job to find evidence on people like him and take them down. But the thought of her charging out of their hiding place to confront Baker scared the red out of his hair. Delaine in any kind of danger set his teeth on edge. He gripped the steering wheel of his Jag until his knuckles turned white.

He pulled into her driveway and she slammed out of the car before he could get the emergency brake in place. She stomped through the front door, stripped off her soiled, filthy clothes in the foyer and sprinted up the stairs.

Justin got an eyeful of a very naked Delaine, cobweb-filled hair flying behind her as she took the stairs two at a time. He stopped short and stared after her. His anger faded as his body tensed with baser emotions. Damn, she had such a nice ass. Would he ever get used to his physical reaction to this woman? Not bloody likely.

He stripped off his dirty clothes, piled them on top of Delaine's and took the whole pile to the laundry room before following her up the stairs.

\* \* \* \* \*

Fuming, Delaine jumped into the gigantic glass brick shower in her bedroom and slammed the door behind her. How dare that man put himself in such danger! She was so mad, she couldn't think straight. He looked more than capable of taking care of himself, but didn't he know how dangerous it was snooping around in The Vault? And he had to be snooping, otherwise he wouldn't have been crouching in that stupid closet. The big question was, who the hell did he snoop for? As a contractor, he could end up working at some other pharma company next week. Perhaps he planned to take Astin trade secrets with him? *'Oh please don't let him be a bad guy.'* She already had one crook to catch, and the last thing she needed was to fall for one. And what if he got hurt in the meantime? What a mess.

One thought led to another, and by the time she angled one of the large shower heads to rush over her body, leaned back against the cool glass brick wall, the bath seat solid under thighs, she was a volatile mix of confusion and fury. Forcing herself to relax, she breathed deeply as the hot water splashed over her head and down her tired, aching body like a warm, gentle waterfall. The steam-covered door swung silently open and a cool whoosh of air washed over her. Justin.

Again, Sapa hadn't warned of his approach. What was up with that?

She opened her eyes and pushed her thick cottony

locks back and away from her face. The soothing scents of rosemary, lavender and peppermint filled the air just as his big hands sank into her curls to lather her hair with her favorite shampoo. His fingers moved expertly through the mass of coils until every inch of her scalp tingled.

"How in the world do you know so much about hair? Black hair at that?" she breathed contentedly. It felt so good, and his strokes were so gentle, working from her roots clear to the ends of her hair. She leaned into his hands and sighed softly with pleasure. He stepped to the side and the waterfall of water flowed down over her body again, rinsing her hair clean.

"Three younger sisters." He kept his reply soft and controlled.

"It feels wonderful," Delaine murmured. How could she stay mad at a man who shampooed her hair? Lather was worked through her hair again and rinsed until all traces of shampoo flowed down the drain and her body threatened to slide off the bath seat along with the puddle of suds.

She started to tell him if she didn't hurry up and moisturize the mop on her head, it would be good and nappy. Instead, she snapped her mouth closed at his attentiveness. One step ahead of her, he was already smoothing a handful of creamy conditioner through her tresses and massaging it through. But now that she thought about it, he always seemed to be one step ahead of her. How?

Suddenly her body cooled and ached at the loss of contact. Justin had stepped away. Her eyes snapped opened and his blazing blue gaze trapped her with its intensity. He held out his hand to her.

"Come here, baby."

Delaine quirked a brow and wondered at the tone in his voice. His jaw ticked furiously, but she did as he asked, stood slowly and stepped into his arms.

He held her close, trembling as he said, "Delaine, I was furious today. The thought of anything happening to you made me crazy." His voice tight with emotion as his hands stroked up and down her back. "I don't think I've been that angry since...hell, I've never been that angry."

"Then you've read my mind," she whispered back. "I know you work for Astin, but The Vault just isn't a safe place to be found right now. I checked the list of authorized personnel and your name wasn't on it, Justin. What the hell were you doing down there?"

"I don't want to talk about that right now. I'm so relieved you're safe, I just want to hold you and never let go. I need to feel you, Del. Let me touch you, baby."

He sat her back down on the bath seat and knelt between her legs. Even on his knees, they were still of a height. He rubbed his nose against hers and whispered all the nasty things he wanted to do to her.

"Baby, I want to nibble and suck on your pretty tits and lick you from the underside to the nipples until you squirm. Then I want to kiss a path from between your beautiful breasts, down to your navel and back up again before I take them in my hands, squeeze them together and slide my dick back and forth between them."

Delaine wanted him to do that and more. His erotic words stoked the low simmer in her womb to a full-blown forest fire.

"I want to suck on the lobes of your ears then slip my tongue up around them. Work my way slowly down your neck to that spot near your shoulder that makes you scream."

"Oh, yes," she hissed through her teeth while her hips moved in a slow restless rhythm as Justin knelt between her legs. One hand massaged the sensitive nipple of one breast while the other found her swollen clit peeking out of its little hood so he could play with it.

He slipped a finger into her mouth and said, "I love how you suck my finger. Your mouth is so hot and wet."

Delaine had never enjoyed oral sex, but suddenly she wanted it with this man. Wanted it almost more than she wanted to feel him moving inside her, more than she needed to breathe.

She stood and pushed him from his knees down to the shower floor. The scent of his body mingled with the steam of the shower into an intoxicating perfume that tickled her nose and made her pussy weep. The second he lay back on the warm, wet tiles she plunged her mouth down over his engorged length with an urgency that took his breath away. He bit his lip, holding back a primal yell when she began sucking his flesh like she wanted nothing more in the world than to take him all the way down her throat and milk him dry.

Her firm lips wrapped tightly around his shaft, swallowing as much of him as she could. Her free hand pumped him eagerly as she pulled her mouth up to the engorged head and swirled her tongue around and around the purple tip before plunging back down.

When she hummed her pleasure the vibration crashed down his sensitive nerve endings to pool at the base of his sac. He almost came on the spot. He sat up swiftly, lifted her high and slid deep in one lightning quick stroke.

"Oh yes! Oh, Justin! Oh, god!" she babbled, an overloaded bundle of nerves but full of a need so beyond the physical, she was humbled by it.

"More!"

"Demanding woman, aren't you?" Justin teased, his jaw clenched tightly as he listened to her demand that he take her harder, give her more, make her scream. Determined to keep his woman happy, he gave her just what she asked for.

He plumbed deep and almost died of the exquisite

pleasure of being surrounded by her tight, gripping sheath. His blood churned thick and hot through his veins as he struggled to think clearly through the haze of bliss that was Delaine. He savored the feel of her strong hands as they touched him everywhere she could reach, blazing a trail up his chest and over his neck to fist in his hair. She yanked and pulled as she rode him.

Up off her knees in a move that surprised him, Delaine put her feet flat on the floor and squatted over him. Nothing touched him but her sweet, shaved core. She rode him like his dick had the antidote to her need loaded inside. He reached between their bodies and found her little swollen knot. His fingers pulled and stroked, drove her higher until the walls of her tight sheath squeezed him unmercifully.

She cried out when Justin lifted her off of him. She yelled for him to put her back. Put her back right now, damn it. Instead, he positioned her on her knees, chest against the bath seat, and plunged deep from behind. Now, she really did cry. The tears flowed down the wet skin of her cheeks as she pleaded for him to fulfill her need. She begged. Demanded. Screamed. And still he rocked into her, his balls slapping against her ass, only to slow down just enough to keep her release at bay.

"Justin, I can't take anymore!" she yelled. "If you don't…oh god…finish me, I'll castrate. Your ass! Over! Breakfast!"

"Ah, baby, you feel so good!" Justin growled in response. "I could fuck you forever. This is my pussy. All mine."

"Yes, Justin. Take it, take it now."

"You sure this is mine, my pussy?" he panted into her hair.

"Yesssssss!"

He pistoned into her, the veins of his thick staff stimulating her beyond reason. She felt her orgasm begin down in her toes, streak up her thighs and circle around her hips. Then it dove straight down and she erupted like a sunburst where their bodies were joined.

Justin filled her completely, pushing himself to the place only he could reach until he was submerged in her. Delaine reached back between her legs and pressed against the sensitive spot underneath his balls. It was over. His head flew back on a loud cry as his seed geysered against her womb, triggering another round of shuddering deep inside her thirsty heat.

They basked in the afterglow of their lovemaking until the water ran cold. Finally remembering Delaine still had conditioner in her hair, he washed it out for her before they washed each other quickly and headed for the big bed to fall into an exhausted stupor. But not before Justin admitted to himself that he was in deep. And he had no desire to be anywhere else.

In the morning he would tell Delaine who he was and exactly what he was doing at Astin Pharma, consequences be damned.

\* \* \* \* \*

Oh hell, it was almost time to meet Pam for breakfast again. After the night with Justin, she wasn't sure she was up to it. She rolled over and bumped into his broad, muscular back. Not only had the gorgeous hunk saved her neck, but he'd laid some sex down on her like she'd never had it before. And she'd be damned if he didn't have the sexiest ass she'd ever seen on a man. Sigh. She hadn't found out what he was doing down in The Vault, but since he hadn't killed or exposed her, she could only assume he worked there. But for who?

"Hey, you," she whispered sleepily, shaking Justin's shoulder on a yawn. It was like trying to shake a mountain. She ran her fingers through his red bed-head and crooned against the back of his neck. "Get up, honey, I need to get going."

Justin groaned, rolled over and smashed the pillow down over his head. She poked him in the ribs in the only spot on his hard body she'd found to be ticklish. He flinched and was out of the bed in two snaps, taking half the covers with him. She watched his eyes drop to her washboard stomach then slide lower to the smooth triangle between her legs. The predator was back with a wicked gleam in his eye and a cock rising to attention before her very eyes.

Oh damn! Delaine jumped out of the bed, snatched a pair of jeans and a tee shirt off the chest at the foot of the bed and fled the room, calling over her shoulder, "I'm meeting Pam in an hour. I'll shower in the guest bathroom, 'cause if I shower with you I'll never get out of here."

He taunted her fleeing back, "Damn straight! Come back here and take it like a man, er, wo-man!"

A buck naked Delaine ran down the stairs and headed to one of the guest bathrooms. Afterward, she went into the kitchen and put the kettle on for tea. She stood near the phone, nibbling on a fingernail, contemplating. Finally picking it up, her nails tap, tap, tapped against the gray granite countertop as she waited for the line to pick up on the other side.

"This is Geri."

"Hey, boss. I'm sending you a package. I got the goods on Baker!"

"Yeah! I knew you could do it. You are, after all, one of the best."

"Flattery will get you everywhere, madam boss."

"So whatcha got?"

"The most foul digital video of Baker doing some interesting things in The Vault. I managed to filch some samples too. They'll need to be analyzed to find out exactly what he's making, but I think it's some kind of synthetic aphrodisiac."

"Are you ready to wrap this up?"

"Not quite. All I need to do is catch him in The Vault, and he's as good as done. By the way, did you get the info on Justin Cooley back yet?"

"It came in last night. Hold on a minute, let me pull it up."

Delaine was anxious and felt more than a little guilty about checking him out behind his back. She kept telling herself that it was just part of the job, but her heart wasn't buying it. And neither did Sapa, who'd been quiet since last night but was now growling her disapproval in the back of Delaine's mind. The one minute she stood on hold seemed to stretch on forever while she listened to the click of Geri's fingers on her computer keyboard.

"Okay, Delaine, some of this info is dated. Let's see, former Marine, black ops, honorable discharge... Here we go, he's D.E.A. Distinguished record with the department for ten years. Hold on, let me check something else."

D.E.A.? Drug Enforcement Administration? Damn it! After their little closet rendevous in The Vault, Delaine was sure he was a thief with a few high tech toys, not a fucking agent!

Delaine heard Geri pick up another line and ask to speak to someone whose name she couldn't quite make out. She distinctly heard the name Cooley, and a few uh-huhs before her boss came back to the phone.

"Delaine?"

"I'm here."

"He's part of Spencer's team."

"Spencer!" Damn, that meant he wasn't just D.E.A., but more like a super covert "Bond. James Bond" type of D.E.A. guy. Shit! This just got better and better.

"Geri, since when does D.E.A. encroach on another agents case? How the hell did I not know there was D.E.A. in my goddamned face?" She felt like a complete idiot.

"Actually, it's our fault. Somehow we missed some intelligence somewhere..." Geri began.

"Yeah, sure it's our fault. We missed something. More like I missed something. Goddamned, son-of-a-bitch, just wait until I get my hands..." Delaine growled in a low voice.

"Delaine, what's wrong?"

"I'll call you back, Geri," she said softly and disconnected the line. She picked it up and dialed again.

"Pam? Hey, it's me. I can't make it today. Something's come up with work. Let's try it next week, all right?"

* * * * *

Justin stepped out of the shower, walked out of the bathroom and came face-to-face with a royally pissed off Delaine.

"You're D.E.A.!"

Damn! Knowing he couldn't lie to her, he simply nodded his head and watched a mix of emotions, including rage and sadness, fly across her beautiful face.

Delaine's heart sank. The bastard had used her. She felt Sapa reach through the bond, trying to calm her.

*Suta Winyan, do not push away our mate unnecessarily.*

Delaine pushed the awareness of the black lioness away. Sapa retreated, with no choice but to wait until Delaine reached out to her. Unless there was danger, the spirit guide could not override her charge's wishes.

"Why did it take a call from my boss to find out who you are?"

"Delaine, I've wanted to tell you, but I couldn't. You know how this business works. You don't expose a cover to anyone without clearance. Besides, baby, when I'm with you the last thing I want to think or talk about is work. I swear I'd made up my mind to tell you, then yesterday with you in The Vault...it scared me, baby, and all I could think about was holding you."

He stepped to her with the need to wrap his arms around her and dip his nose into the hollow of her neck where she always smelled so good. But more than anything, he needed her to trust him. Justin blew out an exasperated breath as she shoved him back, or tried to.

"Nice try," she snapped. "You didn't tell me because you wanted to get the drop on Baker."

"Delaine, don't be ridiculous. After that near disaster yesterday, I planned to tell you everything this morning anyway."

"Sure you did. You can say anything now that you're fucking busted!" She walked back and forth across the carpet with her fist jammed into her hip. "How could I have been so stupid? You wanted a little booty and all of the credit for the bust. That's what I get for falling for..."

Justin shook his head in wonder. Would he ever understand the female mind? He'd saved her life, treated her like a queen, and she was upset because he didn't want to tell her he was undercover? He just couldn't comprehend it. Especially since she'd had no intention of telling him she was undercover herself. It was insane.

But insane or not, he wanted her. Needed her. Hell, he'd even admit falling in love with her, but not in her present mood. He dropped his head on a sigh. Hopefully she'd come to her senses quickly and not do anything stupid in the meantime. Like go after Baker alone. The last thing he wanted was for her to get hurt trying to hurry up and wrap this case before all the ends were tied up. He had one more card to play.

"Delaine, your cover was compromised. I was trying to keep you out of trouble."

"I didn't need you to keep me out of trouble."

"Damn it, you stubborn woman, did you hear what I said? You were compromised!"

"I could have handled it on my own. So tell me the truth, Justin. What were you really after, huh? You've been in this business for a long time. Ready to retire? Needed to go out with a bang?"

"Damn it, Delaine, I told you what I was after. Yes, I was originally sent here to find out if Baker was secretly developing an illegal substance. But after I found out you were involved and in danger I couldn't just leave you for the dogs. Not after getting to know you, baby."

"Riiiight," she drawled sarcastically.

"Look, I won't stand here and be accused of lying," he growled dangerously, his own anger starting to kindle.

"Good! Then get dressed and get the hell out!" Delaine pointed toward the door.

"Fine!" Justin grabbed his clothes off the end of the bed, stepped into his pants and yanked his shirt over his head, wet hair and all. Not bothering with underwear, socks or shoes, he slammed down the stairs and out the front door. The wheels of his Jag echoed in the quiet morning air as he squealed out of the driveway and tore down the street.

## CHAPTER ELEVEN

Delaine's stomach dropped into her shoes every time her phone rang. For the past three days, she'd taken to letting her voice mail get it, but every time she checked her messages it was never the one person she wanted it to be—Justin. She continued to show up for work at Astin and perform her job expertly as if nothing had gone down. Close to getting a sign-off on her hierarchy design, she knew she was running out of time to wrap this case. Geri told her where Justin was supposed to be working inside the Astin facility, but as the days passed with no sight or sign of him, Delaine's ability to rethink the matter finally resurfaced.

She admitted to herself that she was miserable, hated that the two of them had fought. Hated sleeping without him pressed up against her. Her days weren't as bright. Her smile felt brittle, as if the facade she'd perfected was crumbling. Even Sapa was irritated. Her spirit guide came when called, but the warmth that usually flowed through the bond had noticeably cooled. The great huntress sulked behind Delaine's eyes with drooping ears and her grey cat eyes full of sadness.

Perhaps she had behaved foolishly? After all, she'd had no intention of telling Justin she worked for Aegis. So why was she upset that he hadn't confided that he was D.E.A.? Her boss was even willing to take heat since Aegis actually dropped the ball. While uncommon, it wasn't unheard of for intelligence to miss a few key details. It was a huge blunder but nothing that couldn't be fixed. And since they were on the same side, was there really anything to be upset about? Sapa stirred restlessly.

*Suta Winyan, you are being unfair. If you would but think instead of react you would discover your true feelings.*

She thought on Sapa's words and felt somewhat silly. Cutting Justin off cold like that, she'd cut off her nose to spite her face.

*You are sabotaging our chance for a worthy mate. You are running away.*

'Oh, hush already.' Delaine scowled into the recesses of her mind, knowing the black lioness was right. But she didn't want to talk to the big cat about her catapulting emotions. She wanted to talk to a flesh and blood woman. She called Geri.

"Delaine, why are you being such a brick head? Justin is a really good guy. I called Spencer directly to check it out. He told me that as soon as Justin learned from his partner that your cover was blown, he sought permission to cover your ass. He didn't have to do that, you know."

Damn, it had been easier when she thought he was a bastard. Then she could have at least felt less foolish for flipping out on him.

"So who compromised me, Geri?"

"We think it was your tail in R&D. Your paperwork went through Purchasing instead of Human Resources. Some idiot put a code on the requisition used only for the FDA or other law enforcement agencies. Sarah Ann had been dating the main procurement officer in Purchasing. Spencer thinks she saw the code and alerted Baker."

"That would explain why she's been on me since day one."

"Yep, and Justin could have let you crash and burn and continued with his own investigation. It would have been perfectly ethical."

"Thanks, Geri. Gotta run," Delaine said calmly while her guilt ate her alive.

"Hold on a minute. Spencer and I want you two to close this case out together. We think it's safer."

"But the case is blown," Delaine said firmly, hating the words as she spoke them. She'd never failed an assignment in her five years at Aegis, or all her eighteen years undercover.

"The case isn't blown. Baker is not aware of Justin's involvement at all. You just continue to paint yourself as the agent who doesn't know she's been exposed and use it to urge Baker to act. To do something stupid."

"Done. I'll contact Justin and talk to you later."

Delaine hung up and dialed Justin's cell phone. It was three in the morning and wasn't surprised when she got his voice mail. She left a message for him to meet her for breakfast after she got a few hours sleep. Then she hung up and called his home phone just in case.

Big mistake.

\* \* \* \* \*

"Hu-woe?" a female voice drawled on the other end of the line.

"Hello? Who is this? Pam?"

"Yeah, wha'is it?"

"What do you mean, what is it? What are you doing

at Justin's house? And at three in the morning?"

"I'm sthpending the night," Pam slurred and almost dropped the phone from her boneless fingers.

"What!"

"I sorry, girl. I just couldn't help m'self. Don't be mad, 'kay?"

"Don't be mad? You're sleeping with my man and you're telling me don't be mad?"

"Your man? I thought you din't wan him an-more, Del. I mean, you kicked him to da curb, so finers, keepers, girl," she slurred. Pam hung up and smiled when the phone didn't ring again.

Justin appeared in the doorway of his bedroom in a pair of comfy terry sweats. He padded across the living room in bare feet, a towel around his neck to catch the water dripping from his hair. His blue eyes darkened and flashed his annoyance with his unexpected houseguest.

"Who was that on the phone, Pam?" he asked impatiently.

Pam looked up from her temporary bed on the couch and yawned widely. "Naa sure," she lied, her words running together almost incoherently. "I heeerd dit ringed, but I dinn't cath it afore dey hanged up."

"Good, because you don't have any business answering my phone. I'm done in the shower. If you want to take one, hurry up. I just picked up a message on my cell to meet Delaine for breakfast first thing in the morning, so I want to get to bed."

"Thure thing, han-some," she smiled cattily as she rose on unsteady, rubber band legs.

Justin wrinkled his nose when she let all the blankets fall to the floor to reveal her slim, naked flesh. She had a nice enough body, but he'd never been less interested in a woman as he was tonight. The smell of alcohol permeated her pores, disgusting him as she shimmied up to him and ran her hands across his bare chest.

"I—uh, I really 'preciate you lettin' me crash here, Jus. If there's a way I can, uh, repay you, I'm more sthan game."

He shivered, but not from lust. It was a good thing he'd eaten dinner hours ago. Her touch made him want to blow chunks. And this was supposed to be Delaine's good friend? He removed her hands from his chest and spoke through gritted teeth.

"Look, bitch, hit the couch or hit the road. You have ten minutes to get your ass to bed or get out of here. I belong to Delaine, heart and soul."

"Bud you two hadda fight. She duzznt want you."

"It doesn't matter. I want her. And it's a good thing I don't hit women, or I'd beat your ass for betraying her like this."

He turned on a bare heel, stalked into his room and slammed the door shut.

# CHAPTER TWELVE

Delaine took the long way to the restaurant then drove on by. She just couldn't face Justin today. She'd left a message asking him to meet her here, but after that conversation with Pam there really wasn't anything else to say. He'd obviously moved on. If Justin wanted Pam, fine, he could have her. But what started raggedy would end up raggedy. And those two raggedy mogillas deserved each other.

Her heart was in a million pieces, but she refused to feel the hurt anymore. Instead, she focused on her anger and let it consume her until she shook with rage. Bastard! And Pam? She couldn't believe Pam would steal her man like that. She'd sat up in that girl's chair at the salon and told her all of her and Justin's business, so it's not like the woman didn't know Delaine was serious about him. For someone she'd known since their children were in preschool to stab her in the back like this was beyond painful. Oh lord, what was she going to do?

*Suta, you are not using wisdom. This man is not like the puny Gary person.*

128

'But he slept with my best friend, Sapa! Hell, at least Gary slept with someone I didn't know.' She slammed her hand down on the steering wheel then looked down, expecting to see blood on her shirt from her breaking heart.

*Your reasoning abilities are unsurpassed. Use them now. All is not as it appears, Suta. Trust me.*

'I do trust you, Sapa. I just don't trust anyone else,' she replied sadly as a lone tear made its way down her cheek.

Fifteen minutes after she was supposed to meet him, his cell phone number popped up on the caller id. She pressed the ignore button, turned the phone off and threw it in the passenger seat. Heartsick but determined not to cry over a man ever again, she dashed the tears away and instead did something she hadn't done in all the years she'd worked with Aegis. She called in sick.

She flew home, stuffed a weekend bag with clothes, books and nothing related to work, jumped back in her Jag and headed for Nantahala Gorge. A nice quiet cabin in the Blue Ridge Mountains was just what she needed.

\* \* \* \* \*

Justin hadn't called Delaine since she'd gone mental on him at finding out he was D.E.A. But it was only to give her time to cool off. He'd been totally surprised to get her message asking him to meet her for breakfast.

He'd dialed her cell several times, but it just rang and rang. Now it was going straight to voice mail. This didn't make any sense. The woman had called him and left a message saying she wanted to see him then didn't show up? He drove over to her house and rang the bell. At first he thought she just wasn't answering the door, but after walking all the way around the house, noting the closed blinds on every window, he peeked through the small glass on the door that led into the garage from the side of the house. Her car was gone. Damn, she wasn't home.

His shoulders tensed and he felt the beginnings of a nasty headache creep up the back of his neck. Flipping open his cell, he dialed her again. Where the hell was his damned woman? Had something happened that made it impossible for her to meet him? What if she'd run into trouble related to her case? What if she was casing Astin and got caught? And why the hell wasn't she answering her phone?!

He drove toward home, his chest tight with one part anger for the way she'd arbitrarily dismissed him and one part worry at not knowing if she was all right. It wasn't unheard of for someone to die in their particular line of work. Tired of leaving the stubborn woman messages, he finally called Derrick.

"Hey, Derrick. What's up?"

"The usual. Chasing bad guys and doing favors for you."

"Then everything is normal, isn't it?" Justin said glibly.

"What the hell's wrong with you, Jus?" Derrick asked with a bit of a grin in his voice.

"I need to know where Delaine is. She's not answering her cell phone, she's not at home and I haven't seen her since we fell out a few days ago. She called me in the middle of the night and asked me to meet her for breakfast then she didn't show up. She's got the goods on Baker. I need to know she's safe."

"And what if she's safe but avoiding you?"

Justin took a deep breath and his head conjured an image of Derrick, his mouth drawn tight with disapproval. The man had a way of making him feel like the little brother right after the big brother said, "I'm gonna tell dad on you". He steeled himself and got ready for the I-told-you-so. "Delaine found out I was D.E.A. And not from me."

"Man, didn't I tell you to talk to her? I told you sistahs don't play that junk," Derrick said, managing to sound stern and sorry for Justin at the same time.

But there wasn't anything he could do about it now, except try to patch things up with the woman he knew he had to be with at all costs. Whatever it took. He wasn't even shocked anymore at how strong his feelings were for Delaine. He knew he had to find her.

"Look, Derrick, you were right, okay. But right now, I need to know my woman is all right."

"Let me work on it. I'll call you back in half an hour."

"Thanks, man."

"No problem. By the way, Spencer spoke to her boss, which is probably why she called last night. You two are supposed to close this case out together. If you can get her to speak to you ever again, that is."

\* \* \* \* \*

Delaine sat on the back porch of her little cabin and meditated. It was so peaceful and quiet here. No TV. No phone. Not even a decent cell phone signal. Only the rushing of the Nantahala River through the sheer cliffs of the gorge in the distance, and a light wind whispering through the thick towering trees. She'd never seen so many huge trees in her life. They were bare, preparing for the coming winter, but it was still beautiful up here. She shivered, wrapping the extra blankets she'd found in one of the closets more closely around her body.

'What possessed me to literally run for the hills with the thick of winter approaching?' she asked herself.

*Stop running, Suta. Embrace our mate. He comes.*

'Yeah, whatever,' Delaine words were flat and

uncaring, and in truth, she hadn't really been listening to what Sapa was saying to her along the bond.

The sleek mountain cat rolled her eyes and stalked away to a quiet corner of Delaine's mind. Before she retreated, Delaine felt her frustration. Well, she could forget about meditating. All she could think about was Justin. Justin's lips. Justin's hands on her body. Justin treating her like the queen he proclaimed her to be. Cooking for her. Taking her on road trips.

Justin sleeping with her best friend. Rather, a chick that was supposed to be her friend.

She wanted to knock herself in the head. What had she been thinking to get involved with him anyway? He was too nice, too perfect. And you know what they say—if it looks too good to be true, it probably is. So here she was again, in a relationship with a man who couldn't keep his dick out of another woman's pants. Her boss might think he was a good guy, but Delaine saw him as nothing but Gary-Number-Two.

Grumbling under her breath, she rose from the back porch and stomped into the cabin. She hit the sheets early, determined not to lose any more sleep over Justin, Pam or her job.

Bam! Bam! Bam!

What the hell was that? On silent feet, Delaine jumped out of bed with her gun in hand. She checked the lock on the window in her bedroom then edged her way to the small living room.

Bam! Bam! Bam!

Someone was banging on the door like they were the police. That was fine, because if it wasn't the police, whoever it was would limp away with a bullet in the ass.

"Delaine! Open the door!"

She lowered her weapon and clicked on the safety. Justin? Oh my god. How the hell had he found her? Okay, now that was a stupid question, she thought, shaking her head. The man worked for one of the most sophisticated covert organizations in the country. Of course he could find her.

Geesh, Delaine, get yourself together, girl, she grumbled at herself. 'And Sapa, stop all that pacing. It's making me dizzy.' An irritated growl resonated along the bond.

Sapa had told her Justin would come for her. She hadn't believed it one whit, not while he had someone else's warm body to bury his cock in. But Sapa had been wrong, in a manner of speaking. He hadn't come for her. The bastard had come for Pam. And when she was finished with him, he'd wish he'd kept his distance

With her gun fisted on her hip, she yanked the door open and glared up at him under the light of the single bulb illuminating the small front porch.

"What the hell are you doing here? Why aren't you with Pam?"

Justin drew his neck back, arched a brow and looked down at her like she was crazy.

"What the hell are you talking about?"

Delaine ignored his innocent, confused expression and ground her words into his face. "You. Slept. With. Pam! You bastard!"

"I slept with Pam? You've got to be kidding me!" he laughed.

Delaine quirked a brow, not seeing any humor in the situation. His laugh seemed genuine enough, but this was a man whose job was to be an expert at hiding who he really was. As are you. She ignored that little voice and, seeing no humor in the situation, scowled at him and his stupid laughter.

"Well, I'm not kidding! She answered your phone. You know, the one at your house. She said she was spending the night with you."

"And you believed her?"

"Well, she was there, wasn't she? What was I supposed to believe when she answered your phone at three in the morning?"

"But, Delaine ..."

Her voice full of venom and pain, she bared her teeth and poked him in the middle of his chest with the barrel of her 9mm as she spoke. "And she sounded like she'd already been screwed good that night ..."

"Delaine ..."

"You lying, cheating son of a bitch! I should have known better than..."

Justin had enough. He was many things, but liar and cheat weren't on the list. He grabbed a very angry Delaine by the shoulders and shook her until her teeth snapped together. She flung away from him and headed into the cabin, intent on slamming the door in his face. He caught it with his foot just before it hit him in the nose, pushed the door open so hard it banged into the wall. He didn't care. He stomped into the cabin on her heels.

"Delaine, will you be quiet so I can tell you what's going on?"

"I don't want to be quiet! I want to tell you exactly what's on my mind, damn it!" She tossed her gun on the small rustic couch. "Better yet," she snarled and dropped into a fighting stance, "I think I'll just kick your ass!"

Justin's mouth dropped open. She was serious. Balanced on the balls of her feet, her strong arms were up, ready to strike. He watched the muscles in her thighs tighten and flex as she readied herself. His mind flew back to the last time he'd seen those thighs. They were wrapped around his waist, with her head thrown back while he'd sunk to the hilt. He shook his head to clear the distracting image.

All she wore was a little white camisole and a pair of silk bed shorts. To Justin, she'd never looked sexier or more pissed. Delaine's cinnamon skin was flushed with anger, and her chest rose and fell in agitation. The tops of her breasts peeked out from underneath her camisole. A light sheen of sweat made her body appear to glow in the dim lamplight. She was exquisite and fighting was the last thing he wanted to do with her. There was only one way to tame a woman who might be capable of beating you down.

Delaine watched him closely. Her brown eyes clashed with his smoldering blue ones and she knew he was calculating the distance between them. So he thought to take the upper hand, eh? Well, she was determined not to give it to him. She never used her fighting skills on people she knew, knowing she could seriously hurt them, but if he took one more step she was mad enough to lay him out. Damn, he stepped. And she let a right hook fly, ready to follow up with a roundhouse kick to the gut.

Eyes wide, her throat emitted a loud squeak when he countered with a perfectly executed arm figure four move. As soon as she struck, he blocked her punch and grabbed her in the crook of her elbow with his free hand. She had a fraction of a second to wince as he bent her forearm up and back just before he stepped inside her defense and took her down to the floor. Hard.

The air whooshed from her lungs when her back hit the hard wood floor. The next thing she knew, Justin was lying at her side with his right shoulder on top of hers, and her right arm pinned underneath her. She couldn't move. Couldn't breathe.

Damn, that hurt. She instinctively tried to struggle. Justin put all his weight into the submission hold and Delaine went still. The slightest movement caused a funky pain to shoot up her shoulder and neck and then settle behind her eyes. Without releasing her from the hold, he slanted his mouth over hers and kissed the wind right out of her sails.

She had the ability to resist him for all of four seconds before she was lost in the taste of him as his tongue tormented hers. It seemed like forever since she'd enjoyed the way he explored her mouth, sucked and nibbled on her lips. He'd called her his cinnamon candy, and right now she certainly felt like it. He was eating her alive. Mmmm, she missed this. She whimpered when he pulled away from her lips.

He licked the corner of her mouth and rasped out, "Now will you listen?"

She nodded her head, eyes glazed over in a sensual stupor. Lord, the man sure could kiss. But he still hadn't let her out of the submission hold.

"Pam came to my house talking nonsense about how she wanted me. But nothing happened, Delaine. She was drunk out of her mind and it would have been wrong to send her home in that condition. Hell, she was so snockered, I'm still shocked she made it to my house."

"She said she spent the night with you."

"I wish I'd known you spoke to her, baby, because she spent the night with my couch. Before she passed out, I let her ramble on about how lonely she was and it turned out she didn't really want me. She just wants to be happy. I told her she needs to find her own man for that."

"That ho-humping bitch! Wait until I…"

"Delaine, she was so drunk, when she woke the next morning she didn't remember any of it. And I think the hangover was punishment enough."

Delaine looked deeply into his stormy blue eyes and saw nothing but truth. She reached out to her spirit guide. Sapa arose and padded to the forefront of her mind.

*He tells the truth, Suta. Take what I offer,* the lioness lent Delaine her keen sense of smell. Delaine lay still and inhaled deeply. No scent of Pam on him at all. The only female she smelled on him was herself.

"So she slept on the couch, eh?" she asked with a wry grin.

"Delaine, I slept in my bed alone with the door locked thinking about sinking my hard cock into nobody but you. Kind of like I'm thinking right now." Justin slowly released her from the submission hold and began to rub the feeling back into the arm he'd pinned underneath her.

He snickered, mocking himself. Now this was a shame. Here he was on the floor after a fight with a woman who could remove his head from his body, and his cock was hard as marble. It was pitiful, but he just couldn't help it. He slid his body on top of hers, held her arms above her head and pressed a very solid erection into her thigh. He began a slow, tempting grind.

"Oh goodness," she sighed, unable to resist the arousal he was stoking between them.

"Yeah, baby. Oh goodness is right," he whispered against her lips. Her face went up in flames and she blushed from her chest up to the roots of her dark, curly hair. Justin watched the heat move over her skin as his mind conjured an image of chocolate-covered cherries. Damn, but she was delicious.

"Justin, I'm so sorry for the way I acted. About you being D.E.A. and about Pam. I feel really silly, especially since you didn't know what Pam had done. Hell, Pam didn't know what Pam had done." The last words were said on a gasp as one strong hand encircled her nipple through her silky camisole.

"I forgive you, baby." He lowered his head and tongued her sensitive nub through the silk.

"Sssss," she hissed, her neck and body arching into his, instinctively reaching for more of him. "God, that feels so good. Do you really forgive me?"

"Oh yeah. Want me to prove it?" his voice a soft, husky drawl just before he dipped his head and bit her on the sensitive spot on her neck.

* * * * *

Her arms curled around his neck as she arched her back, pulling him to her until her swelling breasts were pressed tightly to his chest. She opened expectantly when he lowered his head to take her in an open-mouthed kiss that stole her senses. He tasted of chocolate and man, and her tongue sought out every corner of his mouth as he kissed her. Sucking on that special spot on her neck, she threw her head back as the breath was pulled from her lungs in long, loud pants. Writhing and moaning at the indescribable sensation that always traveled through her whole upper body whenever he laved her there.

"What the hell?" she asked wildly when he untwined her arms, picked her up and deposited her on the thick rug in front of the fireplace, and rolled her over on her stomach. Her silk boxers slid down over her butt and off. Her camisole followed.

"You've been very bad, Delaine," he said much too softly.

"But you said you forgive me," she said breathlessly, trying to turn back again so she could wrap her legs around him and hold him close. Well, that was the plan anyway. He obviously had other thoughts about the matter. "I do forgive you, but that doesn't mean you haven't earned a little punishment."

"Punish…ooooh!"

His hand landed with a loud smack on her bare ass. Oh damn, it felt good. The pleasure-pain sent a sensual twisting down through the nerves of her bottom and spread from her core outward.

He pulled her up to her knees and leaned forward. His breath tickled her ear, sending new shivers down the side of her neck. Pressing his huge cock into the crack of her ass, he asked in that sexy voice of his, "Do you like that, baby?"

Wiggling her ass to press closer to the hard, throbbing rod with an anxiousness that surprised her, she yelped when his hand landed on her ass again, sending a shockwave of need through her cunt.

"Oh shit! Yes—yes, I like it."

Delicious heat spread across her butt cheeks and settled just beneath her skin. She loved it, but she needed at least one more spank. Had to have it. Oh just one more. The urgency rivaled her need to be filled to bursting with his hard length. She'd never thought something so taboo as spanking could feel so good.

Her chest dropped to the rug and she hissed with pleasure, stretching her arms above her head to scratch and pull at the rug.

"Is there something you want, baby?" he purred against the sensitive skin on the back of her neck.

"Yes, I want it! I want…oh please."

His hands traveled from her warming bottom down to the crease at the back of her knees then around to the front of her thighs. Strong fingers pressed against the mound hiding her throbbing clit and pressed down firmly, while his other hand landed a final stinging smack on her right cheek. She came on the spot.

Unable to support her own quivering weight, she collapsed on the rug, panting like she'd just run an eight-minute mile.

"You don't think you're getting away with that, do you? Baby, you've got some making up to do."

With her pussy still clenching and tightening, her lust was so easily rekindled. All it took was his strong hand pulling her back up to her knees and a deep plunge into her dripping channel.

A scream tore from her throat as he slid inside. The ridges and veins of his steel-hard cock stimulated every inch of her cunt. Every nerve ending fired, making her thighs quake and shiver with need. She'd just come but was already sobbing for him to give her more. Her nipples tingled as her breasts bobbed back and forth under his thrusts. His fingers unerringly squeezed and palmed her sensitive mounds without missing a single stroke. As he rode her hard from behind, not one inch of her skin was neglected as his hands roamed over her ass, her hips, her thighs.

The light sheen of sweat made the rough rasp of his palms feel decadent against her skin. His calluses raised gooseflesh followed by little licks of pleasure wherever they touched. She could feel her climax beginning in the heat centered in her body as her channel sought the eruption only he could give her.

Then he pulled out.

"Noooo!" She howled, looking over her shoulder as his huge body and massive cock poised just outside of her needy pussy.

"Convince me to give you more."

The look in his eye was one of pure male domination...and pain. She realized now how deeply she'd hurt him. After all, she would have felt the same way if he'd thought her low enough to sleep with his best friend. He'd forgiven her quickly enough, but his male ego needed a bit of stroking. Well, stroking was something she could definitely do.

She turned and sat up, taking him firmly in her hand and squeezing gently but firmly. He gasped at the contact, pushing his hips toward her questing fingers.

She didn't speak but used the pressure of her fingers to ease him forward, up off the floor and to the nearby couch.

She pushed him backward and he sat with his knees spread, looking up at her. His fingers wrapped around his cock and he pumped slowly. Her eyes glazed over with pure, unadulterated lust as her gaze shifted from the tempting motion of his cock up to his mouth where his tongue did a sensuous dance across his lips. She sank to her knees.

Without warning she circled the base of his magnificent staff with her fingers and dove over his cock, surrounding him with the warmth of her mouth. She took his feral yell as a good sign and moved her mouth up and down with relentless strokes. His hips moved in cadence with her strokes as his fingers tangled in her hair. She took him deeply and pulled back, allowing her tongue to swirl around the flared head on each up stroke. On the down stroke, she hummed long and loud.

When he began to shake she grasped the base tighter and jacked him harder.

"Del, stop! You're gonna make me cum!"

She stopped her torment long enough to say on a purr, "Well, that was the general idea." Then lowered her head to take him deeply. She never made it.

In a blink, Justin reached down, took her underneath her arms and lifted her onto his lap until she was on her knees facing him. She let out a gasp as he surged forward, seating himself in a single thrust.

"Sink down on my dick, baby! Oh, yeah!"

Wrapping her arms around his neck, she rose up and plunged back down, leaning forward to bite a stiff male nipple. There was nothing sweet or tender in her movements. It was all hard, rough and carnal. And she wanted nothing less. She tightened and released her canal around him with little pulses, bombarding him with sexual stimulus.

"Oh shit! Fuck me, baby! Give me that pussy, Del!"

Moving faster, she flexed her thigh muscles and slammed home, filling herself with his cock until she was sure she couldn't take anymore of him. A subtle shift of his hips brought her clit into constant contact with his rod and her body responded urgently, violently.

Palming her firm ass as she fucked him, she shuddered with anticipation when he reached back and found the spot where their bodies joined. She could feel him spreading her juices over and around her ass, teasing and tickling the tight, untried hole. The sensation was so intense it robbed her of any rational thought. All she knew was that she wanted him inside her in every conceivable way.

Reaching back to where he played with her hole, she singled out one of his long, thick fingers and placed it exactly where she wanted it.

He hesitated. She begged.

Her little tight hole was filled while his free hand rubbed the engorged length of her clit.

The cabin filled with primal, unrestrained shouts as they exploded together.

* * * * *

The cordless phone for Pam's direct line rang. She checked the caller id and smiled. It read Astin PharmaBio. It was Delaine. The woman worked too much, calling her from work on a Saturday. They hadn't talked in days and hoped to plan a get-together soon.

"Hey, girl, what's up?"

"Excuse me, is this Miss Pamela LeDoux?"

Ooops, Pam thought. Not Delaine, just some man calling from her office.

"Yes, this is Pam."

"I'm calling from Astin Pharmaceuticals. We're trying to get in touch with Ms. Jeris. We know she's been ill, but we haven't been able to get her at home. We just wanted to check on her, see if she's all right."

"I'm sorry, but I can't help you. She's not here and I'm not scheduled to do her hair until next week."

"Well, sorry to bother you then. Thank you for your time, MissLeDoux. We'll try her at home again."

"No problem. Bye."

"Oh, wait, I have one more question. Unrelated to work, if that's all right?"

"Sure," Pam said, switching the phone to her other ear as she rinsed the shampoo out of a client's hair.

"A lady friend of mine just moved here and is looking for a beautician."

"This shop caters to women of color. No offense, but you don't sound like a person of color. What nationality is your friend?"

"She's black and very particular about her hair."

"Does she wear her hair natural or relaxed? We don't do relaxers, but I can recommend a good beautician if that's what she needs done."

"She wears her hair a lot like Ms. Jeris. And Ms. Jeris' hair always looks so nice and healthy."

Pam's mouth fell open. This guy must be gay or something to be this into a woman's hair. Especially if the woman wasn't sleeping with him, which she knew Delaine was not.

"How did Ms. Jeris find you?" the man asked. "Were you recommended to her?"

"Me? Oh, no," Pam laughed. "Delaine and I go way back. We're both from California, and we happen to be in North Carolina at the same time."

"Oh, how nice. So you're a very close friend, then?" the voice asked, with a friendly lilt. He sounded kind of English. Pam wondered if he was good looking. But it didn't really matter, because he still sounded gay. The oily quality of his voice flew right over her head.

"Yep. I'm pretty much the closest person to her on this side of the country."

"It's nice that she just moved here and has a close friend to spend time with. Well, thanks, Ms. LeDoux."

"No problem. Hey, what did you say your name was?"

"Uh, Schaller. Bobby Schaller. I'll have my friend call and make a private appointment."

"Sure, no problem. Bye." The call disconnected and Pam went on working. Lots of people promised to call for appointments. She didn't give it another thought.

\* \* \* \* \*

Baker hung up the phone and sat back in his chair, stroking the hair of a dazed Sarah Ann kneeling between his legs under his desk. He thought about his chosen strategy to end Delaine's interference and chuckled before flipping open the cell phone to dial a number in Miami.

"Mr. Tapia, please. Tell him it's Baker."

After a few moments, a thickly accented voice came on the line.

"Tapia, here."

"Hello, Mr. Tapia. It's Baker. We've had an interruption in production, and I could use some assistance getting back on schedule."

"My time is valuable, Baker. Get to the point."

"I need you to send a few more of your associates up to Charlotte. Today."

"I already have twenty men planted in your town. If you can't handle this project, I won't send more. I'll just kill you."

"But that would be bad for business, both yours and mine. Look, I just need some assistance in getting the disrupter, as it were, to either cooperate or disappear."

"Fine. But the next time you call me, Baker, the news had better be good. Comprende?"

"Sí, comprende," Baker responded sharply before clicking the phone off. He hated the man. But he could deal with anything for the power it would bring him. After this project, Tapia would be on his own, and Baker would be king.

# CHAPTER THIRTEEN

The weekend at Nantahala Gorge had been wonderful. Just her and Justin. No work. No interruptions. Just lots of fresh air, beautiful mountain trails, white rapids. And endless, hot, sweaty sex. Delaine couldn't believe how she'd whined when Justin burst her bubble by reminding her they needed to get back to Charlotte.

They packed and left the cabin late that night. Delaine transmitted the digital video of Baker's tests to both Derrick and Geri, then she and Justin talked by cell phone and developed a strategy as he followed her home from their haven in the Blue Ridge Mountains.

Justin opened Delaine's front door and held up his hand to keep her from stepping across the threshold. He signaled her to keep quiet as he pulled his gun out of the holster underneath his jacket and signaled silence. She nodded, retrieved her own sidearm and covered his back as he took the first step into her home.

Before Delaine could follow him, Sapa charged to the front of her conscience. The big cat's presence was so strong, it was almost overwhelming. Delaine took in a surprised gasp as the lioness' protective instincts surrounded her, strongly urging her not to enter the house. But as always, Sapa couldn't overrule her. Any decision of what would be done was up to Delaine. But the lioness made her presence known. If Delaine needed her, she was there.

'Sapa, calm down and tell me what's going on here,' Delaine whispered along the psychic link.

Sapa's response confirmed Delaine's suspicions. Someone had been in her house. Nothing appeared to be missing, but the house had been carefully searched and everything put back in its proper place. Yes, someone had been here all right. Someone meticulous and very careful.

Justin left the lights off and set Delaine's weekend bag just inside the door. He signaled for her to take the upstairs while he searched the downstairs rooms. Delaine took off quietly up the stairs to search her bedroom. They met up in the kitchen and found a neatly folded piece of paper on the breakfast nook table. A note from Baker.

They looked at each other, silently communicating their rage. Both stiff and angry, they stalked to the phone together on the first ring. Pissed that someone would enter her private domain, she snatched the receiver off the hook and snarled a nasty hello. Her eyes went wide at the surprise of hearing Sarah Ann's shaky voice on the other end.

"H-Hi, Ms. Jeris."

"Sarah Ann? It's almost midnight. What are you doing calling me this late?"

"I want to help you. Can I come in?"

"Come in? What are you talking about?"

"I'm sitting in my car across the street from your house. I really need to talk to you. Can I come over? Please?"

"And why should I trust you?"

"Because I hate Brian Baker," Sarah Ann said on a choked sob.

"Well all-righty then. Come on over," Delaine said pleasantly.

Justin stood behind the door fuming as Delaine opened it for a clearly distraught Sarah Ann. He wasn't going to take the chance that Baker's confidante might show up armed, or worse, with Baker himself in tow. Delaine had argued against it, not wanting him to be seen at all. But Justin wasn't having it. He wanted Baker and anyone else to know that Delaine had a big, brawny, mad-as-hell ex-Jarhead at her back.

Delaine led Sarah Ann into the living room. Justin silently stalked behind them.

"Sarah Ann, would you like some tea?" Delaine asked, trying to distract the girl. Hands on hips, looking as calm as she was able, she asked what flavor she preferred.

"Jasmine Green Tea, if you have it," Sarah Ann said, smiling sheepishly. She looked up and her eyes bulged. Now that she was settled on the couch, there was no missing Justin as he stood on the steps that led into the sunken living room. She shrank into the cushions as the huge man glowered at her, the muscle in his jaw ticing furiously. He stood not five feet away, his big muscular arms crossed over his even more muscular chest. His expression clearly read, "One wrong move and your ass is mine".

Sapa sent Delaine a mental picture of what Sarah Ann was feeling. Fear. Anger. Shame. All genuine. Delaine felt sorry for the woman. She'd been thrown into something she never wanted to be involved in. At least she had to guts to try to do something about it now.

"Sarah Ann, let me take your coat," Delaine said, trying to make her feel a bit more comfortable. Now it was Delaine's turn to gawk. Sarah Ann pushed her hood back and unzipped her coat. Delaine felt Sapa's ears prick forward. Sarah Ann's dark brown curly hair was now blonde!

Sarah Ann stilled at the intensity in Delaine's eyes as she stared at her hair. She lifted her fingers nervously, and tugged on an errant curl.

"I didn't want to be recognized, coming over here and all. I colored it just this morning."

Delaine continued to stare. The vision her spirit guide had shown her on that first night out with Justin came slamming back into her mind. The woman with the blonde hair was Sarah Ann! So what about the rest of the vision? Who was the woman tied up in a chair with a bag over her head?

*The woman who seeks to help us is distraught. She is afraid of our mate.*

Delaine silently nodded at Sapa's words and sweetly sent a menacing Justin to fix the tea. He could still see everything going on in the living room, but he still wasn't happy with the idea of leaving his woman alone with Sarah Ann. He gave Delaine his I'll-deal-with-you-later look and stalked off to the kitchen.

"So what's up, Sarah Ann? What can you tell us?"

Sarah Ann shivered with fear and glanced toward the kitchen. Her shoulders hunched forward as a stream of tears overflowed her eyes followed by a bout of rough, ragged sobs. Delaine gave her a moment to compose herself. Sarah Ann squared her shoulders, took a deep breath and pushed ahead.

"I hate what I've become because of Baker and his little experiments. He asked me to help him with research on a new product. After working late one evening he invited me for dinner at his place. We had one night of hot sex, and that's when he first slipped it to me. I'm a good scientist, Ms. Jeris. I had no idea he wanted to use me as a guinea pig."

Delaine felt such sadness at the pain in the woman's voice. Poor Sarah Ann bawled like a baby. Delaine sat down on the arm of the couch and discreetly motioned for Justin to quietly bring in the tea. He set the tray on the coffee table and turned to leave.

The corner of his mouth quirked up when he caught Delaine admiring his tight butt, but she didn't stop looking. She watched him stride back to the kitchen with the grace of a lion. With the exception of his blue eyes and fair skin, he reminded her of Sapa on the hunt. The set of his shoulders relayed his anger at Baker's audacity to enter her home. Delaine was glad they were on the same side. The man looked ready to kill.

"I swear, Ms. Jeris, I didn't know his secret project was a powerful synthetic aphrodisiac. The stuff is highly addictive and I didn't want the drug. When I told Baker I wanted him to find a way to counter the craving for it, he threatened to have me killed."

"Baker threatened to have you killed? Isn't that rather ballsy for him? He doesn't seem the type to want to get his hands dirty." Literally.

"He's got connections with some really bad people, Ms. Jeris."

"So how do you propose to help us?" Delaine asked, sipping her own cup of strong tea.

"I know Baker planned to leave you a note with a phone number on it. Have you called the number?" Sarah Ann asked, blowing delicately into her steaming cup.

"No, not yet."

"Good," she said, sitting the cup down gently on the coffee table. "The directions Baker left you are false. It's a trick. He knows you stole a tape from The Vault. He wants it back, but he's not stupid. He's got your friend, but …"

"Whoa, whoa," Delaine stood to her feet, the tea all but forgotten. "What friend are you talking about?"

"Your beautician friend. His instructions, you haven't listened to them yet. You're supposed to meet him at Astin for an exchange, the videotape for your friend. But she won't be at the meeting place. She's being held at Baker's home on Lake Norman by some Cuban guys who came up from Miami."

"Why would he have people come up from another state?"

"Because that's who he's making the drug for. His connections are Cuban mafia. Some big-time drug lord from down south. From Miami. He contracted Baker to create and make the drug. It's supposed to be the next big thing, the only truly synthetic and powerful aphrodisiac ever made. One that works on women in an explosive manner. If Baker fails to deliver, he'll lose his head and a few other choice body parts. He can't allow you to interrupt his plans, so he asked Tapia to send him some more muscle."

Delaine listened quietly as Sarah Ann confirmed what Justin had told her over the weekend about Baker and his mafia connection. A cold rage climbed up her spine, wrapping around her core with every word Sarah Ann spoke. Bastard. She couldn't wait to send him up.

"If you show up without the tape, he plans to have your friend injected with the drug. He's always tested it with a tablet to control the dosage better. With an injection, she'll have an instant reaction and overdose within half an hour. After his mafia thugs have fucked her silly."

"How do you know all this?"

"I let the creep think I was completely under his control. As long as I played the mindless bimbo, he didn't care if I was in the room while he conducted his business or not. I wasn't a risk."

"So what do you want out of this?"

"I want you to catch him, Ms. Jeris. Take him down."

"Done. Now tell us anything else we need to know."

\* \* \* \* \*

It was three in the morning when Sarah Ann snuck out the backdoor and made her way around the side of Delaine's house to her car. What was it about this assignment and unexpected things happening at three in the morning?

Justin and Delaine called the number on Baker's note and listened to the pre-recorded message. He held Delaine's hand while adrenaline pumped their hearts up into their throats. The threats to Pam were explicit— deliver the tape or Pam was toast. But by the end of the message, both he and Delaine were shaking their heads in wonder. If the situation hadn't been so grave, they would have laughed out loud. Good ole Pam, loud and clear in the background, cussed her head off while telling Baker how she was going to kick his ass for making her miss work. They had to give her credit. The woman had a lot of guts. Now they had to keep her alive.

Justin lay face down on the carpet in front of the fireplace with a splitting headache. He was tense as a bowstring as the events of the night played over and over in his head. He groaned when he felt Delaine sit on top of his butt and begin to work the muscles of his back and shoulders.

"I can't believe I didn't figure this out before," she said quietly, kneading a particularly stubborn knot on his left scapula.

"Hmmm? What are you talking about?" he drawled sleepily. Delaine's fingers worked magic on his tired, aching back and he began to drift into a light doze.

"I still can't believe Sarah Ann was the blonde. And

the bound woman in a chair with a bag over her head was Pam all along. Damn, I can't believe I missed it."

"Okay…so what are talking about?"

"Look, you're probably going to think I'm crazy but I got the information from someone who helps me with this kind of stuff. I was told about the blonde woman asking for help and the tied-up woman, but we weren't sure who they were." Delaine felt the honed muscles in Justin's back bunch and tense just before he turned over. She slid off his back and landed on her butt on the carpet beside him. He was all protective alpha now. Damn if she didn't like it.

"What kind of help? Better yet, who kind of help?"

Oh lord, the man was actually growling at her! Delaine was sure he didn't mean to sound so sexy, but it didn't change the fact that the deep rumbling made her skin ripple and her breath hitch in her throat. He was just so…everything! She instinctively felt the need to calm and reassure him.

"Justin, relax. It's not another man, if that's what you're thinking. It's a she. I have a spirit guide."

"A what?"

"It's a Native American thing."

"A Native American thing?" Cool, as long as it wasn't a man thing, it seemed he could handle it. He rolled to his stomach and Delaine climbed back on and continued her massage.

Delaine explained how Sapa had come to her when she was a little girl. At ten years old while out playing, she'd wandered to far from home and couldn't find her way back. She'd stared with wide eyes at all the cars whizzing by and almost peed her pants when an old streetcar rumbled past, shaking the ground underneath her small feet. On the verge of panic, she spotted a huge cathedral standing out from the rest of the crowded buildings and ran as fast as she could to its towering doors. She ducked inside and looked around frantically but didn't see anyone in the lobby or along any of the long candle-strewn aisles. Curled up in a dark corner, the tears gathered and fell in endless streams until she was all cried out. When she quieted, Delaine heard her grandmother's gentle voice in the far reaches of her mind.

'Meditate, child. Push away your fear and call on your spirit guide,' the voice said.

From as far back as she could remember, Delaine had spent every summer with her grandma on the Rosebud reservation up in South Dakota. Granny had taught her about God, called the Great Spirit or Wakantanka in the Lakota tongue. Whether Delaine was visiting the res or her granny had come to see her in California, she'd always taken the time to teach her little granddaughter of their ancestry, the importance of understanding their natural connection to the land, walking the old paths, and knowledge of natural and spiritual guides.

That day, a frightened and alone Delaine closed her eyes. She cleared her mind the way her grandma had taught her and called out to the Great Spirit with all her strength, heart and mind.

'Great Spirit? It's me, Delaine. Can you help me please? I'm lost and I want to go home. Granny said you would help me if I asked you to.'

That's when Sapa had come to her. The black female mountain lion calmed her with gentle strokes against her mind, sending concern and care through their newly forming bond. The lioness had been with her ever since, guiding her through dangers and sharing her spirit's wisdom through the years.

Justin's mouth hung open, but not because he thought she was crazy. He believed her. In fact, he not only believed her words, he was surprised to find he was somewhat jealous of Delaine and her guide. He'd never had such a close relationship with anyone, human or otherwise. And in his line of work, he'd expected to be alone until he died.

*Since you love us, that will change. You will indeed be close to us.*

Justin flew from his spot on the floor. "What the hell was that?" he yelled in surprise, dancing on the balls of his feet.

*You are a worthy mate.*

"Whoa!" Justin turned around in circles looking for who'd spoken.

Delaine rolled on her back, laughing while Justin looked at her like she'd grown two heads. She laughed harder, holding her stomach as the muscles clenched and spasmed with her giggles. When he turned a ghastly beet red in the face and looked ready to take on a gang of bad guys in a hand-to-hand fight, she calmed down long enough to explain.

"That was Sapa speaking into your mind, honey."

"Sapa?" he gasped, looking around like he expected to see a big black feline stalking around Delaine's living room. Delaine felt Sapa send his mind a calming push. He settled enough to finally ask, "How did she do that? And what did she mean?"

"She said that since you love us...wait," Delaine's eyes went wide on a pause. "You love me, Justin?" After the way she'd kicked him to the curb? The way she'd acted about his job when she hadn't even considered telling him about hers? She cared for him deeply, no doubt about that. But could he really?

Justin joined her on the floor and gathered her into his arms until they were face to face, nose to nose.

"I do love you, Delaine Jeris. I love you more than anything or anyone."

Delaine tried to check the tears gathering behind her eyes. Since they wouldn't listen she closed her eyes and ducked her head beneath his chin as her heart slammed in her chest. He loved her? Already? And after the way she'd treated him?

"B-But we haven't known each other that long," she whispered disbelievingly.

"Baby, I don't know how, but I do know why. You're beautiful, Delaine, inside and out. You're strong, but vulnerable. You're honest, caring. I can't explain how I feel what I feel, but just know that I do, with all my heart, love you, baby. You're my Lakota queen, my dark-eyed love. From the top of your kinky head to the soles of your feet, I love you."

She bawled earnestly now as he stroked her hair, and Justin could have sworn he felt her happiness, her amazement, swirling in his head just out of reach. His large hand stilled, his hand in mid-stroke down Delaine's back. He could swear he heard...purring? Sultry, deep purring.

"It's Sapa, honey. I hear her too," Delaine said, snuggling closer against his chest.

"So what does it mean?"

"It means she accepts you. You love me, so Sapa shares herself with you."

"Has, uh, has this ever happened before? You two ladies, giving yourselves to one lucky man?" For some reason he had to know if she'd felt this close to anyone else, even her ex-husband. He broke out in a broad grin at her response.

"No, she's never, I mean we've never done this before. And there's something else I've never done," she crooned, raising her head from his chest and repositioning her body to straddle him. With trembling fingers, she stroked his cheek while her deep brown eyes locked with his. He tilted his head, wondering at her soft yet serious expression. Then two simple but powerful words tumbled from her mouth.

"My name," she whispered.

He said nothing, but the bottom of his stomach roiled as he regarded her. She couldn't possibly be doing what he thought she was doing, could she? She opened her mouth to speak again and his head started throbbing. Well, no wonder—he'd stopped breathing.

"I-I uh." She snapped her mouth closed, looked down at a spot on his shirt somewhere around his pecs and took a deep breath. When she raised her lashes, he saw everything she wanted to say right there on her beautiful face. The love and care she felt for him was all visible, but would she say the words? He started to tell her that it was okay, that she didn't have to say or reveal anything she didn't want to. Before he could get the words out, their world changed forever.

"Justin, I love you too. And my name is Alesia. Alesia Younglion. The only people in the world who know are my children, my boss. And you."

Justin was sure his heart had never been so full of emotion in his life. This woman floored him, and he was simply undone. A lone tear made a path down his cheek and Delaine, uh, Alesia, gently kissed it away. After a moment, the bands around his chest loosened and he pulled her to him for a tight hug and a quick kiss before easing her back a bit to take in her lovely face.

"How do you say it?" When she tilted her head in confusion, he said, "In your grandmother's tongue. Your name, how do you say it?"

"Younglion? Igmutanka Ojilaka."

"Mmm," he groaned, leaning forward to swipe his tongue across her full bottom lip. "Sounds much sexier than Cooley." Her giggle warmed his insides.

"Damn, you and Ms. Sapa sure know how to sweep a guy off his feet." His voice dropped to a husky drawl, full of emotion and just a hint of smart-ass-ism.

"Oh shut up and kiss me already," Delaine laughed

up into his face. He brought his lips down in a hard, demanding kiss as strong hands dropped to the curve of her ass and slipped underneath to gently finger her jean-covered core. Chuckling into her mouth when she squirmed, he proved that now it was her turn to purr.

\* \* \* \* \*

Their plans were finalized after a last phone call to Derrick and Geri. Too tired to do anything but snore, they made it to bed just before sunup. The instructions on the tape told Delaine to meet Baker at midnight, so they slept in until Justin woke Delaine with tender kisses across the sensitive spot on her neck.

Delaine had spent the afternoon teaching Justin how to call Sapa and recognize the lioness' push against his mind. It was eleven forty-five, and Delaine was in the elevator headed down to The Vault. She summoned Sapa into her corporeal form and sent her ahead to scout. The big cat sent clear images of who was waiting below to both her and Justin.

Delaine stepped out of the elevator and was met by two armed men she'd never seen in the Astin facility before. She knew Baker and ten more thugs waited in and around the lab she'd snagged the samples and videotape from…Sapa's reconnaissance also confirmed Sarah Ann's tip—Pam was nowhere in the building.

She was taken to Baker in the back room. Her two escorts had kept their hands to themselves until now. Suddenly her elbows were yanked painfully behind her back. She instinctively schooled her features into a bored mask as a sharp pain lanced from the joint up through her shoulder blades. Determined to convince the idiots she was powerless, she bided her time with a deep, calm intake of breath and forced herself not to pull away from the men and thrash them into the ground.

Baker turned his steely-eyed gaze on her and smiled nastily. Sapa roared in her head, wanting Delaine to take him down fast. The lioness quieted after Delaine reminded her Justin and the backup they'd called in needed a few more minutes to get into position. Baker's cultured voice interrupted her conversation with her spirit guide.

He stepped much too close and skimmed the backs of his fingers along the underside of her breasts. Delaine ignored him and painted on her who-gives-a-damn face. Her stomach heaved and her skin crawled, but Baker would never have the satisfaction of knowing she was ready to hurl her dinner. He spoke softly, like a gentle lover.

"Where's the tape, Jeris?"

"I didn't bring it, asshole, but it's someplace safe. I didn't trust you to have Pam here. Since I don't see her in this room, I guess I was right." She focused her thoughts and asked Sapa to send Justin a mental picture of what was going on.

"Well, that's too bad for your friend, isn't it?" Baker scoffed. He flipped open his phone and pushed the speed dial. After a few seconds he hung up, his brow furrowed. But he quickly recovered, replacing his frown with a carefree grin.

"So tell me, Ms. Jeris. Who exactly are you? Who do you work for?"

Geesh, what a stupid question, Delaine thought as she looked at him like he was as dumb as a bucket of raisins. She didn't bother to answer. Baker knew damned well who she was. He'd known since the day she arrived.

"You know," Baker drawled, "I don't like your nonchalance. You're in a good bit of trouble, young lady, yet you don't seem concerned." The last word was said as he stepped back and backhanded her smartly across the face. Again Delaine reined in her temper even as her neck snapped sideways. Her calmness only seemed to make Baker madder. Good.

Her lip quirked up into a condescending smile. Bastard. Just wait until she was free. She was going to kick his ass. Blood pooled into her mouth from the small cut he'd opened up at the corner of her mouth. She gathered a nice wad of it and spit it directly into Baker's face.

The wad landed on his right cheek, and he recoiled as if a snake had bitten him, as if her spit was the vilest thing on the planet. He quickly retrieved a sparkling white handkerchief from his lab coat pocket, wiped his face and threw the soiled piece of cloth in the trash bin near his feet. Then he smiled the most chilling, unsettling show of teeth Delaine had ever been on the receiving end of.

"You know, my lovely Ms. Jeris, I've heard that sliding between the legs of a black woman is a life-changing experience. I've never had the pleasure. Until now."

"Please," Delaine spat. "You think I'd give you some of this? You're crazier than I thought."

"No, not crazy. Empowered. And in just a few minutes, you'll be begging me to fuck you."

Delaine laughed outright. Not a cute little chuckle. No, this was an all-out, full belly laugh. He had no idea who he was fooling with. But he'd sure as hell find out, and soon. All he had to do now was make his biggest and final mistake. She didn't have long to wait.

Delaine stoically watched Baker as he walked over to a locked cabinet. He pulled out a large banker's box full of packages that looked like plastic bricks full of little pink candies. He ripped one open and retrieved a single pink tablet before turning his malevolent glare on her.

Baker approached with the tablet balanced on the end of his finger, just as he'd done to the woman on the digital video. But Delaine wasn't that woman. As soon as he stood in front of her, he commanded her to open her mouth.

Then all hell broke loose.

\* \* \* \* \*

Justin and a team of D.E.A. S.W.A.T. crept through the seldom-used tunnels he and Delaine had escaped through before. Justin gritted his teeth as the images of what Delaine was facing streamed into his mind. It practically killed him to allow his woman to face their enemy alone. Hell, he was still trying to figure out how she'd talked him into this cockamamie plan. Slowly getting used to a presence in his head, he was only a bit startled when Sapa spoke into his thoughts.

*In time you will become less surprised at the persuasiveness of your mate, Akicita Justin.*

Delaine had explained to him earlier that the great lioness had nicknamed him, Akicita, "warrior" in the Lakota tongue. He didn't feel like much of a warrior right now, but knowing Sapa had dealt with Delaine's stubbornness since childhood made him feel at least a bit less inept.

*Dealt with her stubbornness? As our Suta would say, you have no idea.*

Justin snorted quietly. If a spirit couldn't rein her in, then he must not be such a bad mate after all. Sapa's calm assurance, lots of deep breathing and fantasizing about what he was going to do to Baker kept him from bursting into the room. His grip tightened on the handle of his gun when Baker backhanded Delaine across the face, but he kept still, hiding in the closet without a sound. When Baker had the drug in front of Delaine's face, on his signal, he and his team burst through the closet doors and filled the room.

* * * * *

One of the men holding her released her arms and ran for the door. The idiot opened the door and ran right into the fists of several armed law enforcement officers. S.W.A.T.! Yeah, she'd know them anywhere. She inwardly winced at the sickening sound of fists sinking into flesh, and the thug was quickly down. His friend, who appeared to be a little smarter, grabbed her by her arm again, but this time she had a hand free.

Her technique was clean and quick. With her free hand she backhanded her captor across the bridge of his nose with a closed fist. His head snapped back on his neck like a rubber band pulled too tight. She stepped back and gave him a clean kick to the ribs and he went down like a sack of potatoes tossed off the back of a truck.

Delaine felt Sapa pushing at her mind with urgency. What was her spirit guide doing? The lioness was supposed to be looking out for Justin. Urgency rushed through the bond and Delaine turned to find herself facing a very angry, charging Baker.

"Noooooo! I won't let you ruin me!" Baker screamed, running toward Delaine brandishing a very heavy-looking, stainless steel lab tool.

Delaine recognized a mad scientist when she saw one. If he was going down, he was determined to take somebody with him. And right now, she appeared to be a perfect candidate. Unarmed, he was on her so quickly she only had time for a single thought.

"Sapa! Help!" Delaine yelled out loud.

*Take what I offer, Suta.*

Delaine felt her body fill with the strength of the lioness. Her skin tingled with untapped power as she saw Baker through the eyes of her spirit guide. No longer the big bad villain. He was now prey.

Time slowed. Even Baker appeared to move in slow motion as he charged her with his makeshift weapon in one hand and the fingers of his free hand tensed and curled like claws. The second his clammy hands wrapped around her neck, she slipped her hands up between his outstretched arms, took a single step in and swept his legs from under him. As he was falling backward, she checked with her hip and he went flying over her back. On his way down to the floor, she slammed his head into the concrete. But the rest of his body continued to fly. In the end, there was an unmistakable crunch when his chest met his face. His neck and every vertebra down to the middle of his back snapped like dry dead twigs.

Sapa roared in her head as Delaine growled low in her throat, breathing heavily. The surge of strength and power slowly subsided as the lioness retreated from the forefront of her mind. Delaine hated taking a life. She'd been raised to always respect life, no matter how rotten or corrupt. She was grateful when Sapa sent peace and pride through the bond. The spirit of the lioness would always fight to protect her loved ones. She was the ultimate hunter and refused to be ashamed of defending those in her care.

Delaine looked down at Baker, his wide green eyes unseeing, and his pale face permanently etched with stunned disbelief. Sapa flashed images to her of what was happening all over the building. Baker's boys had been rounded up, none escaped. The premises were being searched for more evidence, though the box full of pink tablets in the still unlocked cabinet was more than enough.

Then Justin was at her side, pulling her into a warm embrace before hauling her toward the door.

"Justin, wait. We've got to do a mop-up here."

"Not today, baby. Derrick's already called in another team to do it. We've got to get to the hospital."

"Hospital? Why?"

"When our boys burst into Baker's house at Lake Norman, Pam was in the middle of an almost successful escape. One of the bad guys shot her, baby."

"What!?"

"I said, Pam's been shot. Let's go."

\* \* \* \* \*

Delaine stepped into the sparsely furnished hospital room. The orange roses in her hand offered the only relief against the sterile white furniture, walls and curtains. She set the glass vase of flowers on the nightstand and Pam's eyes fluttered open.

"Hey, girl. How are you feeling?" Delaine asked quietly, a slight smile across her lips.

"Like somebody spent the night kicking my ass."

"Well, I'd like to kick your ass too, ya know."

Pam smiled weakly, her words a bit slurred by the wonderful morphine drip on her IV. "I know, and I don't blame you, Del. And I'm so sorry. I was so drunk I didn't realize what I'd done until later the next evening. After lots of coffee and lots of sleep. Justin didn't have anything to do with it. It was all me, girl. But we never slept together. As a matter of fact, he practically ran from me while singing your praises, even though you were mad at him."

Delaine chuckled and said, "I know, Pam, but I wasn't talking about that. I was talking about you trying to get away from several armed men, you idiot." She reached out and gently touched her friend's hand to take the sting out of her words.

"What can I say, Delaine. I wasn't thinking, I just reacted. I couldn't let that bastard use me to blackmail you. You're my girl."

Delaine was touched. She felt so special. She'd never thought to have a man like Justin, nor reunite with an honest, caring friend like Pam. Her chest clogged with emotion and she almost missed the faint scent of Justin's cologne amidst the non-smells of the hospital room. He touched her about the waist and hugged her lightly from behind. She turned slowly, her eyes close to spilling over.

"Hi, baby," he crooned, nuzzling her ear. "How are you holding up, sweetheart?"

"I'm all right, I guess." In fact, she'd refused to allow the events of last night to sink in yet. She'd been on plenty of dangerous missions, but not once had she ever been compromised. And she'd never been in love with the person watching her back. If Justin hadn't insisted on covering her, she could have easily been taken out. If even one part of their plan had gone wrong, her children could have been left without a mom. Or she could have lost this wonderful man who'd stood by her side because he cared enough to put himself in danger, even risk his career, to see her safe. It was a humbling realization.

"Hey, Pam," Justin stepped away from Delaine and moved around the side of Pam's hospital bed. He placed a chaste kiss on her forehead and set a colorful get-well card on her little tray stand.

"Hey, Jus. I apologized to Delaine for that misunderstanding at your house that night. Now I need to apologize to you."

Justin returned to Delaine's side and draped his arm over her shoulder. He looked down at her with a lopsided, boyish grin and said, "It's all right, Pam. We're all good."

The door slid silently open and a short, dark-haired woman called cheerfully from the door. "Hello there, I'm Dr. Lampshire." She removed a clipboard from the slot, checked over the chart and greeted Pam as she entered the room.

"How are you, Pamela?" she asked, adjusting the IV drip. At Pam's grumbled "just fine, thanks", she continued in a friendly tone. "The surgery went well, and there is no sign of infection. If you continue to improve, you can go home in a couple of days. Is there anyone in your family available to take care of you for a few days after you're released? If not, I'll give the okay for you to stay past the required amount of time."

Pam winced as the doctor gently probed the dressing over the gunshot wound high on the left side of her chest.

"Doctor, Pam recently moved here and doesn't have any family. We go way back. She can come stay with me."

Delaine looked up at Justin and found his eyes on her. He winked and said, "Pam, you can come stay with us." Her brows rose, but she didn't gainsay him.

"Us?" Pam wondered aloud. Her eyes widened as much as they were able considering the amount of pain medicine she was enjoying.

"Yes, us. I'm not letting this woman out of my sight, and whether she's at my house, or I'm at hers, she's stuck with me. And you're stuck with the both of us. Or," he added dryly, "you can stay here and enjoy an endless supply of Jell-O."

Pam grimaced and informed the doctor she would indeed be going home with Delaine and Justin.

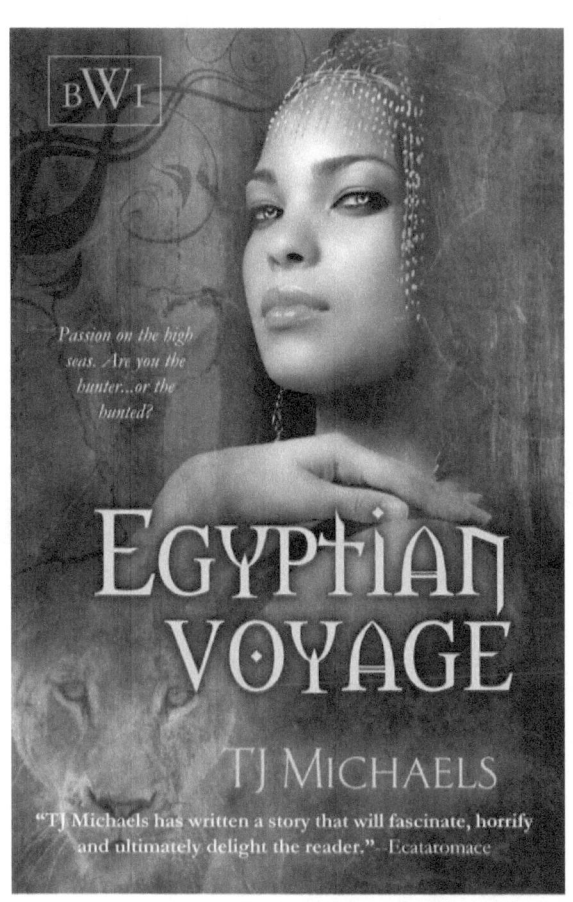

BWI

Passion on the high
seas. Are you the
hunter...or the
hunted?

# EGYPTIAN
# VOYAGE

## TJ MICHAELS

"TJ Michaels has written a story that will fascinate, horrify
and ultimately delight the reader." -Ecatatomace

# DEDICATION

This book is dedicated to the two coolest people on earth, Tamara and Michael. For your understanding, inspiration and lots and lots of midnight tea runs, I appreciate you.

Dear Reader,

This book was originally published by Ellora's Cave during the early stages of my career as a writer. It received a wonderful reception and great reviews.

When the rights reverted from the original publisher back to me, it was republished to ensure that you could still enjoy this fantastic world. So, here is Egyptian Voyage in its entirety and original form. Enjoy!

Love always,

~TJ

# THE EMPRESS III

She is the celestial Isis. Nature, universal fecundity united with spiritual rectitude. She is fertility, creation, intelligence and activity. Whatever the gender, the Empress year brings you in touch with your need to nurture and be nurtured. She is Earth-Mother incarnate. The Empress is not just about love—she's about creativity planted in the realm of the imagination. She is fertile, ripe and blossoming, with ideas, plans, creations.

But know this, my friend—the upside-down Empress III tarot card has a completely different meaning. If the card is drawn by a woman, the upside-down Empress can represent that woman and indicate a partial success in regard to something important to her. But, if drawn by a man, it indicates a loss of love. Negative elements of the Empress are tendencies to be overbearing, vain, and using appearance to sway and manipulate.

And in our story, this Empress is not drawn by a woman. Nor is it drawn in the typical manner of right-side up. Looks like we've got a bad guy to put down...

# PROLOGUE

Eden sat in the dark in his favorite overstuffed chair in the living room. The local news droned on while a small blue ticker scrolled across the bottom of the screen. He usually watched the screen with more than a little interest in the latest mayhem plaguing whatever port the ship happened to dock at. Tonight, the words of the news anchor, spoken in perfect Portuguese, rolled off him as he idly stroked the smooth bald head of the woman sitting quietly in his lap. She was twenty-six inches of porcelain perfection, clothed in the regalia of ancient Egypt and her station. Today, he'd clothed her in the white fine linen of the traditional shendyt kilt, leaving her caramel brown breasts bare.

He'd had her created with the face of the noble pharaoh, Hatshepsut. Perfectly formed lips and cheeks were free of rouge or coloring. Almond-shaped dark eyes were adorned with even darker liner that brought her face to life. Yes, she was definitely his favorite, his harem master, responsible for keeping the males in his harem in line. Not only was she beautiful and damned good at her job, her ability to interpret the tarot made her beyond valuable. Perhaps he'd keep her long enough to give her a name of his choosing.

Tilting his head, he contemplated the large tarot cards spread out on the coffee table. The surface of each was an exquisite work of art and displayed majestic Egyptian symbols of men and women who'd once ruled the ancient world. Their noble profiles brought a sense of kingship and kinship to him. The background of each was a mix of bold gold, turquoise and lapis blues laid over woven papyrus and set against a midnight deep black. Eying the beautiful tarot, the man stretched out a single finger and stroked the intricate borders of two that were separate from the rest of the deck.

Today, he'd drawn Strength and Justice.

*"Yes, beloved, you are both."*

He looked away from the cards and into the lovely face of the woman who'd spoken into his mind. He still hadn't figured out how she managed to do that. He could only hear her when she was near, but none of the others before her had ever been able to do even that much. She spoke again, her voice as clear as a summer sky in his head.

*"The cards proclaim you to be Strength and Justice, to bring balance to this world."*

Everything Eden did had the tarot at its center. He never made a move without consulting them. Today, he looked directly at the cards, saw what they were. But what did they mean? It seemed the interpretation of the cards was almost always different from what he intuitively thought it should be. But his Egyptian golden-skinned beauty always explained it all.

*"Justice,"* she began in her smooth, seductive voice, *"is represented by a woman clad in white, a sword in one hand and a balance in the other. She sits on a throne with two lions at her feet. Strength is shown by a woman with a winged golden headdress, clothed in a white robe*

*trimmed with turquoise jewels. A lion stands before her with the headdress of a pharaoh on his head. Strength holds the beast's mouth closed and he can go no further."*

Okay, so what?

*"Strength, my beloved, is a card of success as long as you retain your instincts and exercise self-control. Justice indicates that all is going as it should. Even if you do not realize it, you're operating according to a divine plan. This plan is in harmony with you, my love, as well as correctness in your relationships."*

Placing a gentle kiss on the top of his harem mistress's head, his mouth lifted in a wide satisfied smile. All of it sounded wonderful.

"So, who is my goal this time?" he queried, as the usual excitement kindled at the base of his gut. There was nothing like the anticipation of what was to come.

*"There is a woman who has unbalanced the life of an important male. Her hair is a burnished hue and..."*

When he'd memorized the description of the female, he rose, placed the harem mistress back on her shelf at the top of the beveled glass cabinet and left the ship. Now he could hunt with precision.

Later that night, as his prey screamed into a hand held firmly over her mouth, he did indeed feel the imbalance of the world shift and groan until it settled into its proper place. The specimen's sticky blood ran out of a fat hole in her back. It soaked through his shirt and streamed hot and thick over the ridges of his stomach, down to his navel. Yes, all was as it should be.

In spite of his ruined clothes, his chest puffed out with pride when the female took her final breath. Yes, once again he'd brought balance to the world and exacted justice on behalf of all those who depended on him as the rightful protector of the faith.

# CHAPTER ONE

Chrysalyn Geyer yanked a large suitcase off the floor and let it bounce on the edge of the bed. Throwing open the top, she yanked out a pair of white capri pants, arranged them so they draped dead center in the middle of the hanger, then snapped them on the pole in the closet.

"What the hell am I supposed to do for three months, damn it?" she fumed, not bothering to send her thoughts psychically to her spirit guide.

*Rest is a novel idea. I do believe it is the reason your employer sent you on this vacation.*

"Adonei, do you always have to be so frickin' logical?" she growled between clenched teeth. Neatly folding her favorite cashmere sweater, she placed it on one of several wide shelves in the walk-in closet.

*Of course. I am, after all, a male. Are we not the more logical of the species?*

"Is this a trick question?" she chuckled, her tone incredulous. A balled-up fist made its way to her hip at the same time her bare foot tapped impatiently on the thick carpet. And how the hell had she wound up with a male for a spirit guide anyway? Perhaps the Great Spirit was testing her?

*I believe it is time for a nap. Summon me if you have need, my dear.* With a yawn and an exaggerated feline stretch, Adonei retreated to a small corner of her consciousness.

"Damned lion," she grumbled, already bored out of her mind.

No doubt this cruise ship was stellar. Everyone on board owned their oversized apartments. And according to the receptionist that checked her in yesterday afternoon, every single one of the units was built specifically for the owner, all of them larger than her whole house back in the States. And priced around a cool million dollars. Her company owned the sprawling condo she would occupy during her vacation. Way to go, Aegis.

Every outfit and its corresponding pair of shoes were arranged by color in the massive closet. Sigh. One more suitcase left, but it could wait until after a wash-up. Chrysalyn made her way to the stylish all-blue granite bathroom and flipped on the shower with a huff.

She had plenty of books but there was no way reading and doing the touristy thing at each port would keep her entertained for three blasted months. Thankfully, they were putting out to sea later on tonight, finally leaving the port in Lisbon, Portugal, behind. At least there would be a change of scenery. She'd also met a dashing older gentleman at the Japanese restaurant up on deck ten last night. Boy, was he a looker—a classic tall, dark and handsome man with a notably square jaw and the most exotic features she'd ever seen on a man.

His chin sported a perfectly manicured goatee over smooth-looking, tanned skin. And the cutest little dimple on his left cheek when he smiled. Salt-and-pepper hair, almost as dark and curly as her own, was stylishly cut.

The man's name was Eden, an interesting name for a learned and well-traveled man. Wherever he was from, he was damned fine, in a sexy, Sean Connery, older gentleman kind of way.

Unfortunately, when he'd strolled over to her table and asked to join her for dinner, a cold streak penetrated the very bones of her spine and chilled the nerves clear down to the backs of her knees. Not fear, but something else, something she couldn't put her finger on. The kicker was the fact that the emotions weren't hers, but Adonei's.

After ten minutes of enduring Adonei's roaring, growling and pacing in her head with no explanations, Chrysalyn pushed the apprehension away and pleaded with the lion to stand down and calm himself. Instead of listening to her, he'd charged to the forefront of her mind with a snarl so ferocious it caught her completely off guard. With fangs bared, the tawny hair on the back of his thick neck stood on end. And Chrys had bitten her lip and forced her butt to stay in the seat rather than jump to her feet in shock. What the hell was wrong with the big cat? He acted as if she was out on a case looking for bad guys, instead of dining in a classy shipboard restaurant, surrounded by highfalutin people and keeping company with a handsome, well-mannered man.

After practically inhaling her dinner and nodding through most of the conversation, Chrysalyn had smiled politely when Eden offered to see her to her apartment, relieved when he departed with a gentlemanly goodnight.

A full day later, she had yet to learn what Adonei found objectionable about Eden. Perhaps then she could see him again. In truth, she had no urge to fuck him whatsoever, but already looked forward to sharing more conversation. Maybe they could take in a movie or go for a stroll when they reached the next port? She was actually feeling rather encouraged about it all…

Until she'd returned from a brief foray into Lisbon, walked through her front door and locked it behind her. One look across the massive apartment reminded her she'd be floating in this private condo complex for another two months, twenty-eight days and four hours. Shit!

Tonight, determined to finish arranging things to her liking, she'd dined alone. The private chef service was awesome. Not only could she skip dressing up to eat, but a gorgeous Belgian chef had come to her room and prepared her dinner. Feeling rather catty, Chrys tried to trip him up and asked for something decidedly non-European. She'd ended up with the most delicious Cajun dishes piled in front of her with no idea where to begin the scrumptious fare. Her favorites, Shrimp Creole, crawfish bisque, hot water cornbread, fried oysters and okra were attacked with gusto. Perfectly seasoned so they weren't too spicy, she'd eaten until she was sure she'd have to summon Adonei onto this plane to drag her to her bedroom. Then the chef had sprung another one on her—fresh bananas foster flambéed to perfection before her eyes. Could she get any closer to heaven than soul food?

Now that she'd successfully waddled to the master bedroom to finish unpacking, she was so full it had taken her a full hour to get one huge bag unpacked. Now Chrysalyn stood underneath the massaging spray of the shower, conjuring up images of her first day back at work. She couldn't wait to return home to Denver and give her boss a piece of her mind. They'd already had the knockdown, drag-out fight of the century, which obviously hadn't done any good, considering Chrysalyn had still ended up on this damned boat headed for a much-too-long vacation on the high seas.

Who cared if she would visit ports in countries she'd

never expected to see in her lifetime? What difference did it make that she hadn't had a vacation in five years? Who needed a vacation when you could spend every day of your life making a difference in the world by taking down bad guys?

Well, according to her boss, Geri, *she* needed one. And like it or not, she was getting one.

\* \* \* \* \*

Dumping the pile of bloodied and soiled clothing into the laundry room hamper, Eden strolled gloriously naked into the luxurious bathroom. The blast of massaging showerheads eased his tense and aching muscles. The woman had put up quite a struggle—funny, his muscles were tight from working out yesterday morning, rather than the grisly business he'd been about only hours before. A perfect smile of perfect, straight white teeth split his lips. It had been the best hunt ever, though too short, too quick. And, like his smile, perfect. Guaranteed to loosen even the most stubborn bloodstains, he washed with the special soap he favored and watched the dried blood mix with steaming hot water and flow down the drain in a froth of pink-tinged bubbles. Eden lathered up again. A deep contentment stole over him as he inhaled. The fragrance was simply inspirational—a blend of vanilla and sandalwood. It was his female's favorite scent. No surprise, since she was the one who'd taught him how to make it.

"*Beloved?*"

"Yes, my dear?" he called over his shoulder, wishing she would leave him alone so he could make his dinner date on time. Truthfully, he couldn't really call it a date, since the woman he planned to meet had no idea he would be joining her. The hunt had taken all damned day. He was in a hurry and now was no time to chatter.

Dressed in classic black dress slacks, tailored black dinner jacket, a crisp white silk shirt and black silk tie, he strode out into the living room. Not bothering to sit down to draw his hand, Eden's long strong fingers stretched toward the deck of gold and black Egyptian tarot cards stacked neatly in the middle of the coffee table. The card on top was snatched up and tossed to the center of the table. The III card—The Empress. Quirking his head to the side, Eden spoke to his faithful companion.

"Why is she upside down? I've never drawn The Empress card upside down before." Actually, he'd never drawn the Empress in any case. A strange chill chased down his spine as he took in the regal form and features of the dark golden goddess pictured on the card.

*"I am sure it is nothing, beloved. Come, kiss me before you go about tonight's business."*

Eden walked over to the display case and gently lifted his most prized possession down from her glass perch.

*"Hurry, beloved."* The sweet caress of her voice eased over his soul like the soothing warmth of a summer sun shower sweeping across the fertile Nile plains. Strange how that same voice sometimes bordered on sheer annoyance. *"Kiss me, so you may go and return to me again."*

Running his fingers over the smooth cool skin of her arms, he looked deeply into the dark, almond-shaped eyes. He loved the charcoal outline on her lids and brows, and the slim angular classic Egyptian features. Eden kissed the pharaoh gently on the top of her head, his emotions catapulting between excitement and sadness. He tucked his nose beneath her chin, careful not to disturb the pharaoh's headdress, an exquisite lapis and gold rearing cobra settled low over her brow.

He knew she cared for him, but while he'd followed

all of her advice, he was no fool and was well aware of her true intentions. Every female she'd directed him to dispense justice upon seemed the perfect lover for one of the males in his harem. She wanted to be the only one to rule their little clan and would do whatever it took to see that it stayed that way. After all, she had the spirit of a man, thus was she pharaoh. Not a queen, but a king.

Thoughts turned to the woman he'd spotted boarding the ship in Lisbon yesterday afternoon. Now *she* was the perfect Egyptian queen. A couple of evenings past, he'd managed to *accidentally* run into her at one of the ship's restaurants. Tonight, he hoped to bump into her again.

While the beauty had been dressed inappropriately for his tastes, he couldn't help but admire her form—and such an itty-bitty thing, perhaps five foot three at the most. Shapely legs teased him from the hem of her sleeveless little black dress down to her cute little sandal-clad toes. Broad shoulders and toned arms supported full, inviting breasts that tapered down to a trim waist. When she'd excused herself to run to the ladies' room, he'd watched every step. Her hips flared lusciously and her ass was indescribably tempting. Round, wide and firm would do for starters. His fingers itched just thinking about touching all that caramel skin. Delicious.

When she'd turned and laid a stunning smile on him, his breathing had deepened on the spot as all the blood in his torso streaked down to his groin. Beauty was too tame a word—the woman was exquisitely breathtaking. Thick black hair was a riot of twists and curls all over her head. He didn't typically like short hair on a woman, but this woman's shiny, healthy-looking waves looked just perfect for running his fingers through. Her eyes were a mix of light brown and gold, contrasting against her dark skin. In the end, he couldn't decide what color they were, only that they were just as lovely as the rest of her.

And the aura emanating from her pulsed with life. Chrysalyn was her name. And she was perfect for bearing strong sons.

*Beloved?*

The voice bounced him out of his reverie. He looked down at the one who called him beloved. The rare creation cradled in his hands was impeccable and unique. Her long braids and golden winged breastplate were indicative of her heritage—a goddess, a daughter of pharaohs. But even her loveliness paled when compared to Chrysalyn, whose very name referred to new life. No, he simply could not allow his harem mistress to ruin his plans to mate another. And Chrysalyn would be that woman.

With that firmly in his mind, he stood and cast a final glance at the tarot card on the table as he made his way across the room. He placed the harem mistress back into the glass display case with his other unique creations.

Her voice trickled over him once more.

*"Enjoy your dinner. Until tonight, beloved."*

On the way out, he looked back at the beautiful work of porcelain perfection and blew her a kiss. Headed for the on-board Japanese restaurant, his step quickened as his thoughts filled with the possibilities between him and the female he was hopefully on his way to meet.

# CHAPTER TWO

Jerked out of a sound sleep, Chrysalyn's eyes flew open as her heart beat wildly in her chest. Lying perfectly still, surrounded by a pile of oversized pillows and warm blankets, she looked around the empty bedroom. There was no sound except the muted splash of the ocean's waves against the hull as the huge ship cut through the water.

She sighed with a bit of frustration mixed with relief. At least they were on the way somewhere and not still sitting in port, as they had the last couple of days since she'd boarded.

"*Adonei? Adonei, come to me*," she silently whispered. Seconds ticked by. No answer. No Adonei.

Where the hell was that damned lion? In all the long years he'd watched over and guided her, he'd never failed to come when summoned.

Well, spirit guide or not, her innate senses told her something was wrong. Reaching out along the psychic bond they shared, she tried again, calling quietly, but firmly, in her mind.

Annoyed, Chrys gave up on the psychic thing and

opened her mouth. "Adonei, get here already," she snapped on an impatient whisper.

Finally, the still air shimmered and shifted next to the bed as Adonei appeared shaking his wild mane on a loud, wide-mouthed yawn. Chrysalyn was glad no one else could hear the racket. Lord, he had a big mouth, all sharp teeth and power. Glad he was on her side, she smiled with genuine affection at her companion as the moonlight streamed through the floor-to-ceiling glass deck doors, reflecting off his two-and-a-half-inch canines. Adonei—African lion and *male* to the bone. No wonder this creature was the king of beasts.

*Chrysalyn, what is it now? Surely you did not summon me to this plane to complain about your three-month rest again?*

Okay, so he was a cynical king of beasts.

'Adonei, I heard something. Well, not actually heard, but definitely felt. Someone's in here.'

He didn't say a word. No change of expression, no smart-assed remark, nothing. Now she definitely knew something was going on. Fine, she'd just have to see for herself.

'Adonei, lend me your sight.'

*Take what I offer,* he yawned.

Geesh, was he ever rattled by anything? Guess not.

Keeping her eyes open and focused on her bedroom door, Chrysalyn embraced Adonei's gifts as they flowed warm and comforting underneath her skin before sinking into her blood. The strength and power of the lion burst forth and filled her. Human eyes took on superhuman clarity as the dim shadows of the night receded and all became perfectly clear. Whispering an unladylike, but appropriate, blue streak of curses, she grumbled under her breath and climbed out of bed. Whoever had disturbed her sleep would royally pay for it. On bare feet, she eased her way across the room to the sliding glass door that opened onto the private deck.

The metal handle was cool against her fingers as she slid the door open. Thankfully, it was well-oiled and moved silently along its rails. Poking her head through the small opening, she eyed the entire length of the moonlit deck before stepping out into the balmy night. All was quiet. The pitch-black sky overhead was blanketed with a sea of stars so vast it rivaled the twinkling of the moon off the surface of the water stretching out before the ship. If she hadn't been scooting across the deck in the middle of an emergency, she would have sank down into the nearest cushioned deck chair and slipped back into her dreams under those stars.

But nooo! Instead of enjoying the relaxing atmosphere, the lull of the waves, the pearlescent glow of the moon, she had to kick someone's ass tonight for breaking into her apartment.

Kneeling down, she peeked through the far deck door into the dim living room.

"Oh, you just wait," she ground out between clenched teeth, her spiking temper directed at the dark shadow easing into the guest bedroom. Her head cocked sideways in surprise when the shadow reappeared and moved toward her closed bedroom door.

She eased the glass door open a crack, thankful for the lack of sea breeze. The last thing she needed was for the drapes to billow and warn the bastard of his impending ass-kicking.

The second his head disappeared through the opening of her bedroom door, the living room pane slid all the way open and Chrysalyn flew toward the encroacher on silent feet.

The closer she got to the shadow, the more it stretched toward the high ceilings. It was a man, and whoever he was, he was tall and well-built. Fine, she'd just have to take him down hard and fast. Damn it, now she wished she'd asked Adonei for his strength instead of just his exceptional sight. But she didn't have time for that now.

With a well-aimed kick at the common peroneal nerve running along the intruder's right leg, she struck out with all her strength. In a fraction of a second, the leg went numb and buckled, unable to support the man's weight. As he went down, a solid uppercut connected with his jaw, followed by a lightning-fast left to the mouth. But before she could finish him, Chrysalyn found herself wrapped in a tangle of arms and legs, and heading swiftly toward a meeting with the hardwood floor. The intruder rolled with her until the legs of the coffee table blocked their progress, with him on top. Damn.

She looked up into a handsome face a mere three inches from her own. Holy shit! Even in the dark, there was no mistaking the perpetrator's identity. After three years apart, there still wasn't another male who looked like this. Felt like this. Smelled like this.

"Rahn!" she gasped, from both shock and exertion. "What the hell are you doing here?"

"At the moment, I'm bleeding. How are you, Chrysalyn?"

Oooh, and his voice was still dead sexy. Double damn!

\* \* \* \* \*

"Rahn? What the hell are you doing here?"

"Well, now that you've asked so sweetly," he huffed sarcastically, a bit winded by their tussle. At least his leg was beginning to get the feeling back. Ow! His ribs hurt too. She'd kicked the shit out of him. He took as deep a breath as he was able, and said, "I have a case to close in

Rome. Since the ship was headed there anyway, Geri thought I might enjoy a little holiday first. It's been awhile since the last one."

"Vacation? Here? With me?" The woman was practically screeching. If he didn't know better, he'd swear she was nervous about him sharing the huge apartment. He'd have to ask his spirit guide about it later. Man, she felt good underneath him. Time to move before he gave away just *how* good she felt. Rolling away, he immediately missed the warmth of her body.

"This is the company's apartment. With three bedrooms and a couple thousand square feet, it's more than big enough. Our boss figured you wouldn't mind."

On his feet now, Rahn headed for the nearest couch. A glance over his shoulder made his body shudder. The woman was still spread-eagled on her back. Her itty-bitty nightshirt didn't cover much, bunched up just below her sex as it was. He cocked his head and spoke silently to his spirit guide.

'Mahpiya, lend me your senses.'

Immediately, the lioness's gifts flooded into him. Ooh, big mistake. He tightened his thigh muscles, trying to keep from coming on the spot when his eyesight sharpened and Mahpiya's sharp sense of smell flooded through his body until it became his own. His eyes took in the sleek, smooth length of Chrysalyn's lovely legs. His nose told him she lay sprawled on the floor, minus any kind of panties. The scent of her pussy wafted through the air and practically sucked all the common sense right out of his head. Sweet, deliciously sensual, her scent was reminiscent of honeysuckle and dark red wine.

"Shit," he grumbled, realizing the couch wasn't nearly far enough away from her. He eased toward a chair clear across the huge room. He flopped down into the overstuffed cushions, snatched a pillow from behind his head and smashed it down over a suddenly painful erection. Where the hell had the hard-on from hell come from?

*Did you not ask for my aid, my charge?*

'Oh shut it, Mahpiya,' he quipped at his psychic companion. Damned cat had no mercy.

*Do not be angry with me, youngling. I gave you just what you asked for. 'Tis no fault of mine you received more than you bargained for.*

Then she laughed! How the hell did a lioness laugh anyway? Damn it, she was supposed to be his spirit guide, not his tormenter.

*You torment yourself, young one.*

Rahn was thankful when she retreated into a small corner of his mind to nap. But not before she sent a genuinely amused and toothy grin through their psychic bond. Damned cat.

Chrys' words broke through his thoughts. "So, why are you going to Rome?"

His eyes were drawn toward the lovely body projecting the silky voice across the room. Lifting his head, he glanced her way. Shit, she was still on the floor, only now her arms were crossed behind her head as she looked toward the clear glass doors that led out to the deck.

"Rahn? Did you hear me?"

Hell no, he hadn't heard her. He was too busy trying to drown out the blood rushing through his ears as it streaked toward his dick.

"What did you say? My head hurts from the pounding you did on it. Hard to focus," he lied—about the focus part, not about the pounding. He watched her roll up from the floor and stomp her way to the chair across from him. She flopped down in it, completely nonplussed, comfortable in her practically bare skin and obviously unaware how delicious she looked.

"I asked what you're going to be doing in Rome, Rahn," she said.

Okay, time to get his head together to make this lie sound convincing. As much as he hated to tell her half-truths, if the woman ever found out the nature of the case he was on his way to solve, he'd never be able to keep her nose out of it.

"There have been a string of murders there. They seem to be centered around a certain area. The international police have asked us to look into it for them. Less complicated if we investigate the matter, since our organization flies well below the radar." The last few words were said with a grunt as he shifted on the chair and tried to rearrange his cock in his pants.

"So," he gasped as his fingers wrapped around his raging hard-on, pushing it to the left. "How's that gorgeous cousin of yours?"

"Delaine? She's fine. Getting married soon."

Now that snapped him and his cock to attention. Delaine Jeris was getting remarried? Whoever had landed that beauty was a lucky man. Rahn was glad she'd finally let go of that idiot she'd been married to for so long and moved on. Everyone in their agency had been tempted to help the asshole have a little accident after word got around about what he'd done to Delaine. If their boss, Geri, hadn't expressly forbade any late-night ass-kickings for the man, he would have been nothing but a pile of sore bones for ages to come.

"She met someone soon after she moved out to Charlotte," Chrysalyn said, her voice somewhat wispy, as if she longed for something. But she was getting married herself. So why did she sound so...forlorn?

"Speaking of married," Rahn said quietly, watching her closely. "You've been engaged for a while now. When is your big date?"

As quickly as she'd sat down, she was back on her

feet. Back stiff with what could only be a major case of ticked off, she stomped across the floor, into her bedroom and slammed a solid wood door on him without a word.

"Well, hell, that didn't go as planned," he grumbled to himself.

Mahpiya's powerful presence surged to the forefront of his mind until he could see the outline of her majestic feline form just behind his eyes.

*Do not fret, my charge. It is not your fault. She is lonely.*

"Lonely?" What the hell kind of sense did that make? The woman was getting married. How could she be lonely?

*She is lonely because she is not getting married. She is alone and in need of comfort.*

His eyebrows rose so fast, surely they would fly off his face and hit the ceiling. With narrowed eyes and more than a bit of serious curiosity, he practically growled at his psychic companion.

"How do you know she's not getting married, Mahpiya?"

Rahn sent utter shock resonating down the bond he shared with Mahpiya. He rolled his eyes in frustration as the image of the majestic lioness, lying in a comfortable heap licking her huge paws, faded from behind his eyes without answering his question.

\* \* \* \* \*

The ship was underway on the three-day sail from Lisbon to the Balearic Islands in the south of Spain. It meant hunting on board until they made port. He didn't particularly care for it. There weren't enough dim or dark nooks to hide, which meant there just weren't as many opportunities to genuinely enjoy stalking his prey.

189

His breathing quickened at the remembered thought of how the last woman had looked over her shoulder, her body stiff with fear when she'd realized that someone followed her. He'd stalked her for the entire time they'd been in port in Lisbon, all ten days. Each evening she'd walked from the middle of town to a small flat. Each night, her apprehension had grown more and more acute until he'd thought he might be able to reach out and eat a piece of it.

His cock swelled as his mind conjured the wide-eyed dread etched across her lovely features when he'd finally shown himself. He'd known the exact second she realized her life approached its end. Her last gasp, the last thump of her heart had brought with it such a heady rush of adrenaline, accompanied by a high so consuming he felt it down to his shoelaces. And he craved it again, would have it again.

Eden moved quietly through his bedroom to the closet where he gently stroked the black silk he so loved to wear. It never showed the blood and cleaned up nicely.

At sea, there were no pretty little females to follow through the darkness of the night or stalk from dark alleys. No overconfident, swaggering young men to approach in the gathering dark. No matter. There were plenty of people who considered themselves high class, and too good to mate with the men in his harem. It would be easy to keep his skills sharpened on them. He would simply practice on a hand-picked pawn aboard ship. After all, it was the sole reason they were on board, for his pleasure.

"At it again, I hear," he mumbled to himself with a shake of his head and gently closed the bedroom door at the first screech of his harem mistress's voice. She was no doubt on the case of one of the men again, scolding in a tone she never, ever used with him. Then again, she may be scolding them all.

"You will say nothing to our master," her hard voice practically cut the air around her. "I am responsible for all of you and this is not outside the realm of my authority. I will deal with it," said the lovely Egyptian female who called him "Beloved". She was indeed responsible for the harem. In spite of her tendency to dominate those she was supposed to care for, she'd said nothing that caused him concern. Eden ignored the conversation. Whatever the issue, let her deal with it.

Dressed in severe black, the only break in the darkness around his body was a crisp, blinding white silk handkerchief expertly tucked into the top pocket of his dinner jacket. Clasping an onyx cufflink onto the sleeve of his black shirt, Eden made his way through the living room and over to his most prized possessions to make sure all was well before he stepped out for the evening.

They were sullen, but otherwise unharmed. Eden picked them up one by one and allowed them to touch his mind, speak to him about their troubles. First was the porcelain, bronze-skinned male he called Shaman. A prized Native American warrior, with a body so perfectly sculpted even he would have been tempted if the man were flesh and blood. He was beautiful, standing at almost twenty-four-inches tall, with perfect porcelain skin and jet black hair down to his solid waist. And as usual, the first thoughts he shared with his master were of how much he resented having to bow to the whims of a temperamental female harem mistress, no matter how exquisite.

After a few assuring words, Eden put Shaman back on the shelf and reached for the next work of perfection.

Celon was a blond-haired Viking if there ever was one. A little shorter than Shaman, he stood at twenty-three inches of porcelain perfection. Dressed in classic Norwegian garb reminiscent of the early ninth century, he sported a wide muscular chest, a narrow waist and thick legs. His expression was one of seduction. His creator must have been a female. Even one painted eyebrow was raised in invitation and one side of his perfect mouth tilted up into a sly smile. He was a predator, plain and simple. Yes, he was Eden's favorite.

After listening to Celon's short, clipped complaint about the pharaoh harem mistress, Eden smiled at the man as a final thought slipped into his mind. Celon wanted nothing more than to fuck the harem mistress silly until she gladly got on her knees and begged him to take her. Poetic justice, since that was her favorite position for all ten males in the harem—on their knees before her.

But Eden could not regret her behavior. He needed someone ruthless to keep his stable in line. And what was more ruthless than a female?

Last, he picked up Daven. The dark-skinned male reminded him of the Egyptian kings. More than once, he thought he'd spotted the figure of this doll on one of the tarot cards he studied. Egypt was, after all, in Africa. It would be no surprise to find a man like this exquisite creation as a former ruler of that amazing place. Skin as darkly smooth as his favorite coffee, Daven was a master of temptation, as were all of the men in his collection. Dark brown eyes set under even darker brows practically beckoned females to his bed. If he were standing before him in the flesh Eden might have even considered asking him for advice on securing the female, Chrysalyn.

Tonight Daven was clearly not in the mood to play. And, for once, he didn't want to fuck the harem mistress. He wanted to beat her senseless. Why? The bitch had again selected a female for elimination that would have made a perfect mate for one in the harem.

His Japanese doll, Saraka, was enraged and distraught. The last woman the harem mistress had instructed Eden to hunt and ultimately destroy should have been Saraka's mate.

Oh well, nothing to be done about it now. Eden said goodnight to all of his men and lifted the harem mistress from her perch. With her in his arms, he made a beeline for the couch in the massive living room and reached out to the stack of tarot.

What the hell? The Empress upside down again. Pinning his harem mistress with a hard stare, he pushed the words out of his mouth.

"What does this card mean when it's not upside down?" he asked with an even, calm tone, though apprehension slipped down the backs of his legs.

*It represents the woman who is important to you. As a male, it may be a woman you know or will meet who may become your friend, lover or mate. It may also mean that you are entering a time of overflow, abundance and prosperity.Opportunities may very well come upon you from out of nowhere*, she replied quietly, carefully.

"Yes, but if all this comes about when the Empress is right side up, then the upside-down card must mean I am headed for trouble," Eden pressed roughly, unfamiliar with the apprehension twitching around in his gut. And he didn't like it one bit. He knew only one thing—his Egyptian flower had better tell him what he wanted to hear.

*If this card pertained to you, then perhaps what you say is true. However, I do not believe you are selecting this card for yourself, but for a person you have yet to come across. Perhaps this card tells us the future of your next task?* she said in a soothing timbre.

"You'd better fucking be right," he said calmly, kissing her lightly on each brow. With less than two hours before the ship left port, tonight he had to be precise in order to handle his business and get back on board in time.

Easing open her resting place, Eden set her gently on the top shelf of the glass cabinet and asked, "So, who shall it be tonight?" He stroked the top of her glossy head, loving the silky slide of her ethnic braids through his fingers. He paused mid-stroke and pinned her with a level stare. "And no more targeting the females who are meant for the men."

Her angry sigh echoed in his head, but he knew she would not gainsay him. At least not out loud.

# CHAPTER THREE

"Nope, definitely not a morning person," Rahn moaned to himself. Damn, even floating on water with the sun beaming into his room, warm and bright, he still wanted nothing more than to stuff the pillow over his head and tell the day to go to hell.

Well, no hope for it. He had a case to solve and a woman to protect. And that woman, who had always risen with the chickens, was no doubt up and about. Too bad he couldn't protect her in bed. Hmmm, then again, she was single again. Just maybe…

Kicking the covers off with a loud huff, Rahn pushed to his feet and stood there a moment. The view through the huge beveled glass window no more than three feet from his bed was incredible. He could see past the private deck and out to sea, where the sun shone down from a clear sky. The light reflected off the dark blue water, causing it to sparkle like the finest London blue topaz gems. And there was nothing else but ocean and more ocean. God, he hated deep water. Anything deeper than a bathtub was out of his comfort zone. If the ship went down on its way through the Mediterranean straits, it would be all he could do to stay afloat long enough to be rescued. And it was going to take three whole days to get to Ibiza? Damn.

Well, at least the ship was large enough that he wouldn't be constantly bent over the railing feeding the fish every time he had a bite to eat. With a snort, he dragged himself to his private bath.

Already bored, his mind sought for something to think on besides the case that brought him here. But until he checked in with his boss, Geri, for an intel update there was no need to dwell on it.

His thoughts drifted to Chrysalyn and the bomb Mahpiya had dropped on him last night. Chrysalyn was lonely? He still didn't understand it.

"Mah, come to me," he whispered around his toothbrush. At least his eyes were open and he was beginning to recall how to focus. Damn, he was tired. Mahpiya eased to the forefront of his mind, the slabs of dense muscle under her tawny coat flexing as she moved. He closed his eyes a second and grinned when the great cat flopped down on her stomach, raised her amber eyes and waited for him to speak.

Glad no one was around, so that he could speak out loud, Rahn jumped right in and said, "I wonder what the hell happened to Chrysalyn, Mah. I mean, the last time I saw her, she was engaged to that asshole, Kevin or Calvin or something like that. What the bloody hell went down? It's times like this I wish you could pop over to wherever she is and read her mind."

Shaking his head in wonder, he was still unable to believe the one woman he knew he couldn't live without was somewhere around this sprawling apartment. And she was available. Heading for the shower, he stopped short at Mahpiya's next words.

*There is no need for mind reading. Chrysalyn Geyer is your mate.*

Whoa! Back up. Rahn spun around so fast the clear glass door to the huge stall he'd just opened smacked him soundly on the knuckles. Rubbing the now-tender skin, he reached into his mind, demanding an explanation.

"Mah, how the hell can you know that?" When she didn't immediately reply, he summoned the feline onto this plane so he could look her in the eyes. "Mahpiya, come to me. Right now."

The sleek African lioness disappeared from behind his eyes and shimmered into her corporeal form right in front of him. Damn, she was huge—four feet tall and almost four-hundred-eighty pounds of raw power. At the top of the food chain, her earthly cousins were the perfect hunters. And Mahpiya was no less formidable. With the ability to speak mind-to-mind with those in her care, Rahn tended to forget how majestically imposing Mahpiya was. He immediately lowered his head and asked her forgiveness for his impertinence. After all, she served him at her pleasure. He was blessed to have such a wise companion.

Stepping into the shower, he dunked his head under the lukewarm flow and exhaled sharply. The scent of his favorite sandalwood soap filled the oversized stall.

"Okay, Mah, what do you mean, Chrysalyn is my mate?" Could it be? Chrysalyn, the woman perfect for him? He should have been shocked, so why wasn't he? Because Chrysalyn had been everything he'd ever dreamed of in a woman, a real class act. All he'd had to do was pursue her. But noooo, he'd been an idiot and allowed himself to be, uh, distracted by woman who'd chased after him instead. He'd learned later that same woman not only pursued him, but any other cock she could get her hands on. Hell, she had even slept with his best friend. Claimed it was all part of the job as an undercover. Yeah, right.

Obviously, their relationship hadn't lasted, but by the time he'd pulled his head out of his ass, Chrysalyn had moved on to someone who treated her like she deserved. The two had been engaged to be married and the woman seemed happy enough. So what happened?

He was snapped out of his musings by Mahpiya's sharp words and sultry voice.

*Get dressed, hoksila. You must be about your business. Your mate awaits you.*

With that, Mahpiya herded him out of the shower and back into his room with an urgency that had him moving double time. Was something wrong? Was Chrysalyn in danger? And where the hell was the woman, anyway? And hadn't Mah mentioned a spirit guide before?

*If you stop thinking, you can move faster,* Mahpiya growled before swatting him across the backside with a large paw.

"Ouch! Damn it, that hurt," Rahn yelped, hoping the impending welts didn't cause him too much discomfort later. A faint sound caught his attention as he fished around for underwear and a pair of sport socks in his dresser drawer. Lifting his eyes toward the quiet splash, Rahn spied an unlikely vision through the glass doors leading out to the deck.

Holy shit! Chrysalyn basked under the early morning sunshine, her body partially hidden by the swirling rush of hot water in the oversized hot tub. Arms spread out to her sides, the swell of her breasts was just visible above the waterline. Her delicious, cinnamon skin gleamed enticingly, wet from the steam and droplets peppering her beautiful body. The leopard-print swimsuit plastered to her curves sent a rush of heat straight to his cock. Her hair was loose and little curls framed her strong jawline as she laid her head back, eyes closed and...puffed? On a cigar?

His cock screamed as he stood there, mute and

unable to get a single muscle in his body to move. She was so damned sexy. And here he stood with another chance to have her and he couldn't draw his eyes away from the window.

Another swat across his buttocks took care of that.

"Okay, already! I'm going, Mah."

*Excellent,* she purred as her corporeal form shimmered away.

Not like he needed any further encouragement. One peek at the exquisite woman lounging in the tub had his dick stiffer and hotter than a fireplace poker left sitting on top of a burning log.

The next moment found Rahn moving toward the doors with sheer determination in his stride. He headed across the deck and straight toward the hot tub and the succulent woman awaiting him.

* * * * *

The second the hair started dancing on the back of her neck, Chrysalyn's brows drew together in a fierce frown. Forcing the muscles of her face to relax until she was the epitome of absolute calm, she called to her spirit guide.

Reaching out with her mind, she asked, 'Adonei, who's approaching?'

*Do not worry, my charge. There is no danger.*

'I don't give a shit if there's danger. I don't like people sneaking up on me.'

And who the hell wanted to admit the man was making plenty of noise. The loud snap of the glass doors to his room and the soft flap of his bare feet on the wood deck told her who approached. His fresh masculine scent stole over her, carried on the easy ocean breeze. Oh great! Now her stomach was doing the butterfly samba. What the hell was there to be so giddy about? It was only Rahn, right? It was only the man she should have married three years ago. The man whose smooth tenor English accent sent little strokes of heat up the back of her knees. Whose sexy smile and killer physique made her want to do all sorts of nasty things to him.

The bastard who fell for a horse-humping bitch who wanted nothing more than to prove she could steal him. And he'd fallen for it, the idiot.

*Ease yourself, Chrysalyn. You are screaming in my ear,* Adonei scolded with a deep growl. His annoyed expression was crystal clear in her head, along with the bored roll of his eyes. How an African lion managed to roll his eyes, she would never know. And she was *not* screaming, damn it!

"Chrysalyn?"

Sitting up, she opened her eyes and watched Rahn approach. Tangy ocean mist drifted up from the wake as the huge ship cut gently through the waves. It tickled her nose. She liked the way it smelled. The sun had risen only an hour before, but the deck was already nicely warmed and comfortable. Add the barely perceptible rocking of the sea and her day was perfect. But the vivid blues painted across the sky, the smell of the sea, the opulence of her private dwelling, all of it paled in comparison to the gloriously naked man coming her way. His stride was long, but easy, kind of reminding her of Adonei when he was hunting some imaginary prey.

The sweet chocolate and coffee smoke of her Kahlua cigar drifted like silken threads of aromatic decadence. The scent of the indulgence she enjoyed every now and again made her think of how long and thick the hand-rolled treat was, which in turn carried her wayward thoughts to other similarly shaped objects that would fit nicely perched between her lips. Aw, hell.

Reaching up, she plucked the fat Kahlua cigar from

her lips and set it in the sleek ashtray just off to her left. Sounding as bored as Adonei's eye-rolling looked, her voice lacked any kind of warmth as she answered his call.

"Yeah, what, Rahn?"

*There is no need to be rude, Chrysalyn.* Adonei again. Didn't the cat have somewhere to go?

'Says who? I was perfectly fine out here all by myself. What the hell does he want anyway?' she grumbled back at her spirit guide, who was becoming more and more a pain in the backside lately with all his male logic.

*He is not a danger to you, woman. However, that black-clothed fellow does concern me.*

'Who? What black-clothed fellow?' she wondered.

*The one who insinuated himself into your company when you were dining alone. That one is dangerous, I am sure of it.*

'Eden, hmm? Seems harmless enough. But you've never steered me wrong. I would be a fool to totally ignore your warning. I'll be careful.'

*Thank you. Now, in the meantime, you have company.*

Hell, she'd almost forgotten about Rahn.

Geez, what a blatant lie. But that was her story and she was sticking to it. By the time her conversation with Adonei was done, Rahn was climbing into the hot tub with a determination in his eyes she was sure she'd never seen unless he was after a bad guy.

He was very close now. So close that if the water hadn't already been one-hundred-two degrees, she was sure the heat emanating from his body would have taken care of any tepidness. She sat up and looked down.

*Oh dear lord.* The man was gloriously naked, with a cock so long, broad and hard that the game of baseball came to mind. Hell, he was at least a foot away from her, but the thick-veined tool jutting her way put him a whole lot closer.

One more step and his erection thudded against her stomach, just underneath her breasts and partially hidden by the frothing water. Her heart rate kicked up into overdrive and breathing was a whole lot higher on the scale of important things to do. Okay, time to go. So, why weren't her legs carrying her the hell out of the damned hot tub?

"Chrysalyn?" he asked, seeking her permission to touch with a whisper-soft plea against the side of her face. With her butt rooted to the spot, she watched one of his large, strong hands move toward her face to remove her sunglasses as the other tipped her chin up just before his lips brushed sensuously against hers.

"Chrys, baby, I've missed you so much." His breath was a barrage of peppermint flowing over her cheek, followed by Eskimo kisses. When was the last time she'd rubbed noses with a man, or anyone for that matter?

His perfectly chiseled body scant inches from hers sent the blood dancing in her veins as the heat in her own skin threatened to out heat the bubbling tub. God, why had he always been able to get to her like this? Especially when she should totally hate the bastard—the dark-haired, tawny-eyed, gorgeous and seemingly sincere bastard. The knowledge that he could move her like no one else pissed her off.

*Or perhaps you are more angry with yourself?* Adonei queried as he faded to a little corner of her mind.

Nope! She was not angry with herself. Even if she had made every dumb decision possible during that rocky period while on the rebound from Rahn. Even if he would have crawled back, she'd simply been too proud to forgive him, determined to stay with the fiancé from hell just to prove a point.

Oooh, but now he nibbled that little spot he knew she liked while whispering her name between little bites.

"God, Chrysalyn, you taste so good," he murmured against her slightly parted lips before covering her mouth with his. Any gentle intent dissolved into pure lust as he entangled his tongue with hers. She felt herself slip under his spell, felt the petals of her sex tingle and burn, and it had nothing to do with the heat of the hot tub.

Then she was suddenly empty. Rahn was there, but in her mind, she was utterly, totally alone.

Usually an expert at schooling her features, her emotions slipped out of her grasp and ran away from her. The panic that reared up to press against the middle of her chest was etched clearly across her face. Adonei! He was gone. They'd never been apart since the day she'd met him as a child. Why? Why now?

*I am here, Chrysalyn, bu tI would not disrespect you or your mate by intruding upon your mating.*

'What? Adonei, don't you dare leave me!' she wailed in her head.

*Your mate will take good care of you. Do not worry. I will be near.*

'My mate? What's with this mate stuff? Adonei? Come back!'

"Hey, sweetheart, what's wrong?" Rahn asked, letting her push away just a bit. The concern in his voice, accompanied by a little shake, broke through the wall of fear quickly erecting itself around her heart and snatched her back to the present.

"Are you all right?"

Her gut clenched painfully. All right? Hell no, she wasn't all right, but it would be a seven-below-zero day in hell before she admitted it. He couldn't possibly understand the emptiness in her head, the little void in her heart that was always filled with Adonei's presence.

Just the thought of being alone inside her own mind was downright terrifying.

Rahn crooned into her ear, holding her tenderly, gently massaging the muscles of her back. "You look afraid. You know I won't hurt you, love."

Still shaken from Adonei's absence, she snapped, "I'm not afraid of you, Rahn." And moved to jump out of the tub.

Rahn's hand wrapped firmly around her biceps just as her toe hit the edge of the Jacuzzi. She froze.

"I'm sorry, Chrys. I didn't mean to upset you," he said quickly, his smooth voice full of concern. The pained expression in his deep amber eyes moved something buried inside her she'd thought long dead— the ability to receive comfort from a man. That comfort eased through her heart, mind and body, worked its way to her head and calmed her fears.

She went willingly into his arms, allowing herself to be cocooned against the solid wall of his chest. He picked her up and the natural masculine scent of his skin enveloped her as he eased her into his lap to straddle his hips.

Mmm, and his lips, soft and slightly damp from the steam rising from the water, tasted of fresh air, mint and warm aroused man. Then again, perhaps the meaty, throbbing erection bobbing up and down between them indicated the aroused part.

"Oh, baby, I've missed this. Missed just being close to you." The edginess in his voice made her thighs, draped over his, quiver like Japanese mochi pudding. The skin where their bodies touched melted clean away when he moved in for another kiss, this one hot and unapologetic. His need conveyed through the movement of his lips and tongue, the motion smooth, but hard, full of desire and heat. It made her want, made her need. Chrysalyn moaned wantonly as he practically inhaled her.

"Damn, woman, I want you more than I want to breathe," he whispered against the damp curls plastered against the side of her face.

"Really?" she gasped when he moved away from devouring her mouth to nip the sensitive spot just underneath her jawline. "You want me? Even more than…?"

"Yes, baby, I want you more than I ever wanted her."

How had he known what she was going to say? Then again, he'd always known what she was feeling, thinking. It was as if they'd simply picked up where they left off three years ago. Last night, she'd fled from him, hadn't wanted to explain her breakup with her ex-fiancé. And she certainly hadn't wanted to acknowledge how the old spark between them emerged to hum just below her skin the moment she'd come up on him sneaking around her apartment.

Now that spark flared like a newly lit stack of charcoal doused with lighter fluid. The strong feelings she'd stuffed under mounds of work and duties crashed to the surface as if they'd never been buried.

His hands slid across her steam-slick skin, pausing to knead a muscle here and there, reminding her of the most decadent massage she'd ever had in her life. One he'd given her long ago. One she'd never forgotten and never thought to experience again. And there was nothing she could think of to compare it to. Hell, she could barely think at all.

"Baby, please. Let me taste you?" he asked in a way that wasn't really a request. And boy, did she ever want to feel his mouth on her. Her teeth snapped together with an audible *click* at the feel of his tongue, wet and hot, sliding up her neck to lick away the moisture along the way.

"Chrys?" he asked again. "Let me?"

Yes, oh, yes. She wanted to give him permission, but when the slightly roughened pads of his fingers eased underneath the wet fabric of the slinky little two-piece and skimmed along her ass, she couldn't get a single word out. All she could do was nod her head and hope he was paying attention. Could he taste her? Hell yes!

With Mahpiya's subtle retreat to the outermost reaches of his mind, Rahn's head was strangely empty, yet at the same time, full of Chrysalyn—the way her short silky curls reflected the morning sun, the contrast of her milk chocolate skin against his tanned fairer tones. And her height, the little firebrand was so much shorter than him. Even when he lifted her out of the water, set her on the edge of the hot tub and kneeled on the seat in front of her, they were still of a height. Her breasts were just enough decadent flesh to fill his hands and were at the perfect angle for sucking. He palmed, squeezed and toyed with them until she squirmed, then he zeroed in on the puckered nubbins at the tips of those firm mounds and let his teeth have their wicked way. She'd always been partial to biting.

He lapped and nipped her beautiful breasts through her swimsuit while his fingers ran up and down toned, muscled calves and thighs, all on a five-foot-two frame. Chrysalyn was strong, compact and hippy, just the way he liked his women. Small package. Whole lot of beautiful female.

"Time to lose the swimsuit, Chrys," he groaned around a succulent mouthful of her lovely areolas. Her stupefied "what" made him chuckle. He repeated his request, each word said with a little pluck to her nipples. She appeared ready to swoon.

"Chrysalyn, do you want me to stop?" he growled, backing off just enough to allow a cool stream of air to pass between their bodies. "Do you want me to stop, sweet?"

"Oh god, no!"

"Then. Remove. The. Suit."

With trembling fingers, she reached up and with a flick of her wrist undid the string secured around her neck. The top of her halter-style bikini fell free, revealing the tasty treats Rahn had been suckling through the fabric. And they were beautiful. Her breasts were full and firm, the color of caramel cappuccino with Hershey's Kisses nipples. Damn. With his chest wedged between her knees, he couldn't resist feasting a while longer and pulled the entire crown into his mouth while his fingers ducked into the warm flesh between her thighs.

There he found so much honeydew pleasure, he wanted to drown in her. The sounds echoing from her throat as he explored with lips, tongue and questing fingers were seductively sexy. But he wanted to push her over the edge, kick her ecstasy up a notch until she screamed to the heavens from now until the end of time.

Fingers slick with cream, he raised them up to her parted lips and pressed them inside.

"Taste yourself, love." Her tongue snaked out and wrapped around his finger, pulling and sucking until he felt the sensation clear down to his swollen balls. "God, woman, your scent is so sweet I can't wait another minute to sink my tongue into that pretty pussy."

She nodded dumbly, but didn't move, just sat there on the edge of the bubbling Jacuzzi, trembling as her chest heaved up and down. He would just have to be patient, because if he dared put his hands to her swimsuit bottom, it would be a shredded piece of no-good fabric when he was done yanking it off her succulent body. A succulent body with too many clothes on it!

Clenching his hands, he ground out, "Chrysalyn. The bottoms, sweet."

"Uh, yes. Okay." The words were breathy, lost. Hungry. And all for him.

She stood on the submerged seat and peeled the wet bottoms over the curve of her ass, down her lovely legs and dropped them on top of her sodden top on the deck. Settled again on the tub's edge, she spread her legs and flashed a siren's smile. The smoldering heat in her light brown eyes said come fuck me now. The engorged lips of her pussy, spread wide for him to see, screamed even louder. But no cock for her. Not yet.

He called quietly to his spirit guide one last time before he gorged himself on Chrysalyn's dewy folds.

'Mahpiya, lend me your senses.'

The reply was so faint, he almost missed it.

*Take what I offer, my charge, and enjoy your mate.* And then she faded away completely, leaving him and Chrysalyn truly alone.

Closing his eyes, he allowed the power and aura of the lioness to fill him until the very essence of his spirit guide whistled through every pore in his body. Then he lowered himself down into the water until only his chest was visible. The aroma of her sex, heightened by the lioness's keen senses, smelled of clean, fresh woman. And something else he couldn't quite pin down, like honey syrup and cardamom spice.

He kept his gaze pinned to hers as he pushed her thighs as far apart as they would go. The woman was practically doing the splits on the edge of that tub and he would take full advantage of it.

One swipe of his tongue up her dewy slit caused a strangled cry to erupt from between her lips.

"Oh dear god!"

A second pass brought on a shudder so intense, he thought she might keel over into the tub.

"Rahn! Oh, yesss!"

A third sent her spiraling toward release.

When the two of them had spent time together years ago, she'd never given him complete access to her body like this, saying she wanted to wait until the time was right. He'd been frustrated then, but now he was glad. This did feel, for lack of better words, right. Not forced or awkward. As if the pieces of their lives snapped together with perfect precision. The response to his touch was something he'd never dreamed of. It was as if he'd unwrapped a beautiful present, uncovered a rare jewel. And if her wild cries were any indication, the idiot she'd been engaged to had never gifted her with this kind of loving. Pride filled his chest as his lips and tongue continued to work her over.

"Oh god! Rahn! No more! I can't take it," she screamed. Mmm, what beautiful music. The cries torn from her throat as her orgasm peaked and consumed her filled his head as she exploded. The climax was forceful enough to set her slick channel clenching around the tip of his tongue and her legs trembling even while her knees wrapped tight around his head and her fingers gripped the edge of the tub.

Head thrown back, spine bowed, she gave herself up to his attention until she was a trembling mass of pliable flesh. Finally, Chrys collapsed backward onto the warm deck.

When her breathing returned to normal, she sat up and looked at him. What was that? Confusion? Fear? He couldn't tell.

The next instant, she snatched her wet swimsuit up off the deck and headed through the glass doors that led to her bedroom. The definitive snap and *click* told him she'd locked it behind her.

What the hell? Just as he started to go after her, Mahpiya's powerful presence charged back into the familiar place in his head.

*Hoksila, *leave her be for now*.*

Fuck.

'No worries, Mah. I can tell she needs a minute alone and so do I.'

His mate. Wow, he'd never expected such a thing. With that, Rahn climbed out of the tub and went back to his room. He flopped backward onto the bed, wrapped his fingers around his aching erection and closed his eyes. What would Chrysalyn's hot cunt feel like wrapped around him? Would she grip him tight? Would she yell like she'd done a few moments ago?

With his mind full of fantasy and his cock as hard as iron, he pulled and stroked himself until his balls drew up tight against his body. His come geysered onto his chest. The eruption provided scant relief, knowing he wouldn't be fully satisfied until he'd sunk into Chrysalyn's sweetness, binding her to him completely.

But why hadn't he realized this years ago? Mahpiya chimed in.

*Because you were not ready to receive such a gift*, hoksila. *Certain events in your life have brought you to a place where you can appreciate her. Rest assured, Chrysalyn is the one.*

'Thank you, Mah. Thanks for looking out for me.'

*My pleasure and my duty,* she whispered, retreating to her favorite corner with a yawn.

After a catnap, Rahn rose, showered again and headed to Chrysalyn's room. He was determined to win her, heart and soul. May as well start now.

It was still early enough, couldn't be much past ten a.m. Perhaps she would have breakfast with him?

"Chrys," he called quietly, tapping on her door.

No answer. Maybe she was napping as well?

"Chrys, love?"

Easing the door open, he was hit square in the chest by her scent, followed keenly by a disappointment so palpable he could have torn it in two and thrown it overboard. The room was empty. Chrys was gone.

# CHAPTER FOUR

Over the years, he'd thought of Chrys often, but never contacted her out of respect. After all, she had someone else in her life, or he thought she had until this morning. But after tasting and touching the woman, after being in her presence again, he had to have her.

"Mahpiya, come to me," Rahn grumbled, deep in thought. He walked across the expanse of the living room and sat in the overstuffed chair directly across from Chrys' bedroom. His arm hung over the side of the linen-covered chair and was immediately propped up by the sleek back of an African female lion. Rahn's fingers automatically smoothed over the thick pelt, but stilled at Mahpiya's irritated growl.

*May I remind you I am not one of your pathetic home cats.*

"That's housecat, Mah," Rahn said with a grin. He knew where this conversation was going.

*Whatever.* She yawned with a muted roar. *I am queen of my domain and have no need of petting.*

Yep, she was proud all right. And beautiful and strong. But Rahn knew every woman needed a little stroking, no matter the species. "So, what if I need to do the petting? What if it soothes me? What then?"

*If it is something you need, then I shall, of course, allow it.* She sniffed and stretched her big body out on the plush carpet and Rahn buried his hand in her fur. Corded tendons and thick muscles bunched and twitched when his fingertips slipped over the spot just above her left shoulder. That was her sweet spot.

She rolled over on her side.

*So why have you summoned me, my charge?* the powerful spirit guide asked on a purr. Direct and to the point had always been her style. Rahn wished all females were this way. At least with Mahpiya, he always knew where he stood. If all was well, she said so. If he was being an idiot, Mahpiya had no bones about telling him. No second-guessing required.

"When I went to look for Chrys, she wasn't in her room. Is she running from me?"

*Hoksila, you know I am not allowed to touch the thoughts of one who is not in my charge. I can only sense the emotions of others, however, with Chrysalyn I may be able to see somewhat deeper.*

"Mah, what are you getting at?" Rahn asked, his eyebrows bunched in question.

*If I answer your question, it would mean revealing a secret that is not mine.*

With a frustrated sigh, Rahn pushed out of the chair and paced in front of the corporeal body of his guide before flopping back into the cushions.

"You can trust me, Mah. You know that."

*Yes, I know, but I am not the one who must trust you. It is someone else.*

"Chrys?"

*In a manner of speaking.*

"Is Chrys okay? Is everything all right?" He was no longer easing his hands along Mahpiya's back, but sat ramrod straight, brow knotted with tension. If something was wrong with Chrys, he wanted to know about it.

*It is not what you think, hoksila. It is, in fact, a wondrous thing.*

"Then tell me, before I go out of my mind with worry, damn it," he pressed. Rahn knew he was being less than polite with a female who tolerated no disrespect. But she did recognize that, while she was his spirit guide, he was all man. It was second nature to him to demand what was needed.

The lioness's tawny-eyed stare bore into his. Rahn couldn't have cared less.

"Tell me, Mah. Right this instant. What the hell is this secret that involves Chrys? You know I'm trustworthy, now out with it."

*If you insist.*

Seconds ticked by. Felt more like eons as they sat, holding each other's gaze. Suddenly, Mahpiya's expression softened, and she grinned as only a feline could.

*I told you earlier Chrysalyn is your mate. What I did not tell you is that she has a spirit guide. An African lion, like me.*

"What?" Rahn couldn't believe it. What were the odds of that? Of all the women he knew, the one he wanted more than anything had a spirit guide. But the realization raised more questions. If he and Chrys did get together, would the two spirit guides get along? Which one of the lionesses would lead their little pride? It was too amazing to conceive and sent his thoughts tumbling one over the other until they gelled enough to form a logical question.

"So what's her spirit guide's name?"

*Adonei,* Mahpiya said fondly. Rahn's brows rose. Well, it was obvious Mah already got along with the other lioness. Strange name, though.

"Adonei? What kind of a name is Adonei for a female?" he queried. At her response, his mouth fell wide open and practically hit the carpet.

*Adonei is not a female. Adonei is a male, and he is my mate, as Chrysalyn is yours.*

"You have got to be shitting me!"

Mates? Mah and this Adonei lion? Finally, his faithful companion would have someone especially for her. She was such a good guide, she deserved another who would love her, hunt with her and maybe even give her little spirit babies, if there was such a thing. Wait a minute. How did he know this Adonei was a good spirit? Sure, Mahpiya could sense such things, but they'd been together for years and he wouldn't just let anyone waltz into her life. After all, she deserved the best. Perhaps it was time for a little interview with Mr. Adonei.

"So," Rahn said evenly. "When can I expect to meet this Adonei?" Fingers steepled under his chin, the tips tapped together as he pinned Mahpiya with a glare. "If he's your mate, then as your only male relative, I demand to have a talk with him."

*I appreciate your concern, hoksila. I love you as well.*

"Mah," he growled impatiently when she didn't answer his question. She laughed! And when he was totally serious too!

*You cannot speak directly with Adonei because you and Chrysalyn have not joined yet. But once your bond begins to form, you will be able to talk with him as easily as you speak with me. And there is more.*

"Hell, Mah, I don't know if I can take any more news."

*Adonei and I offer our assistance in securing your mate.*

"Huh?" he asked as his mind tried to wrap around what his spirit guide said.

*I said, we wish to help you win Chrysalyn.*

Boy, this just got better and better. He felt an idiotic grin spread across his lips, but couldn't seem to control his facial muscles.

*If you want her, that is.*

"Of course I want her. I've always wanted her. What man in his right mind wouldn't want a woman like Chrys?" Regret had been his constant companion since he'd blown his first chance with Chrys. The woman evoked such strong feelings in him, she was the only female he knew who made him feel so…unsteady. But like a fool, he'd allowed himself to be distracted by other things. By the time he'd figured out she was everything he'd ever wanted in a woman, she was engaged to what's-his-butt.

So what happened between the two of them? Why hadn't they gotten married?

*I know you have questions, but until Chrysalyn accepts you, spirit, soul and body, you must speak to Adonei through me. I will do my best to ensure we communicate well.*

"Thanks, Mah. I love you, you know that, you big beautiful cat?"

*Big cat? Humph!*

"Okay, you and Adonei fill me in." A noticeable pep in his step, Rahn made his way to the kitchen, listening to Mah's sultry voice. All this news about mates and spirit guides made him hungry. Not to mention the wonderfully intimate time he'd spent with Chrys early this morning.

After a bit of rummaging around, he found everything he needed to make a nutritious brunch. Slicing a sushi-grade filet of Ahi tuna, Rahn made a quick dish of Hawaiian poké, complete with fresh ginger, spicy soy sauce, fragrant green onions and a dash of sesame oil served up on a bed of crisp lettuce. He sat down at the dining room table, picked up a single bite of the delicacy and froze with his fork in midair.

Suddenly uncomfortable, his eyes immediately scanned the area for the source of the sensation, but it seemed to come from far off and was unfamiliar as it flowed down the psychic bond he shared with his spirit guide. His skin felt stretched tight and almost itchy. His gut churned until it felt pulled inside out. An air of deep disgust settled in, so strong he wanted to rip off his t-shirt and jeans, run back to the shower and scrub until he felt clean again.

"Mah, what the hell's going on? What's wrong?"

*It is not me, my charge. Adonei is uneasy with the company Chrysalyn is keeping.*

"Show me." Understanding dawned the second he closed his eyes and Adonei shared the situation with Mahpiya, who then shared it with Rahn. A lovely image of Chrys filled his mind, so clear he could see each individual strand of her short wavy hair. Her cocoa skin was so flawless, it reminded him of a smooth river of milk chocolate. And he'd learned this morning that it was just as sweet. The need to touch her almost overwhelmed. But if he reached out, could he brush his fingers over the curve of her shoulder?

Then the vision shifted and the hair on the back of Rahn's neck stood at full attention. He didn't hear his fork clatter into his plate, then down to the tiled floor. A burst of adrenaline hit his bloodstream. The urge to take off at a dead run had him clenching his leg muscles as Mah sent the unfolding situation into his mind. He wasn't sure he'd ever felt such apprehension, even when pursuing the nastiest of villains. And these feelings came from Chrysalyn's spirit guide through Mahpiya? And so strong?

He was out the door in two shakes.

Once on the elevator, he wished he'd taken the stairs.

The damned thing was moving too slow. Surely he could have run faster than this. The thoughts flowing into his mind gave a whole new meaning to the phrase slower than molasses.

Damn, he had to get a hold of himself. Dealing with the thoughts of three entities—Mahpiya, Adonei and himself—he'd be so worked up by the time he got to Chrys, he'd simply deck the man who was causing such concern. Then he'd toss Chrys over his shoulder and carry her back to their apartment, caveman style.

The idea had merit, but it would certainly bring more attention than he wanted. Before he could say anything, Mahpiya once again proved why she was the spirit guide and he was her charge. The cat was one step ahead of him, as usual.

*I must cease sharing Adonei's concern with you. We do not wish for you to behave irrationally when you arrive at your destination. Adonei and I wish to assist you in winning Chrysalyn, not make her angry.*

Thankful for the calm reassurance, Rahn took a deep breath and stilled himself.

'Thanks, Mah,' he whispered along their bond as the elevator doors opened with a quiet swish. 'I'll call if I need you, but before you stand down, ask Adonei one more question for me.'

*Yes?*

'The name of the man with Chrys.'

*Adonei says his name is Eden Pall. They met shortly after Chrys boarded a few days ago. Something about him simply does not smell right to Adonei.*

'Thanks, Mah. You can stand down now.'

*As you wish,* she whispered, retreating to the special little corner of his mind where she liked to nap.

Slowing his stride, he made his way into the restaurant. One look at Chrys' beautiful self and his tongue stuck to the roof of his mouth. The woman was dressed in a formfitting sports bra and matching cropped workout pants. All curves and luscious skin, yet she screamed strength and ability. Damn, even her tennis shoes looked sexy. A glance at the man with whom she kept company stripped the slight smile from his face. His jaw began to hurt. Well, no wonder—he was grinding his teeth. The Eden fellow sat looking like he wanted to eat her up along with whatever he had on his breakfast plate. But not today. Or any other day, for that matter.

The second she spotted Rahn making a beeline for her table, she looked like a deer in the headlights. He hoped she'd close her mouth before something flew into it. But as for the dark look he received from her temporary partner, Rahn had seen it before, and always on someone up to no good. Oh yeah, that's just what he was looking for and would make sure to call his boss, Geri, today to check this guy out. The man looked normal enough, but the veneer was too smooth. His pasted-on smile, too perfect. This guy was bad news. Rahn felt it down in his gut and, obviously, Chrys' spirit guide did too. So why was she here? If Adonei had sent even half of what he'd shared with Mahpiya down his psychic link with Chrys, how in the world could she sit here looking so calm?

Rahn strolled right up to the couple, ignored the encroacher and leaned down to plant a kiss just at the corner of Chrys' decadently tempting mouth.

"Hello, love. When I awoke, you were gone. I missed you. Everything all right?"

\* \* \* \* \*

God, if Adonei didn't quiet down, she was going to go bonkers. His displeasure at Eden popping up to share her brunch was beyond palpable. The lion's anger and agitation, like the scraping of sharp claws across a chalkboard, filled the inside of her skull. Chrys' teeth were set on edge and had her more than ready to plead a very real headache and flee the table. Something about her present company rubbed Adonei completely the wrong way.

Head down, pretending to study the breakfast menu, Chrys tried to get Adonei to talk to her. Her churning stomach made her queasy. Something made Adonei's skin crawl. She felt it through the bond, as if a dark and demented presence traipsed a slimy finger up her arm leaving goose bumps in its wake. Oh god, she was going to be sick. Had she remembered to pack her migraine medicine? She sure as hell hoped so. And she couldn't get mad at Adonei. He wasn't trying to hurt her, but whatever had him ready to pounce swooshed down their psychic link and slammed into her mind like the pounding of waves against the sand in the middle of a storm.

"Chrysalyn, you seem ill."

Eden's thick accent was exotically sexy in her ears, but slid over her soul like rancid oil. When her company reached over and gently covered her hand with his, the sick swirl in her belly intensified and sweat broke out on her top lip.

She eased her hand from underneath his, swallowed the bile racing into her mouth and picked up the glass sitting in front of her. Chrys didn't think she'd ever been so happy to see iced water in her life. Even the condensation dripping down the side of the crystal goblet called her name, invited her to cool the suddenly feverish skin on the inside of her palm.

God, the liquid felt so good sliding down her throat to calm her stomach.

"Chrysalyn, are you all right?" Eden asked again.

"Uh, sure, I'm fine," she sputtered and forced a smile while waving down the waiter. She placed her order and then took another sip of water, followed by shallow breaths. Out of the corner of her eye, she caught sight of a tall, wide figure moving her way with a determined posture. The man, intimidating body language and all, wasn't a danger to her. If he were, Adonei would have put up even more racket than he had since Eden sat down a few moments ago. God, and those moments felt like eternity.

Suddenly, Adonei went still. He continued to pad back and forth across the forefront of her mind, but other than that there wasn't a single roar. Not even a sniff or a yawn. And her nausea, headache, goose bumps and shivering disappeared as if they'd never been. Strange.

She turned and locked gazes with one of the most beautiful men she'd ever known. Rahn. The second their eyes met, Chrys could have sworn she felt a light brush of relief against her thoughts from her spirit guide.

His long legs ate up the distance between them as he approached, all brawn, class and a nice tight ass. Oh, goodness, had she really thought up a poem in honor of Rahn's backside? An unusual tightness encircled her tongue as she watched him come. Resisting the urge to roll her eyes at her own goofy line of thinking, she snapped closed the mouth she hadn't realized was wide open. A heated blush crept up her neck.

Rahn's dark hair, though tastefully cut, was slightly mussed, as if he'd taken a shower, dressed quickly and come straight to her. The sexy smirk that had always made her knees tremble was firmly in place. And the gleam in his golden brown eyes screamed to the world that he wanted nothing more than to get next to her.

There was no subtlety about his intent as he stepped to her side. A soft musky scent filled the scant space between them. God, he smelled good. Looked good. Felt good. Licked and sucked good.

She squeezed her eyes shut and tried to push the

thoughts away. She couldn't sit here with Eden and think about how deliciously Rahn had feasted on her still-throbbing pussy just after sunrise. It just wasn't right. Chrys didn't like Eden *that way*, but it felt naughty to think on such intimate details in the presence of another man.

And Rahn wasn't making it easy on her. Especially when he leaned forward, his breath tickling her ear just before he dropped a kiss dangerously close to her lips. Her mouth almost fell open again when he started talking about how much he'd missed her when he woke to find her gone. And the man made no attempt to keep his voice down, either. Damn it, he'd have everyone thinking they were sleeping together! They were in the same apartment, but they weren't sleeping together. Hot-tubbing maybe, but definitely not sleeping, though the idea was beginning to have merit.

God, she was really losing it.

Rahn eased into a pub chair. His thigh brushed against hers as he reached across the table and extended a friendly hand to Eden. A glance at her tablemate stilled the blood in her heart. She almost called his name to see if she could snap him out of his...whatever he was in. Lips set in a stern line, Eden didn't move, didn't blink, showed no expression at all. The man looked as if he were carved from stone.

"Hello," Rahn said in as friendly a tone as she'd ever heard. "I'm Rahn. Traveling with Chrys for, ah, work." The urge to kick him in the shin when he turned and winked at her almost overrode her common sense. There was no missing the implication as the knowing smirk reappeared, accompanied by a slyly arched brow. How did he pull that off without looking like a smart-ass? And now that he was seated next to her, his presence swirled around her, reached for her. Focusing on her spirit guide, she was surprised to find Adonei settled down, watching the byplay. The big cat had ceased pacing and now sat on his huge haunches, watching curiously to see what would happen between the two males sharing her table.

Hmm. What was going on here?

'Adonei, is there something I should know? You're awfully calm all of a sudden,' she whispered in her mind, sneaking another peek at Rahn from underneath her lashes. Geesh, the man was gorgeous even when he ordered coffee. And if the big grin spread across the face of the perky little waitress was any indication, Chrys wasn't the only one who thought so.

A bagel and cream cheese was hustled to the table along with a small bowl full of sweet, sliced melon. Chrys found her eyes glued to the sinewy play of muscle in Rahn's forearm. Skilled fingers moved gracefully as he spread some strawberry cream cheese over the toasted bread. The lightly tanned skin exposed by his dark blue three-quarter-sleeved t-shirt was smooth, but heavily veined and stretched over thick ropy tendons. The bulge of biceps pushed against the fabric, hinting at the raw power of his honed body. Damn, he was sexy.

And could have anyone he wanted. So what the hell did he want with her? The answer lit her mind like a beacon.

Chrys sniffed and turned away. She was nobody's fool. Rahn may have alluded that he was more to her than a coworker, but he was just posturing because Eden was there. Typical male. He might not want her, but he didn't want anyone else to have her either. So what about the stint in the hot tub? Again, typical male. What man could resist a half naked woman in a hot tub?

*Here we go*, she thought with a silent snort. *Two men all cocksure over a woman neither of them have any right to.*

Eden hadn't gotten anywhere near being intimate

with her. And Rahn obviously thought a few perfectly placed licks of his talented tongue meant he could pick up with her where they'd left off three years ago. Now that pissed her off.

Besides, their previous estrangement was all his fault. He was the one who'd decided to get so wrapped up in his cases that he didn't have time for her. And he sure as hell gave no indication he'd intended to ask for her hand while getting himself caught up in the agency's floozy of the year. So Chrys had cut her losses and moved on. Shortly after she'd become engaged to Sean, Rahn had moved back to London and pretty much disappeared from her life. All she knew was he occasionally worked out of the Miami, London and Rome offices. He'd only tried to contact her once since then.

On a trip back to Denver, he'd managed to get her alone in the office for a minute. He'd wanted her back. But, hell, at the time she'd been too busy trying to figure out what was going on with the idiot she was engaged to.

Yep, she'd picked an insensitive blockhead to get over Rahn and ended up cutting off her nose to spite her face. It wasn't something she'd advertised after the wedding was called off. In fact, no one except her cousin, Delaine, and her boss, Geri, had even known the real deal until almost six months past the wedding that never happened.

So what was Rahn really doing here? Was it just work? His possessive overtures and attempt to seduce her—an attempt that was working quite well until a few seconds ago, by the way—said it was nothing more than just an investigation in Rome. But if he needed to get somewhere, why take the long way 'round on a cruise ship with her?

Her suspicion grew as she watched him. The smile plastered on Rahn's face certainly didn't reach his eyes. In fact, she couldn't recall spotting such a cold, calculating look on the man.

And now that she was really paying attention, Eden got more and more fidgety the longer he sat in Rahn's presence. So what was Eden's problem? He'd practically come right out and said he was interested in her. Now that Rahn appeared, he was just going to up and back off? Now she was really annoyed.

'Adonei, come to me,' Chrysalyn called across their bond. The fully mature lion rose and stalked forward until his image practically filled the very forefront of her mind.

'Adonei, what is going on with Rahn? He's being civil enough, but he seems to be feeling Eden out like he'd do with a suspect on one of his cases.'

*He has every right to be protective of you, Chrysalyn,* Adonei said quietly, seriously.

'Really? Why is that?' she snarled sarcastically along their link.

*He is your mate.*

A sip of coffee slipped down the wrong pipe into her lungs. "Oh please!" she hacked around rough racking coughs. Oops, she hadn't meant to say that out loud.

Rahn's head snapped around and his golden brown gaze captured hers. No mask. No schooled features. No pretense. Only true and genuine concern was mirrored there.

He reached out a hand and covered hers gently. "What was that, Chrys? What's wrong, love?" His words were pitched low in his throat with a smooth and inviting timbre, laced with care. Bastard.

Before she could answer, Eden wiped his mouth on a crisp linen napkin and tossed it gracefully onto the table next to his half empty plate.

Chrys frowned as she watched him tidy up his area as if he were leaving. What the hell did Eden have to be uncomfortable about? She was the one sharing an apartment with the most striking man in all of creation. And that damned English accent of his made her body shiver until she clenched her thighs together to keep from coming in her fitness pants. And she wasn't supposed to want him, damn it! Eden was a welcome distraction, damn it.

"If you'll excuse me, Ms. Geyer."

She schooled her features, wanting nothing more than to snap her neck to the side and settle her fist on her hip. Ms. Geyer? What happened to calling her Chrysalyn?

Eden rose smoothly to his feet. "I believe I shall go and see about arranging a tour for our next port of call. Perhaps we can finish our conversation later?"

And now her welcome distraction extracted himself from her presence. Sigh. Maybe she could still salvage the situation? She smiled and opened her mouth to agree, but Rahn cut her off.

"You know, love," he crooned, turning to her. "I was thinking perhaps we could take a private tour of Ibiza when we get to the Balearic Islands. One of the owners brought along a few toys, including a jet boat. You game, Chrys?"

Raising a hand in the universal I surrender gesture, Eden gave a slight bow and left as quickly as he'd appeared.

Rahn grinned like a rogue. God, she wanted to smack the cocky grin off his face. Besides, he had no intention of taking her anywhere. He was just trying to head off Eden. Damned man.

With schooled features and a plastic smile of her own, she eased her plate back and away, along with the coffee she hadn't finished.

"You arrogant, self-centered, son of a…"

"What? What'd I do?" Rahn asked with wide-eyed innocence. If she'd been a novice she would have actually believed the sinless-as-an-angel reaction. Out of her seat, she stilled when he swiveled around in his chair and wrapped his fingers firmly around her biceps, preventing her from leaving.

"Where are you going?"

"Last I checked, I was on vacation and not reporting to anyone. Not even our boss," she growled quietly, not wanting to draw attention to their little quarrel in the middle of a packed eatery. Especially since the restaurant was on-board ship and she'd surely have to see at least some of these people again.

"Chrys, baby, don't be mad."

"Don't be mad? I'm stuck on this damned floating palace for three months and you just chased away my potential hang-out buddy. Now what the hell am I supposed to do? Just sit around with my thumb up my ass, bored out of my head?"

"Sweetheart…"

"Don't you dare sweetheart me, Rahn."

"Chrys, I meant what I said. I do want to spend time with you, and I really did look into some private tours for us. Just last night, actually, right after I came aboard."

"Wha…?"

"When I joined you in the hot tub this morning, it wasn't meant to be a one-time event."

He pulled her closer until she stood between his long legs. Aw, hell, her insides were going all gooey. *Come on, girlfriend, snap that spine in place.* Hmmm, the spine wasn't listening. Just great.

"I intend to make up for all the time I spent without you."

"Oh, be real, Rahn. You were just postulating, doing the mark-my-territory thing."

"You want me to be honest, Chrys?"

"Yes, damn it." She almost lost her train of thought when he took both her hands in his and kissed each knuckle. The heat of his inner thighs burned through the fabric of her workout pants and scalded her legs where they connected with his knees.

"Here's real for you, love. I plan to seduce you. And most importantly, I plan to keep you. Period."

# CHAPTER FIVE

He released her hands and slowly eased his strong arms around her waist. His gaze was hot, unwavering as he slowly eased her even closer. Oh god, he was going to kiss her right here in the restaurant! Her stomach danced wildly, and like a puppet on a string, her feet followed his direction without her permission. Her lips tingled in anticipation of feeling his mouth on hers, his wide solid chest pressed against hers. Oh, dear god. She had to go right now. Either that or melt into the glossy varnish of the hardwood floors.

She pushed away.

"Chrys?" he asked, his voice full of what she could only describe as expectancy. And not only did she know what he wanted, she actually wanted to give it to him. What the hell?

"I'm going to the spa, Rahn. Alone."

"Fine. I'll walk you to the elevator."

"Rahn, I don't need..."

But he was already out of his seat, guiding her through the fancy glass double doors and toward the elevator with a hand at the small of her back.

He steered her into a little nook she hadn't noticed on her way into the restaurant. The second her body disappeared into the shadows, his big body blocked out the rest of the light as he swooped in for the kiss she hadn't allowed at the table. And, lord, could he kiss.

She tried to resist, but after a few seconds of deliciously intimate nibbling, the quiet moan locked in her throat slipped through. Then Chrys let him take her very breath away. His lips were insistent as they moved over hers. His earthy male scent mixed with the chocolate mocha coffee he'd been drinking and stole her very senses. Her body arched into his and earned a ragged groan as his rapidly swelling cock pressed against her belly. He held her so tight. How wonderful to be engulfed in his embrace, held so securely against his honed body.

It felt good to know she was the cause of the flex and ripple of muscle under her fingers. His pecs and abs tightened and fluttered as she explored his body through the kiss.

Reluctant to come up for air, Chrys let one of her hands slip up the side of his neck and bury itself in his thick, silky hair. She almost tightened her grip to the scalp and pulled him back to her mouth when he eased away.

"Chrys, baby, I've missed you so much. I don't know if this is the right time, but I've got to tell you this."

Suddenly, apprehension bit at the base of her spine. What was he going to say? Had he changed his mind about his intention to seduce her? Considering the fact they'd been estranged until just last night, should she be surprised if he walked away?

Then her spirit guide, without her having to ask, sent reassuring care and love through their bond and she instantly relaxed. What did Adonei know that she didn't? She'd have to have a long talk with that damned lion as soon as she got some time to herself.

"Chrys, listen, I know I practically disappeared after you got engaged to what's-his-name." The way he spit out what's-his-name made her smile. "But I've never stopped caring for you. Wanting you. The only reason I asked for a transfer to London was because I couldn't stand to see you with someone else. I still can't."

He leaned down, pressed his forehead against hers and waited.

"So," she said on a sigh as his hands gently caressed the tense muscles of her lower back. "What do you want, Rahn?"

"I want you, love."

She went still as stone. Now why hadn't she expected such an answer? Because she hadn't believed anything he'd said this morning. And now she felt caught in the headlights. It had never been a feeling she enjoyed, whether the situation was good or not.

But, damn it, if she was going to be a deer in the headlights, Chrysalyn Geyer wasn't going to stand in traffic alone. Her hands dropped away from his chest as she tried to create some space between them. She would have succeeded except for the wall at her back.

"Why are you really here, Rahn? Is it because you have a murder to investigate, a case to solve? Are you here for work or for me?"

He gritted his teeth and hesitated. And she had her answer.

"Bye, Rahn."

"Damn, it, woman."

Squeezing past him, she'd made it almost a whole foot away when she was snatched back against a wall of a rock-hard chest. Then the marvelously muscular man planted a sweet peck on her cheek.

"You know I can't tell you. But I will say I've learned from losing you the first time. Work will never take your place. Not this time, love." He kissed her again, this time so gently she felt tears gather behind her eyes. She pushed him back with a deep, though purposely annoyed-sounding, intake of breath.

"Check in with me after you're done at the spa."

She started. He held up his hand in a conciliatory gesture and continued. "I know you can take care of yourself, but I mean it, Chrys. Be careful off by yourself." This followed by a ground-out "Please", before he strode away.

Gaze glued to his retreating back, Chrys allowed herself a moment to admire his ass. Damn, he looked good in jeans. A lopsided grin tipped up one side of her mouth as she stepped inside the elevator.

Reaching out to her spirit guide, Chrys called to the big cat.

'Adonei, did you catch that?'

*Of course. It is my task to look after you, is it not?*

'Well, yeah, but it looks like you might have to fight Rahn for the job. By the way, you've never been so silent while I was in the company of a man lately. Only with Rahn.'

*He is your mate. It is only right to give him that respect.*

'Mate, eh? But why now? Why not years ago?' Maybe the knowledge would have kept both of them from making stupid mistakes.

*Because neither of you were ready to accept what you meant to each other then. Hence, it was not made known to me the importance of this human male.*

'And we are now? Ready, I mean?' she asked with a snort and a grin.

*It would seem so, yes.*

'Well, mate or not, if he thinks he's gonna start ordering me around, he's got another think coming.'

The elevator stopped and slid silently open. Chrys

stepped out and her mouth, which seemed to be falling open often these days, made the trip again. The entrance to the opulent spa was a set of wide gold and glass doors with Clinique La Paris written in elegant frosted script across the panes. A massage, manicure and pedicure awaited her, but thoughts of the interactions with Rahn intruded. That, along with Adonei's words, ran rampant through her brain. Mate. Mate. Mate?

It was useless to try to hide the chemistry with Rahn, especially when her body responded so eagerly to his touch. Not to mention he was genuinely a good guy. Hell, who was she kidding? If there was a word for beyond attracted, it would almost sum up her feelings for the man.

She checked in with the technician and was shown to a plush private room to change. Her toes wiggled as the warmth from the heated tile eased into the soles of her feet. It was so soothing, she was almost reluctant to climb up on the massage table and pull the sheet over her naked body. Her mind strayed to Rahn again, to the desire she saw in his eyes when he looked at her, the softness with which he touched her. The fierceness of his loving as he took her with lips, teeth and tongue. Immediately, her nipples tingled and soon stabbed into the warm blanket she lay on.

Three months of vacation, eh? But that was her predicament, not his. He was, after all, working on a case. Would he rejoin her on the ship after he wrapped up his investigation in Rome, or simply fly home alone? She had no idea, but she had the whole crossing of the Mediterranean before she had to worry about it. If she played her cards right, at least some of her too-long trip would be interesting. If she could just manage to keep a little part of herself from falling.

\* \* \* \* \*

Eden took the elevator up to his sprawling apartment. Ignoring the call of both the pharaoh and her charges, he whipped off his day clothes, neatly folded the cargo pants and t-shirt and left them on top of the washing machine. He strode to the master bedroom and yanked on his customary all-black hunting garb, then changed his mind. Where he was going, the slacks and silk shirt would stand out. He opted for a black sweatsuit instead and was out the door in less than five minutes.

In the fitness area, he walked around the large wide-open rooms. Finally, Eden spotted a woman who fit the description of the last one he'd been instructed to correct. As he followed her from the fitness area to the indoor pool, he sighed inwardly. The female didn't exude any apprehension or concern. In fact, she didn't seem to notice being followed at all. No thrill to the hunt. No exhilaration or surge of energy as on other forays. Strange.

"This is fucking boring," he mumbled to himself. His steps were silent, but he'd spoken too loudly and caused the specimen to turn around and look behind her. Damn it. He knelt and pretended to tie his shoelace.

He waited for his pharaoh to speak to him while surveying the occupants. Nothing. No hints or clues as to who he was supposed to exact justice upon. Now he wished he'd taken a moment to answer her when she'd called to him while he changed his clothes.

But that damned hybrid infidel who'd practically accosted Chrysalyn at the breakfast table had him charged up and wired for sound. Seething didn't come close to describing his agitation.

He chastised himself while resisting the urge to roll his eyes toward the ceiling. "Get your mind into the game, Eden." But his brain wouldn't cooperate. It kept turning back toward the beautiful and exotic Chrysalyn.

Their time together at breakfast had been pleasant until her big coworker showed up. Chrysalyn seemed completely comfortable with the man. If Eden wasn't mistaken, the fellow appeared to be of Egyptian birth. But no, his skin was too light, his speech too Western. But he couldn't take the chance that this Rahn person came from the same homeland. If the bastard was indeed a kinsman and saw Eden acquiring Chrysalyn the way he intended to, his plans would be foiled. He'd become an outcast.

For the first time in ten years of cleansing the world of the unworthy, Eden was nervous. A bizarre and unwelcome sensation. Why was this happening to him, and why now?

He let his intended prey go on alone and sat down on one of the cushioned seats along the hallway. Quieting his mind he called out to his pharaoh. Again, nothing. The voice of his devoted pharaoh and harem keeper did not penetrate the morass of confusion that assailed him. No spiritual awareness. No voice in his head. Just a big black void.

Inwardly, his heart pounded at the prospect of something having happened to his beloved tarot reader. Never one to bring unnecessary attention to himself, Eden forced his feet to take calm, measured steps back to his apartment. Suddenly a thought flashed into the forefront of his mind. The Empress. The apprehension grew. He had to know what the hell was going on with that damned card.

Eden stepped over the threshold into his foyer. Once inside, he pulled a deep cleansing breath into his lungs and let it whoosh out. Again, in and out. The third time around, he finally felt the tension begin to leach from his limbs and relaxation take its place. His harem keeper was where he'd left her. All was well.

*Beloved, what is wrong? You are tense?*

Eden removed his shoes at the door, strode to her case and gently removed her from the shelf.

"I needed you while I was on the hunt and you did not respond. I did not like it."

*But, beloved, I never accompany you on the hunt. We always speak before you depart...*

Yes, damn it, he knew that. But this time he'd needed her, needed her presence in his head. Who the hell cared what she always did or didn't do? The only thing that mattered was right here and now.

Easing down into his favorite oversized chair near the coffee table, Eden set his harem keeper down on the coffee table, picked up the black and gold tarot deck he kept there and shuffled it.

The Empress. Upside down.

Again, he shuffled, yet drew the same card.

Last time he'd asked about this card, his lovely pharaoh blew him off. Not this time.

"I want to know what this fucking card means and right now."

She remained quiet a moment. Eden knew she was preparing some kind of bullshit answer, but he wasn't going for it. His gut churned. Sweat erupted from his brow and crept down the side of his face, dampening the skin all the way down to his neck. He had a feeling Chrysalyn might be affected by this particular draw as well as himself.

"Tell me what this card means or you will find yourself in need of an heir to take up your rule."

Snapping her lovely brown porcelain neck was no hardship for him. He'd simply have another made. Or better yet, allow one of her charges to take her place. They were growing tired of her heavy-handed tactics anyway.

*Beloved, there is no need to be angry. I do not believe you have selected this card for you, but for someone else. Someone you will meet or have recently encountered.*

"Just tell me what the fuck it means," he growled. His nostrils flared as the tip of his nose smashed against her dainty little porcelain one. Then silence. Finally, she spoke, though her exasperated tone made him feel more like a scolded little boy than her master. Fine, he'd deal with it later.

*As a man, it indicates the weakening of the figure of your beloved, either because you are experiencing your feelings and sentiments less intensely, or the woman is losing love because she is physically or emotionally distant. That is all.*

Her voice trailed off.

Eden leaned his head against the backrest of the chair. With understanding came relief and the knots in his stomach loosened. It was so clear to him now. The man who wanted Chrysalyn, the Rahn asshole, was losing her. The woman was losing love for him. She must be coming to realize how good she and Eden would be together. After all, she did appear to be a smart female.

With a bit more pep in his step, Eden kissed his harem keeper on the very forehead he'd been ready to smash moments before. Setting her back in her case, he touched his fingers to his lips and blew her a kiss, not bothering to hide a grin.

Yes, she would have to be destroyed. He simply couldn't have his little taskmaster trying to make Chrysalyn's life difficult once they got together.

And get together, they would.

# CHAPTER SIX

Rahn paid a courtesy visit to the ship's captain, Todd Laurens. Thankfully, the shrewd and experienced man was more than pleased to have a discreetly armed and qualified agent on board. After dismissing the lower-ranking officers from the bridge, Captain Laurens and his First Officer, Lt. Spans, offered to provide any assistance Rahn needed. He'd been ordered to keep a tight wrap on the details of the case and they were all on the same page. The captain and the government of the ship's origin wanted nothing more than to keep it quiet that this vessel might be connected to a string of grisly murders spanning the Mediterranean and beyond.

After the brief meeting, he returned to the apartment he shared with Chrys, had a quick lunch, then scouted the ship from top to bottom. He noticed nothing out of the ordinary, but Mahpiya's constant growling in the back of his mind let him know something was more than wrong.

The sun was setting by the time he made it back to the spacious suites. Damn it, Chrys wasn't back yet. And there was no message on the voice mail from her, either.

Rahn prowled from one end of the huge apartment to the other. Through the living room and dining room, into the kitchen and back. The next trip took him from his bedroom, out the sliding glass doors onto the deck and into Chrys' room. Her enticing spiced ginger scent was everywhere. He stood next to her oversized bed and couldn't resist reaching down to grab one of her pillows. Face buried in the center of it, he inhaled deeply, drew her rich, womanly scent into his lungs.

The smell brought the memory of how perfectly her thighs cradled his head while he lapped at her succulent pussy. How her soft moans wrapped around his cock and squeezed relentlessly. The honeyed taste of the soft skin of her lips, the curve of her neck and her breasts with their chocolate cherry nipples. His fingers itched to bury themselves in the cottony down of her hair and pull her lush, inviting mouth against his. Wanted to feel her sharp teeth nibble and nip all of his sensitive areas as she explored his body.

She was such a beautiful female. All dark skin, light brown eyes and short midnight silky hair. He wished she'd let it grow out to its former length so he could wrap it around his hands while he rode her from behind. Chrys was a succulent treat, like syrup dribbled over cinnamon ice cream. And she was his. His woman. His damned stubborn woman who hadn't bothered to let him know where she was all day.

He tossed the pillow haphazardly into the center of her bed and stomped back to the kitchen. He hit the speakerphone button on the satellite phone hanging on the wall, punched in a number and listened to the line ring while he pulled out the bowl of leftover poké.

His boss picked up the phone and Rahn confirmed their worst suspicions. Each of the murders had indeed occurred in a port of call right before this particular ship departed for its next destination. And it was getting more and more difficult to keep the information from leaking out to the public.

"So what do you have?" Geri asked. Her fingernails click, click, clicked on her computer keyboard in the background.

"Captain Laurens wants to accompany me into town at the next port. I'm having a hard time convincing him not to get involved. I wish you'd warned me he's a former Navy man. Getting him to stay out of this is proving difficult," he said around a mouthful of food. It was quickly washed down with a swig of iced tea.

"Is difficult? Does that mean you haven't succeeded?"

"Hardly. I reminded him that our agency's survival depends on our ability to remain secret. Blend in with the populace. I pointed out that it would be strange for him, a man who's sure to be recognized by both crew and passengers, to be seen with me in the seedier parts of each town."

"Didn't work, eh?"

"Not even close. *He* reminded *me* that nothing about the victims or the places they were found was seedy. Still, only he and his first officer know why I'm here."

"And what about Chrys?"

"I told her I'm investigating a case in Rome."

"And she bought it?" Geri asked with disbelief.

"Doubt it. She's a smart woman. I'm sure she's already figured that if I needed to be in Rome for something important, I'd be there by now, and not tooling through the Mediterranean on a luxury cruise ship."

"Any leads?"

"Nothing other than a few vague descriptions of a possible suspect," Rahn reported. "But something odd is going on, something off. I can feel it. By the way, there's someone I want you to check out for me. A man named Eden Pall. Five foot, ten inches. About a hundred and seventy pounds. I'm not sure where he's from, but he looks and sounds of Egyptian descent."

"Egyptian? Why don't you use your own contacts to run him down?"

"I already put a call in to my aunt. She's working on it. I'd already planned to stay a couple of days at her house in Alexandria when we pull into port, anyway. She'll have something for me by the time we get there."

One of the advantages of having a family full of law enforcement specialists. Whether at home in England or Egypt, there was the benefit of contacts who happened to be relatives.

Finished with his snack, he set the bowl in the sink and rinsed it quickly.

"Geri, I'd still like you to pull a report on him. It couldn't hurt. And it'll be days before we get to Egypt and Aunt Suman won't call me on board, no matter what. It would be just my luck that Chrys would answer the phone. My aunt never could lie to Chrys."

Geri's "uh-huh" of agreement was quickly followed by a nosy, "Any chance you and Chrys might hook up?"

"Speaking of hook up," Rahn deliberately blew her off. "What happened to Chrys and what's-his-name? Why didn't they get married?"

"Well, I'm not sure if I should tell you this, but knowing Chrys, she probably won't spill it." Geri paused, sounding a bit uncomfortable with the subject. Rumor had it his boss felt personally responsible for Chrys' unhappiness. "You know I introduced her to Sean, right? After she decided you would never ask her to marry you, I was just trying to help her move on. He'd held some of the highest positions on the Department of Justice payroll. And now we know why. The man was an expert at keeping secrets, especially his own."

"What are you getting at?" Rahn asked impatiently.

Fingers raked a path through his hair as he snatched the phone off the hook, put it to his ear and paced. The carpet on the living room floor was so spongy and thick underneath his boots that he left tracks. He hated leaving tracks. Geri continued.

"Well, Chrys found out he had a whole 'nother family right here in Denver. She'd met a young boy named Alex, who Sean introduced as his son. Chrys thought it was just some kind of 'Big Brothers-Big Sisters' thing. After all, Sean is white as the driven snow and Alex is African American, like Chrys. Turned out Sean was married to the boy's mother and had been keeping Chrys a secret. Not to mention Chrys would have been wife number four, which he'd also neglected to mention, though she'd asked him flat out how many times he'd been married. Hell, if he couldn't be honest, hid a wife, a son and a daughter, and couldn't stay married after three tries, Chrys certainly didn't want to get saddled with someone like that. Especially not at twenty-five years old. So, she canceled the wedding and cut him off."

"So, did you cut his balls off slowly, or in one quick swipe?" Rahn asked, bristling at the thought of someone hurting Chrys in such a callous way. Bastard. Perhaps Rahn would look him up when he got back to the States.

"I don't know how, but we managed to keep it quiet. There would have been plenty of agents upset about the way it all went down. They all love Chrys. Of course, she threatened to 'disappear' both me and Delaine if we touched Sean. She just wanted it to all go away, so she simply pushed it to the back of her mind and threw herself into her work. She's been working herself to the bone ever since, which is why I forced her to take this vacation."

"About this vacation, Eden Pall is supposedly taking a holiday. But he's a bit too interested in Chrys."

And speaking of Chrys, where the hell was the woman?

Mahpiya's voice slipped into his mind. *She is near.*

'Near and here are two different things. I told her to check in with me, damn it. Doesn't she know it's dangerous?'

*Chrysalyn senses an odd darkness in the spirit realm, but cannot determine whether it is focused on her or not, so no, she does not realize it is dangerous. She returned here after her spa treatment, but it was during the time you spoke with the leader of this vessel.*

Rahn's attitude instantly reduced from an angry tyrannosaurus rampage down to miffed male seethe. At least Chrys wasn't avoiding him. Wait a minute. How did Mahpiya know where Chrys was if she couldn't speak thought-to-thought with her yet?

*Adonei told me,* Mahpiya replied in a sultry purr. *He has been keeping me…company.*

'Oh, yeah? What kind of company, Mah?'

*Do not play games with me, cub. You are aware we are mates. And while you have yet to secure your female, Adonei has wasted no time securing his.*

Oh, god, he didn't want to know any more. Just the thought of mating was a seriously nasty turn-on. What the hell was wrong with him?

*I always believed you were more lion than human,* Mahpiya crooned. The transparent image of the majestic beast slowly groomed its paws.

Geri's voice streamed through the earpiece of the phone and broke through the private conversation between Rahn and his spirit guide.

"Rahn, are you there?"

"Uh, yeah, sorry, boss. Just thinking up various ways to keep Chrys off this case and out of danger without tying her up," he said, pacing again. But tying her up held a certain appeal. At least he'd know where she was.

"I don't envy you, Rahn. If she finds out you're spying on her, she may just kick your ass," she said glibly.

"I'm not really spying on her, just trying to keep her ass out of trouble. And if I recall, you sent me on this assignment, so my being here is your fault. I'll let her kick *your* ass," he chuckled. "I'll check in with you before I leave the ship at the next port."

"No problem. Talk to you later."

The second he clicked off the satellite phone and strode into the kitchen to hang it up, he called for his spirit guide again.

'Okay, now where is she?'

*Did we not promise to help you, shall we say, ambush Chrysalyn? And so we shall.*

With that, the air in front of the pantry shimmered and shifted until it solidified into Mahpiya's corporeal body. She was such a powerful creature, so regal and perfect that Rahn almost regretted that no one could see or hear her except for him. He'd love to get a photo of her rolling from her side onto her back with her tongue lolling out. He'd never seen her so playful. That Adonei must be one hell of a man, er, lion.

*Do not concern yourself with my mate. We must help you win yours.* Then Mah stood with all the grace and attitude of the feline she was. She padded silently away. Rahn watched with curiosity. Where was she going?

The second the thought formed along the bond, the lioness swung her large head and pinned him with an amber stare.

*Are you not coming*, hoksila? *Your mate has gone to dinner. Surely you do not plan to go after her dressed like that.Besides, after your day of scouting, you smell...interesting.*

Then she laughed at him. Again. How the hell did she

do that? And all at his expense. Good thing he knew she had his best interests at heart.

Less than half an hour later, Rahn and Mahpiya left the apartment. Rahn had to admit, it was pretty cool to walk down the wide civilized hallways with a bad-assed African lioness at his side.

Now all he had to do was capture a flesh and blood female hunter—Chrys.

\* \* \* \* \*

Unlike this morning's breakfast bistro, this restaurant was dimly lit with an intimate atmosphere. The place was decked out for a performance of some kind of mystery song-and-dance dinner theater. A carpet of artificial fog crept across the floor, disturbed by the incoming crowd. Slightly scented votive candles glowed in the center of each table. The mystery in the air complemented the props and background music. Not creepy, but seductive.

Regardless of the lighting, two steps through the door, he spotted Chrys across the room and stopped short. She sat at a table with Eden Pall. Again. What the hell was she doing with that guy?

'Mah, you're aware of how I'm feeling?'

*Aren't I always*, hoksila?*

Yes, it was a stupid question, but he was pissed the hell off and couldn't say he was thinking rationally. But he was a master of pretending to be coolheaded.

'Be a dear and give Adonei a glimpse of my fabulous attitude so he can pass it on to Chrys, hm?'

*I will do as you ask, my charge, though you may want to reconsider.*

'Because?' he asked impatiently.

*Because there are times when it is better to be wise rather than right.*

'Perhaps. But not tonight. And while you're conversing with Adonei, lend me your senses. All of them.'

The raw power of the lioness surged through him, amplifying his own ability to see, hear, feel, taste and smell.

Rahn immediately regretted his request. Several women mingled in the small crowd between his position and Chrys' seat across the room. Their strong, much-too-flowery perfume stung his nose. Gah, how awful. He practically gagged.

Yet the strongest of the lioness's talents was sight. From this distance, he saw the nap of the viscose used to weave the cloth of Chrys' dress. The glittery lotion on her skin made the cinnamon shade appear dusted with diamonds. The candlelight reflected off the strands of cropped waves and curls on her lovely head.

He didn't miss the sudden rise of Chrys' chest. The quiet gasp told him the exact second Mah and Adonei passed his emotions on to her. She was getting more from him at this moment than either of them had bargained for. More anger than he'd ever expressed in word or deed. More raging possessiveness. More raw, erotic need.

Her big brown eyes found and then followed him as he wove his way around the tables. The place was packed with patrons who had no idea that a volatile situation had just walked in on two legs. Chrys' expression was a mix of confusion and apprehension and he knew she hadn't realized until now just how much he saw her as his. And she'd have an even clearer picture before the night was through. That was for damned sure.

The Eden creep spotted him as he made a beeline for their table. Why the hell did they have to pick one all the way on the other side of the room? Well, at least it was close to an exit door. Wait a minute. The Eden creep probably intended to whisk Chrys through that fucking door for a little evening interlude under the stars.

"Hello, love," Rahn whispered. A quick kiss on Chrys' cheek was followed by a steel-laced, "Eden, how nice to see you again."

Both occupants were doing a hell of a job schooling their features. Chrys' mouth hadn't fallen open nor had her eyes widened to the size of tea saucers. And Eden's distinct deep golden features were a blank mask. But this time, when the older man started to rise, Rahn moved smoothly with a gesture of conciliation.

"Please don't get up on my account. I'm not staying." *And neither are you*, he thought, taking in the display of Chrys' luscious curves, courtesy of a dazzling deep purple spaghetti strap dress. "Chrys, would you step outside with me for a moment. I called into the office today and I have a message for you." Well, it was true, just not in that order.

*Ah, what a dazzling smile*, Rahn grunted. He didn't appreciate she was giving it to the wrong man as she rose gracefully from the table, telling Eden she'd be right back. Rahn motioned toward the exit door not five paces from her chair.

The second she was over the threshold, he grasped her by the forearm, pulled her into the nearest alcove and completely lost his mind.

Chrys rounded on him, and hissed, "I was just about to have dinner, Rahn. This had better be important, damn it. So, what's the message?"

Angry didn't begin to describe her current mood, but he sensed she was more upset about her deepened breathing and the inability to suppress the flush of her skin. He inhaled deeply and was rewarded with the scent of her arousal. Mmm, the unique fragrance of her sex was just beginning to waft up from between her thighs. He grinned. The smell hadn't been there while she sat at the table, so at least she wasn't creaming for the Eden creep.

She'd asked him a question, but there was no way he could respond. Not now. Not when her sweet pussy called his name with its honeyed aroma. Not when his fingers itched to slide over her bare arms, the skin so smooth and soft, like endless candied silk stretched over sleek muscle. He almost cried out for God to help him when the tips of her nipples beaded and plumped under his gaze. His eyes followed the movement of her strong, slender fingers as they knotted into a fist and settled over her hip. And such a lovely hip—lush, full, wide and connected to a succulent, spankable ass that he wanted to grip, and then guide to his quickly rising erection.

"Rahn?" she asked grumpily. Now her left foot tapped on the floor of the alcove. Her perfectly polished nails peeked out of the tip of her strappy sandals. Painted to match the royal purple of her evening dress. Damn, even her feet were pretty. Each little digit looked just ripe for sucking. The image of his lips wrapped around each one made him look away and out toward the deck. The lacquered wood was awash in bright starlight, while the deep waters of the ocean reflected the bright moon like an endless sapphire pool. Definitely a night for lovers.

He remained silent. Her toe tapped faster.

"Rahn, I asked you a question."

Aw, hell.

"What's the message from Geri...mmmphff!"

It was moments like this when he was grateful he'd only asked Mahpiya to lend him her senses. If he'd asked for her supernatural strength, the rough way he'd grabbed Chrys might have bruised her tender skin. But damn, he needed to touch and he needed to touch her *now*. Smashed against his chest, her nipples tightened into teasing little treats hidden by the top of her dress. The sensual stab of the swollen points rasped against his skin through his linen shirt. Teased and tormented him because of his enhanced senses. His hands traveled the length of her back, following the curve of her spine as he dipped his head and took her mouth in a kiss so hot it singed the tips of his ears.

Her flavor burst upon his tongue. She tasted so good. Felt so good. As her apprehension melted away, her lips softened underneath his. Strong fingers sank into the front of his shirt and held on as she gave herself up to the kiss and let him feast as his tongue twisted and twined around hers.

He groaned into her mouth. His hand wandered up over her ribs and confirmed a niggling suspicion—she wasn't wearing a bra. The firm breast filling his palm was all her. God, such a curvy little thing. Perfect, pleasingly plump. And his.

Rahn left a trail of heated nips over the shell of her ear and down the slope of her neck. Her breathing deepened and he reveled in every rise and fall of her chest, the slight flush under her skin, the fullness of her kiss-swollen cherry lips.

One hand slid down over her hip and around to the plump globes of her ass. And he did exactly what he'd been thinking moments before. He pulled her hard against his groin and ground his hips forward. She looked surprised, thunderstruck and just a bit wary of her reaction to him. The woman seemed unsure whether to kiss him again or run like hell. His mouth kicked up into an irrepressible grin. He wanted to preen like Mahpiya did after a successful hunt. Why? The unflappable Chrysalyn Geyer was completely out of sorts and it was all his fault.

"Uh, so…my goodness," she said on a rush of breath. It took her a second to get it together. Then she let her artificial career agent's face slide into place.

She took a half-step back and said, "So, what's the message from work?"

She was too quick to recover. He'd have to work on that.

A rough edge he'd never experienced before with a woman rode him hard. The need to mark her, mate her was like a vise wrapped around his lungs that he'd never be free of until the deed was done. He'd never felt so predatory, so dangerous. Ever.

"First, I said I called in today. However, I did not say the message was from work."

"What?"

"Our boss says hi and enjoy your vacation. But the message, Chrys, is from me."

"Rahn, I don't understand. What message?" she said curtly, brows knitted with irritation. He knew what that meant. She wanted to know what was up. Right damned now. And Rahn wanted nothing more than to oblige.

"The message, love, is this—lose the Eden guy and meet me in our apartment in ten minutes. Or else."

"Or else? Really?" she said as the fist slammed back onto her hip. She couldn't tap her foot because he stood too close. "And what's the or else, asshole?"

One strong arm under her bottom lifted her clean off the floor, the other held her firmly, but gently, by the nape as he covered her mouth once again. Her legs automatically wrapped around his waist, causing her dress to ride up in a bunch around her hips. A single step had her back flush against the alcove wall as he kissed her hard, hungry. Miles and miles of gorgeous thigh and ass were bare to his questing fingers. And the scrap of cloth she called underwear was no barrier at all. A fingertip skimmed her left butt cheek. The nerves underneath her skin quivered clear down to the slit of her pussy. So he followed that quiver with his hands and allowed himself to play. Mmm, what a wonderland her body was.

Burning with need for this woman, Rahn poured the energy from the fire in his blood into the kiss, into each touch. God, he was going up in smoke. The ragged moans rising up in her throat told him she wasn't immune.

He eased away a bit and let her down. Her feet touched the ground and she wobbled. Well, maybe she didn't quite wobble, but it was an excuse to keep his hands on her a while longer. Unable to keep the rasp from his voice, he spoke through gritted teeth.

"Ten minutes, Chrys. Don't make me come looking for you."

Chest heaving, he backed away and disappeared out onto the deck. He didn't wait for a yes or no, didn't plan to give her a choice. And by the time he was done with her, she would only want to make one decision. Him.

The man was too damned bossy, but he sure had a talented tongue. Never mind the fact her heart had belonged to him for too many years to count. Even after he'd broken it, the bastard. She'd forgiven long before he'd ever apologized, so why did her heart and her head have such a hard time agreeing? One said he was the one for her. Even her spirit guide approved of the man. But the other said no way, that he would just hurt her again. She really needed some help here. She looked down at her watch. Seven minutes left to make up her mind.

'Adonei, come to me.'

Immediately, the semi-transparent image of her spirit guide's regal form appeared behind her eyes as she made her way back to the table where Eden waited. Other than Rahn, Chrys didn't think she'd ever met a more handsome man. And from Egypt, of all places, his home was just outside Alexandria, one of the ports of call on this trip. Maybe he would give her a personal tour of the

Lighthouse of Pharos once they reached port?

A muted snuffle sounded in her mind as Adonei shook his maned head. *Your mate would not approve, woman.*

'But I haven't accepted him as my mate. I'm not sure I even want to.' Now why the hell had she bothered to say those words? Even if she tried to lie to herself, lying to Adonei was just plain impossible.

*I cannot assist you if you are not willing to be honest.*

'Yes, I know, Adonei,' she admitted with a sigh. She'd known the second Rahn laid down his little ultimatum what she would do. Would he always get his way? Hell no. After all, she was no punk bitch. But tonight, the man looked like a hunter after her hide, and she wanted to give it to him. She'd never felt such an innate need to submit before. Even when she'd been engaged to Sean, she would have laughed in his face if he'd ordered her to be somewhere. The difference was she wanted to be exactly where Rahn asked—no, told— her to be. In five more minutes.

"Hi, Eden. Sorry about the interruption," she said with the brightest smile she could muster. She didn't bother to sit down.

"Is something wrong, Chrysalyn?" he asked pointedly, but politely.

Honestly, she replied, "No, nothing's wrong." Adonei's rumble of approval resonated down their bond. "But I have to go. My coworker called into the office today." Which was true. "Something's come up." Yeah, Rahn's king of the jungle act, along with his thick cock. "I'm sorry, but I won't be able to stay for the dinner show. Maybe another time?"

*There will be no other time, woman,* Adonei shot down the bond. But she couldn't take the words back now and would just have to deal with it later.

Eden stood, graciously took her hand and kissed it gently. "Another time, then. Do you require an escort?" he asked sweetly.

Adonei growled.

"No, thanks. I'll be fine. Goodnight, Eden."

She was sure he responded in kind, but she'd already made for the door.

Their condo was close now. If she hurried, she'd make it at exactly ten minutes. But running for any man was out of the question. Oh, she'd be there all right, honest enough with herself to admit she couldn't resist Rahn's call to her body, and had no desire to. But that didn't mean she couldn't take her time. Besides, she wore a formfitting dress and high heels, right?

*Woman, if you were dressed in fitness wear and tennis shoes, you would still manage to be late, if only to prove a point.*

'Adonei!'

But that was as far as her outrage carried, since the big cat was right.

# CHAPTER SEVEN

The woman would choose now to be stubborn. Her ten minutes had come and gone. Rahn wished he could say the same for his Rock of Gibraltar erection. Walking over to the front door for the fifth time in as many minutes, he kicked his shoes off and paced back across the apartment.

Hands on hips, he stared out the sliding glass doors and past the private deck to the dark rolling ocean. He fisted his fingers in the thick drapes just to give his hands something to do. He wanted to play in her soft hair. Wanted to cup her firm ass and lift her against his throbbing cock. Fuck, he was going absolutely nuts.

Damned woman.

'Mah, where the hell is she?' Rahn growled silently.

*I do not know, hoksila. There has yet to be an established bond between you and Chrysalyn, so I cannot yet touch her mind.*

'Well, what about Adonei?' he snapped. 'Can't you just ask him?' He tore his hands away from the curtains, only to run them roughly through his own hair. The insistent need gnawing at his belly for this woman bordered on insane. If it was this bad now, how would it be after they established a relationship? She was five minutes late and he was practically out of his mind. Not something he was familiar with where a female was concerned. With the exception of Mahpiya's occasional absence from his head, Rahn had never been so impatiently alone.

He almost thrust his fingers down to his scalp again, but stopped himself, knowing what Chrys would see when she arrived—a wild-haired, crazed crackpot from the worst B movie he could imagine.

'Damn it, this is ridiculous, Mah. Why do I feel so out of control?'

*It is the mating instinct. The need to claim your mate. Trust me, this is natural.*

'How the hell would you know what's natural? First off, I'm a human, and second, I'm a male.'

*Yes, which only makes you more irrational, cub. I suggest you calm yourself before your mate arrives.*

Cub? Had she called him a cub? Rahn rolled his eyes. The lioness would choose this moment to remind him that he was no more than a child in her eyes. Her endless years and, of course, endless knowledge of dealing with humans gave her just a bit more of an edge in this situation.

He took a deep breath, closed his eyes and reached out for his guide, silently calling her onto this plane. Her big muscular body materialized, stretched out on the living room floor between the glass coffee table and the overstuffed couch. Rahn walked over and sat down on the floor next to her.

"I'm sorry, Mah," he said softly, reaching out a hand to rub her thick muscled shoulder. "I didn't mean to disrespect you. Forgive me?"

*Of course, hoksila. As I said, you are less than rational. It is the mating heat and will ease once you *claim your female. She is quite the prize. A strong hunter, though Adonei does not approve of her choice of casual companions.\**

"Her choice of what?"

But there was no answer. Without warning, Mahpiya's pelt shimmered and shifted. Her body faded until nothing but a faint dusting of her essence floated on the still air before disappearing all together.

"Mah?" All was quiet. Even the small, constantly occupied place in the corner of his mind was silent. It had only happened once before—this morning in the hot tub. He knew exactly what Mahpiya's sudden absence meant.

His cock twitched in anticipation as he sat there cross-legged on the floor, waiting for Chrys to turn the knob on the front door to their apartment.

\* \* \* \* \*

Why did she feel like she was sneaking into her own place? Couldn't possibly have anything to do with the fact she was practically tiptoeing into her own foyer with her shoes in one hand and easing open the door with the other.

Rahn sat on the floor in the dark with a strange light in his eyes. Drapes pulled back, the wide glass panes allowed the evening light to flood into the room. The angle with which the beams reflected off his light amber orbs made him look like a cat caught by a flash of light.

He rose slowly, all sinewy grace and barely leashed power. Damned sexy.

Even the movement of his long legs and wide muscular torso reminded her of one of the big cats out hunting on the Serengeti. So entranced was she by the easy sway of his lean hips, the slight flex of biceps and pecs as he moved, Chrys didn't realize he was practically on top of her until they were toe to toe.

Then he had to go and open his fat mouth and ruin the moment.

"You're late. Where the hell have you been? And why didn't you check in with me earlier like I asked you to?"

*Well, somebody wasn't happy*, she mused sarcastically. At that exact moment, Adonei's presence diminished in her mind until he was barely a speck on the radar. Obviously backing off to leave her to deal with the miffed male towering over her.

'Traitor,' she hissed along the link. Good thing she didn't expect a response because she received none.

"Chrys, I asked you a question, woman."

She snapped her neck to the side, knowing her eyes were wide with incredulity. Talk about a pissy attitude, the man was almost unbearable. The way he snarled down at her, she half expected him to start thumping his chest before tossing her over his shoulder while doing the Tarzan yodel.

Was this Rahn? The same Rahn she'd worked with for years? Cool, level-headed agent, laid-back, easy-going? Puh. Obviously not.

"You didn't ask me a question, Rahn, you asked me two," she snapped back, refusing to be treated like a damned child. Then again, she didn't recognize such behavior from this man, so she wasn't sure what he saw her as. Well, sizzling kisses and hot tub action aside, of course.

"Yeah, and you haven't answered either one of them."

The urge to submit to him while he'd held her up by her backside in a dark alcove just a little while ago faded as completely as Adonei had from her head. Challenge was the new word of the day.

"You're the one working here, Rahn. I'm on

vacation. I'm playing."

"If you play with anyone, it sure as hell better be me!"

"What?" She couldn't believe what she was hearing. "Who the hell do you think you are? I am not accountable to you and owe you no explanations. I'll do what the hell I want, when I want. You're not my man, Rahn. Not anymore, if you ever were in the first place."

She was as hot as a Hawaiian volcano, and not with lust. Anger kindled so fast and high she expected his eyebrows to singe away any second now.

She dropped her shoes on the tiles next to his in the foyer, stepped around him with a humph and headed for her bedroom.

Who the hell did he think he was, anyway? She didn't have to take this macho crap from anyone, damn it. *Even if you need a strong man to handle your stubborn female self?* She couldn't even scold Adonei for the comment because he hadn't made it. Damned conscience. It would choose this moment to show up.

Rahn was so close on her heels she'd swear she felt him breathing rough and hard down the back of her neck. Her arm froze in mid-reach for her doorknob when a firm, but gentle, hand teased her shoulder.

"Make no mistake about it, Chrys. I am your man."

The words were softly spoken, seductive with a hint of a growl. The deep rough timbre sent a thrill through her body. The enticing thrum began at her ankles, eased up the back of her calves and drilled into her thighs just below her butt. The flesh covering the sensitive spot between her ass and her pussy tingled and itched in anticipation of what would follow such a fierce declaration. A declaration he'd never made to her in all the long years they'd known each other.

She found herself spun around and eased back against her bedroom door. Mouths joined in a burning conflagration of lust, but she needed more than her lips on fire. She needed to completely go up in flames.

Chrys reached up to twine her arms around Rahn's neck, pressed closer and relished his shiver when iron-hard pecs made contact with puckering nipples. His chest muscles jumped and flinched. The involuntary movement made her peaks harden faster, stiffer.

Her own soft moans sounded eager and oh-so erotic in her own ears.

Rahn's arms tightened, totally engulfing her with his big beautiful body.

"Mmm, Chrys, baby," he moaned into her mouth, deepening the kiss, tasting, savoring. Overwhelming. "God, you taste so good."

Chrys broke away and rested her forehead against his chest, trying to get her catapulting emotions, not to mention her breathing, under control. But that didn't stop him from exploring her body with a knowledge that should be forbidden to any man on earth. It was just too devastatingly delicious.

He lowered his head and licked her overheated skin from her jawbone down to her collarbone. It felt so good, she could think of nothing to compare it to. When his hands cupped her ass, she didn't protest. As he teased and nibbled along her ear, her dress was hiked up past her hips to settle in silken rolls around her waist. Rahn's strong fingers continued to knead the flesh of her sensitive round cheeks. She gasped when a single finger eased into the cleft of her ass, then lower to the slick folds of her cunt.

It dipped and played until it was completely coated with the juices making their way down the inside of her thighs. Her hips made a perfect figure eight as she sought more of the intense pleasure.

When he removed his hand, Chrys caught the scent of her own dewy arousal. Damn, what a turn-on.

Rahn ground his thick erection against her hip as two fingers slipped up into her juicy pussy. With a subtle curve, the tips hit an overly sensitive bundle of nerves deep inside she hadn't known was there. He stroked once. Twice. Three times.

"Oh my god!" she screeched as that special little spot sent a crackling zing exploding through her womb. Every cell in her body screamed. Thigh muscles quivered while her ass clenched wildly and her fingers dug into Rahn's chest through his shirt. Head thrown back, it hit the door with a thump as she came on the spot.

Rahn dropped to his knees, buried his head between her legs and lapped up the fragrant evidence of her release. All the while, he hummed his approval as he wrapped his tongue around her throbbing clit, gently easing it out of its cowl and into his eager mouth. The combined vibration and suction shot up her slit and kicked off a new round of quivers stronger than the first. The earth shattered around her until she expected the ground to open up and swallow her whole.

"Rahn, please. I need you inside me."

He didn't stop moving his mouth over her flesh. Didn't stop humming over her clit. Didn't stop tormenting her with the long laps of his tongue or the fingers buried inside her.

Oh, and it was good. But damn it, she needed to be fucked. Hard, deep and long.

Reaching down, she sank her fingers into his hair, clear to the scalp and pulled. Easing him away from her soaked flesh, Chrys looked down and her eyes went wide. The man's mouth, nose and cheeks were covered with her own essence. His light brown eyes flashed with hunger and the hard set of his mouth told her she'd interrupted something he relished. And she'd better quickly replace it with something else.

He flashed a wicked grin while he massaged the backs of her knees. "You have interrupted my meal, Chrys."

Her mouth opened and snapped shut on a silent plea. God, he was so damned sexy she couldn't even form the words to describe his tousle-headed, handsome self. She tried to speak again just as his touch moved from the back of her right knee up to the juncture of her thighs and pressed into her swollen lips. Her breath hitched instead. Finally able to string more than two words together, they tumbled out as a strangled plea.

"Oh, Rahn, I need it. Please. Give it to me."

She needed this. Wanted this. Wanted him more than…hell, she couldn't think of anything or anyone that had ever made her feel so desperate. Not even the thrill of hunting and bringing down bad guys.

He grabbed a handful of dress and yanked. The sound of rending threads and popping straps resounded through the huge living room. The little scrap of soaked cloth partially covering her sex went next. Then she was underneath him on the floor.

Only one small problem. He still wore all his clothes.

Chrys sat up and pushed Rahn back on his knees. In a flash she'd unzipped his pants and pushed them down as far as they would go. Instead of taking his dark green silk boxers down with them, she bared his skin a scant bit at a time, nipping as she went. Her tongue flicked out and licked a spot just below his pelvic bone. He jerked, almost doubling over. So she tongued him there until he moaned nonstop.

"Chrys, god, baby! That feels so good."

But it wasn't nearly enough.

Finally her goal, his glorious hard cock, was completely uncovered. It bobbed in front of her face, the shaft a deep mottled caramel. The flared mushroom head wept. She could almost see the fat veins twined around it throbbing in time with her own rapidly beating heart.

The moment her fingers grasped the thick rod, a primal urge rippled through her soul. The need to mark herself with his scent. To be his, and for him to be hers. Leaning forward, Chrys gently rubbed the smooth hard length of him against her cheek. Then across her forehead and down the other side of her face before turning to take him down her throat in one gulp. His scent filled her nostrils even as he filled her mouth.

He yelled. Thighs shook, hands clenched wildly at his sides. The taut tendons of his throat stood out from his neck as he hissed through gritted teeth.

"Aaaah, shit! Chrys!" he pleaded, took in a large gulp of air and begged some more. Just as she'd begged moments before. "Woman, you're killing me."

Humming around his cock certainly wouldn't make it any easier on him, but she felt particularly evil just now and planned to drive him as insane as humanly possible.

He must have caught on when she didn't stop sliding her tongue over him, didn't stop stroking him. She knew the jig was up when he eased her away from his cock. Pants were kicked off, shirt yanked over his head and hands reached out for her. In a split second, she was settled with her creaming slit directly over his hungry cock.

And just when she thought he would plunge to the hilt, he scooped her up in one hand and flipped them both until he was dominant.

Her pussy was so swollen, it throbbed to the point of pain. If he didn't fuck her soon, she would lose it. Her lower lips were so puffy and wet, dew dribbled and pooled into the crack of her ass, making her cheeks clench spasmodically.

Finally he pressed into her sopping entrance.

Only the head of his cock dipped into her scalding pussy, yet it almost did him in. Rahn couldn't believe how close he was to totally losing control and coming right then and there. Gritting his teeth, he reined in the wild urge to surge to the hilt and camp out there for the rest of the night.

Then she moved.

Shit. So much warm slick flesh slid against his, while her cunt pulled on him, begged for the very thing he was trying to hold back. Lowering his head, Rahn sought her lips and poured all his desire and every downright nasty inclination into that lip lock. Her tongue boldly tasted his, joined in a magical dance that sent his head spinning as he slowly eased deeper into her body.

The walls of her sweet channel closed in around his length and squeezed. The woman was absolutely delicious. So wet, tight and his.

The exquisite friction of sliding his hardness into her hot, sopping flesh sent a tremor clear down to the fine hairs on his toes. Rahn couldn't let another second tick by without having them joined lip to lip, chest to chest and cock to pussy.

The inside of Chrys' strong thighs rubbed against his hips as she wrapped her legs around him. Settling her heels into the base of his spine, she tightened her grip and urged him deeper. God, the woman squeezed him everywhere—cock, waist, spine. Not to mention the arms wrapped firmly around his back, holding him so tight, he struggled to breathe. Then again, the demanding rhythm of Chrys' hips keeping time with every thrust of his rod may have had something to do with the lack of air in his lungs. She sucked the very life out of him. And damn, he liked it.

"God, love, you feel so good wrapped around my cock." Rahn eased out slowly, his throbbing erection coated with her dewy juices. "Come for me, Chrys." A ruthless, balls-deep plunge back into her depths. "Come around my cock. Milk me, love."

Her eyes were glazed over with passion. Her answering pant and moan preceded a gentle nudge against his shoulders. Reluctantly, he eased his weight off her and pushed up on his palms. Rahn sucked in a shallow breath at the rush of air flowing between them, cooling the heated flesh of his pecs. That single breath remained locked in his airway after Chrys' hand disappeared into the space between their bodies.

His stomach muscles clenched wildly as her fingers traipsed over the ridges. But she didn't stop there. The woman teased past his abs and wrapped her fingers around the base of his cock just as he pushed forward into her pussy again.

"If I go, you go…oh, oh," she squealed.

The inviting "O" of her luscious lips made him wish he had two cocks, one for her mouth and one for her pussy. Eyes closed, he knew the moment her fingers reached her clit. The quiver and pulse of her sex was immediate.

Death was imminent. There was no way he'd survive such exquisite pleasure. The sensation of her cunt encircling him, combined with the fingers traveling from her clit back to the base of his cock over and over again, shredded any bit of imagined control.

"Oh god, fuck me!" she demanded.

He drove into her, then pulled back until just the flared head remained inside. Then buried himself again. Fast. Faster.

She panted and moaned, mixing an occasional "Oh my god!" with Rahn's own wild grunting.

Just before he went up in flames, Rahn lowered his head and sank his teeth into the soft flesh between Chrys' shoulder and neck. Not enough to draw blood, but enough to still the wild thrashing and clawing as she sought her own release.

With a final thrust of his hips, he slammed into her

cervix with a mix of pleasure and pain. Sleek pussy walls pulsed around his erupting cock and they came together with an intensity that yanked a roar of completion from his throat and a sensual scream from Chrys.

His arms gave out and he collapsed on top of her. He sighed while her fingers lazily traced the bones of his spine through the light sheen of sweat cooling on his skin. Sliding toward what he knew would be the sweetest sleep he'd had in a while, he was taken by surprise when Chrys flipped them over, her sweet cunt still clasped around his softening cock.

Mimicking his behavior of only moments before, she bit into his thick trapezius muscle between neck and shoulder. The sting of the bite sent a blazing rush of blood to reawaken his cock. He'd never recovered this quickly before, yet here he was instantly hard and just as hungry for the woman as the first time.

Thank god Chrys was already impaled on his flesh. There was nothing to delay him pumping like a madman while she kept a grip on his neck.

She bit down harder. He bucked like an unbroken bronco and she rode him like the most experienced cowgirl until they once again fell apart in each other's arms.

# CHAPTER EIGHT

Rahn rolled over with a groan. The goofy grin on his face disappeared when his hand made contact with a cold pillow where Chrys' head should have been.

"Damned woman. Why can't she stay where I put her?"

Mahpiya yawned big in his head. *It will take more than a bite on the neck to tame that one. Then again, perhaps you do not wish to tame her at all.*

Hmm. Well, maybe not. After all, the whiny doormat type had never appealed to Rahn. Chrys was his equal in every way. She was a hell of an undercover agent, educated, honorable, loyal. She didn't take any crap off anyone for any reason, but also knew when to negotiate. And she'd try her best to kick his ass if he ever pissed her off enough and then was stupid enough to let his guard down. Yes, she was a challenge. A worthy mate.

Their mating was far from complete, but last night had certainly been a fabulous start. Now all he had to do was get her to accept him completely, to accept what they were to each other. And he was certainly up to the task.

He ducked back into his bedroom for a quick shower. Dressed in nothing but a pair of comfortable jeans, Rahn grabbed his secure satellite phone off the nightstand and spoke into the voice recognizer.

"Dial Mother Hubbard."

After a few *clicks*, ringing sounded through the earpiece.

"Stud, here."

"Hey, Geri. Just checking in."

"How's the investigation going?"

"The captain has provided me with more good information. And since I can't get him to stay out of this, we've come up with a plausible excuse for him to accompany me here and yon. He's going to play tour guide."

"And how's Chrys?"

"A handful if ever she was, Geri."

"Has she figured out anything since the last time we talked?"

"Hell, no. But if I know Chrys, she's just not saying anything."

"You've got that right, Rahn. Just be careful. If you get hurt on this mission, Chrys will have your head. If she hasn't, er, had it already."

"A gentleman wouldn't dare go there. But I will say that I certainly have a better reason to be on this ship than finding a serial killer."

"Is that reason about five-foot-nothing with a muscular build, short wavy hair and brown eyes?"

"Actually, yes. I'll call you when I have something more to report, all right, boss?"

"Right. Mother Hubbard, out."

He snapped the phone closed and stuffed it in the back pocket of his jeans. Barefooted, he padded to the kitchen, pulled some fresh greens from the fridge and sat them on the built-in chopping board on the counter.

Suddenly, he wasn't in the mood to cook. In fact, he didn't want to eat either, not unless Chrys was on the menu.

Leaning against the nearest wall, Rahn reached out along the bond with his spirit guide.

'Mah?'

Her ears perked forward. *Yes, hoksila?*

'Where is my mate?'

*Shouldn't you know?* she teased.

But, yeah, he should know. And if he had anything to say about it, he would know from now on.

'Mah, would you mind…'

*Yes, I know, my dear. Would I mind asking my Adonei where she is?*

He felt like a little kid again, but smashed down his pride and muttered, 'Uh, yes, ma'am.'

After a moment of silence, Mah's thoughts filled his head along with the images she'd borrowed from Adonei. Chrys was in the exact spot he'd found her yesterday morning—in their private hot tub.

He picked up the phone and dialed the food service people.

"Hello, this is Rahn Benson in 15E. We require the service of the personal chef for breakfast, lunch and dinner. I have a menu in mind. If you can have a chef arrive within the hour, he can fix all the meals and we'll reheat them later. Oh, and I'll leave the front door unlocked. We'll be busy."

Rahn hung up the phone, strode to his room and dropped his jeans in the middle of the floor. The glass doors that led from his room to the balcony moved on silent tracks. He stepped out and there she was. Arms spread wide, head thrown back and resting on the edge of the tub, Chrys looked to be asleep. Then a forearm moved, bent at the elbow until a hand settled on her right breast and caressed with care. Her head rolled from one shoulder to the other. She sighed and dropped her hand back to the side of the tub.

Damn, she had such lovely breasts. Rahn could see the outline of her nipple straining against the fabric of her royal blue bikini from here. And the stiff little peak called his name, begged him to come set it loose so it could greet the morning sunshine.

Rahn padded to greet his mate.

\* \* \* \* \*

My god, what was she going to do? How the hell was she supposed to make it through this whole vacation with both her heart and pussy intact with a virile man like Rahn sharing her apartment?

Did she want him? Absolutely. But what if it didn't work out again?

The man seemed to be all into her right now, but what if he changed his mind?

Chrys tilted her head back to rest against the ledge of the hot tub. She tried to relax and let the hot bubbling water melt away her troubles. A glass of her favorite juice sat at her fingertips. A wisp of smoke from her favorite Kahlua mini-cigar floated up and mingled with the steam of the hot tub. And she hadn't taken a single sip or puff. None of it appealed, given the butterflies dive-bombing her stomach.

Then she thought of how she'd tiptoed from her own bed in the early hours of the morning, and the butterflies were driven off by a band of ravaging ravens. She really needed help here.

'Adonei?'

*I am here, Chrysalyn. Shall I come to you?*

Her throat clogged with unexplainable tears. 'Yes, please.'

Adonei's powerful tawny body shimmered into view

next to the hot tub just within arm's reach. Chrys stretched her arm toward him and sank her fingers into the thick dark mane. He turned questioning brown-sugar eyes on her, and suddenly she wanted to hide, to sink under the turbulent water until it was over her head.

*Why are you so upset, Chrysalyn?*

'Because I don't know what to say or how to act the next time I see Rahn. Sure, he did the you-my-woman thing last night. In fact, he did it quite well.' Her womb fluttered at the memory of what a fantastic lover Rahn had been. Every touch had brought her pleasure. No awkward moments. No missteps or blunders. It had been, in a word, perfect. 'But that doesn't mean he'll be as sure about this, this…whatever it is between us now that morning is here.'

*Woman, you make no sense. You had no problem facing him after coming together in the warm pool before.*

'Hot tub, Adonei,' she huffed.

*As you wish. However, if you were able to face him then, you can face him now. He is your mate, you are meant to be. He knows this as well as you, yes?*

'Yes, I know he's my mate.' A deep sigh followed the admission she didn't think she'd ever make, simply because she hadn't expected to have Rahn.

*Then why would he not want you as much in the light of day as he did under the light of the moon?*

'It's just that before, when we had a chance to be together, it didn't work out. And, well…hell, you know what happened. You were my spirit guide, after all.'

*Yes, the spirit guide who tried to tell you…*

'I know, Adonei, I know. You tried to tell me I was tripping and that he wasn't serious about the woman he was working that case with.'

*Yet you still chose to become engaged with that dreadful what's-his-name.*

Chrys grimaced. Sheesh, talk about the disaster of a lifetime. And she'd been so determined to walk into the disaster just to make Rahn jealous, it took her almost-mom-in-law disclosing the secret from hell to shake her resolve—she would have been wife number four. And it wasn't just the number of marriages that made her back up and take stock, it was the fact the asshole hadn't told her then, and still wouldn't own up to it. Not to mention the way he'd gotten rid of wife number one. The sneaky bastard had movers come while he was at work, pack the woman up and ship her off. When he got home that evening, he was happily wifeless.

Unfortunately, by the time Chrys had come to her senses and broken off the engagement, Rahn had moved back to London.

Now here she was with a second chance to be with the man of her dreams and fear had her damn near paralyzed...unless she was in his arms being fucked silly, of course. In truth, other than the constant state of horny-ness since Rahn showed up on her doorstep, Chrys was scared down to her toes.

*Do not worry, woman. There are events in motion larger than yourself. And they are all good things. Trust your instincts and listen to your guide. Neither of us has ever led you astray, yes?*

'Yes, you're right. Thanks, Adonei.'

*Of course, I am right,* he sniffed, all smug male lion.

His ever-present place in her mind lessened and the big cat's corporeal form glimmered and faded. Her stomach knotted nervously.

Chrys scented Rahn as he approached and almost groaned. She hadn't had time to completely process the meaning of the explosive bout of lovemaking—scratch that—no-holds-barred jungle fucking they'd done on the living room floor. There was no way she could handle a confrontation with him right now.

Adonei popped back in long enough to say, *And you know it will be a confrontation because…?*

'Oh hush, already,' she admonished.

Her eyes flew open on a squeak when she found herself hauled up against a hard chest, then set on her feet on top of the bath seat. Rahn nuzzled her navel as she stood in front of him.

"I don't like waking without you, Chrys."

Tilting her head to the side, she settled a fist on her hip. Was the man growling at her?

Ignoring her posturing, he continued. "It makes me think…"

She sucked in a breath when her bikini top flew across the deck and the ocean breeze teased her nipples.

"That you regret our time spent together last night."

The man skipped all the preliminary niceties. Hell, he hadn't even kissed her. Just picked her up and dove for her pussy like his lifetime supply of breakfast, lunch and dinner oozed from her rapidly swelling sex.

He backed off long enough to ask, "Do you regret it, Chrys?"

"I-I, no. I don't, uh. Oh god."

How the hell was she supposed to think, talk and feel all at the same time, damn it?

His warm tongue slipped between her pout folds, wreaked havoc on her senses. Fingers eased up and down her bare thighs as his mouth devoured her on the spot.

With her bikini bottom scrunched off to the side, he soon grumbled his frustration at the fabric impeding such important progress. But he couldn't bear to let her move more than an inch from his questing mouth. She tasted so good. Felt so good. He knotted his fist in the stretchy fabric and yanked. The remnants of the bottoms joined the bikini top across the deck.

Her very loud "damn it" told him she wanted to fuss. Instead, it came out a moan as his fingers found a home deep inside her gripping heat. He looked up in time to watch her mouth fall open. Wide enough to slip a nice wide cock into. His breath caught in his throat and rumbled around in his chest as he fought to keep his feet planted on the floor of the hot tub rather than springing up and tackling her to the deck.

He'd always had finesse with his lovers, but Chrys sent his brain into overload. He had no class, no James Bond-type subtlety where she was concerned. It was all out there for her to see, laid bare and downright greedy for her. But he was a man of control. Puh. Right.

"Touch your beautiful breasts, baby. I love it when you touch yourself."

His gaze settled on the palms of her hands as she caressed and weighed the caramel-tipped beauties. Mmm, and the way her fingers tweaked and rasped over the sweet nipples until they were stiff and distended had his eyeballs bulging along with his cock. And her soft moans and writhing hips? Aw fuck.

To hell with it. Grabbing her by the waist, Rahn carried her, with her delectable ass pressed against his cock, to the nearest balcony door. Setting her on her feet, he pressed her up against the sliding glass doors.

"Rahn, what the hell…?" she demanded. But that was as far as she got.

The man palmed the sides of her firm succulent breasts as he smashed her against the cool panes. A needy cock plowed into her from behind in one frantic stroke.

"Oh yes. Oh dear god, that's so good." The wicked swivel of her hips pulled him deeper. "Mmm, yeah. That's it, baby, fuck me."

He grinned at the smudged fingerprints on the glass where she clawed at the window with each deep stroke.

There it was again. Perfect, exhilarating friction and heat wrapped around his rod on each glide in, each slide out. He looked down to where their bodies came together. The sweet cunt gobbling up his cock provided the first course of a succulent erotic feast for the senses. Engaged in every way, he reveled in the sight, sound, taste, feel and scent of her pleasure. Thick honeyed dew became a froth of cream at her entrance. More. He had to have more.

"Give me that cream, love. Come for me, Chrys."

He gripped a thigh, lifted it high and was rewarded with a deep gasp as her sugared walls tightened and fluttered.

"Oh god. Sssss, Rahn. Oh yeeeesssss!"

Rahn scooped her up just as her knees buckled. Planted firmly in her still-twinging pussy, he eased open the glass doors and stepped into her bedroom.

They never made it to the bed…but the lovely floor-to-ceiling mirrors on her closet door provided some nice images he would remember until the day he died.

* * * * *

Mahpiya stretched out on her stomach, paws crossed lazily as she purred. Adonei laved the base of her neck with long swipes of his rough-textured tongue. An occasional nip of his sharp teeth produced a quivering in her stomach and a satisfied rumbling in her throat.

God, the lion sure could groom.

"So," she hummed. His tongue eased over a particularly sensitive spot just below her ear. "I do believe our charges are getting along rather nicely."

"Yes, I agree. My Chrysalyn can be rather stubborn at times, yet I believe she understands the significance of her attraction to your Rahn."

"I am glad they have finally reached the point in their

lives where they can accept a mating. When they were together before, I did not sense you as I do now," Mahpiya whispered around a yawn.

"Perhaps the Great Spirit meant for us to help train our charges, ready them for a time such as this? It would not have been possible to keep me away from you if I had been aware of you back then. The results would have been less than helpful to either Chrysalyn or Rahn."

Mahpiya thought it over and decided her mate's words made sense. If she and Adonei had gotten together before Chrys and Rahn were ready to mate, one of them would have had to give up being a spirit guide.

It was uncommon enough for a female guide to be given to a male human. But the Great Spirit simply wouldn't have allowed Mahpiya to continue to guide and protect Rahn if she mated with Adonei, but Rahn didn't accept Chrys. So to avoid such an incident, it made sense that the Great Spirit had simply hidden Adonei and her from each other. Until now.

Sigh. And what a lovely now it was.

Thoughts of Rahn's case intruded on her contentment. Adonei immediately picked up on it and settled his big muscular body down next to hers, pressing his sides against her. The significance of the simple act reassured and infused her with warmth. He truly was a magnificent animal, her lion.

"Adonei, I am concerned about the killer my charge is tracking. It is a dangerous business. We have always worked well together on things such as this, yet I feel as if I am blinded from things I would typically be aware of."

"Yes, I understand. It is the same with me. And more concerning is that Chrysalyn knows your charge is here for more than a simple ride to Rome. Yet she says nothing because she is afraid."

"Afraid of what? The Eden fellow? He makes it no

secret that he wants her."

"No, Chrys thinks nothing of him. My charge is not easily frightened, but her desire for her mate is almost overwhelmed by fear of losing Rahn now that they have found each other again. But speaking of the Eden fellow, he seems to appear whenever she is not with your charge. There is something about him that bothers me. I am sure he is a danger to Chrysalyn."

"Yet you have chosen not to tell her this. Why?"

"It is not my place. It is for your charge to discover the danger and keep her from it."

"Ah," she said. "Perhaps my Rahn's mission and the danger surrounding your Chrys are one and the same. If this is the case, I see why we would be prohibited from interfering too much. Looking after Chrys is something Rahn would wish to do with as little interference from me as possible. It is in his nature to want to protect his female."

"And I will protect mine," Adonei growled as he moved to cover her.

Mmm, there were times like this that Mahpiya more than appreciated being a spirit guide. Unlike natural lions, Mahpiya and Adonei could shift into a human representation of their lion selves, and couple for much longer than just a few moments And right now she reveled in the tantalizing sensation of her lover moving inside her, hard and fast, just the way she liked it. Strong teeth sank gently into her neck, keeping her immobile for his ravishing. Instinctive behavior for a male, but it was far from necessary. The loving felt so good, staying like this as he plunged into her hungry core was no certainly hardship.

# CHAPTER NINE

The second the chef finished preparing their meals, Rahn shook the man's hand with a grin and practically shoved him out the front door. He was already on his way back to Chrys' bedroom when Mahpiya brought a message from Adonei. Chrys was still asleep. The male spirit guide would have usually roused her when the chef, a stranger, arrived. This time, he deliberately didn't wake her.

'Mah, ask him why he didn't warn Chrys that I was in the apartment the night I came aboard and Chrys almost whipped my ass in the dark?'

*He says because he felt me, sensed my essence within you. He, he...scented me.*

Well, this was a first. Mah was embarrassed. Another question for the list of things to ask God when he got to heaven—how the hell did a lioness blush?

Rahn chuckled. Mah growled.

'Oh, don't be offended. It's funny.'

Eyes closed, he grinned at the faint image of the majestic cat licking her paws with a disgruntled snap of her tongue. Her tail swished up into the air. He knew if she'd been on this plane, she'd have swatted him with it. She was such a doll.

*On to more important matters, shall we? You have a concern, do you not, hoksila?*

'Actually, I do. I'm just not sure how to approach Chrys with the whole mating, bonding thing. I'd never expected to find a mate who had a spirit guide like me. A spirit guide I'm not supposed to know anything about.'

He shucked his robe and let it fall to the floor next to the bed as he joined his woman under the covers. Chrys' warm body instinctively snuggled up to his.

*Your Chrysalyn may be skeptical at first, but Adonei and I are both here. She will believe you because she believes Adonei. Now is as good a time as any other to discuss such an important subject.*

'I know you're right, Mah. I just wish I knew what Chrys was thinking.'

*You are a wise man. You will choose your words carefully and all will work out in the end. Besides, your female is just as wise.*

'Thanks for the encouragement, Mah. Stick around in case I need you, all right?'

*Of course.*

Mahpiya turned and padded away. Her image, but not her presence, faded from behind his eyes. At ease, yet ever watchful, the huge cat settled into her favorite spot.

Reassured, Rahn sent one last thought to her before he woke his mate.

'I love you, Mah.'

*Yes, but not as much as you love her, which is as it should be.*

Wow. Was Mahpiya right? He had strong feelings for Chrys, but was he already far gone in love with her?

It was a stupid question. He'd always loved her, even after they'd shattered each other's hearts.

He lay there for long moments, contemplating how to go about what he knew must be done. Chrys shifted in his arms. A satisfied sigh escaped her lips as the fragrance of their loving wafted from underneath the sheets. Their scents mingled and Rahn came to an immediate conclusion—he smelled damned good on her.

Easing his fingers along her jawbone, he gently tapped her.

"Chrys, sweetheart, wake up."

"Mmmnnn, no wanna." She grumbled, turned over and scooted her lovely backside up against his thigh.

Instant erection. Damn.

Ignoring the throbbing cock now tenting the sheets, he hauled her up against his chest and whispered in her ear.

"Chrysalyn, do you believe in spirit guides?"

He almost laughed when her neck jerked back as if he'd smacked her. Honey brown eyes snapped open, along with her lush kiss-swollen lips. She quickly painted on a plastic smile and a bland expression, but too late.

Well, he certainly had her attention.

"Do I believe in what?" she asked, her tone one of incredulity mixed with a bit of agitation. And was that a hint of fear in her eyes?

Wrapping her in his arms, Rahn settled her more comfortably against his chest in a gesture he hoped was reassuring.

"Spirit guides, sweetheart." When she didn't respond, he sat up, taking her with him. Her warm, moist pussy settled right against his raging hard-on. Damn, it was difficult to hold a conversation when all he really wanted to do was melt into her.

Instead, he looked in her eyes and said, "Look, Chrys, I want to share all of myself with you. And that includes my spirit guide."

She still hadn't said a word.

'Okay, Mah. Help me out here…'

*Adonei says Chrys is wondering how someone of your origins could have a spirit guide.*

Duh. Made sense. Of course she would wonder. Spirit guides were a Native American thing. Chrys' Lakota Sioux grandma made sure she and her cousins grew up with a clear understanding and appreciation for both natural and spiritual things. He knew this because, even though he was a blue-blooded Englishman and half Egyptian, it was Chrys' cousin's fault he'd met Mahpiya in the first place.

"Chrys, you're probably wondering how someone like me could have a spirit guide, right?"

"Uh, er, well…" she sputtered, pulling the sheets up to obstruct his view of her beautiful plump breasts.

"No worries, love. After all, spirit guides are a Native thing, while I'm white and Egyptian."

"But, Rahn, you don't have to…"

"Hush, sweetheart, I do indeed have to. Now listen, all right?"

Rahn was pleased when the woman snapped her mouth shut and listened as he recounted a case he'd worked as a young agent. Chrys' cousin, Delaine Jeris, had been assigned to mentor him, and took him along on one of her cases. One particular mission involved corruption, murder and, unfortunately, federal agents. To this day, neither Rahn nor Delaine had ever spoken a word of the happenings of that incident to anyone except their boss. Until now.

Thankfully, his heritage came with the luxury of a deep tan during the summer months and allowed Delaine and him to go deep undercover on a reservation in South Dakota. The same reservation both Delaine and Chrys had visited often during their growing-up years.

During his extended stay on the res, Delaine quietly

took him to spend time with their grandma. She was a wise old woman, wise in the ways of spirit and life. She'd patiently shared her experiences with him between cups of strong coffee and piles of homemade fry bread sprinkled with powdered sugar or honey.

The Lakota believed that the Great Spirit, Wakantanka, created all things and was no respecter of persons. Granny often laughed when she said, "Wakantanka will not hold it against you that you were not born a Sioux."

Rahn had gained a new respect for the land and nature. Learned about spirit guides and himself, as well as the importance of understanding his place in the world. The time Delaine and Granny spent teaching him about Lakota beliefs and customs not only helped him understand and have patience with others, but it saved his life.

"While checking out a lead, I was snatched out of my car, bashed over the head and dragged out into the middle of nowhere." Chrys winced. With a chuckle full of mirth, he said, "It got better. I was then shot and left for dead almost fifty miles from the nearest warm body. I called out to the Great Spirit with all my heart, just like Granny, *your* Granny, taught me. In that moment, Mahpiya came to me."

Chrys' eyes gleamed with unshed tears as he described the calm that had enveloped his mind. A peace so encompassing, he knew he was going to die. Just when he thought he'd taken his last breath, Mahpiya spoke to him.

*I have come to protect and guide you*, hoksila. *I will be with you for as long as you wish. Do you accept me?*

At his mental nod, the image of the most majestic creature he'd ever seen, a huge and powerful African lioness, appeared behind his eyes. In that instant, the connection, the bond they shared to this very day, snapped into place.

*Take what I offer, my charge.*

The words preceded a ferocious surge of power that slammed into his physical body, giving him the strength to make it to the nearest road. Thankfully, a stranger stopped and took him to the hospital.

"Chrys, baby, are you crying?"

She shook her head, but a loud, slurpy sniff gave away how touched she was by his story.

"Chrys, you're my mate and I want you more than anyone or anything. But..." He paused and took a breath. "My spirit guide is important to me. Can you accept both of us? I understand there are old fears that make you want to pull away from me and not trust me. I'm sorry for that, but can you let it go? Especially since neither of us meant to hurt one another."

Her eyebrows rose a good inch.

"Yes, Chrys, you hurt me too. But I know you didn't mean to and I forgave you a long time ago."

Rahn sat quietly, stroking the short silky curls she sported so well. He swore he heard the gears turning in her head as she worked out her feelings. No problem. There was only one thing left to say.

"Chrys, I swear I'll be yours for as long as you'll have me, love. Take the time you need to think about it, but let me be clear. I don't intend to take no for an answer."

Chrys tried to stem the flow of tears, but simply couldn't. She knew what it took to share something as intimate as a spirit guide, how important it was to guard such a special connection with a creature not of this world. But Rhan shared his Mahpiya without hesitation. Knowing Rahn's spirit guide must have sensed Adonei by now, the tears ran faster down her cheeks—the man hadn't asked a single question about her own special circumstances.

The fortified walls around her heart crumbled. All the fear and pain she'd kept closed inside melted away. Chrysalyn wanted him more than ever. But…

'Adonei?'

Warmth trickled down their psychic bond.

*Go ahead, Chrysalyn. Share yourself with your mate. The result will be a love you have never imagined.*

It was all the encouragement she needed. She took in a shuttering breath and resisted the urge to wipe her face on the warm skin of Rahn's chiseled pecs.

"Rahn," she blubbered, so moved it didn't enter her mind to be embarrassed. "I don't need time to think about it, I know what I want. And that's you. And I have a spirit guide too. His name is Adonei, an African lion."

Rahn shifted enough to reach over to the nightstand and pass her a handful of tissues. Blowing rather unceremoniously, she cleaned her face, wiped away the tears…and her logical agent's brain jumped into the silence.

Wait a minute. How much of a coincidence was it that Rahn's spirit guide was an African lioness and hers was an African lion? Was she missing something here?

Suddenly, a pair of strong hands picked her up and placed her chest to chest, thighs spread, with a meaty erection pressed against her clit. Every curious thought trickled right out of her head when the man slid his hard cock back and forth across the little bundle of nerves, urging her body to release its slick, moist dew. Didn't take long.

Oh lord. What had she been thinking about? Wait, Rahn's lioness…

"Mate with me?" he asked softly. Leaning forward, a warm tongue wrapped around a plump nipple and tugged lightly. His hips moved slowly, sinuously, back and forth, rubbing, sliding, encouraging. "Chrys?"

"Oh god, yes," she sighed. Head thrown back, she rose up on her knees just enough to make clearance for his upright shaft. She laced her fingers behind her head and watched his skilled fingers move over her sensitive skin. One hand gently spread her swelling pussy lips while the other eased the tip of his cock inside.

Then came a faint stirring in her mind. Adonei? How strange. This time her guide hadn't left her as he had the other times she and Rahn had made love. This time, the second Rahn's hard length disappeared inside her hungry pussy, she felt a presence join Adonei.

*Hello, wicincala. I am Mahpiya, come to aid our mates in your protection and guidance. I will be with you for as long as you wish. Do you accept me?*

'You've come to aid our mates? I don't understand,' Chrys gasped as the head of her man's cock parted her flesh.

Mahpiya answered her question almost before it fully formed in her head.

*Adonei is my mate. My charge, Rahn, is yours. I would join with both of you. And no, the males cannot hear us. This is a moment for just the two of us.*

'What about later?'

*All will be explained in due time. Now is the time for mating. Do you accept me?*

'Yes. Yes, of course.'

Suddenly the flame of desire between her and Rahn erupted into a conflagration of care and flat-out lust. Strong enough, powerful enough to singe her very soul. It was the merging, the mating of their spirit guides combined with her and Rahn's joining.

Mahpiya's rumbled purr subsided and Rahn's rough-edged voice filled her ears.

"Ride me, Chrys. Ride my cock, love."

Hands cupped underneath her backside, he lifted her until he was nothing more than a tease at her entrance.

Raising his hips, he slammed her body down to meet his and sank deep inside. Again. And again. Until she was a trembling mass of need.

"That's it, Chrys. Take it, take all of me."

Hell, she didn't think it was physically or spiritually possible to take anything more. Inside her head, she couldn't see Adonei and Mahpiya mating, but she sure as hell sensed it. The loving was fierce, untamed. Wild. The sensation of feral heat zinged back and forth along the psychic bond with Adonei, now made doubly strong by Mahpiya's presence.

It called to her and she opened herself to it completely, allowed it to surge through her blood. The need was so strong, she was filled with it. Brimming over until she expected the very cells underneath her skin to catch fire.

Her pussy tightened and clenched around her lover's thrusting cock. Oh god, it was so good. So hot. So deliciously wanton.

"Damn, woman! Oh, yeah, just like that," Chrys heard Rahn growl. His words only ratcheted up the heat as his molten length pistoned into her wet cunt with supernatural speed. And she received him with supernatural endurance. Whoa. Their guides had given them their power without asking? Reassurance flooded her soul and she knew this was part of the mating heat between them and their lions.

And it was damned near too much. Chrys couldn't remember ever being this overwhelmed by a bout of sex in her life. It was out of this world. Literally.

"God, Rahn, you feel so good."

"Then come for me, sweetheart. Bathe my cock."

Her stomach muscles trembled and tightened in cadence with her pulsing sex. When his fingers left her breast and focused on her clit, she yelled to the rafters.

"I can't," she wailed. "It's too much. It just feels too

good. I can't take it!"

"You can," Rahn asserted. "And you will." His voice was tight, rough. His fingers trembled and his chest rose and fell with deep, but erratic gusts. Well, at least she wasn't the only one losing her mind.

The friction between their bodies was exquisite. He slammed into her, out of her, so fast that her juices ran down the inside of her thighs like the froth on her morning cappuccino.

"Oh god. Oh, shit. Rahn!"

"That's it, baby. Give it to me. Give it to me, now."

They orgasmed as one. His cock pulsed and exploded deep inside her just as her channel squeezed and milked him. Their worlds collided, bright and cataclysmic, leaving the earth trembling in the wake.

As Chrys drifted toward sweet oblivion, her mind was bathed with a soothing blanket of love. Mahpiya's, Adonei's. And Rahn's.

* * * * *

Rahn rolled over and reached for his new mate. A satisfied sigh became a frustrated groan. Chrys was gone. Again.

"Damn it, what is it with that woman never being where she's supposed to be?" he grumbled to himself. After reviving from her faint—something she swore never happened, period—the woman wore his balls into the mattress with a fierce loving that lasted well into the night. They'd barely gotten out of bed long enough to enjoy a meal or two. Instead, they'd reveled with awe in their joining, getting to know each other, their guides and good lord above, their bodies.

Rahn's mouth stretched wide in a loud, tired yawn. Quieting his mind, he reached along the bond he shared with Mahpiya. And now Adonei.

"Mah, come to me," he sighed aloud, replete and beyond satisfied.

The sleek corporeal body of the African lioness shimmered into view. And for the first time, Adonei appeared with her. My god, he was a huge cat. His mane was thick and full, a dark chocolate brown that contrasted with his tawny coat. Easily twice as large are Mahpiya, with massive paws, a well-defined chest and eyes the same honey color as Chrys. Adonei stretched out beside his mate. Both of them showed an impressive set of canines as they dropped their jaws and half yawned, half roared rather loudly. Obviously, they were all bone-deep tired.

After the initial joining, Adonei and Mahpiya had given him and Chrys some privacy. If their sleepy demeanors were any indication, they hadn't cut out so they could go to bed early.

"Well, Mah, I would ask why you didn't wake me when Chrys left the apartment, but it's obvious you were sleeping on the job," Rahn chuckled.

Mahpiya sniffed indignantly. Adonei licked his paws.

"Either of you know where my mate is?"

*Of course we know where she is,* Adonei replied. *Yet even a fully grown lion cannot manage to keep her in one spot.* He swung his huge head toward Mahpiya and said, *Perhaps her mate will be more successful than her spirit guide.*

Sarcasm colored every word. Rahn laughed outright. Chrys would do what she damned well pleased, mated, guided, or not.

Up and headed toward the master bathroom in Chrys' suite, Rahn inhaled deeply. Her scent was everywhere—on the towels, in the air. And all over his skin.

He looked back over his shoulder and motioned to the two lions lying lazily on the floor across the room.

"Come on, you two. While I shower, you can fill me

in on what Chrys is up to, as well as what to expect now that we're mated. I can't hear her in my head, but I can hear the both of you well enough."

Mahpiya padded after him.

*It is the same with Chrysalyn. The bonds are fully formed, but they do not create telepathic abilities in humans. Chrysalyn can hear and see both Adonei and me. She can see anything we wish to show her, but she cannot hear you, nor you her.*

"That makes sense," Rahn replied. Grabbing a washcloth off the rack, he inhaled the feminine scent of his woman before he lathered up with whatever soap she had in the shower. It smelled a bit girly, but he didn't care. Anything that reminded him of his Chrys was just fine with him. Anyone who had a problem with it could kiss the end of his fist.

"So where is she?"

*Chrysalyn has gone ashore. She is on a tour of Ibiza.*

So they'd reached the Balearic Islands during the night. Damn it, he didn't like the idea of her venturing out alone with a murderer on the loose. The woman could probably take down the culprit, but that wasn't the point. She was his to protect.

Sigh. Well, at least he didn't have to do it alone.

"Can the two of you keep an eye on her? One of you stay with her while the other scouts ahead of her? Keep her out of trouble while I do a bit of snooping. Captain Laurens has a lead for me. I need to check it out without worrying about running into Chrys on the island."

*And what of you?* Mahpiya asked, her tone abrupt. Obviously, she didn't like the idea of Rahn going about his duties with no one to watch his back.

"I'll be fine, Mah. I'll call if I need you. But what I need more is for you to keep Chrys far away from me while I'm scouting. Hell, even if she's with that Eden asshole, at least she won't be alone."

Adonei jumped to his feet and looked as if he wanted to pounce on Rahn. The lion's snarl was so ferocious, Rahn almost took a few steps back. But he was there to aid and assist, not attack.

But then again, he'd felt Mahpiya's sharp claws across his ass on more than one occasion. Usually right after he'd done something stupid. Hmm, he might have to rethink this whole spirit guide thing with Adonei in the mix. His female cat could get away with swatting him on the backside, but there was no way in hell he was going to let a fully grown, big-assed male do the same. Not without a fight.

Turning off the shower, he toweled off quickly and strode naked through the living room, heading for the closet in the guestroom suite.

Stifling a chuckle, he asked, "Problem with the Eden asshole, Adonei?"

*I do not care for the human.* But he said nothing more.

"Chrys may be stubborn, but she'll listen to you if she's in danger. She'd better or I'll have to paddle her ass. Go join her on her tour, all right? Tell her I said good morning and I'll catch up with her for dinner."

With that, the air around the two majestic beasts shimmered and shifted until they faded before his eyes. With their essence still vaguely present in his head, Rahn dressed, grabbed a quick bite then headed to the ship's bridge to see Captain Laurens.

# CHAPTER TEN

Chrys forced her eyeballs to remain uncrossed as the tour guide's deep monotone droned on, and on.

"Welcome to Ibiza. Third in size of Spain's Balearic Islands, Ibiza's charms include a magnificent bay that rivals that of Naples. There's also a chain of golden beaches and an ancient and picturesque main town. As much a colony of discerning artists and writers as it is a popular tourist destination, Ibiza still offers many areas of charm, tranquility and stunning natural beauty..."

Blah, blah, blah.

Adonei stalked into her head. About damned time.

'Adonei, where in the world have you been?' she scolded.

*Getting to know your mate. He sends a good morning greeting and looks forward to your company for supper.*

Immediately, sweet warmth infused her soul and brought a smile to her lips. Her mate had sent her a message, even though she'd snuck out of bed this morning. Her mate—amazing how two simple words could be so soothing, yet conjure the most wicked images in mind, like the fierce loving of the previous night. There'd been such an urgency to be mounted, stroked inside and out, that she'd lost her mind under a barrage of feeling. The depth of hunger sunk so deep, it had sent her emotions reeling. Even now, it was almost too much to fathom.

A tremor snaked through her body. Her temperature soared while her stomach tripped. Ears burning, Chrys wondered how long it'd been since she'd actually blushed from thinking about a man. Rahn. God, he simply had her undone.

"Damn it," she muttered to herself. Her head had been so wrapped up in the man, she'd missed a step and stubbed the hell out of her toe. Guess sandals weren't ideal for sightseeing in the old medieval stone pirate towers of the island.

Okay, time to get a handle on herself.

The tour guide's dull voice intruded once more.

"Ibiza and Formentera have been a popular destination for visitors from overseas for thousands of years, but unfortunately it is only during the last few decades that these frequent visitors have brought money with them on their visits to the islands."

Hardy har har. Chrys winced at the dry humor.

'I am bored out of my head. I think I'll go off on my own,' Chrys whispered along her link with her lions. Strange how Mahpiya occupied the same space now, yet the feline was separate and apart from her awareness of Adonei. Almost like they had their own special connection without excluding "the guys".

*Chrysalyn, it is not wise to venture off alone,* the lioness said firmly.

Apprehension snaked through the link and Chrys felt compelled to listen to the big cat and do exactly as she suggested. She pushed the strange feelings away.

'I've got two bad-assed African lions with me. What

do I possibly have to be afraid of?'

The uneasiness of the previous moment surged into full-blown protective instinct. Mahpiya was concerned for her. But why?

'May I call you Mah, like Rahn does?' she asked respectfully.

*Of course.*

'Thank you. Now, Mah, what's going on? I can feel you're on full hunter alert. And shouldn't one of you be with Rahn?'

Neither lion said a word for what felt like eons. Their postures seemed easy enough, but tension wrapped around the bond like a tangible thing. They were hiding something. But if Mahpiya was anything like Adonei, no amount of harping in the world would get her to spill.

Sigh. Well, perhaps she'd try anyway. Even picking away at the patience of a spirit guide had to be less boring than this stupid tour she'd signed up for.

'Well, since neither of you are telling, I guess I'll drop it.' For now. 'Meanwhile, let's go into the heart of town and explore. Maybe get some lunch.' Chrys didn't wait for them to answer or give permission. With a farewell wave to an older couple she'd met while debarking off the ship, she turned and left the droning tour guide and the group of tourists behind her.

Down the road was a row of modern restaurants and shops, all top-notch according to her research. There was one that specialized in rare gifts. Oooh, and they carried Dominican Republic hand-rolled cigars. Wow. Would Rahn enjoy something like this? He'd never smoked in her presence, but a man of such impeccable taste might appreciate a seasoned mild cigar. For her, there was nothing better than a Tatiana groovy-flavored smoke with an after-dinner dessert. Or the coffee-flavored smoke of a Kahlua cigar mixed with the cool smoothness of a cream-laced beverage. Yum.

With her purchases tucked into her day bag, Chrys walked up a hill, turned down a quiet street and settled for a small mom-and-pop cafe for lunch. Suppressing laughter at Mah and Adonei's antics, she stepped through the door and was immediately shown to a table out back with a clear view of the sea's crystal blue waters off in the distance.

The food was fabulous. She'd never been a big fan of Mediterranean food, but this stuff was wonderful. With every kind of cuisine under the sun to choose from, perhaps the French five-star restaurant down the street would get a visit before she headed back to the ship later. After all, Ibiza was no backwater island, but a place where the young and chic came to vacation.

Her companions were quite a pair. The faint image of the two lions grooming each other lovingly as she sipped a cup of espresso produced an inward smile. Then the next instant, Mah swatted at Adonei's head after he'd said something so totally male even Chrys grimaced. The lioness was quick-witted and even quicker with her claws. And, of course, Chrys had to throw in her two cents, usually on Mah's side. Soon Adonei was mumbling about catty women who were too smart for their own good, and perhaps he would go and keep Rahn company after all. Chrys bit the inside of her cheek and tried to keep her mirth under wraps—not smart to have the locals thinking she'd gone bonkers by laughing at someone they couldn't see.

After lunch, she stepped out into the bright afternoon sunshine. The sun was dazzling, shining off the many white stone churches common in every town on the island.

Then the hairs on the back of her neck hit orbit, standing on end as the bottom fell out of her stomach. Someone was watching her.

After waltzing around the island with no set

destination, Chrys had no idea how far away or where her nearest shipmates were hanging out. Yep, it was times like this she sure as hell appreciated having a spirit guide. Correction—two spirit guides.

At the first twang of apprehension, both Adonei and Mah bolted up into sitting positions, ears pricked forward. Adonei's presence faded and she knew he'd gone to investigate what, or rather who, was both ahead and behind her. There was no doubt that in the second she stood in front of the eatery, pretending to explore the beautiful potted plants, Adonei had scoped out each possible route in and out of the area as well as surveyed every person in close proximity.

Meanwhile, Mah's calm power-infused presence radiated down their newly formed bond. Someone might be tailing her, but she sure as hell wasn't alone. Far from helpless, Chrys readied herself, reached for and caught the calm focus required to quickly measure and take down an enemy.

The air off to her left rippled in waves just before Adonei's huge corporeal form shimmered into view. Mahpiya remained out of sight, but clearly visible in her mind's eye.

*You are indeed being hunted.*

Hunted? Who would dare?

*It is the Eden person. I do not like it.*

'Well, that sure as hell makes two of us,' she hissed back. Why would Eden be tailing her? He'd always appeared to be so nice and gentlemanly. Not to mention damned good-looking. Did he really mean her ill? Perhaps Adonei was simply overreacting. Or, as usual, he'd been correct in his first assessment of the man.

Well, time to find out.

'Adonei, please lend me your senses.'

Immediately, eyesight and hearing sharpened. Natural ability increased many times over as every cell was infused with the lion's raw power. Taking her time, Chrys and her two invisible escorts turned down a narrow road and out onto the main boulevard.

Eden was a good enough distance away that a typical person wouldn't have noticed his presence. The man was awfully good at tailing, which meant only one of three things—she and Adonei were both paranoid, Eden was a bad guy or he was a special ops person like herself. Odds on that first one were highly doubtful and the thought of him being either of the other two sent a chill up her spine.

She kept moving. With her enhanced senses, not only did Chrys catch the musky scent of his body, but she could have heard his soft footsteps a mile away.

Then, as suddenly as she'd sensed Eden behind her, he was gone. Only to be replaced by the presence of another man she hadn't expected to run into.

Rahn was across the wide boulevard. He stalked—it was the only word she could think of to describe the graceful and dangerous way the gorgeous man moved—down the stairs of what appeared to be the town hall and headed her way.

Two men were at his side. One was a local cop. In her line of work, she could spot a government gofer a mile away, even if he was dressed casually in cargo pants and a button-down shirt. The other man, taller than Rahn, but not nearly as well-built, was none other than the captain of the ship. So what was Rahn doing with these people? His case was supposed to be in Rome, not on Ibiza.

'What the hell is Rahn up to? I'd recognize that I'm-on-duty look anywhere.'

Not expecting either cat to actually tell on the man, Chrys ducked into the nearest shop and waited for him to pass by.

This direction headed right for a crowded town

market her tour group had passed earlier. If she was careful, it would be the perfect place to tail him without being noticed. She hoped. After all, Rahn wasn't one of the most distinguished undercover specialists in her unit for nothing. But she was damned good at her job too. And at the rate the men were walking they'd passed by now.

Chrys stepped out into the street on silent feet.

And ran right into Rahn's chest.

"Chrys?"

She watched the expressions on his deeply tanned face morph from surprise to understanding to flat-out pissed off. His jaw tightened and ticced. The lips that had kissed her so wonderfully every day and night now pulled back in a snarl, baring sharp white teeth.

Shit. So much for following him at a discreet distance.

"What the fuck are you doing up here by yourself?" he growled quietly. One look at his face and the men accompanying him gave sympathetic smiles and got the hell out of Dodge. The man looked like a volcano.

"Woman, get your ass back to the ship right fucking now. Better yet, I'll take you my damned self." He grabbed her by the hand and practically dragged her down the hill.

What the hell was going on? She didn't think she'd ever seen Rahn so angry. Not even after the time he'd been shot in the ass by a bad guy while diving for cover in the middle of a shootout.

And who the fuck did he think he was talking to? She was a grown woman who didn't require nor allow a babysitter.

"Slow the hell down or let go of my damned hand," she snapped. "I'm wearing sandals, not running shoes."

His answer was a grumble she couldn't quite make out. Sounded something like having to get his woman back where she belonged?

*Well, my mate, shall we leave these two alone for a time?* Adonei asked Mahpiya. His tongue lolled out of the side of his mouth and Chrys could have sworn he was grinning. With that, his corporeal form vanished and his presence dimmed. Mahpiya disappeared all together.

Damned cats.

\* \* \* \* \*

Eden bit back an eager grin. His thoughts were fixed on the beautiful prize of a woman walking ahead of him. Chrysalyn's smooth caramel skin glistened with a light sheen along her shapely calves. His mouth watered at the strong compulsion to taste the crease at the back of her knee to confirm the moisture was a film of sweat mixed with the tangy humidity of the island.

Chrys called to him—mind, body and soul. She was only a short distance away now, barely a block. If he could get to her before she reached the town square, he'd have a chance to, uh, persuade her to spend a bit of quality time with him before it was time to return to the ship to leave port.

Eden wasn't sure why, but just as he was about to pass the steps of the town hall, he came to a halting stop and stayed put, just out of sight.

Seconds later, the Rahn asshole came down those steps accompanied by a local cop he recognized from his last trip through here, along with the captain of their ship.

His pharaoh hadn't said anything about peace officers, captains or assholes in her interpretation of the upside-down Empress card. And if both the Rahn person and Chrys were in this very same spot, did that mean they were here in port together? As a couple? No, not possible. According to the cards, Chrys was supposed to have lost interest in Rahn and leaning toward him instead. Hmm. He'd have to have a talk with his lovely tarot reader when he made it back to the ship.

Risking a peek out of the little alcove he'd ducked into, Eden watched the Rahn asshole rake his hands through his hair. At this angle, the man reminded Eden of one of his own cousins. A strong chin, even stronger body, deeply tanned skin. An air of nobility and honor clung to him like a second skin. His stance screamed royalty. Just like himself.

Listening intently, Eden's spine stiffened at the words of the three men who stood talking on the steps. His lungs seized as if they were afraid to breathe. Heart kicked up into a wild rhythm. Stomach twisted into a sick knot.

Eden's Catalan language skills were somewhat rusty, but he recognized the words "dead" and "killer" in any language.

The Rahn asshole's jaw clenched tight as he questioned the peace officer. "The woman found early this morning. Same description? Same type of wounds?"

"Yes, sir. She was found just after the ship pulled into port. Wealthy female, Caucasian, blonde hair. Not a resident of the island. A visitor…"

"Who didn't come here on our ship," Rahn interrupted. "Naked and bound, but other than the knife wounds, she was untouched. No rape, no assault. Damn it, just like the others."

Eden pressed closer against the wall between him and the other men.

"Anyone else know about this?" Rahn asked quietly.

The captain of their vessel replied. "Absolutely not. I've spoken to all of the officials in every port we've touched. They've all agreed to let your agency handle the situation."

Agency, eh? So the Rahn asshole was some kind of

high-up law dog? And if he worked with Chrys, did that mean she was a cop too? Eden backed up the way he'd come and took the long way around back to the ship. His harem mistress needed a talking-to. And he obviously needed a change of plans.

* * * * *

Rahn was practically on her ass as they both stormed through the door into their apartment. She rounded on him, her face lined with confusion and her fist jammed into her hip.

"Rahn, what the hell are you so upset about?"

The image of his beautiful mate flashed into his mind. She lay in a crumpled, bloody heap, her lifeless eyes glazed over, seeing nothing. The woman they'd found earlier could have easily been Chrys. Just the thought of not having her at his side sent a rush of heated fury through his soul. He teetered dangerously close to the edge of sanity just now. Simply couldn't handle losing her. Not again.

"Damn it, Chrysalyn, how the hell can I protect you if I can't manage to keep your ass where you belong and away from danger?" he yelled.

Yelled? He never yelled. The wide bug-eyed shock on Chrysalyn's flushed, but lovely, face was enough to embarrass him down to his toes. He took a step back, appalled by his own behavior. Didn't last long, considering there was a murderer on the loose and she was prize pickings.

Sobering quickly, he snapped his mouth shut, knowing the wheels of her agile mind hummed from the implication of his words. Damn, he couldn't believe what he'd just let slip. And Chrys wouldn't forget it. In fact, the woman was probably weighing the importance of each word he'd just said.

But instead of giving him the argument he expected, she turned to duck into the sanctuary of her bedroom.

He wasn't having it. Anger flared. Control didn't seem to be anywhere near at the moment, which seemed to be the case more and more of late when in her presence.

"Woman, do you hear me talking to you?" Rahn growled, reaching for her. He had to feel her, had to hold her in his arms. A deft pop of her knuckle in just the right spot had his muscled forearm numb in seconds.

"Yeah, I heard you all right. How could I not? And keep your damned hands off me."

"What? Well, you haven't seemed to mind my hands on you every night we've met up in bed." Ouch. He hadn't meant to say that. The hurt look on her face told him she hadn't expected him to, either. "Chrysalyn, baby, I'm sorry. I didn't mean that. It's just…"

"Save it, Mr. Benson."

Aw, hell. She'd called him Mr. Benson. Definitely not a good sign.

"If there's one thing I can't stand is a man who throws something in my face. Someone who takes a special moment and turns it into a guilt-inducing negative," she fumed.

A grumbled "asshole" reached his ears as she stomped over the threshold of her room and slammed the door in his face. He stood there with his nose pressed against the smooth lacquered wood and tried to gain at least a bit of composure. With a sigh, he sucked down his pride and let the groveling begin.

"Chrysalyn, I'm sorry," he called through the door. "I was just so worried about you, I lost it for a minute. A body was found just this morning, not an hour after we docked."

Her door slid open. Well, he'd gotten her attention, but the flint-hard look in her eyes clearly said he wasn't getting any forgiveness. He prepared to spend a lot of time on his knees making up for this blunder. But god, was she worth it.

Lowering her head, she glared up at him with a "you'd better have a good explanation" look. Damn, she was so sexy. Even more so in her anger. He must be nuts. Raking a hand through his hair, Rahn backed up a step, blew out a frustrated breath and spoke as many words as he could string together. Which weren't many.

"Chrys, you know the position I'm in." He shot forward in just enough time to get his boot wedged into the space between the doorjamb and the open door. "Listen, I'm working. I'm undercover. I lied about going to Rome. My case is right here aboard this ship. We didn't know the danger or what was going on until after Geri sent you here on vacation."

Arms crossed over her tempting bosom, she snapped. "Why didn't she just have me work the case since I was already here?"

"Because you're supposed to be on vacation. If you don't believe me, then call her. But I can't divulge the nature or details of this case without her permission. I'm sorry, sweetheart, as much as I love you, I can't…"

Oh hell. Had he just let that slip too? God, he couldn't seem to keep anything behind his teeth when Chrys was around. Perhaps it was her fierce spirit that kept him off balance. Or the way she gazed at him with those lovely almond-shaped eyes of hers. Or that luscious ass that winked at him every time she walked by. Or her scent. Or…hell, he could go on forever. The list of what he loved about her was simply endless.

"Rahn? Did you say…? No, never mind. It doesn't change the fact that you lied to me. What else did you lie about, huh? Did you just want to get a bit of bedtime distraction while you're working your case, just to disappear from my life again after it's over? Son of a bitch."

Again, he was presented with her back. But there was no way he was letting her go. She might not believe what he said, so he'd just have to give a bit of action to go along with them. He reached out, careful to get her by the wrist so she couldn't do that pressure-point arm-numbing thing on him again.

Instead, he found himself rolling across the floor into her room. His head made contact with the foot of the large platform bed with a thud. And all the air whooshed out of his lungs when a pissed-off sistah landed hard in the middle of his chest.

Thighs spread wide, Chrys sat high up on his pecs. Arms trapped at his sides, the woman used the odd angle of his neck for leverage. A strong thumb pressed into the base of his trachea and delivered a most uncomfortable sensation that made him want to gasp and gag at the same time. He couldn't move without injuring her or himself.

"And I told you to keep your damned hands off me," she growled.

Skirt bunched up around her hips, the subtle scent of her delectable pussy tickled his nose. His cock shot to attention. A lethal agent sat on his chest, a thumb in just the right position to cause his windpipe considerable damage, he couldn't move…and he had a hard-on?

Yep, he was definitely crazy.

# CHAPTER ELEVEN

Chrys instinctively eased the pressure off his throat when Rahn gagged. But only a bit.

How dare the idiot bring up their lovemaking. He clearly didn't trust her to walk down the street alone. Then another thought bloomed in her mind—murders. He'd insinuated that they were tied to this ship somehow. They had to be or he wouldn't be as ridiculous about her being off alone when he knew she could take care of herself.

On the other hand, spirit guides for company or not, Rahn had let her waltz around unarmed and unaware of the true danger.

Adonei and Mahpiya stirred in the forefront of her mind for the first time since she and Rahn had literally run into each other on the hip, upbeat avenues of Ibiza. A wisp of thought eased through their bond and she felt like an instant fool.

Trust between her and her mate had nothing to do with this situation. After all, she'd suspected the man had been working a case all along. The rules that applied to Aegis agents, unfortunately, didn't apply to relationships. He wouldn't and couldn't share with her. The more she knew, the more danger she was in. The man was protecting her. Not to mention following protocol and orders. Just as she would have done had their roles been reversed.

Mahpiya gave her a glimpse of what her man was feeling. A flood of insecurity and heart-seizing fear streaked through their bond. Every emotion she could think of flooded her consciousness, caught up in a tangle of uncertainty, followed by determination and fierce protectiveness—and it was all Rahn's.

Except for this man, no one other than her cousin, Delaine, had ever looked out for her. And he loved her. Sure, it may have slipped, but it didn't change the fact that he'd said it.

This man put every male she'd ever met to shame. Sexy. Fearless. And just a little bit vulnerable. What an arousing combination. Sitting on his chest, their bodies pressed together in this position, she felt every flex and twitch of his rock-hard pecs. The sensitive flesh between her legs gave an answering tremor. Instantly aflame, the roaring heat of desire for Rahn consumed her. With a tone she'd never heard herself use before, Chrys gave him a new set of orders.

"Don't fucking move," Chrys growled. As if he could with his neck at such a wild angle. Chrys removed her thumb from the notch of his throat and settled her hands on the floor on either side of his head. But she was and would remain in charge. She needed to take him, rather than be taken. And he would move when she told him to, damn it.

Rahn flipped her off his chest and pinned her underneath his big body. No way. Wasn't happening. She rolled him off and landed on top again. By the time the dance was done, they were halfway across the room, dizzy, out of breath. And laughing like two loons with carpet burn.

Side by side on the thick rug, their chests heaved and fell from exertion. Turning to look into the other's eyes only resulted in more chuckling. On a dime, Rahn's twinkling, whiskey brown eyes grew smoky, hungry. His jaw tightened along with the intensity of his gaze. That look reached through her clothes, clear down to her soul. It was like lying on the floor with Superman, complete with X-ray vision and sex appeal that stirred up a longing so raw that it had her exploding off the floor again.

Mahpiya's wild roar sounded in her brain. The huntress had come out to play.

And this time, things would be seen through to their rightful conclusion—Rahn naked underneath her with his powerful cock thrusting deep. And loving it.

This time, when she planted herself on top of him, his fingers sank into her hips and held her there. Thighs splayed wide, Chrys scooted up his chest so she could reach his lips. A split second before she slanted her mouth over his, his fingers began to undo her blouse. To hell with niceties or preliminaries. Swatting his hand away, she ripped the damned thing down the middle. Between her and Rahn, they sure seemed to be destroying a lot of clothes lately. Shucky darn.

Buttons flew in all directions, landing around the room with soft thuds, followed by the soft swish of linen as the shirt joined them on the floor.

Screw the skirt.

With the crotch of her little slinky panties pushed aside, Chrys dry-humped the bulge in Rahn's pants. Fumbling for the zipper of his jeans, now damp with her own cream, she almost breathed a sigh of relief when Rahn pushed her hand aside and freed his steel-hard cock.

Damn, could the man get any more perfect? Not only

was he built like a six-foot tank covered with perfect tanned skin, but his cock was literally a golden rod. Wide at the base, thickly veined and delicious. And just the perfect length to fill her to bursting without pain.

"Does this mean you forgive me, love?"

"Shut up and fuck me already," she panted. The shaft of his cock brushed the inside of her thighs and scalded. God, she wanted him.

Hot. Nasty. Rippling pleasure whirled from her soaked pussy around to the nerves at the base of her spine, and back again. The flared head of her lover's staff teased her entrance before sinking inside.

Rahn met her thrust for thrust as her hips slammed frantically, seeking, craving.

"Sssss, yes. More, baby. Please." The wild hunger to mate, to be pumped full of his seed drove her relentlessly toward the pinnacle of climax.

Chrys balanced on the balls of her feet and each plunge of his cock met nothing but pussy. Gaze lowered, her eyes were riveted on the erotic sight of his flesh disappearing inside hers. Hard met soft as Rahn's flushed, marble-hard cock sank into her sopping core with purpose.

She looked up. Rahn's gaze followed hers.

"Damn, baby, you're so wet. Look at all that cream dripping down my cock." He surged into her welcoming body.

She gasped, "All your fault."

Through gritted teeth, he replied, "I'll gladly take the blame for making you so hot and juicy."

She swiveled her hips, forcing a cry from both their throats.

"God, woman, you're going to kill me."

"Yeah, but you'll die a happy, happy man."

In her mind's eye, she couldn't see the fierce mating of their spirit guides. Instead, there was a faint hint of

Mahpiya's pleasure as her mate took her ferociously. And that little bit of bliss, the sexual heat generated by both couples, added to the energy of her lovemaking with Rahn and pushed the swelter up a notch, or two. Then three. Good lord!

"My god, do you feel that?" she panted.

"Yes," Rahn hissed in sync with the surge of lust thrumming down their bond. "Oh god, yes."

Strong, slightly roughened fingers wrapped around the globes of her breasts and weighed and palmed them before gently pinching the diamond-hard nipples. A streak of pleasure-pain sent her pleasure streaking toward the rafters.

"Bite me, Rahn. Please."

He sat up, grabbed her by the hips and raised her body up and down on his cock. At the same time, his lips closed over the sensitive spot where neck met shoulder and bit down.

Rahn's fingers dug into her ass and hips, sending a sensuous zing down the back of her thighs as he pounded her pussy. Teeth and tongue claimed her. His other hand squeezed and teased her nipples. And the untamed feral heat of the spirit guides stampeded through the psychic connection.

Good lord, could she possibly take any more stimulation? Rahn bit down harder. All she could do was be swept along for the ride.

Chrys' whole body stiffened as she came on a strangled cry.

* * * * *

With a receiver in his hand, Rahn moaned helplessly as the hot flick of a wet tongue tormented the base of his balls. That special spot just below his sac, but not quite to the pucker of his ass. Chrys found it during their earlier love play and was clearly determined to drive him out of his bloody mind every chance she got.

He lay on his back, shivering, trying to hold it together. One hand held a secure satellite phone tight to his ear, while the other buried itself down to the scalp of the head moving up and down between his legs.

"Yeah, lick it, baby." The words slipped past his lips before he could catch them.

"Well, damn, I love you too," echoed an amused voice through the earpiece. Shit, he'd been so distracted by the smooth glide of his woman's tongue, he hadn't realized he'd hit the speed dial, and was even less aware of the line ringing.

He covered up the phone and tried to extract his cock from his mate's oh-so-lovely mouth.

"Chrys, baby, I can't think when you do that."

She opened wide, took both his balls into her mouth and gently suckled. Oh, damn.

"Chrys. God, woman, if you don't stop, our boss is gonna hear me come."

Stilling immediately, her lips fell open on a gasp and his sac fell heavy against the inside of his thigh. He'd never seen Chrysalyn blush such a lovely shade of red-infused caramel. If she hadn't looked so mortified, he would have laughed.

With a final swipe of her tongue over the weeping head of his throbbing staff, she crawled up his body, sat up long enough to pull the covers over them, then settled down with her cheek pressed into the crook of his shoulder.

His arm automatically circled her body and pulled her closer until her short silky curls brushed his chest. It tickled. A satisfied sigh escaped her lungs as she settled in. Stray fingers plucked and played with his nipples. The sensation spread out from the taut nubbin across his pecs, only to dive-bomb for his cock. He closed his eyes and prayed.

*Lord, please help me to not drop the phone and hump my woman senseless with our boss on the line.*

Mahpiya's subtle chuckle sounded in the recesses of his mind.

Geri's amused words blared through the earpiece. "Well, are you back, Rahn?"

"Yeah, boss, I'm back. I'd like to put you on speaker so Chrys can hear too."

"So that's who has you moaning like a moose in heat, eh?"

Rahn hit the speakerphone button and the voice of the woman who'd been more friend than manager to both him and Chrys filled the room.

"Good morning, Chrysalyn."

"Mornin', Geri."

"What's up? How are you?" Geri asked. Even if Rahn had been both deaf and blind, it would have been hard to miss the cheeky sarcasm lacing her words.

"I'm fine. At least I'm not bored. As for what's up…well, Rahn is."

Rahn's mouth fell open.

"Chrys!" Damned woman.

"What?" she queried, then had the nerve to cast him an innocent-as-a-new-kitty stare. "Well, I can't help it if you're sexy as hell."

The two women giggled like schoolgirls at the mall on a boy-watching trip. Rahn felt his cheeks go up in flames. His mind's eye filled with Adonei, who had no problem grinning at his expense. What was this, torment Rahn day or something?

With a gentle pinch to Chrys' gorgeous round ass, he sucked up the embarrassment and chuckled along with the ladies. Besides, he was too damned sated and happy to stay upset over his woman bragging about his cock. There were certainly worse things she could have said.

Giggling up at him with a wicked waggle of her eyebrows, Chrys toyed with him as her hand traveled from his pecs and skated over his twitching abs on a clear path to his still-full rod. Rahn sucked in a wild breath as his stronger grip eased hers back to its semi-harmless position on his chest with a muttered curse.

"Enough, you two. Let's get down to it. Rahn." Geri's tone was all business. "Report."

"Captain Laurens accompanied me into Ibiza to see the local law dogs. And another body was found. Same profile as the others, same description of a possible suspect."

"This is just awful," Chrys whispered with genuine distress.

He met her gaze and frowned with a shake of his head. She wasn't supposed to know anything about his mission. A certain protocol had to be followed to get what he wanted, regardless of the fact that they lay skin to skin.

Geri overheard her quiet anguish anyway.

"Chrys, what do you know about what Rahn is doing?"

"Well, the man constantly fusses at me for doing what I always do, which is take care of myself. Then there's all the growling he does whenever I'm with my friend, this really good-looking man named Eden…"

Rahn's entire body stiffened involuntarily. Mahpiya's and Adonei's growls joined his. Just the mention of the man's name irked him. Irked all of them, except Chrys.

"Geri, with Chrys so close to danger, I request permission to brief her on my current case. She doesn't need to take part in any of the activities or investigation, but I'd be much more comfortable if she were in the know."

"I agree," Geri replied.

Chrys pushed up on her elbow and glared at him.

"Well, I don't."

"What?"

She narrowed her eyes and snapped, "I said, I don't agree."

The woman would choose now to be stubborn. Rahn gritted his teeth as she explained.

"I'm a trained professional with the same clearance as you. I'm on vacation, not inept."

"Yes, and on vacation means no work. It's my job to see to your safety, mate."

"Mate?"

Geri's question went ignored as Rahn's irritation flared. Did the woman always have to be so difficult? A few choice curses colored the air and aura about them to a few shades of blue as she plowed on.

"Look, Rahn, you may as well stop trying to use this mate business to put me on lockdown. I'm not some soft flower that needs protecting any more than you are. I'll walk and work by your side or not at all."

"What?" Rahn's brows snapped down into a frown. "Are you threatening me, woman?"

"Look, this isn't up for debate," Chrys continued.

Geri stepped into the fray with a chuckled sigh.

"Here's the skinny, Chrys. For the past year, there's been a murder near every port that ship has traveled to. All of the victims were similar in regard to their stations in life, though their physical profiles differed. The last four or five incidents, witnesses have provided a partial description of a possible suspect. Always the same, a man dressed in all black who walked with distinction and a certain presence. Medium height and build. Hell, could be anybody."

"And," Rahn chimed in, "just because this ship is full of nothing but privately owned, high-end, multimillion-dollar condos and wealthy people doesn't mean the killer isn't one of them."

Surprisingly, Chrys didn't say anything. But with every port they passed, the unsolved mystery brought with it a smothering oppression that sat heavy on Rahn's shoulders. Made him wish he could skip this investigation all together, shadow Chrys off the ship and go back home to London. Even if he had to truss her up like a turkey and toss her into a sack to do it. But it simply wasn't an option.

Last night the ship had moved back into open sea. In no time they'd be pulling into the port in Athens with only two more ports-of-call until they reached Alexandria. And for some reason he couldn't quite fathom, the closer they got to Egypt, the more concerned he became.

# CHAPTER TWELVE

No fucking like bunnies—or in their case, lions—in the hot tub. No cuddly kisses and sweet words with breakfast in bed. Mr. Romance was nowhere to be found.

In his place was some tyrant Chrys wanted to skewer. Since when was Rahn all business this early in the damned morning? She was supposed to be on vacation, damn it. Not dragged out of bed in time to meet the sun coming up over the horizon. Even if the view was brilliant.

Chrys stood in her room at the glass doors, gazing toward Athens. Greece, garden of gods and kings. Ancient. Unique. Beautiful. And too fucking bright. The terra-cotta buildings plastered with sparkling white façades reflected the light of the sun so brightly it was like staring directly at the largest star in the solar system. Chrys closed her eyes and watched myriad orange-white sparkles dance against the black backdrop of her eyelids. Even if she did crawl back into bed, she'd never get back to sleep now.

Dragging herself away from the deck doors, she

snatched the curtain closed and stomped into the oversized bathroom for a quick shower. Rahn hadn't told her where they were going or what he was up to, only that they weren't going ashore. So, if they weren't going anywhere, why the hell did he wake her up so early? And why had he left workout clothes on the bed for her? And where the hell was the man, anyway?

It would have been so simple to ask Adonei. But she just didn't feel like bothering with anything male, whether spiritual or logical, right now.

Dressed, and grumpy enough to growl obscenities at her hairbrush, Chrys pulled the hood of her sweatshirt up over her non-cooperating bed head, slipped on her tennis shoes and socks and headed for the kitchen. No Rahn, but the distant sound of running water and the steaming plate of food sitting on the dining room table answered at least a couple of her questions. He'd cooked breakfast for her before jumping in the shower. How sweet.

Didn't do a damned thing for her mood.

Instead of the cholesterol-laden, high-fat meal she craved, there was a light breakfast of two slices—two little measly slices—of smoked bacon and a boiled egg. Her spirits lifted a bit when she spotted the wheat toast with a smattering of butter and her favorite peach preserves. One bite had her sighing with pleasure. That and a cup of gourmet coffee to die for, with just the right amount of cream and sugar.

Wait, back up. How did Rahn know she loved peach preserves?

*Of course my Adonei told him. There isn't much those two don't discuss these days,* came Mahpiya's sultry voice floating into her head. An image of the regal cat appeared in her mind. Her golden fur shimmered, slightly translucent as Mah settled back on her haunches and licked a paw.

'Those two sit up and talk about me?' Chrys inwardly

gawked around a bit of the heaven-covered toast.

Mahpiya's lack of response, in addition to a "duh" expression, told Chrys all she needed to know.

Aloud, Chrys asked, "Well, what else do they say about me and how much detail are we talking here? So, Rahn knows I adore peach preserves. Does the man know the color of my favorite underwear too?"

*My child, I would not be surprised if you found a few dozen new pair of said underwear in your size and your three most favorite colors. After all, Rahn has plans for each pair. Strange, each scheme seems to end with the scraps of cloth either in shreds or perched on top of his head...with you still in them. Hmm. His lack of finesse where you are concerned is somewhat comical.*

Chrys sputtered and her coffee projected itself a foot across the top of the lovely lacquered table.

Sensing her distress through Mah, Rahn flew out of the room that had served as his former bedroom—these days all he kept in there were his clothes. In a few fleet steps, he was across the living room, through the kitchen and in the dining room, pounding her back with firm, effective whacks.

"Chrys, love, are you all right?"

She just nodded jerkily between lung-wrenching hacks as Mahpiya's smug and totally self-satisfied image faded from behind her eyes.

*Excuse me, young Chrys. Adonei is calling to me.* With a wink, the damned cat was gone.

Chrys, on the other hand, blushed furiously. With a croaked "I'm all right", she left a concerned Rahn staring after her and hurried to change her coffee-stained t-shirt.

\* \* \* \* \*

Exactly thirty minutes after Chrys' breakfast, Rahn

took his still-grumbling woman down to the fitness area. He'd purposely avoided her questions last night when she'd asked him about heading into port. Most of the owners had gone ashore for an overnight excursion in Athens.

Vacation or not, she needed to keep her skills honed and sharp. The gym was usually reserved for basketball and volleyball, but today the place was all but deserted. They could spar and, if she wished, talk about the case with relative privacy.

Rahn looked her up and down. He loved the way her workout pants hugged her hips and that lovely, lush ass. The sweatshirt covered up just about everything else, but he knew good and well what was under it—a little gray sports bra. And nothing else.

Before his body could react to the thought of stripping her bare and nibbling on her candy nipples, he pushed the temptation away and focused on the task at hand—sparring.

He dragged her fully into the gym, dropped his gear bag by the nearest wall and squatted to unzip it. Chrys was a petite little thing, but strong in body and character. And he wouldn't go easy on her, knowing the woman would go for blood from the second he signaled "go".

"Name your weapon."

With a roll of her eyes and a sigh, she finally said, "Give me the Japanese bo. For starters."

Her glare spoke volumes. Guess she really wasn't a morning person. Keeping her up half the night exploring every sexual position known to man couldn't possibly have anything to do with her grumpiness.

Rahn dug a pair of bokken out of the bag, tossed her one and walked to the middle of the floor. "On your mark."

Chrys gave a short bow, and it was on.

And damn, the woman was good with the thing. The

slim sword-shaped piece of smooth wood sliced through the air with a hiss. A loud clack echoed through the wide-open space as their weapons met. He countered a blow to his upper thigh, but her strike was so hard and solid that the vibration traveled up his arm and settled in the joint between shoulder and collarbone.

A loud "yaaaahhhh" erupted from deep in her being, as if she'd gathered all her chi, all her life force, just for this moment. Three swift kendo blocks warded off his attack, then she flowed into a high diagonal cut, followed by a half-cut, full-cut combination that nearly took his head off.

Chrys signaled a break and took just long enough to strip off her sweatshirt. Then she jumped back into the fray with skill, grace and undisguised intent. Next came a good solid bout of exchanged blows. They both landed several good whacks. No doubt a good soak in the hot tub would be in order later.

With a step back, slightly winded with exertion, Chrys signaled that she was dropping her weapon. But if he thought she was giving in, he was quickly disabused of the notion. Chrys? Quit? Not bloody likely.

The second their weapons clattered to the floor, Chrys left the ground with a flying kick to the torso and landed lightly on her feet. He stumbled backward, quickly regaining his balance. Time to change tactics.

Then again, considering how much had happened in so little time, Chrys must be up to her eyebrows with frustration. Why not let her use this practice time to work it out on him? But he'd better remain focused or she'd pound him into a big greasy spot on the floor.

Chrys stood cool-headed and composed in a perfect horse stance. The perfect fit of her stretchy pants outlined the muscle of strong thighs. Sleek thighs. Delicious thighs. Damn, the woman was hot.

Moving in close, she engaged him in hand to hand

with a strange combination of Aikijutsu and Krav Maga. And she gave everything she had, and then some.

Just then he inhaled deeply, trying to catch his breath. And got a whiff of Chrys in all her sweaty glory.

The way the perspiration glistened on her skin called his tongue, urging it to lick a path through it. The ferocity with which she defended and attacked turned him on like nothing else.

This was fucking ridiculous. Even in a fight, he wanted to make love with her. He backed up, trying to ignore the uncomfortable ridge pushing at the front of his sweats. Good thing he wasn't wearing boxers or he'd have a tent in his pants.

A surge of plain old lust swept him from toes to nose. When Chrys let a punch fly for his jaw, he caught her little fist in his larger one and yanked her to his chest, then flipped her around.

His cock pressed into the crack of her ass. She tilted her head and tried to look back at him.

"Rahn?" The way his name rolled off her lips held just a hint of confusion with a splash of arousal. Enough to push him right over the edge.

An open-mouthed lick across the back of her sweaty neck reduced them both to panting, horny-assed agents.

Turning slightly, whatever she was going to say was cut off in the ferocity of Rahn's kiss. A kiss so blatantly carnal, hell, he even shocked himself by the urgency with which his mouth moved over hers.

In seconds, she was squirming, trying to turn around to circle her arms around his waist and grind the flat of her belly against his hardening cock. Peeling the bottom of her damp sports bra up, her lovely breasts spilled into his hands. He teased, palmed and stroked them until she wriggled. She broke the kiss on a groan, whispering her need.

"Mmmm, oooh…" she panted. Her head rolled to the

side and he couldn't resist biting and laving the ultra-sensitive spot where neck met shoulders. A series of wild shudders racked her body and her pants became desperate moans.

"Rahn, baby, I need it. Please…"

And he wanted nothing more than to give it to her. But there was no way in hell they'd make it all the way back to their apartment.

Instead, he straightened her bra, tossed her sweatshirt into his gear bag, then scooped her up in his arms. Headed out of the gym, he didn't set her on her feet until they reached the room he'd spotted at the end of the hall on an earlier trip down here.

From this day forward, whenever Chrys thought about aerobics, her face would blush a shade of caramel apple red every time. He would see to it.

The man's kiss was like rich dark chocolate, potent, rich, a pure aphrodisiac. Better than the best cup of hot cocoa in the morning. Better than fine aged port wine. Better than…than peach preserves!

And it only took ten seconds of his delicious mouth on hers to make her want him so bad she ached with it. Her pussy bloomed, swelled and moistened in anticipation of his lovely cock spreading her open and sinking deep.

A moment of concern intruded when she saw where he carried her. It was the damned aerobics room. Obviously, no one was scheduled to use it today since the shades were all down and most folks had gone to Athens. But still, it was a public-use room.

"Rahn, wait. No way." But her body screamed yes when he set her on her feet and a broad palm kneaded her tingling breasts through her sports bra. Her nipples peaked and stiffened, wanting more. More of his touch. More of his cock pressing against her ass cheeks. More of everything.

The *click* of the door lock echoed around the room. It was just the two of them. In a room with mirror-covered walls.

Care melted like snow underneath a hot July sun. Chrys didn't think she'd ever seen a human being strip so fast. In seconds, Rahn's clothes sat piled at his feet. The raw, hard glint of his whiskey brown eyes reached through her soul and pulled. Hard. Speaking of hard, the man was that, and then some. The muscled peak of one biceps rose and fell as his hand stroked the mouth-watering length of his cock. The other arm reached for and caught her.

From between clenched teeth, his desire spilled from his lips.

"Chrys, damn, I want you so much I'm almost crazy with it. Even without asking Mahpiya to lend me her keen sense of smell, your scent reaches out and grabs me by the gut. I need to fuck you."

Dayum!

What the hell could she say to that, other than "Jump me, now"!

But first, she had to taste him.

Dropping to the floor, her knees landed on the soft pile of clothing. Her lips opened in anticipation of his unique flavor. Mouth wide, eyes closed, Chrys leaned forward, so ready to feel him bumping the back of her throat.

With a squeak, her lids flew upward as her hands grabbed for whatever she could get a hold of. Flipped onto her hands and knees, palms flat on the floor, a stream of cool air flowed against her skin as her pants and a pair of skimpy underwear were peeled down and off. Rahn's warm breath came out in a rush against her ear.

"If you touch me, I'll blow. I'm so hot and hard for

you, I just need to get inside. Are you ready, love?"

Boy, was she ever!

No man had ever wanted her so much, needed her so badly. The knowledge alone had her soaking wet, swollen and achy.

The tip of his cock nudged her weeping folds apart. Damn, he was so hot the velvety skin stretched taut over the fat head practically scalded and sent her own temperature soaring. With one surge, he was seated to the hilt with his chest plastered against her back, panting like he'd run a marathon.

Chrys' adrenaline ran so high, it barely registered that she held them both off the floor. The only thing she cared about was…more. Hips squirming uncontrollably, she silently begged for him to put out the fire he'd kindled in her womb. Her flesh tried to hold him inside as he slowly, deliberately withdrew.

"Unggh," came his ragged cry as he slammed back inside. His breath whooshed out of his lungs while hers felt corked up in her chest.

Out.

"Rahn, oh my god."

In.

"Oh, yes!"

Out. Too damned slow.

"Rahn, fuck me, damn it."

Chrys felt her lion rise up and push against the surface of her thoughts like never before. It was more than Adonei's consciousness. It was Adonei in pursuit of Mahpiya.

The entire length of Rahn's rock-hard staff disappeared into her body and triggered an explosion of stars. Light streaked across the back of Chrys' mind as the two majestic beasts pounced and came together like the swirling vortex of a summer storm. Both were hunters. Neither was prey. And the mating of spirits was fierce and beautiful, echoing the maelstrom of emotions streaking along the bond to surround Chrys and her mate.

They cried out together, both caught up and caught off guard by the intense rush of sensation.

"Shit!" came their echoed cries.

Then the man became a literal fucking machine.

Eager for every inch, Chrys' body took over and instinct ruled. Her chest hit the floor, leaving just her ass in the air as she clawed frantically for anything to anchor her. Rahn's fingers dug into her flesh, pulling her hips back to meet each stroke.

"Yes, baby. Give it to me," she gasped.

He moved deeper, harder.

"Is this what you want, Chrys?" The words were gravelly, harsh.

She yelled her response. "Yes!"

"My cock and only mine?"

"God, yes!"

"Then come around my cock, love. Let me feel that sweet pussy milk me. Touch yourself, sweet."

Just as she began to stroke her slick, swollen clit, Chrys turned her head and caught their reflection in the mirror. Hell, she didn't think it was possible to get any more turned on than she already was.

She was wrong.

The sight of Rahn's marble hard girth sinking into her willing flesh, along with the fingers plucking and rubbing her slick, swollen clit sent her out of her mind.

Orgasm gathered low and tingled at the base of her spine. It burst through her entire being—mind, soul and body. Chrys came on a loud wail, with Rahn's roar echoing in her ears.

\* \* \* \* \*

Eden plopped into the nearest living room chair, panting from the morning's activities. He surveyed the room and sighed. Perhaps he'd taken it a bit too far. A slew of porcelain arms and legs littered the floor in front of the specialized curio cabinet. The beveled panes of glass lay shattered into fine pieces amidst the array of special-ordered shirts, kilts, blouses and trousers. He admired the hand-sewn moccasin still on a dislocated foot.

No. There was no way he'd accept the meaning of the cards. She had to be mistaken. Everyone made mistakes. Even pharaohs, right? Yes, even pharaohs. And like everyone else, pharaohs passed from this plane to the next. And many went before their appointed time. Like this one.

And now who would give him direction?

Perhaps he could guide himself? He'd never possessed the level of skill with the tarot as his harem mistresses. Especially this last one. But now he'd ripped her and all her males to pieces in fury as her words echoed in his head.

She'd claimed the upside-down Empress hadn't meant Chrys was losing interest in the Rahn asshole. In fact, his pharaoh had left important information out of her first readings of the damned card and neglected to tell him that the reading was accurate…if the person who'd consulted the cards was a woman.

In that case, the upside-down card could represent that woman and indicate a partial success in an important area of her life.

But if the person consulting the cards was a man, it could indicate a weakening of the figure of his beloved, either because the man experienced sentiments less intensely, because the sentiments of the woman had weakened or because she felt physically or psychologically distant.

But he'd been operating under the presumption that Chrys was losing interest in the Rahn asshole, not feeling physically distant from Eden himself. Not to mention he'd been feeling distant from his harem mistress for some time now. The cards could have easily meant his disintegrating tie with his now-in-many-pieces beloved.

But then again…

Damn it, he just wasn't sure. And he'd become so enraged when his porcelain beauty revealed the other possibilities of the card's meaning, he'd snapped her neck like a chicken before she could finish the explanation. And now she was gone. Still, her absence was not his concern as much as the possibility that he'd missed something in her interpretation or misunderstood what she had been trying to say.

Sigh.

And it would be months before his next pharaoh was completed. He'd just have to make do until then.

# CHAPTER THIRTEEN

"I can't believe you're not ready to go," Chrys teased, moving into the kitchen to turn off the lights.

As she passed, Rahn eased up behind her. He pulled her into his arms, planted a loud smack against her temple and held her tight.

"Not my fault. When Captain Laurens ran into us on the way back from our workout, he said he wanted to speak with me for a few minutes. I couldn't possibly cut the man off mid-sentence when he had such important information to share."

"Mid-sentence?"

A fist balled up on her hip while a foot tapped out a cadence on the hardwood floor. And that foot was dressed in the sexiest damned high-heeled, ankle-wrap sandals he'd ever seen. And her dress? Shit, she was going to dinner in that? A black backless halter affair that molded perfectly to her luscious curves until it hit her waist. From there, it flared out with a little flip that made him want to peek underneath it. Surely it was designed for a midnight interlude on a private deck…with her leaning over the railing with it hiked up over her hips as she wiggled her ass at him.

God, at this rate, he'd never make it to dinner. He shook his head to clear it and returned to a safer, less freaky subject.

"So, the good captain's few minutes turned into almost an hour. But the details he passed to me were good ones. Someone got a decent look at our suspect."

"What? That's great news." She turned in his arms and hugged him around the waist. Pushing away, she headed into the dining room and snapped off the light. Rahn trailed behind her, watching her check and double-check that each light was turned off.

"Still annoyed I'm not ready and dressed for our dinner date?"

"Me? Annoyed? Never," Chrys laughed playfully. "Now hurry up and shower already. Every owner I've spoken to has complained about how hard it is to get reservations for this place, and we own the whole damned boat. Our seating time is 8:00 p.m."

"What time is it now?"

The roll of her eyes should have answered the question clearly. "It's 7:58 p.m., sir."

"Well, why don't you go on ahead? I'll meet you downstairs at the restaurant. The fancy highfalutin Japanese one, right?"

"Yep, that's the one." She still moved around the apartment in an endless stride. Now she was checking the locks on the glass doors that led to the deck.

"Hey, I turned on the shower for you already. Move it, handsome," Chrys called from across the expanse of the den and disappeared into his old bedroom, now termed the "guestroom", to complete the security check. He couldn't blame her. If she hadn't done it, he would have. In their line of work, it became second nature after a while, almost a nightly ritual of sorts.

Shucking his clothes on the way to the master bath,

Rahn couldn't ignore the sense of foreboding that rode him like a damned cowboy rode a bucking bronco. He simply couldn't shake it.

*Mah, go with Chrys and your mate to the restaurant. I'll shower quickly and meet you in about ten minutes.*

Mahpiya's presence dimmed. Chrys' giggle from the living room told him that she and Mah were probably teasing the hell out of poor Adonei about something or another.

Males. They just couldn't get a break. And god help them when the two women got together and ganged up on them. Witty, smart. Damned merciless. And he wouldn't have them any other way.

Soothing hot water felt good sluicing over his sore muscles. He and Chrys had sparred every day for the last three days that the ship had been in port in Greece. The woman packed a wallop and gave as good as she got. If he'd had time, he would have rather soaked in the hot tub to loosen up the tense muscles and soothe the knots and bruises up and down his back. The woman had really worked him over. He'd taken it easy on her, but Rahn was sure there were a few choice spots where she could stand a soak.

He was soaping up when Chrys walked in. Neatly arranged on a set of hangers were his favorite suit and a shirt-tie combination that matched her dress. She headed straight to the closet and hung it up. On her way out, she stopped, did a double take then backed up five steps.

"Dayum! You look so yummy." She slid her fingers over the glass, leaving trails across the steam-covered glass. "Too bad the Mastersens are meeting us for dinner, otherwise…"

The words hung in the air as those same fingers teased over the swell of her breasts, as her little pink tongue peeked at him from the corner of her mouth.

Heat crept up Rahn's neck, and it wasn't from the shower. When the woman touched herself like that, said things like that, he couldn't help but feel...well, flattered. Nobody affected him like Chrys. No one could make him feel sexy, cherished and wanted like she did.

"Well, that's all right," she sighed dramatically. "I'll get mine later. On top."

His cock shot to attention.

She grinned and practically skipped from the bathroom. "See you in ten minutes."

Damned tease. But she was his damned tease.

A few minutes later, he stepped out of the shower and stood for a moment, breathing in the thick humid air. Chrys had left the bathroom door open, but her scent lingered. It never ceased to amaze him what a simple whiff of the woman did to his nervous system. His poor cock should be crying out for mercy by now, rather than begging him to call her on her cell and tell her they were having dinner in bed.

Drying quickly, he ducked into the cedar-lined walk-in closet. A smile kicked up one side of his mouth when he saw the underwear and socks sitting perfectly folded on the shelf for him.

She was such a neat freak. Good thing she didn't expect him to be one.

He'd just zipped up his pants when a faint rustle caught his attention. Chrys must have forgotten something.

Rahn walked out of the closet. His stocking feet touched the steam-dampened tile of the bath area when he met pain so intense, the breath froze in his throat. The muscles of his back seized and twitched. From behind, cold steel twisted and plunged deep into his body, separating his ribs to pierce the organs underneath.

And he knew he was a dead man.

* * * * *

With a smile at the light banter going on in her head, Chrys followed an immaculately clean waiter through the restaurant. Rice paper lanterns sent a gentle glow from the center of each large circular table. Japanese kanji symbols strategically placed along the walls and the rich red cinnabar ornaments here and there, gave a feeling of "rightness" to the atmosphere. She wasn't really into Feng Shui, and doubted the decorators of this Japanese restaurant were either, considering the art was of Chinese origins. Either way, her spirit guides seemed to love the energy of the place.

Chrys settled down in her chair, sat back and allowed a sense of peace and relaxation to envelop her— something she hadn't felt since she learned of the case Rahn was working.

The Mastersens were seated and already sipping on frozen, delicious-looking green cocktails. Several couples Chrys didn't recognize were in the middle of ordering the same thing when Mrs. Mastersen spoke to her.

"Chrysalyn, dear," Mrs. Matersen beamed. "I'm so glad you could join us for dinner. You must try one of these. It's a Midori Sunrise and tastes like tropical paradise."

Mrs. Mastersen was an all-out chatterbox. On the way back aboard ship on Ibiza, the woman had amused Chrys when she'd spotted the bag of specialty cigars she'd purchased. She'd introduced herself and her husband, then asked to try one without an ounce of shame. Gray-haired, feisty and carefree, the two were enjoying their retired years sailing around the world. Chrys had loved them on sight.

"Your dress is downright sexy, young lady. Now where is that delightfully handsome beau of yours? And

329

he let you out looking like that? He'd better be careful or Harold here might put the moves on you. Mr. Mastersen was quite the rake in his day. Still has great skill…"

Chrys wondered if the woman had taken a single breath.

"And even after all these years, he still makes sure I come before he does."

Chrys coughed on the iced water she'd been sipping. Way more information than she needed to know. Clearing her throat, a quiet giggle escaped between words.

"Thank you for the compliment on my dress, ma'am. As for Rahn, an earlier outing took a bit longer than he thought."

Captain Laurens sat down at the head of the table and said, "That would be my fault, I'm afraid. Hope we didn't put too much of a dent in your plans."

Chrys smiled and said, "When I left, Rahn was getting ready. He sends his apologies and should be walking in the door any minute now. So, I think I'll order his drink for him. Waiter?" Chrys called, and another smartly dressed young man headed her way. "I'd like a glass of your best chilled rice wine for my, er, friend. And I'll have one of those green things, please."

"Friend, eh?" Mrs. Mastersen gawked excitedly. "How fabulous for you, my dear. You've dated a while, have you?"

"We've worked together for more than six years and know each other well." The rest of it was none of anyone's business. Out of nowhere, the image of Rahn in the shower burst into her thoughts.

*I am sure my charge would blush if he knew what you were thinking just now. Can you think of nothing but his cock?"* Mahpiya whispered to Chrys, her tongue lolling to the side.

'Oh, hush up, you. You're not supposed to tell all my

secrets, and I can tell from the way the bond feels that Adonei is listening in.'

*Of course I am listening in. It is my job, is it not?* Adonei sniffed indignantly, then turned to Mah, fussing. *And do you have to speak so boldly regarding your charge's private parts?*

Chrys almost laughed out loud. Didn't he know by now not to set himself up like that? Before she could form a single smart-assed response, Mah was all over him.

*My dear Adonei, I believe you are in need of schooling, and given your old age,* Mah paused for dramatic effect, *you know I certainly do not have to use the word cock. I have been a spirit guide for eons. There are many other ways to express myself, mate.*

Chrys clamped her lips together, picked up her water and sipped, trying to hide the smile at the corner of her lips. Oh, boy, here it comes.

*I could have called it by some of the other words I have heard over the years, like bacon bazooka...*

*Bacon what?* Adonei queried, his brow pulled down in a confused frown.

*Do you not like that word? 'Tis much better than cock, don't you think? No? Perhaps pork sword?*

*What is it with you and pig meat?* Adonei groaned, clearly wishing he hadn't said anything.

*Fine. No more pork. So what about tally whacker? Tickle-gizzard? Wanker? Tube steak?*

Chrys' own eyebrows flew up at that last one. Tube steak? Eww. Adonei swiped a huge paw at Mah, but the lioness dodged it with a laugh and simply kept right on.

*Maypole? Meat whistle? Milk bone? Mr. Happy?*

Adonei rolled his eyes and grumbled something about the Great Spirit's sense of humor and boneheaded mates.

Suddenly, the muscled body of the tawny-haired

lioness stiffened. Alarm and no small amount of fear streaked down the bond and settled in the pit of Chrys' stomach.

'What? What is it?' Chrys demanded, thinking the lions were upset because Eden was headed their way. The man walked right up to the captain, bowed low and managed, yet again, to insinuate himself into their plans. But it wasn't Eden. It was something else.

Mahpiya's head swung from side to side as if she were looking for something. After a moment or two of soft, seeking roars, her shaken gaze turned inward to Chrys and Adonei. The lioness's answer was laced with undisguised panic. Something Chrys never imagined to see or hear from the great huntress.

*My charge! He is gone! I cannot feel or hear him,* Mahpiya wailed even as Adonei tried to sooth his distraught mate with broad strokes of his tongue just behind her ear.

Chrys squirmed in her chair in a subdued version of the pee-pee dance. "Excuse me, you all. I need to take a trip to the powder room." Glad no one questioned her, she grabbed her little clutch purse and scooted back from the table, keeping her movements slow and deliberate.

Out in the hallway, Chrys ducked past the entrance to the ladies' room and hurried down the hall, speaking to her spirit guides. She tried to ease Mahpiya, who paced nervously at the forefront of her mind,

*It'll be all right. Nothing short of death could take a charge from his spirit guide,* Adonei reminded them both.

*That's what I am afraid of,* Mahpiya screeched.

Adonei nipped the skin just above her shoulder with a muted growl, steel grit behind every word. Mahpiya stilled, startled into a quiet contemplation.

*You will cease this negative talk of your charge. Speeding negative thoughts or energy his way

*will gain you nothing.Come with me, now,*\* he demanded with the quiet authority only an alpha could pull with one so great as Mahpiya.

Before Chrysalyn's eyes, the air in front of her shimmered and blurred as the two big cats took on their corporeal forms. It was the first time Adonei had ever come to her in this form without being summoned. She didn't hesitate.

'Both of you go ahead of me. Find Rahn.'

Adonei turned to Mahpiya and said, \**We hunt, my love.*\*

With a nod of her large regal head, Mahpiya agreed and let out a ground rumbling roar that would have frightened the stoutest heart. They turned and took off in opposite directions.

Walking as quickly as her high-heeled sandals would allow, Chrys moved quietly down the hallways and toward their apartment.

Moments later, Adonei pushed into her mind. What he reported made her strip off her shoes and tuck them under her arm. Her slender fingers dipped down into the front of her dress to retrieve her apartment key as she ran like the wind.

'Oh, no, Rahn. Rahn, don't you dare die, damn it,' Chrys ordered along the bond with their spirit guides, knowing they would both send her thoughts and feelings along to Rahn the same way they sped his current state to her. He was there, but just barely hanging on to the edge of consciousness. But based on Mahpiya's slight sighs of relief, it was more than there had been when she'd reached out to him mere moments ago.

Chrys burst through the front door, dropping her shoes and purse in the foyer. A quick stop in the kitchen for the first-aid kit, and she was off again, following Adonei's specific directions through the apartment. She knew exactly where to find him—on the master bathroom floor, bare-chested in a pool of his own blood. The tile was so slick with it, she almost skidded as she sped over the threshold. Dropping to her knees, the first-aid kit landed next to his too-still body with a loud clank. The gash in his side bled profusely. Afraid to move him, but knowing she must, Chrys called to the spirit guides waiting to aid her.

*Adonei, lend me your strength,* she grunted, trying to roll Rahn over on her own.

The lion's brute strength rushed into her muscles, filling them with supernatural might, heightening not only her own strength, but all of her senses as well. The scent of Rahn's blood and freshly showered skin and hair filled her nose and mouth. The sound of his shallow, barely there breathing spilled over her and filled her with an urgency mixed with a strange dose of melancholy.

She pushed it away and focused on the task at hand.

Now able to easily maneuver the dead weight of Rahn's densely muscled body, Chrys gently rolled him to one side and packed the wound with clean linen to staunch the flow of thick, hot, blood. His lids fluttered, but he didn't make a sound.

'Mahpiya, can you nudge him closer to consciousness?'

Chrys knew they had to pull him back to this side of the spiritual plane so he could call Mah. Rahn had to request her help. It was against the spiritual laws for a spirit guide to aid without being asked. They could not impose their will on their charges. But if they didn't do something fast, Rahn would be lost to them. He'd die.

Leaning forward, speaking directly into his ear, Chrys pleaded for him to call to Mahpiya. To ask for her aid, even if he asked with his mind and not his mouth. Rahn's eyes opened for a moment.

"Mah. Help. Please." The words were barely a whisper, but she heard them all the same. The fear that had been riding her released the bands around her heart and allowed it to beat again. Mahpiya's silent relieved response flooded the bond. Rahn would be all right.

Mahpiya disappeared all together from Chrys' consciousness and she knew the lioness focused all her healing energies on Rahn. It was hard work mending flesh and replenishing blood, even for a spirit guide. But she'd saved his life once before. Now she would do it again.

But now Chrys was flat-out pissed off. Someone had done this to her mate. Someone had tried to take Rahn away from her.

Grabbing one of the thick bath sheets off the rack, Chrys covered up Rahn's bloody body and left the bathroom. Not bothering to wipe the blood off her feet or remove her ruined dress, she flew for the nightstand across the huge bedroom. Almost as an afterthought, she spoke to Adonei.

'Guard the apartment, will ya, boy?'

The moment the words left her lips, Adonei's hackles rose. A deep menacing growl rumbled in his chest as his stance took on one of attack, gaze fixed on a point behind her. Chrys went still.

Unease snaked its way down her spine, and the nerves along the bottom of her stomach danced in time with Adonei's growling. But she wasn't afraid. The strength of her spirit guide still flowed like fire through her entire being. Whatever, whoever it was, bring it on.

She turned, ready to drop into a fighting stance if need be.

"Eden, what the hell are you doing in here?" she demanded. Unsure of his intentions, Chrys instinctively calculated the difference in their body weight and the moves required to take him down fast. He looked slightly crazed, but as soon as the expression appeared, it was gone again.

"Chrysalyn, your dress, what happened? You're covered with blood."

Now he appeared genuinely alarmed. Adonei wasn't buying it, but her man needed help and she didn't have time to deal with this right now. A faint groan caught her attention. Rahn. Heading toward the phone, she tossed the words over her shoulder in a rush.

"Rahn was attacked. He needs a doctor."

"Really? Here?" he gasped. "Go to your friend. I'll get the surgeon and call the local emergency." And Eden was flipping open his cell phone on the way out the door.

Back in the bathroom, she held Rahn's hand, stroked his beautiful fingers and ignored her tears as they splashed on the palm clasped gently in her own.

In mere minutes, Eden was back and the apartment became a hive of frenzied, but calm, activity as the ship's surgeon came in and tried to extract her from Rahn's side. Captain Laurens hauled her out of the bathroom, explaining how both her and Eden's fast thinking had saved her mate. Rahn was placed on a stretcher, covered with blankets and gently lifted from the cold tiled floor. All the while, the ship's doctors, along with the Grecian medics, marveled over the fact he was still alive.

# CHAPTER FOURTEEN

The ship was delayed in Greece while a full investigation took place. Nothing. No leads, no suspects. A week and a half later, with the aid of both Mahpiya and Adonei, Rahn was good as new. And while Chrys was relieved, she was so ready to get off the damned ship.

Upon arrival in Alexandria, she was up with the chickens and ready to head ashore. First stop, Qaitbay. Perfect starting point since Rahn was scheduled to meet a contact there anyway. And even better, since she couldn't sit in on that meeting she'd get some much-needed time alone, even if only for an hour.

High up on the imposing limestone walls of the Citadel, the tang of the salty sea air tickled her nose as Chrys took in the beauty literally surrounding her. A crisp breeze off the water took the edge off the midday sun. She raised her face to the sky as it blew over her, ruffling her short curls and cooling her skin from neck to knees.

What a mystical, soul-stirring place. She'd always wanted to see the Sphinx and the Pyramids of Giza.

Maybe even the monumental statues of Ramses the Great at Philae. But now that she stood on the banks of the Mediterranean, looking out over the crystal waters, Chrys couldn't believe she'd never looked into coming to Alexandria before.

The sparkling isthmus caught the eye of Alexander the Great more than twenty-three hundred years ago. Founded in 332 B.C., the city still carried his name, though Cleopatra, the last queen of Egypt who happened to be Greek, ruled her kingdom from here during the first century B.C.

Amazing was this fortress built by Sultan Qaitbay in the 1480s. Erected on the very foundation of the famed queen's Lighthouse of Pharos, one of the seven wonders of the ancient world. She wondered what Cleopatra looked like. Imagined the queen spending the night in her lover's arms as they gazed out to the sea toward Rome together, planning, dreaming of a life together.

But Julius Caesar and Cleopatra's love wasn't enough to save them from their own stupidity or the ill wishes of others.

And now Chrys was here with her own warrior lover. A lover who'd recently been nearly gutted.

The same foreboding she'd experienced in Ibiza and the night Rahn was stabbed slithered over her skin. The possibilities tumbled end over end through her mind. True, the attack on Rahn didn't fit the profile of the bad guy he was after. But what if the intrusion wasn't random, like Rahn, Geri and the others speculated?

As soon as the thoughts formed, she pushed them away. She hadn't survived as an undercover agent this long by allowing her life to be ruled by fear. Besides Rahn worried enough for the both of them.

Her thoughts turned toward home. Just where would that be for her when all of this was over? Lately, Rahn had been too busy luxuriating in her more-than-willing body to discuss it.

*Do not blame your mate,* Adonei complained. *It is not as if you have tried so very hard to speak to him about it.By the way, he expects you to remain where he left you, up on the wall.*

Males. They sure stuck together…which, of course, had nothing to do with whether she was right or wrong. Nor did it matter that she hadn't pressed the issue out of simple self-preservation of her tender heart. Skip it, they'd get around to it.

Shielding her eyes, she looked to the south toward a stone-enclosed harbor so large it resembled a sea full of boats, yachts and ships of various sizes, small to gigantic. To the north was the blue jewel of the Mediterranean. She gazed up to the main building, soaring seventeen meters skyward. When lookouts were stationed here, they could spot invaders an entire day's journey out to sea. On a clear day, perhaps she could see all the way to the Greek isle of Crete.

And this truly was a fortress, complete with inner and outer walls, gardens, courtyards and the towered fort of Qaitbay itself. No wonder it was referred to as the pearl of the Mediterranean.

Wandering around the impressive structure, she found her way to some of the coastal tunnels and passages under the walls that looked more like cave entrances. Thankful for the small windows set at intervals along the way that looked out to sea, Chrys wound her way around and through the dimly lit halls under the structure.

"Huh. Interesting," she mumbled to herself as she huffed and puffed her way up the steepest flight of stairs in all creation. Thankful she was in halfway decent shape, her journey ended—well, almost ended—on the first floor of the famous Qaitbay Citadel's main building.

There was no way in hell she was going to even attempt finding her way through the long, though interesting, passages. She'd just have to find Rahn from here. Better yet, she had two spirit guides watching her back. One of them would just have to go get him. As for Chrys, she was determined to sit her butt down in a chair and enjoy the silent company of the guards looking after the place.

Better yet, she was sure she'd spotted a bustling bazaar on the way here. Nothing like a good bout of shopping to get a girl back in a good mood.

Interrupting a heated debate between Mah and Adonei about the importance of post-sex conversation, she passed a thought to her companions.

'Adonei, let Rahn know where I am, will ya?'

*He is already aware and nearing.*

Then to the guards, she said in perfect Arabic, "Excuse me."

They eyed her askance, probably because she was an unescorted female. But these men would respect strength in a woman, even a foreign one. Motioning in the direction she wished to go, the bell sleeve of her white linen blouse fell back a bit to reveal taut skin stretched over well-honed biceps as she firmly, but respectfully, stated her request.

"Can you please assist me in the proper direction to hire a *hantour* to take me to the bazaar?"

One of the men passed a friendly smile, but before he could open his mouth, a stern-faced Rahn stood at her side. The soldier's smile became a full-blown grin.

"Sir, how good it is to see you again. It has been a long time."

Rahn gave the guard a slight bow and extended his arm to a gawking Chrysalyn. She had no idea why she was so surprised to hear Rahn converse in Arabic. After all, she'd just done it and she was a sistah from Colorado with no ties to this country to speak of. Rahn, on the other hand, had family here.

"Your aunt asked us to look out for you and your fiancée. She has been expecting you."

"Thank you, Lieutenant." A quick glance down at his watch was followed by a polite, "We must be going. We're due to meet my relative at the bazaar in less than half an hour. Thank you for escorting my, er, fiancée. It is much appreciated."

Chrys didn't say a word as he hustled her out of the building, across the courtyards and through the gates. No complaints here—the bazaar was exactly where she wanted to go anyway. She couldn't decide whether to grimace or roll her eyes when Mahpiya let a taste of Rahn's irritation slip through the bond they shared with both spirit guides. He was a very unhappy camper. Might have something to do with her exploring on her own. Oh well.

Linking her arm through his, she flashed a blinding smile and walked beside him to the carriage that would serve as their ride.

Rahn's anger crackled in the air. But damn it, she would never be a fragile flower. When would he see that? She hadn't intentionally upset him, but it was simply in her nature to do things on her own. Something Chrys was willing to work on, but certainly not changeable overnight. Besides, what was the harm in wandering around an old fort? The place crawled with guards anyway.

"Rahn, won't you speak to me?"

His answering growl spoke volumes. Damn, the man was otherworldly hot and hunky, even when he was pissed off.

"Baby, stop worrying. I was fine by myself. Besides, you've been attacked on this trip, not me."

Oops. The stiffening of his spine screamed "wrong

thing to say". She tried to clean it up.

"Rahn, I'm not trying to diss you. It's just that I've been on my own forever. Taken care of myself forever. Even with Delaine for a mischievous cousin, we grew up in different states. I only got to enjoy getting into trouble with her once a year, on our annual trip to Grandma's on the reservation. I don't want you worried about me, and I promise to try harder to let you protect me. Just realize that my independence isn't meant to make you worry. It's just who I am."

Anguish was painted across his brow, but the expression in his clear brown eyes said he understood.

"And let's not forget I've got two big bad African lions in my head with their power at my call simply for the asking."

With a frustrated sigh and a rake through his stylishly cut hair, he said, "I guess I can't expect you to do all the adjusting in this relationship. I'll try to be a bit more understanding when your need to get into trouble surfaces. I can't promise I won't spank you afterward."

The man had the yummiest smile this side of creation. *Yep. Sin on legs*, she thought as his grin did her in.

With her arm still twined around his, she leaned in close and inhaled. Mmm, he always smelled so good. All male musk and spicy love. He must totally exude some kind of kinky pheromone, because she couldn't think of a time since they'd been reunited that she didn't want to jump his bones. With a husky sigh, she whispered in his ear.

"Besides, right here, right now is the last time we'll be alone for a while. Don't waste it being angry. We'll be at your aunt's house for three days? Three whole days of sleeping without you? Damn. I can't wait to get back to the ship so I can strip you and bathe every inch of your rock-hard body." Had he stopped breathing? Good.

She grinned secretly and continued. "Then I'll straddle your perfect, manly, muscular thighs and slide down onto that delicious cock of yours."

Rahn met her gaze with a deadpan expression. Chrys wondered what he was thinking until a flash of pure lust zinged from his light brown eyes. That stare became potent enough to singe her eyebrows. A quick peek downward revealed the ridge rising in his pants.

All on their own, Chrys' slender fingers found their way to his groin and encouraged that ridge to grow a bit harder. All the way to the bazaar.

At their destination, the driver pulled the *hantour* up to a post where several other horse-drawn carriages were parked. Rahn paid the man, climbed down and tried to discreetly adjust himself.

"Damned woman."

"What?" she asked innocently. "What'd I do?"

"I don't have anything to cover this up." He nodded discreetly toward the impressive bulge pushing against his zipper. "I'm almost tempted to go buy some traditional men's clothing to hide this damned thing."

"Well, I happen to like that damned thing."

"While I'm glad you enjoy my cock, I don't particularly want it on display. And I don't even want to think about trying to walk right now."

She laughed. Couldn't help it.

A few clouds rolled in from the west, but it was still warm and balmy as they moved along. Turning a corner, Chrys screeched to a halt, biting the inside of her lip to keep her mouth from falling open.

The fabulous and unique scents and sounds of the bazaar hit her square in the face. Row after row of stalls and tents stretched out before them. This was heaven. Had to be. She'd never seen so many different items available in an open-air market. This was like the flea market from God! And she could haggle with the best of 'em.

Music floated from various directions. Some fast, some slow, all with the telltale hypnotic sounds of drums and pear-shaped stringed *oud* present in most music from this region. And so many oils and fragrances, it boggled the mind.

Aside from colorful hieroglyphs and drawings on leaf papyrus, there were paintings of pharaohs and their queens, ankhs, camels and such on black, brown and even bronze dyed leather. Rugs in every color and pattern imaginable, brass lamps, spices and perfumes, mother-of-pearl, silver and resin jewelry boxes. Another peddled heavy blown-glass oil lamps in a slew of vibrant colors with accompanying sweet, spicy and floral scented oils. Her favorite was a hand-blended mix of jasmine and vanilla with a touch of sandalwood and lemon. The aroma was so delicious, it even caught Rahn's attention for a second.

The stall next door was packed with curio accessories, including lead crystal tea sets and water pipes. Chrys snatched up a royal blue *hookah* pipe along with a small brick of mango and orange sticky tobacco from an endless selection, determined to try it. Maybe she'd become a *shisha* connoisseur instead of a flavored cigar lover.

So wrapped up in shopping and purposely ignoring the shuffling drag of poor Rahn's feet, Chrys almost missed her own stomach grumbling.

"Sounds like you could use a little something to eat."

"Gee, you think? Snarky doesn't become you, Rahn," she muttered with a smile as she pulled him to the next tent.

"Oh yeah? Since when?"

Good question.

But when they ran across several booths with intricately designed, embroidered head covers called *galabia*, Chrys just had to look around some more. The women manning the booth explained that the head cover was usually black or white when outside the home, but could be myriad colors when worn at home. She bought four of them.

"Woman, where in the world will you wear those when we get home?"

Wicked incarnate, she turned to her mate. "For your information, I can wear them all the time with…nothing else."

Rahn instantly relieved her of her mountain of purchases before his iron grip wrapped around her biceps. Rahn eased her around and through the milling crowd to a less populated section and into an empty booth. He released her long enough to tie the flaps closed and crowd her into the back room, again tying the flaps. God, he hoped this booth was empty for the day and not just empty for, say, the next five minutes.

"Rahn, what are you doing?" Chrys whispered, the corner of her mouth tipped up into a barely there grin.

"Minx. How 'bout showing me what you look like in that scarf right now…and nothing else."

"What? No way. What if somebody comes?"

"Should have thought of that before you decided to tease me," he grinned with slow and deliberate intent.

"Oh please, give me a break," she snorted, growing hotter by the second. Brown eyes practically aglow with sizzling heat, the man moved with purpose and grace, stalking her all the way across the tent. The back of her knees began to sweat. *Oh god, please send a strong breeze to cool me down*, she prayed. Because in a few more seconds, her little white linen pants outfit would be soaked through with more than just her own sweat.

Stiff with concern of getting busted having sex in an Arabic country in someone else's tent, Chrys bit her lip to keep from moaning. Didn't help at all.

"Aaaah." The groan slipped out as she was turned around and bent over the nearest object. Rahn's warm, wet tongue left a cooling trail across the skin on the back of her neck as his strong hands reached around her body. God, she loved when he did that.

Her breasts were at instant attention. Hell, even if he hadn't lifted her blouse to caress them, they swelled so quickly she could almost feel the blood pumping through the veins underneath her skin.

The heat of the day couldn't hold a candle to the temperature spike caused by the hard flesh pressed against her ass. Correction, the bare crack of her ass.

When the hell had the man taken her pants down? But she was so wet so fast, when he pressed into her yielding flesh and filled her in one stroke, Chrys didn't give a damn about the methods he used to undress her.

The man was a machine, all hard, unyielding and perfectly tuned. And so totally able to hit the sweet spot deep inside her creaming pussy.

"Damn," she panted. "God, that's so good."

"This is all I think about if you're within a hundred meters of me. Sliding into your hot pussy. Diving into this cunt as deep as I can go. Then holding you close after."

"Oh god," she wailed. He was fucking her like she was his last piece of ass before he died. He took her hard and fast. And her orgasm spiraled up out of her belly just the same way—hard and fast.

And she loved every minute of it.

Nothing like an afternoon quickie in a public place to invigorate a sistah. Hell, it was even better than shopping.

\* \* \* \* \*

Later, Rahn breathed an audible sigh of relief when

he spotted his aunt moving through the crowd. She waved and smiled as she made her way over to them.

Slightly taller than Chrys, her hair was covered with a beautifully embroidered *galabia*. Smooth skin, barely a shade lighter than Chrys' cinnamon tones, was visible on her face and hands. So this was a relative, eh? She knew it was probably a girl thing, but found herself wondering if the rest of Rahn's relatives had such beautiful skin. With his half-British, half-Egyptian heritage, Rahn sported more of the too-much-cream-in-the-coffee tanned tones, and boy, did he wear it well. Chrys was sure she'd never met such a handsome, gorgeously built, muscle-toting, kissable man as hers. Okay, time to quit staring and drooling at Rahn and greet his aunt like she had some sense.

"It is so nice to meet you, Chrysalyn."

"Chrys, please."

"Thank you. Chrys it is. I am Sumanjah el Hattal. You may call me Aunt or simply Suman will do."

The barely noticeable crinkles around her eyes and mouth brought to mind a mix of mature wisdom and a zest for life. She kind of reminded Chrys of her own aunts back home, who still lived on the reservation in South Dakota. Women who looked after their family, passed on wisdom and stood firm in the face of adversity, smiling all the while. And even though those women were friendly and sweet, they didn't miss a thing and wouldn't hesitate to tell you about yourself. And you'd better not call them by their first name, either.

Aunt Suman turned to Rahn. "I cannot stay long, but I do have news for you. Unfortunately, none of it is heartening."

Rahn looked back and forth between the two women.

"Maybe it can wait until later? We still plan to stay with you and Uncle a few days."

"Yes, but…"

The man was clearly torn between wanting to get the news on a possible suspect, but not wanting to leave her side to do it. Chrys tried not to roll her eyes, honest she did. But off they went, rolling upward in frustration before she could stop them.

"Rahn, why don't you find me a cup of that delicious thick-as-axle-grease stuff you guys call tea. Or better yet, I'll get it. We passed a stand with some goodies just down that way."

"Chrys, no…"

"I'll get some tea. You talk to Aunt Suman and do your job. I'm not officially on this case and I know you can't discuss details while I'm present. It is kind of cool that your aunt is your informant." Then she turned with an outstretched hand and said, "Ms. Sumanjah, I look forward to spending time with you and your family."

"Chrys," Rahn warned, the words pushed through gritted teeth.

Oh, please. She chuckled. He scowled and she reminded him that it was unlikely that she was a target.

Rahn practically bellowed, "And you know that how, exactly?"

Chrys' blood ran cold, simply because she couldn't answer the question. Yet she was determined that he not worry so much about her. Besides, in all her years of service, she'd never fallen prey to a criminal or became a target. This case was no different. If anything, Rahn was more likely to be in danger, considering he was actually "working". She was just along for the ride.

"Rahn, on the way here you promised to try to give me a little breathin' room, remember? Look, what could possibly happen to me here? The place is stuffed with people hawking and buying wares. And I promise to stay within screaming distance, okay?"

He looked ready to take his promise back, but he snapped his mouth shut. Judging from his clenched teeth and matching fists, Chrys knew it had probably taken all his mental and physical strength to pin his lips together. Good, 'cause she'd said all she had to say about it.

Giving him her back, she went off in search of something to drink. The tea served here was so strong that even though it was meted out in a cup barely bigger than a shot glass, it required at least three teaspoons of sugar just to get it down. But it was delicious and would stave off her hunger a bit longer. Not to mention the wonders of caffeine.

Standing outside one of the small cafes with a permanent location at the bazaar, she sipped the steaming brew and winced. Damn, it was potent stuff. Mahpiya and Adonei had been on high alert ever since she left Rahn's side and it was beginning to get on her nerves.

*Can't you two settle down? Or at least close down the link a little bit. Your edginess is making me nervous.*

But Chrys' words only seemed to agitate them more. The next instant, both imposing spirits settled into a lion's most common battle stance—feet planted firmly, eyes pinned on what they perceived as a threat, and ready to pounce.

# Chapter Fifteen

"Avoiding me?"

Chrys almost dropped her tea when the cats pacing around in her head upped their roaring and growling.

'Don't worry, you two. I'll be careful around him. He acts like a nice guy, but I'm beginning to have my doubts.'

For the first time in weeks, Chrys admitted to herself and her guides that there was something just a bit off about Eden, no matter how suave he appeared. Six years of undercover training kicked in and Chrys painted on a plastic smile and a serene façade. If she played her cards right, maybe she could get some answers in regard to what rubbed her companions the wrong way.

"Hi, Eden. Where've you been hiding lately? We didn't get a chance to thank you for helping after Rahn was injured."

"I thought I should give you and your friend some privacy to heal. I'm sure it was traumatic for you."

For her? Rahn was the one who'd been attacked. He was the one someone had tried to carve up like a Sunday baked turkey. Her man had lain in a pool of blood that night. If anything, it was traumatic for Rahn. She looked at Eden sideways, not caring for the irritation, however slight or unintended, when Eden called Rahn her friend.

Then there was Adonei. Damned lion was pacing the well-worn trail across her mind again.

Eden ordered a tea and asked, "So where is Mr. Benson?"

"Who? Oh, Rahn?" she asked with her best oblivious-as-a-blonde expression. "He's off shopping for a surprise for me," she lied. "Hey, what was that?"

"What was what, Chrysalyn?"

"That noise. Sounds like someone is in distress."

Instinct had her legs moving toward the sound. With a confused-looking Eden tagging behind her, Chrys silently sent Adonei ahead to scout.

When the mighty lion returned, his news hit her straight in the gut.

*It's a female. She is under attack. Two males, both masked. Neither as strong as you, even without the infusion of my powers.*

Chrys turned a corner into a dim alley and took in the scene before her. Just as Adonei said, two men yanked at the clothes of a kicking, screaming woman. She was completely covered from head to toe, like a Bedouin woman, but the creeps harassing her were trying to make sure she didn't stay that way.

Well, watching someone get raped in an alley just didn't float her boat. Without a second thought, Chrys moved in to protect the female and walked confidently into the fray. The men looked up and she could see their leers through the scarves over their ugly faces. One of them licked his lips. Ewww. Nasty bastard.

Eden's hastily mumbled "I'll go get help" made it more than clear she was on her own. Fine. Coward.

All their attention on Chrys, they released the woman who promptly took off at a dead run. The two would-be rapists began to circle Chrys. No worries. With no weapons, her body would simply have to take these assholes down.

Surrounded, Chrys didn't doubt she could still beat the hell out of them, especially with Adonei's strength. All she had to do was call.

Or that was the plan until Mahpiya shouted a warning into her skull. Too late. Someone snuck up behind Chrys and poked her in the kidneys with a very heavy, very cold piece of steel. Hell, even with lion super-strength and speed, there was no way she could dodge a bullet this close.

The order to shut up or else was an unfamiliar muffled hiss against her ear. And these bastards looked more than capable of following up on the "or else" part.

"Turn around."

Hands up in surrender, Chrys obeyed and mentally kicked herself in the head for not being more careful.

"What the hell?" she demanded, unable to keep the incredulity out of her voice. Eyes narrowed in disbelief, she stared at her abductor—Eden and the woman she'd just rescued. Even after swearing to be careful she'd allowed herself to be duped.

One of the bad guys wrapped several thin, but strong, twine ropes around her wrists and tossed a simple dress-like garment over her, effectively hiding her from the world. The victim had been nothing but bait and Chrys was well and truly caught. For now.

In the meantime, a call for Rahn was in order.

'Adonei, come to me. I need your assistance.'

*I am here, my charge.*

'Please go find Rahn. Show him what's happened. I need help.'

*I am sorry, Chrysalyn, but I cannot.*

'What?' she almost yelled aloud. 'What the hell do you mean? You can't scout him out and bring him back to help me?'

*We both promised your mate we would not leave your side for any reason.*

'You're my spirit guide, not Rahn's. Since when do his wishes carry more weight than mine?' she snarled along the bond as Eden's goon squad hustled her through the empty alleyway and away from the bazaar.

*Since you mated him,* Adonei responded frankly.

'What? Oh, this is fucking ridiculous. Mah, can you go?'

The lioness refused. But it made more sense for her to refuse a request than Adonei.

*I cannot disobey my charge any more than I can interfere in his choices. I was asked to stay with you and gave my word. But I promise to lend you my hunter's strength the moment your body is far enough away from the weapon trained on you.*

*You cannot lend her strength. Only I can do that,* Adonei huffed indignantly.

*Yet you will not do as your charge asks and go to her mate? Could you possibly get any more hypocritical than you are at this moment?*

An argument ensued. Chrys couldn't believe it. She was being taken who-knew-where thousands of miles from home while her two supposed bad-assed lions fought over who should do what. Obviously, mating among humans with mated spirit guides was rare, but right now, Chrys couldn't care less about their hierarchical rules and laws.

'Somebody do something, damn it,' Chrys demanded. That stopped the argument but didn't get her any further. So it was time to talk some sense into these boneheaded cats once and for all.

Patience all but done, she argued the case that because they were joined, Mahpiya was as much her spirit guide as Adonei, and vice versa for Rahn. By the time the three of them got a decent plan formed between them, the sun was setting and they were well outside of the city.

From the front seat of the vehicle, the woman who'd lured her into the alley turned, pulled off her head cover and leaned over the seat. It was then Chrys realized that none of her captors, save Eden, were Egyptian. They were all Eastern European with classic Euro features. Made perfect sense.

Rahn had explained to her how men of his culture believed they were caretakers of the earth and their faith, which included women. No man worth his salt in this country would sit by and watch if she were in trouble. So, Eden had gotten someone else to do his dirty work.

Eden's arms came around her to hold her still as the woman stuck a needle into the fat vein at the side of her neck. Shit, it hurt. And she'd better not get an infection or she'd have to kick their asses twice, damn it. A slow burn spread from the injection site, erupted straight into her brain and sent her into oblivion.

\* \* \* \* \*

Damn it, they'd looked everywhere. Mahpiya had been feeding Chrys' anger, and then her fear, through their bond. He at least knew the woman was all right. Then suddenly, it winked out. It was as if Chrys had disappeared off the face of the earth. He started to summon Mahpiya, but didn't want to call her away from his mate's side. Surely she was better off with two spirit guides rather than one.

All of his local family had gathered at Aunt Suman's home in anticipation of Rahn's homecoming, only to be met with the news that his fiancée was missing.

His aunt walked out onto the porch and put an arm around him.

"We will find her, Rahn. I promise."

She meant well and Rahn appreciated it. But it did nothing to quell the deep guilt he felt at allowing the damned woman to go romping around the bazaar alone. It didn't matter that she now had two spirit guides to keep her safe. He was ultimately responsible for her safety and happiness. Period.

"Thanks, Aunt Suman, I appreciate that." He knew his words were hard and angry, but he simply couldn't help it. Damn it, he was angry. Angry at himself for letting her out of his sight. Angry that someone had managed to tail her here, someone he should have caught by now. Angry for not realizing Chyrs was even in danger. She didn't fit the profile of the others who'd had their lives terminated at every port that damned ship stopped at. Why Chrys? Why her?

"I think I'll go for a walk, get into my own space so I can think a bit."

His aunt smiled in understanding and said, "All the family is here for you. And we are expecting a bit of help from an unexpected source."

"What unexpected source? Who?"

Rahn's eyebrows quirked in question, but she waved him off with a simple, "I'll tell you when you return from your walk if they have not arrived by then."

Rahn looked up at the sky as he went. It was so beautiful here. The sky was so clear, he didn't doubt he could see all the lights of the entire universe. But nothing compared to the sweet light in his woman's eyes. The way she brightened when he walked into a room. The way she reached for him, accepted him, both in and out of bed. And he realized Chrys would never allow him to lock her away from life, away from the world. She was a free spirit. But could they find a way for her to be both free and safe?

He kept walking, thinking of the sunset he'd watched

alone and how Chrys would have enjoyed seeing the clouds morph from vivid reddish-orange to pinkish-purple to deep gray.

Down the block and around the corner, Rahn sucked in a deep, startled breath as Mahpiya's imposing presence literally roared into his head.

'Mah? What the hell are you doing here? You're supposed to be with Chrys.'

*Adonei is watching over her. Since I am as much her spirit guide as I am yours, I must grant her request under these circumstances.*

'What circumstances, Mah? What are you talking about?'

Mahpiya told him the whole sordid tale from beginning to end, starting from the supposed bumping into Eden at the tea stand, to the woman Chrys had gone to help, to her present location and direction.

From hopeless concern to jubilation, he could barely contain himself. Because of Mahpiya, he now had everything he needed to rescue his woman. He was so damned grateful he couldn't even be angry at Mahpiya for leaving Chrys' side. Besides, Rahn was no fool. If Mah was here, she had good reason to be. The lioness was not just a great hunter, she was one of the wisest entities that walked the earth.

'Mah, show me what's happening now.'

*As you wish, my charge.*

Immediately, Mah's image faded from his mind and was replaced with the scene of a slumbering Chrys slouched in the backseat of a car.

Mahpiya's quiet voice caught and pulled him out of the vision she'd sent to him.

*You are growling aloud, Rahn. Do not bring unnecessary attention to yourself.*

And she was right. It wasn't as if he was the only one out on the streets of Alexandria tonight. He couldn't help

Chrys if he was locked up in the loony bin for walking down the street talking to himself while *not* drunk.

Focusing again on the images flowing into his brain, Rahn understood one thing immediately. Chrys was asleep, but not because she wanted to be.

'What did they give her, Mah?'

*These are some of the thoughts Chrysalyn sent me before she passed out.*

Injectable sedative. Great. At least she would sleep through most of her ordeal.

'Show me the signs on the road.'

They were headed south on the main road toward Cairo. Considering the amount of time Chrys had been missing, Rahn was sure they'd almost completely covered the scant one hundred or so miles. If they hadn't already, they would soon.

Rahn's heart went out to his woman as Mah explained Eden's part in this play. And he'd bet his life that the bastard's role was bigger than they realized. But appearing to be helpful when Rahn was injured put Eden in Chrys' good graces, even against her better judgment. Now she was paying for it. And according to Mahpiya, his little hellion wasn't the least bit happy about it.

But he was still going to paddle her ass for walking into danger instead of calling for help. He'd do it with some understanding, of course, then follow up with hot sweaty make-up sex.

*Your mate is more distraught for you than she is for herself.* Then Mah opened the gate of her memories and let them flow through the bond shared with her new charge.

Chrys' thoughts and feelings poured into him. They completed and filled every nook and cranny of his soul. Rahn shook his head in awe, moved by the depth of love and anger his woman carried on his behalf.

'Mah, thank you for sharing my mate's feelings with

me. But we have another problem.'

*What is that, my charge? You will go to her infused with strength and purpose, a gift from your spirit guide. Adonei will do the same for your mate. I see no problem here.*

'Except the one Chrys might create. I felt the heat behind the images you showed me. I know she's pissed off. And she's not afraid of a damned thing, even when she should be. I just know she'll say something stupid to those idiots holding her.'

*There, you have a point. Adonei and I will see what we can do to keep things under control until your arrival.* The cat sighed. *I must say, you are much less of a handful than Chrysalyn. And you are a male.* This was said with disbelief and a wink.

Rahn snorted.

The lioness was gone.

Rahn ate up the distance back to the house at a dead run. Simmering with anxiety, he tried to keep his anger from rising to a full boil. He would have his woman back and Eden would go down for the count. At any cost.

Toeing off his shoes, he rushed over the threshold and headed to the living area, where he knew his Aunt Suman, her sisters and all their husbands, along with a horde of cousins waited.

"Aunt Su..." His words trailed off.

Talk about shock. The room was not only full of his family. Off to one side stood six dark-haired men he didn't know personally, but could see a resemblance that spoke volumes over the sudden silence.

Eden's relatives. His brothers, to be exact. Last he heard, the apple didn't fall far from the tree. So if Eden was a pathological liar and psychopath, what were his brothers?

"Aunt Suman?" Rahn asked in a near snarl, nowhere

near ready to trust these strangers, not with his woman's life.

"They have been, shall we say, assisting me in gathering intelligence for you. On their own brother."

"What?!"

She grabbed him by the ear—he'd hated that since he was a little boy—gently eased his face down to hers and whispered for his ears only. "They do not know who you work for or the details of your case, but when I ran the information past them on the possible suspect, all of them agreed that their brother, Eden Pall, fit the profile."

As Rahn listened carefully to his aunt's words, his gaze remained plastered on the man he perceived was the oldest. When she finished, she took a step back and waited.

"Why are you doing this?" Rahn asked, not bothering to keep the edge or skepticism out of his voice. He had no reason to trust these men. Not with his mate's life.

The eldest, a man named Adel, replied. "Because we are bound to protect life, just as your family is."

With a neutral expression, he silently wondered if the man knew that he, his family and his woman were all agents of one kind or another?

"Even if it means reining in one of our own. We understand your woman is missing. Our youngest, Nasir," who waved his hand so Rahn would know who they were speaking about, "saw Eden at the bazaar today about the time your aunt says your woman disappeared. I know what it is like to lose a mate to unfortunate circumstances. We cannot support the actions of our sibling. We wish to assist."

The remaining men didn't say a word, just nodded their agreement.

Rahn accepted their help. They were here because of his aunt. The woman was no fool. She would have checked them out six ways from Sunday. Even down to their underwear size if need be. And because he trusted his aunt, he would extend the hand of friendship to these men. Until they blinked wrong.

He flipped open his emergency satellite phone and hit the speed dial.

"Geri, Chrys has been taken. I have a feeling her captor might be responsible for more than just making off with her. I've just received intel on where she is." He left out the part about being told this by his spirit guide. "Boss, I need a few favors."

With Mahpiya's road map imprinted firmly in his mind, a seething, determined Rahn and a small horde of equally determined males headed for Alexandria's El Nohza airport.

\* \* \* \* \*

Awake, groggy and somewhat stiff, Chrys resisted the urge to stretch. The needlelike sensation shooting down her numb left butt cheek was a pretty good indication of just how long she'd been asleep.

It was comforting to have Mahpiya back in a quiet corner of her mind and Adonei standing watch ready to wake her if needed. As they slowed to a stop, she cracked her lids open just enough to realize it was pitch black outside. She almost grinned evilly at the big wet spot that spread from just underneath her chin to soak into the fabric of the man next to her. She might not be able to fight Eden, his goons and the goonette right now, but she'd sure slobbered on him good.

Mahpiya's chuckle sounded behind her ear and Chrys bit her lip to keep from answering in kind. It was childishly funny, but hell, she'd take what she could get right now.

The car slowed to a stop, then took off again. Chrys sat up with a jolt.

What the hell? Or rather where the hell?

Unlike the more traditional old-styled neighborhoods of Alexandria, this place was a bustling, brightly lit, tourist-filled metropolis. Street vendors pushed their carts along. Couples strolled the boulevard holding hands, some shopping, others having coffee or tea in one of the many outdoor shops. Wow, a soaring statue of Ramses III sat atop a pedestal that seemed to rise up out of nowhere and was lit from underneath by small spotlights. The walls of shops and apartments were covered with colorful paintings and mosaics.

The foliage-lined, wide sidewalks were full of life, both old and young. But the streets? Holy shit, it was worse than driving in New York!

Chrys almost wished she'd stayed asleep. There wasn't a stoplight to be seen, and even when someone was crossing the six lanes of traffic, none of the drivers slowed. Only honked loudly and continued right on through what should have been crosswalks.

Just when she thought they'd splatter someone all over the pavement, they turned off the main road, left the more populated streets and headed into a quieter neighborhood.

Hmm. No hustle or bustle here. Instead, all was eerily quiet, almost tomblike.

Their car pulled over and parked near a low arch cut into a high wall. Eden and the skanky female hopped out of the car. Left in the backseat alone, panic pushed at the edges of Chrys' mind when the two goons approached the still-open rear door. Adonei sent soft reassurance through the bond.

*Rest easy, Chrysalyn. Your mate will arrive shortly.*

The typical quiet calm that encompassed her in times of danger was under siege by an almost unreasonable fear. Fear of never seeing Rahn again. Fear of never resting her back against his chest as he held her, surrounding her with his strength and warmth.

And that pissed her off.

Chrys twisted and pulled against the still-tight bonds. Searing pain sizzled through the nerve endings of her wrists and hands, clear down to the fingertips. Damn, that hurt.

'How long before Rahn gets here?'

*An hour perhaps.*

'Good,' Chrys growled along the link. 'Then I have an hour to get free and kick some Eden ass.'

Mahpiya padded forward in Chrys' head and sat down beside Adonei. *Your mate does not doubt your ability to win against your captor, but he would rather you do something more important.*

'Like?' she snapped.

*Like getting this Eden person to talk.*

Understanding lit through her. Determination to assist her mate and take Eden down pushed every other thought from her mind. Chrys gritted her teeth and forced herself not to pull away from the man reaching into the car. He hauled her out of the vehicle, down the street and through the arch into bleak nothingness.

# CHAPTER SIXTEEN

'Adonei, please assist me.'

The tawny head of the regal lion nodded in acknowledgement of her request. Agitated and beyond ready for action, Adonei growled, *Take what I offer, my charge.*

A burst of raw power pumped into Chrys' body, blitzed through her blood and burst through each muscle fiber. Her senses flared alive. The outline of the tombs and dimly lit narrow pathways, when met with the infusion of the lion's enhanced sight, appeared sharper, more defined. Crystal clear was the stern jawline of thug number one as he jerked her along and the wide back of thug number two walking ahead of them. The putrid stench of rotting garbage and raw sewage forced her gag reflex to tighten her throat. Taking shallow breaths, Chrys parted her lips to breathe through her mouth. Bad move. She could practically taste the muck on her tongue.

Overflowing with the strength of the mightiest hunters, Chrys snapped the bindings around her wrist with a simple flick, careful to keep her hands in a bound position. The garment they'd tossed over her earlier while hustling her out of the bazaar hid her freedom.

Vermin scurried out from underfoot as their party ducked through an entrance and into a small dwelling. The escorting bad guy gave her a shove. Pretending to stumble, she fell into a chair in the center of a shadow-shrouded room. A light clicked on and Chrys froze.

They were in a fucking tomb. Literally.

"Eden, where the hell are we?" Chrys demanded.

The thugs and thugette disappeared through an exit across the room, leaving her and Eden alone.

Sitting stiffly, back ramrod straight, Chrys demanded answers as Eden circled her like a buzzard waiting for the fresh meat to drop. Moments ticked by and she wondered if he would answer at all. Finally, the man spoke in a quiet, emotionless flat tone. So flat it brought to mind a vivid image of some poor soulless automated robot, unfeeling, uncaring as it floated in the blackness of space toward nothingness.

A single finger trailed over her shoulders and across the back of her neck as he moved around and around her still body.

"We are in Qarafa." At her blank stare, he continued. "What Westerners would call The City of the Dead."

"The who?"

"The City of the Dead," he repeated in a disconcerting flat-sounding timbre. "This place was an important burial ground hundreds of years ago, now the poor gather here. Thousands of them. Just think, among soaring minarets, mosques, elaborate tombs of sultans and their families, live ordinary men and women. In fact, a lovely widow lives in a tomb room just a few doors down with her children."

"But, but how?" Chrys stammered. Not from nervousness—she was too angry for that—but from the simple inability to fathom anyone living in a place like this.

"We have not so much thought of cemeteries as a place of the dead, but rather a place where life begins," Eden replied. "The new tenants have adapted where the families of the dead used to come to spend time with their departed loved ones. Now the grave markers serve as desks and shelves, while strings hung between gravestones are used to dry laundry. As for the light, they've brought in the electricity by wires over the roofs coming from the nearby mosque. Pity, really."

Well, the name certainly fit the place. The City of the Dead—northern Cairo's four-mile-long walled necropolis that now housed thousands of families and countless small businesses. In this day and age? Amazing.

But it didn't explain why the hell he'd brought her here. Not to mention he seemed too refined to have a "room" in this place for any virtuous purpose.

"But why…?"

"She thought I was wrong, you know. But I wasn't, it was her. She'd made the mistake, stupid bitch."

Okay, the words insane and crackpot came to mind. Chrys bit her tongue and let the man rant.

"Even pharaohs make mistakes. Sometimes deadly ones. But it really doesn't matter. With you at my side, I have no need of another pharaoh or harem mistress. The tarot was connected to the Rahn asshole after all."

Then Eden threw back his head and laughed as if the funniest joke in all of creation had just been told. Oookay? When the cackling ceased, Chrys took a slow breath, forced her words to emerge meek and humble.

"What tarot, Eden? I'd really like to understand."

Hmm. That seemed to please the walking nut job.

With a smile, he stopped circling and stopped in front of her. From his left breast pocket, he removed a beautiful card covered with gold, black and lapis blue

Egyptian symbols and hieroglyphs.

"It was the Empress. This card represents the Empress, see? I always selected different, and sometimes unusual, suits of cards, but she always explained them to me. But after I saw you for the first time aboard ship, I kept selecting this same card over and over. And always upside down. Stupid pharaoh had me believing it was because you were losing interest in the Rahn asshole."

The bottom of Chrys' stomach danced with unease. Now this was getting freaky. Right, as if Eden weren't already in that category. She held her thoughts to herself, demanded her fists to remain still. Giving away the fact that her hands were no longer tied would probably make the man stop talking.

And that simply wouldn't do. Her mate wanted a confession and, damn it, she was going to get him one.

"But you weren't losing interest in him," Eden rounded on her with a snarl. "You had no interest in me. But that will change, I promise you. I still don't understand why he didn't die." Eden's head tilted just a hair to the right, his expression one of genuine bewilderment.

"Die?" Chrys uttered in shock, and this time was no act.

"Yes, die, damn it all. He was supposed to die. I know I cut him in the right spot. But you came and did something to him. What did you do to him? All I wanted to do was stomp his brains out when I came into your apartment and saw you covered with his blood. You were moving toward the phone to call for help while that damned Rahn moaned like a foaling cow on the bathroom floor."

Chrys fought for calm, begging her spirit guides to send her a large dose and fast. Adonei's power still pulsed through her body and she fought to keep her temper under control, fought to keep the fierce force of the lion leashed.

But the more he talked, the more she wanted to rip his head off.

*Keep calm, Chrysalyn. He baits you,* Mahpiya crooned. *This must be finished before your mate arrives.* Then she flashed a quick glimpse of Rahn and a whole host of mean-looking men with him. And they were close.

Eden was pacing again, his words distant and far away, as if he were trying to work something out in his head. "I just don't understand. I cut all the other specimens in the exact same spot, and they all died within minutes. Perhaps it was because Rahn is more muscular, larger than the females I gutted? Or maybe I missed the spot all together."

"What specimens, Eden?"

"The women. I know you know about the women, Chrysalyn. My pharaoh hand-picked them all, one in each port of call. All strong, independent, capable. None of them needed to be led, but none were willing to follow. Too eager to step on the back of a male. Not like you, Chrysalyn. You are strong, yet understand the need to walk beside a man as an equal. Not afraid to be a real woman loved by a man. There is no desire to trample on him. On me."

Boy, did he have that last part wrong! She'd trample him, all right. Son of a bitch. The bastard was behind it all—the attacks at each port, the attack on Rahn and now, her abduction. By appearing to be helpful, he'd diverted suspicion away from himself. And since the spirit guides had never liked him, Chrys had simply gotten used to them going ballistic whenever the man was in the room.

And Eden had almost succeeded in adding Rahn to his list of victims. While her man had lain prone on that bathroom floor, bleeding to death. Spiritual law dictated that spirit guides be called or summoned onto this plane. Their assistance had to be requested. Something Rahn couldn't have done while unconscious.

Bad guy or not, without Eden's help that night, Rahn could very well be hanging around in the spirit realm with Mahpiya and Adonei.

And this idiot, perplexed and angry because Rahn hadn't kicked it that night, now confessed everything. She had all they needed to bring this asylum candidate to justice.

Just then, Eden moved in close enough for her to hear the air move in and out of his lungs. Then the man began moving down a different, more bizarre path. With a gentle touch, a single finger lovingly traced a path along Chrys' jawbone.

"Chrysalyn, I am pleased with you. You will be my queen forever, and bear me strong sons."

His eyes were alight with love and determination. Shit, the man was serious. How could someone so handsome, articulate and educated turn out to be such a nut job?

A slithering crawl eased along her skin when Eden's hand came in contact with her shroud-covered breast.

Waiting for Rahn dropped off the list of options.

\* \* \* \* \*

Adonei broadcast everything going on in that damned room right into Rahn's head as he and his backup waited outside the tomb room door. The second he saw that Eden bastard put his hands on Chrys, it was all he could do not to rush in and just start shooting. Except gunfire was a last resort for all of them. It was illegal to live in this place, but it was packed with people. Every empty tomb sheltered a person or a family, all very much alive. They couldn't risk having shots sound here. The

Egyptian government might turn a bit of a blind eye to the people squatting here, but gunfire was something they would definitely investigate. And fast.

*There are three armed humans in the back room,* Adonei warned.

'Any other way in?'

*There is no other entrance to this dwelling.*

'Well, we can't go in with guns blazing. Not with Chrys in the line of fire between us and them. Tell her to duck 'n cover. Right fucking now.'

The lion's presence winked out and Rahn called out to his guide. Mahpiya immediately responded, pouring supernatural strength and ability into his mind and body until it overflowed every nerve, every cell. Seconds later, he kicked in the door and rushed the room along with all six of Eden's brothers.

Eden snatched his hand away from Chrys' breast as if he'd been well and truly caught...which he was. The flash of recognition that lit his dark eyes was quickly replaced with a hard look, full of resentment and crazed determination.

Time slowed to a crawl. Chrys hit the floor and covered her head at the exact moment Rahn stormed in. Two big rugby-looking, rough-hewn European trees and a dark-haired woman flew in from the other side of the room and threw themselves into the fray.

Infused with the strength of the lion, an unarmed Rahn took evasive action and was across the room before the obviously inexperienced bad guy wannabe could get a shot off. But when he did fire, it echoed around the tomb with a deafening boom. Eden's brothers took down the other two and headed for Eden.

But not before he'd practically climbed on Chrys' back while she was still in a crouch on the floor.

"Hold it right there. One more and she joins the others."

All eyes, except the ones of the unconscious rogues, focused on the glint of the wicked blade pressed just underneath Chrys' jaw.

"Hold on now, brother," Adel called softly. "It's us. We are all here."

Eden's wild-eyed glare raked over his brothers.

"Why are you here, Adel?"

"We have come to help you."

"Really? It seems more as if you were helping him." Eden motioned his head toward Rahn, who managed to take a couple of steps his way while he'd been focused on his siblings. Just another step or two and Rahn could take him. Had to.

As if he'd read Rahn's thoughts, he pulled Chrys tighter against his body and pressed the blade closer. Close enough to cause an almost imperceptible thin line of blood, almost as fine as a cat's scratch, to appear.

Oh god, what could he do? What should he do? One wrong move and his woman would die before his eyes. Before he'd had a chance to say and do all the things he'd missed out on for the years they'd been parted.

No, this was simply unacceptable.

His fists flexed and his heart drummed in his ears. He'd pounded one of the rogues into a pulp in no time flat. He'd just have to find a way to do the same to Eden. With Mahpiya's strength, he just might make it.

Shit. The odds simply weren't good enough.

'Mahpiya, I need your wisdom.'

*Your mate has a plan.*

'Share it with me.' In a flash, the details streaming through Chrys' mind moved from her to Adonei to Mahpiya to Rahn. Rahn felt the color drain from his face.

'No. Tell her no fucking way is she to try…'

Then Chrys moved, infused with Adonei's essence.

One hand grabbed Eden's wrist so fast and hard that

the knife clattered to the stone floor. Before anyone could get within two strides of Chrys, she had the man knocked out, subdued facedown on the floor with her knee jammed into the back of his neck.

And she was shaking like a leaf.

He went to her then, gathered her up in his arms and held her tight. He felt the exact moment when shock and reality of what could have happened gripped her. With her face buried in his shirt, he spoke in hushed tones.

"Take deep, steady breaths, baby. It's all right. It's over now."

"Rahn, he tried to take you away. And he, he killed all those women…"

"I know, love. But you stopped him. Stopped him cold."

Her teeth were chattering now as the adrenaline crash let her down hard. Adonei and Mahpiya both retreated slowly, careful not to jar either of their charges.

God, he would never let her out of his sight again. Not even to take a pee. If he had his way, he'd just keep her chained to the bed with his head buried between her legs. He'd make her come so hard she couldn't walk or talk, let alone leave by herself on a mission.

Shit, he'd never been so scared. Twice in his career he'd faced certain death, and he'd rather face it again than see Chrys in the hands of a criminal.

Adel bounced him out of his current train of thought.

"Quickly, go now. We will take care of cleaning up. You must clear the area before the police arrive. You cannot be found here."

Rahn reached out and clasped hands with each man, from the eldest to the youngest. "I understand. Thank you for your help tonight. We are in your debt. We couldn't have done this without you."

"I'm not sure about that, friend," Adel said with a grin. "You and your woman move like nothing I have ever seen. Perhaps when we meet again, you will teach me this, yes?"

With a smile and a slight bow, Rahn bundled up a shivering Chrys and disappeared into the darkness.

# EPILOGUE

Now this was heaven.

No phones. No laptops. No work. Just Chrys moaning her pleasure around his cock as she flexed her jaw muscles while her mouth surrounded him.

Back arched into the moment, Rahn briefly—very briefly—thought on the events of the past three weeks.

After taking Eden down, Chrys had given all the details of the man's bizarre killing spree to Rahn's family and Eden's brothers. Before the Egyptian secret police arrived in the City of the Dead, Chrys had been spirited away—wouldn't do for an American agent to be caught "working" in Egypt without permission. Rahn and his Aunt Suman looked on with respect as Eden's brothers turned him over to the police. To tie up any loose ends, Eden's oldest brother walked into a holding cell and got the man to repeat, with chilling detail, every murder he'd committed. Some they hadn't even known about. And with diplomats present from several of the countries where the crimes were committed, including Portugal, Spain, France, Italy and Greece, Eden hadn't had a chance of fighting extradition. In the end, they'd all agreed he was beyond rehabilitation. Eden Pall was currently enjoying a full range of sedatives and anti-hallucinogenics in an undisclosed location.

And Rahn lay on a towel in the solarium on the top floor of his, now *their*, London flat. The sun warmed every inch of his gloriously naked body, with the exception of the parts the future Mrs. Chrys' torso cast shadows over. And those parts were warmed by her talented tongue and deep throat.

Damn, but the woman knew how to suck a cock. Went down on him like she'd never get enough. The perfect O of her lips encircled the tip the same way they did one of her favorite flavored cigars. And the woman knew her way around a good cigar.

Her tongue flicked over, teased and licked his lollypop before covering him completely. Over and over again, she sucked and laved until his balls practically crawled up his back.

"Damn, Chrys. God, that feels so good. Yeah, suck it, baby."

Her hums and moans became frantic, sending a wicked vibration through his cock and sac. Rahn loved the way she got all hot and bothered from giving him head. He knew if he reached down and stroked her pussy, she'd be soaked and ready for him.

A strong hand slid over the ridges of his abs and up to tweak a stiff male nipple. The other followed her talented mouth up and down his stiff length. The woman's whole body was into what she was doing, hips wriggling, back arched. She mumbled around him, her breath both cooling and warming his throbbing length.

"Mmm, you taste so good," she panted. "All male and musky and…mine."

Between wet swirls of her tongue and equally wet draws on his flesh, the words spilled out and sent his heat level soaring.

"I'm so hot right now." Suck. "My pussy is aching." Slurp. "Oh god, I need it."

How he loved it when she talked dirty. He loved it even more when she followed through. Chrys crawled up his body. The next instant, Rahn gasped with pleasure, balls-deep inside scalding-hot, wet, willing woman. And she rode him until the cream of her cunt frothed around the base of his rod.

"Oh yeah, Chrys. Give me that pussy, baby. Fuck me."

"Yes. Rahn. Mmmm…" Each word rose in volume and intensity until she yelled her pleasure. He shattered into a million pieces as her juicy sex rippled and gripped, pulling his own orgasm from the base of his cock.

Holding her tight to his chest, Rahn kissed the wild riot of curls on top of her head. The Great Spirit had truly blessed him.

He had two African lions, strong and regal, for spirit guides. A job he loved. And the most special woman on earth, his equal professionally, spiritually and definitely in the bedroom. And he loved her to the depths of his soul. More than he could have ever imagined loving another human being.

And he'd found her in the most unlikely of places.

On an Egyptian voyage.

## AVAILABLE NOW:
## FOREVER DECEMBER
## BY TJ MICHAELS

Michael had never before seen Melaniece's mouth fall open as her skin went pale. It would have been comical if it hadn't been so important for her to be happy to see him. He strode into the living room in his socks. Though his steps were deliberately slow and easy, he was so eager to wrap the woman in his arms that it still felt like he was practically running.

"Michael? What the hell are you doing here?" Melaniece gasped, still sprawled on the floor in front of the fireplace. Damn she looked sexy. It was just like he'd imagined in his dreams—her lying in front of the fireplace waiting for him to ravish her lush, beautiful body.

Suddenly she sprang up from the floor with a wild-eyed expression like she'd been caught with her hand in the cookie jar. And she didn't look happy to be caught, at least not by him. But that was just too bad. He'd come all this way only for her, and he'd be damned if he wasn't going to have her.

"Hi, Mel," he deliberately crooned, knowing how much she loved his "deep" voice. "Aren't you glad to see me, babe?" he asked stretching out his arms to her. Arms that had become well acquainted with holding her during her last trip home. And there was nothing like cuddling with Melaniece Matthews. But this time, there was no need to leave it at cuddling. No need for her to assure him he was more than ordinary in spite of his crumbled marriage. Self-confidence restored, he was all man standing in her house with outstretched arms. Hell, screw a cuddle, she looked so deliciously surprised standing there in her skintight tee and comfy sweats, her hair all over her head, nervously nibbling on her bottom lip. He wanted to strip her bare with a smile, right here, right now.

Her tongue seemed stuck to the roof of her mouth. But Michael, being his old self once again, didn't wait for her to acclimate. Instead he pulled her into his arms and wrapped them around her until his nostrils were full of the scent of delicious, mouthwatering woman. And it was absolutely decadent.

"Mmmm, it feels so good to hold you again, Mel. Merry Christmas, beautiful."

# JAGUAR'S RULE
# EXCERPT
## BY TJ MICHAELS

## Chapter One

The big male swatted at the female's head but missed. She'd eluded his huge paw, jumped to the side of the unconscious human lying face down on the ground, his blood mingling with the wet grass. The female crouched again, ready to spring and prepared to fight for the human. He didn't doubt he could take her, but the set of her powerful shoulders and the gleam of the moonlight off her bared canines made him think twice. He'd seen this particular female before, often out in the jungle. None of the other males ever approached her. Perhaps she was a formidable foe?

But he wasn't just another male. He was a prime of his species, a jaguar, a fully grown *panthera onca* who always got what he wanted. He decided he wanted her.

She thought he was after the body she guarded. Good, let her. He would back off for now, taking the opportunity she'd unknowingly given him to watch her closely and see just what kind of female he was dealing with. But he had no doubt that in the end, she would find herself underneath him while he thrust with powerful strokes into her body. Oh yes, she would yield. He would see to it. And perhaps afterward, he would keep her.

\* \* \* \* \*

*Uhhnnn, owww.* Aaron was sure someone had split his head open and used a metal baseball bat to work sand into the wound. And those voices! God, why wouldn't they just shut up? The buzz overlaying the words of whoever needed to shut up drilled through his brain.

Each breath sucked into his lungs felt shallow, as if he couldn't drag in enough air, and every breath out left behind a tight burning sensation. Why couldn't he take a deep breath and hold it? Pain this intense could only mean one thing—he was dying.

The voices were louder now. Damn it. Ready to glare at the people talking when his head pounded like a drum at a rock concert, he was somewhat surprised at the gritty feel behind his lids as he forced them open. He blinked then blinked again, but the blurry images wouldn't clear. They just moved back and forth in the dimly lit room. The sound of a million cawing birds filled his ears, and the sweet scent of wet grass floated on a cooling breeze across his skin. His *bare* skin. Did they have bare skin in the hereafter?

He blinked a few more times, wincing as the side of his head exploded with a new round of pain. And who was the bearded old man leaning close to his face? He wanted to lift his hand to smack the man and tell him to back up a bit. The garlic on his breath made Aaron's stomach lurch but the pounding in his head was so fierce, just the thought of blowing chunks made him grit his teeth to hold back the bile while the vein in his forehead threatened to burst. The old man was speaking. What? Sounded something like mud, or blood, or…he just couldn't make it out, his thoughts were too scrambled. Oblivion had been pretty sweet compared to this. Perhaps he could slip back into it?

But not before he caught a glimpse of the angel standing just behind the garlicky old man. Now he remembered, sort of. Lightning. His plane had gone down in the jungle after the engine under the left wing caught fire. The image was blurry but he knew an angel when he saw one. Was she here to take him to heaven? He was sure he'd done at least a few good deeds to warrant making it through the pearly gates.

This angel had milk chocolate skin and a set of piercing, almond-shaped, light gray eyes that made his pulse skip a beat or two. And her hair, a shoulder-length mane any woman would kill for. Thick and curly, it hit her shoulders at the perfect length and made his fingers want to reach out and touch the silky black-as-sin tresses before he floated away to the hereafter. The image of his angel wavered.

"Wait! Come back, beautiful! Can't we spend some time? Maybe talk awhile before I leave this plane?" Could she hear his urgent whispers? Of course she could, all supernatural beings had great hearing. So why didn't she respond? Instead, she just looked at him with a strange mix of pity and irritation. What the hell kind of angel was she anyway? She was supposed to be smiling at him, preparing him for his journey. Well, she obviously wasn't interested in doing her job. Maybe if he lodged a formal complaint with God, she'd get fired.

The garlic master was back. His stomach lurched. *Damn it, old man*, he shouted in his head, and immediately regretted the ferocity of his thoughts. Now his neck, shoulders and ribs joined his head, pounding relentlessly against his skin from the inside out.

The older man stuck him on the top of his hand with something and the beauty faded away fast, but not before he got a good glimpse of the swell of the angel's breasts and the curve of her shoulders. Since when did cherubs wear tank tops? It sure looked good on her. And how could be he in so much pain and still manage to achieve a hard-on? *Damn, she's sexy*, he smirked at himself as his eyelids fluttered closed. Hell, even in his state of impending death, he was thinking with his cock instead of his brain.

*I'm no better than the half-assed angel*, he thought as sleep claimed him.

\* \* \* \* \*

Reya followed Dr. Matons out of her bedroom and closed the door with a quiet snap. After brewing herself a cup of tea, she joined her old friend out on the screened veranda and plopped down in her favorite plastic patio chair. The smell of the passing storm was heavy in the air, along with the scent of charred wood and jet fuel. In spite of the evening's hair-raising events, she was calm and determined.

Vanilla and clove scented smoke floated up from Dr. Matons' pipe. She should have never asked her Aunt Sulu to send the stuff. Now the old curmudgeon would never again settle for the local tobaccos.

"Well, our little patient was lucky tonight," Dr. Matons drawled around his pipe.

"*Little* patient?" Reya queried with amusement. She was sure she'd never met a man so long his feet practically hung off the edge of her bed, or a more muscularly perfect specimen as the one lying in her bedroom. She and Dr. Matons had spent the past several hours removing glass and plastic from various patches of skin. They'd stitched the deeper cuts across his back, wrapped his chest tightly and cleaned off all the blood. She'd seen every inch of his magnificent body and there was nothing, and she meant *nothing*, little about him.

"It's a good thing you were out on patrol when his plane went down. I don't know if he would have made it otherwise," the doctor said, blowing out a ring of thick smoke. "He is certainly handsome, as men go." His eyes crinkled at the sides as he watched her. The old matchmaker. Always looking for someone to pair her up with. Even an unconscious man in serious condition.

When she didn't answer but stared out into the night, he continued. "I gave him a strong painkiller, but he's not out of the woods. Do you mind if I sleep here so I can check on him during the night?"

"No, I don't mind at all. Why don't you take the office? The futon in there is pretty comfy. I'll take the couch." Her eyes hadn't strayed from the tangle of ferns and vines leading into the dark canopy of jungle no more than a hundred yards from her back stairs.

"You're not planning on going back out in this deluge, are you?"

"The storm is almost past. I'll be fine. Besides, something weird happened out there tonight. If you're still awake when I get back, I'll tell you about it."

The moon, pale and obscured by dark thunderheads, was the only light shining onto her second-story veranda. Reya unlaced her boots, toed them off and set them beside the screen door that led down the back stairs. Dr. Matons continued to puff on his pipe while she peeled off her tank top and blood-spattered pants, tossed them in a pile and loosely tied a small bundle around her neck.

"Be careful, my dear. Wake me when you return," Dr. Matons called quietly. Extinguishing his pipe, he rose and slipped through the sliding glass door and into her living room.

Reya watched his retreating back until the subtle snap of the office door told her she was alone. Shirt, pants and shoes in a neat pile on the floor, she dropped to her knees. Muscles rippled and bunched as raw power surged through her limbs—heady, thunderous power as her body shortened then stretched. Her tall frame shuddered as thick fur burst through her pores, replacing smooth skin. The cooling breeze ruffled the sleek fur on the tufts of the ears of a black jaguar as she stalked down the stairs and loped into the surrounding jungle.

# ALSO BY AUTHOR TJ MICHAELS

Carinian's Seeker, Vampire Council of Ethics Book One
Serati's Flame, Vampire Council of Ethics Book Two
Hatsept Heat, Vampire Council of Ethics Book Three
Seeker's Solace, Vampire Council of Ethics Book Four
Silk Road, Seals of Destiny
Spirit of the Pryde, A Pryde Ranch Shifter Story
Niah's Pride, A Pryde Ranch Shifter Story
Jaguar's Rule
Forever December
Egyptian Voyage
On the Prowl
Entwined Hearts
Shards of Ecstasy
Caramel Kisses
Death and Roses
Mastered: Ten Tales of Sensual Surrender
Juicy, A Twilight Teahouse Tale

## ABOUT THE AUTHOR

TJ is an award-winning author of several romance genres, including paranormal, fantasy, sci-fi and urban fantasy romance. Writing like a madman, TJ hasn't lost steam. Her mind? Yep, that's gone, but steam there is a-plenty. A true Taurus, TJ isn't slowing down and she's definitely too stubborn to stop when she sees the fence!

No matter the genre TJ is penning, her favorite thing to do is build worlds. To take you somewhere extraordinary. To transport you to a place where you can close your eyes and slip into your fantasy...

Visit T.J. Michaels online at her Website.
http://www.tjmichaels.com/